EDGE OF WAR

THE ETERNAL FRONTIER BOOK 2

ANTHONY MELCHIORRI

Eternal Frontier (The Eternal Frontier, Book 2)
Copyright © 2017 by Anthony J. Melchiorri. All rights reserved.
First Edition: April 2017
http://AnthonyJMelchiorri.com

ISBN-13: 978-1545165010
ISBN-10: 1545165017

Cover Design: Illustration © Tom Edwards, TomEdwardsDesign.com

This is a work of fiction. Names, characters, places, and incidents either are the
product of the author's imagination or are used fictitiously, and any resemblance
to locales, events, business establishments, or actual persons—living or dead—is
entirely coincidental.
10 9 8 7 6 5 4 3 2 1

ONE

GRAY SCARS ALONG THE RIGHT SIDE OF THE ALIEN'S FACE stretched as it snarled at Commander Tag Brewer, former chief medical officer and now captain of the SRES *Argo*. The alien's single working golden eye narrowed as if it was scrutinizing him, already predicting his every move. Tag knew the Mechanic was intelligent. He had spent plenty of time on the *Argo* getting to know the strange alien who looked something like a human and snake chimera. Slitted nostrils broke up the angular, elongated head of the Mechanic. His serpentine limbs, extending from his thin torso to his six-fingered hands, could bend in ways that made Tag's stomach turn.

"Coren," Tag started, dropping into a fighting stance. He bent his knees, prepared to pounce, his hands held in front of him, ready to grapple the skinny alien. "I never thought it'd come to this."

Coren scoffed. "What? You thought you could just let me onto your ship, drag me across the galaxy to help your people, and then not let me show you what a true Mechanic is made of?"

The duo circled like two male lions. Tag had clashed with Mechanics before, and the memories surfaced in his thoughts. Those Mechanics, enslaved by self-assembling nanite antennas residing in their brains, had been acting at the behest of some mysterious entity he still knew nothing about. After surviving the attack on the *Argo*, he had taken on three of those Drone-Mechs alone. They had been wearing power armor, and he had fought with only the tools and weapons he could scrounge up while sneaking around the ship. And even then, he had reigned victorious.

I can certainly handle Coren, he thought.

His eyes traced the Mechanic's lean body. Coren had been the chief engineer of his ship, not a battle-hardened warrior. He might be flexible, but his muscles were hardly thicker than a power cable, and he was skinny enough that Tag thought if the Mechanic sneezed too hard, he would break his own ribs. Tag grinned. While he hadn't spent as much time in the *Argo*'s gym as the marines who had once called this ship home did, he lifted weights enough to feel confident he could throw Coren over his shoulder like he was nothing more than a heap of leftover IV bags.

"Are you going to admire me all day, or do you plan on striking, human?" Coren said with a sneer.

Tag lunged. This would be over in a few seconds, max, with Coren lying on his back, giving Tag the victory he deserved. His fingers found Coren's thin wrists and wrapped around the fur-covered limbs. He forced one of the Mechanic's hands behind his back then swept one of his legs behind Coren's ankle, knocking the Mechanic off his feet.

Boom. Done, Tag thought.

This was the same basic move that Tag had learned from his

hand-to-hand combat training in boot camp. The same training every human citizen of the SRE underwent during their compulsory military service. And as Coren flew feet over head, Tag commended himself for remembering that training after all these years. He threw all his weight into carrying Coren backward, leaving nothing behind. No retreat, no defense necessary. This was too damn easy.

But right as Coren's shoulders touched the floor, the Mechanic's arms curled backward, pulling Tag forward. Coren twisted to the side. With his fingers still secured around the Mechanic's ropey limbs, Tag's elbows were bent to their limits, and he yelped in pain. Coren turned to land on two feet and let Tag's own momentum carry him to the ground. Pain scattered through Tag's skull when his head hit the deck, his vision crackling as if he was traveling through hyperspace. Instead of going anywhere, Tag groaned and lay on his bruised spine.

"Damn you, you bloody Mechanic," Tag managed.

Coren laughed, standing over him. "Is this cockiness a trait all you humans share? Or is it unique to you and Sofia?"

From the corner of the training room, Sofia laughed. She placed a hand over her chest as she strode toward the sparring mat. "Coren, you know damn well I can take you down. That's not cockiness; that's just honesty."

Coren held out a hand, and Tag took it, hoisting himself back to his feet.

"When we first started training together on Eta-Five, you fell just as easily as him," Coren said.

"Sure, but that was a one-time thing. Fool me once, shame on you," Sofia said. "Fool me twice..."

"Yes, yes, I know how these human sayings go," Coren said.

"Damn right you do," Sofia said. "Never pulled that move on me again, did you?"

Coren let out a low huff.

Tag rubbed the back of his head. "For a scrawny creature, you pack quite the punch."

Again, Coren emitted a derisive laugh. "It's not the power behind *my* punch. It's the power behind yours. From what Sofia tells me, our standard hand-to-hand combat is similar in concept to your human jiu-jitsu. It relies on leveraging the opponent's strength and momentum against them."

"Makes sense," Tag said. He thought to test the limits of Coren's humor and clapped the Mechanic's shoulder. "It's the only way weaklings like you stand a chance without power armor."

Coren didn't laugh. His lips remained straight. "There's more truth to that than you may realize. We are far too logical and intelligent a race to neglect our weaknesses. Something you humans could stand to learn for yourselves."

Tag grinned when Coren's thin lips curled slightly.

"Would anyone be willing to spar with me? I would gratefully accept the opportunity," a voice called from another corner. Alpha, the sentient half-machine, half-biological being of Tag's creation, cocked her silver head slightly, and her servos whirred as she stepped forward.

"No!" the others said in unison. Alpha's screen-like eyes glimmered dully as if she were disappointed. Out of everyone on the four-person crew, Alpha by far possessed the most intrinsic strength. Her mechanical limbs would make short work of any flesh-and-bone beings, and she had even torn the alloy shell off of an exo-suit Drone-Mech pilot when they had saved the SRES capital ship, the *Montenegro*, from a massive assault. Tag had downloaded the entirety of the *Argo*'s encyclopedic databases into Alpha, including more fighting styles and techniques than all the fully biological beings on the crew could ever hope to learn in their lifetimes combined.

"How about we take a break from physical training and get some work done instead?" Tag asked. "I'm not interested in breaking any more bones today."

"Captain, between your medical skills and the regen chambers, it would be no problem for us to treat any broken bones," Alpha said.

"Count yourself lucky you don't have pain receptors," Tag said. "Otherwise you wouldn't be saying that."

"I will, as you say, take your word for it, Captain," said Alpha in a robotic tone that sounded vaguely glum.

Tag wiped off the sweat beading on his forehead with his sleeve. "You do that. In the meantime, we've only got a couple days until we hit normal space outside Eta-Five. Back to the bridge."

The mention of Eta-Five cut any air of good humor that had been shared within the group. Tag could almost feel the apprehension radiating off his crew as they made their way up the ladders to the bridge. The last time they had been on Eta-Five, they had been chased off it by a barrage of torpedoes, warheads, and pulse weapons. And now, with nowhere else to turn, they were headed straight back.

TWO

O N THE *ARGO*'S BRIDGE, A HOLOSCREEN CAST ITS WAN BLUE
glow over the crew members seated around the chart table.
The resulting light and shadows playing over their faces accentuated the grim expressions they wore. None looked forward to
what they might encounter, and Tag did his best to appear more
confident than he felt, hoping to inspire a bit of the same in Sofia,
Alpha, and Coren. He gestured to the image of a planet rotating
on the holoscreen. Spinning in the air with its wispy atmosphere
forming soft, snowy tendrils around it, its serenely white appearance belied the true nature of the planet. Beneath that beautiful
exterior was an unforgiving landscape riddled with more ways to
kill a person than cannons on an SRE Behemoth-class capital ship.

"Alpha," Tag began, "I want you to chart a flight path that
keeps us in the cover of one of Eta-Five's moons as long as possible." He circled a spot on Eta-Five, and the area expanded. "Here's
where we'll land. We've got to touch down near the wreck of the

MES *Stalwart*." Despite their best efforts, Coren and his crew just didn't have the parts to fix the *Stalwart*. They had barely gotten away from an encounter with the Drone-Mechs in the first place, and even then, they had been lucky to survive the crash on Eta-Five. Now, years later and unable to leave, the planet that had been their refuge had turned into their prison. Coren and his crew of uninfected Mechanics wanted nothing more than to shatter the chains of the nanite menace enslaving the rest of their people, but they stood no chance of doing that if they remained stuck on Eta-Five. "We should have enough scraps from the battle between the Drone-Mechs and the *Montenegro* to make the ship spaceworthy again."

"Guaranteed," Coren said hungrily. "One way or another, I'm getting my people off that planet."

"What? You guys don't like the snow?" Sofia asked.

"I have had enough of it for a lifetime."

Alpha's silver fingers splayed across the chart table as she peered at Eta-Five. "Captain, I am worried we aren't considering our main mission. Admiral Doran charged us with uncovering what Captain Weber was supposed to be doing out here."

"I haven't neglected that, Alpha," Tag said. "But I'm at a loss. None of my searches through the ship's logs showed anything out of the ordinary."

"Likewise," Sofia said. "If Admiral Doran was right and he was on some covert mission, I'm not a damn bit closer to figuring out what it was. All we've got is that it could have something to do with the nanites, Eta-Five, and that old generation ship that disappeared out here."

"The UNS *Hope*?" Coren asked.

"Yep," Sofia said. "Something fishy is definitely going on, but I'm stumped."

"I haven't found any trace in our computer systems that might point to a covert operation. I have also been unable to determine the nature of *cargo* and torpedoes that the Drone-Mechs stole from the *Argo*," Alpha added.

"Yeah, thanks for rubbing it in," Sofia said ruefully.

If Alpha had had eyebrows, Tag guessed that she would have raised one then. "I don't understand that expression."

"Point is," Tag said, "we've got nothing. But my gut tells me that following the nanite trail is our best lead. And to do that, we could use some help. Getting the *Stalwart* up and running again is going to be crucial. It's better that we don't do this alone. Whatever is out there is worse than we ever imagined." Tag grimaced. The nanite technology had infected almost an entire alien species with self-assembling antennae that were being used by *someone* to control their minds with grav-waves. "This is beyond anything either humans or Mechanics could've come up with on our own."

"I'm sure *we* would've come up with it on our own at some point," Coren objected, appearing indignant.

"Regardless, we need all the help we can get," Tag said. "And, if you agree, I think the first step toward figuring out who is behind the nanites is finding any surviving Mechanics that might be out there. I'm not just talking about the ones on Eta-Five, either."

Coren's chest seemed to swell at that. He didn't quite smile, but he gave a single enthusiastic nod. "I am obviously biased, but I fully support that course of action. I'll do whatever is in my power to ensure we find any surviving Mechanic strongholds and, machines be willing, track down whoever inflicted the nanites on my people."

"I'm assuming we'll have the full support of the free Mechanics in this mission too, right?" Tag asked.

Coren sat silent for a moment as if mulling the question over. "You can be assured my people will seek retribution for what has been done. They will want to see this through, and if that means supporting the *Argo*'s mission, then I'll ensure we do just that."

"Good to know," Tag said. Internally, he processed the full meaning of Coren's statement. The nanites shared striking similarities to a human technology that had long ago been developed and then banned before the SRE ran Sol System Prime. The officials Tag had discussed this with claimed the SRE had always supported the ban on biowarfare and mind-control weaponry. But there was a nagging worry in the back of Tag's mind that someone in the SRE might have continued the development of these nanites. And for all he knew, a human in the SRE might have been responsible for deploying them.

Tag was nothing more than a commander in the SRE Navy, and prior to that the chief medical officer of the *Argo*. Covert operations and weaponry technologies were not his specialty, nor was he privy to whatever classified weapons systems research and development the SRE had going on. And while Coren had learned to trust Tag, the Mechanic still openly voiced his skepticism of the SRE government. Tag feared what kind of retribution the Mechanics might seek if the nanites were indeed an SRE plot. But, he reasoned, postulating and worrying about possible conspiracies wouldn't help them find the actual culprits.

"Coren, would you mind running a final diagnostics array?" Tag asked. "I want to ensure the bots have finished all essential repairs."

"Yes, Captain," Coren said with a slight nod. He bent over one of the terminals.

"You got plans for me, too, Skipper?" Sofia asked.

"I do," Tag replied.

"Better not involve cleaning the heads."

"I believe that's what we have the maintenance bots for, is that not correct?" Alpha asked.

"It's a joke, Alpha," Sofia said. "Humor, remember?"

Alpha tilted her metallic head, growing still for a minute. "I remember humor. I still do not understand it."

"Probably because it's a shitty joke," Tag said.

Alpha's screen eyes seemed to narrow. "Is that a pun, Captain?"

"Yeah," Sofia said, smirking. "A crappy one, too."

"I'm sensing there are layers to this conversation that I may be missing. I'll record our conversation to analyze later."

"You do that," Tag said. He couldn't help the slight grin crossing his face. "No heads duty, Sofia, but we do need to get our new additions to the crew caught up on everything."

THREE

Tag led Sofia past the mess hall.

"I thought we were meeting with the new marines," she said, eyeing the hatch.

"We will, but not yet," he replied. Admiral Doran had initially told them she couldn't spare much more than supplies. The *Montenegro* had lost far too many crew members from the Drone-Mech attack, and she needed all the surviving hands to take care of the maimed ship and other injured crew members. However, while the *Argo* was being repaired and undergoing preflight preparations, Doran had managed to scrounge up a squad of marines to help fill the ghostly corridors. Initially the ship had held a full crew of sixty-four, satisfying all the necessary redundancies to ensure that if an integral crew member was lost, their skills at least were not. There were others that could step into their place. Tag didn't have that luxury now, but at least he had a few more guns in case things got ugly on Eta-Five or another run-in with the Drone-Mechs led to an unexpected boarding.

"I really was joking about the heads, you know," Sofia said. "You're not making me do the cleaning, are you?"

"No," Tag said, opening the hatch to the med bay. He led her in. The familiar sterile smell greeted his nostrils. A tinge of burned plastic drifting in the recycled air served as a constant reminder of the working air scrubbers and filters. The buzz of laboratory equipment provided soft background noise as Tag leaned against one of the cylindrical regen chambers. He crossed his arms over his chest. "I want to talk about Coren."

"He's a good fighter," Sofia said with a wry smile. "You can't win every match."

"I'm not after your sparring tips. I'm talking about what happens when we find out who made the nanites."

"You mean what happens if we find out the SRE is responsible."

"Yeah, that."

Sofia drummed her fingers on a silver examination table. "Let's hope it doesn't come to that."

"But if it does," Tag started, "then what's he going to do? We're bringing a load of Mechanic ship parts back to the *Stalwart*. It's bigger than us. It's got better weapons than us. He's got a crew that's exponentially larger than ours sitting on Eta-Five and waiting to fly again." Tag paced in front of the regen chambers. "I've known the guy for a matter of weeks now. And even though he's about as emotional as a statue most of the time, I can still tell he goes through bouts of wondering whether he can trust us. He's a part of the crew one moment then distant the next."

"Wouldn't you be if you were him?" Sofia asked.

"Without a doubt," Tag replied. "I don't find his behavior strange, but...you know him better than I do. What I want to know is what you think he'll do if—and three hells, I hope this is a big if—if we find out the SRE *is* somehow involved with the nanites."

Sofia let out a long exhalation as if she was buying time before delivering bad news. "I want to say I think he'd spare us. That he'd spare the *Argo*. You know as well as I do that he's true to his word to a fault. The Mechanics are bound by two things: logic and honor. And while he might honor our lives, honor the fact that we're going back to help his people, logic might tell him we're the enemy. That it's more advantageous to stop his enemy whenever and wherever he can find them."

"That doesn't bode well for us."

"Nope," Sofia agreed. "But I'm with you. I can't believe the SRE would be behind this. Maybe it's some rebellious colony. Then we shouldn't have to worry about the Mechanics at all."

"Maybe." But Tag doubted it. The genetic integration technologies involved with the nanites were so advanced that they were practically magic to Tag's scientifically trained mind. It would take a colony with exceptional access to the best scientific resources and brains. "Keep an eye on him for me, will you? He probably trusts you more than he does me. After all the skepticism I threw at him, I wouldn't expect anything less."

"Will do," Sofia said. "Anything else?"

"Sure you don't want to clean the heads?"

"Positive."

"Then let's go have that chat with our marine friends."

———

"Son of a bitch!" A grizzled voice boomed from the open hatch of the mess hall. Something slammed against the bulkhead, and the noise of the impact reverberating through metal brought back memories of the Drone-Mechs' initial attack on the *Argo*. Tag's heart immediately thrashed against his rib cage.

"You good, boss?" Sofia asked, giving him a curious glance.

"Peachy." Tag recomposed himself.

They entered the mess and were greeted by the raucous yells of marines. A game of Turbo was playing on the viewscreen showing the Weir City Mars Razors playing against the Rome New Union Juggernauts. The 40–20 score showed a clear lead by the Razors. Tag watched a player sail over another's head to launch what appeared to be a game-clinching hammer-down, though he wasn't sure which team the player belonged to until the viewscreen pulsated with "Razors WIN." While the voices of the five marines watching echoed in a mix of celebration and disappointment, a hollow feeling crept into Tag's chest. The mess normally fit forty crew members. Scientists to run experiments. Marines for security. Engineers to keep the ship in pristine shape. All of them were gone. The sense of loneliness Tag had first experienced at finding himself alone on the *Argo* still haunted him, fueled by the memories of his former crewmates, including Staff Sergeant Kaufman. A vague memory of her proudly declaring her loyalty to the Razors cropped up in his mind.

"Commander!" The olive-skinned, mustachioed Giovanni 'G' Mezo snapped to attention. Tag had spent enough time mingling with the crew of the *Montenegro* while the *Argo* was being repaired that he recognized most of the new additions to his command. Giovanni had boyish looks that underscored his nascent career within the SRE and belied the typical genetically enhanced athletic frame so characteristic of the navy's foot soldiers.

Rebecca "Lonestar" Hudson, blond hair shaved razor short and dyed with a shocking line of blue, yanked on Giovanni's sleeve. "Give it a break, G," she said with a drawl that made Tag think of all the Texas stereotypes people had ascribed to him when they found out he was born in Old Houston. Unlike him, Rebecca had never been to the SRE province that now encompassed Texas, instead hailing from a homestead on a colony planet.

Giovanni paused, unsure what to do until Tag said, "At ease."

A woman with braided hair black as the space between stars shook her head at Giovanni. Fatima "Sumo" Kajimi. "Commander says we're not an uptight ship, then we're not an uptight ship. Relax, G."

Marvin "Gorenado" Goreham turned off the viewscreen with a simple hand gesture. The movement, despite its subtlety, made the nano-ink dragon and fire tattoos on his dark skin pulsate with color.

"Thanks," Tag said.

The fifth and final marine strode over from a corner, where he had been studying something on his wrist terminal.

"Briefing time, Commander Brewer?" Sergeant Ryan "Bull" Buhlman asked.

He brushed a hand over his short red hair, and his green eyes narrowed. The self-described station rat had spent his life growing up in SRE navy-controlled space stations with intermittent gravity, never so much as traveling down the gravity well toward a planet. He was a full head shorter than Tag, which made him an unusual physical anomaly in the otherwise genetically enhanced and bulky people that composed the majority of the marine population.

"That's right, Bull," Tag said. The call sign came out awkwardly when he said it. The marines had insisted he use the nicknames. They hadn't let him in on any of their origin stories, so every time he talked with them, it felt like he was a stranger trying to make sense of an inside joke. "Sofia's got a presentation on the xenos you're going to see on Eta-Five—and some that I hope you don't see."

"Oh, we got some scary monsters there, huh?" Fatima—*Sumo*, Tag corrected himself internally—asked.

"Monsters or not," Lonestar said, "I reckon it'll be nice to set foot on an actual planet. Been too long since my boots touched solid ground."

Gorenado simply huffed in agreement.

"Let's get on with it," Bull said, his eyes never wavering in intensity.

"All right then," Sofia said, sauntering to the mess's main viewscreen. She rubbed her hands together like a professor starting class, and a wide smile crossed her face. "This is the first real presentation I get to give on Eta-Five and the Forinths. Studied these suckers for the past five years, so you have no idea how much I've been waiting for this moment." Her smile faded. "Only problem is I didn't think I'd be giving it to a bunch of jarheads, so if I go too fast for you all, feel free to stop me and ask questions."

"Yes, ma'am," G said attentively.

Sumo rolled her eyes.

"You're already familiar with the Mechanics," she began. "You've met Coren, and he's told you more about them then I ever could. I don't have too much to add other than to say watch your tongue around them. They pride themselves on their mechanical aptitude and their honor. They're a pragmatic species, so don't go insulting them or questioning their intelligence."

"Why are y'all looking at me?" Lonestar said, looking shocked.

"Doesn't take a scientist like her to pick out which one of us always starts the bar fights," Sumo said.

Lonestar raised her hands in mock innocence, but Bull shot them both a serious look, and the duo quieted, their attention returning to Sofia.

"Anyway, you might accidentally insult a Mechanic, but they aren't the dangerous ones. It's the Forinths you need to look out for. They're the indigenous race," Sofia said, gesturing across the viewscreen. A 3-D projection of one of the octopus-like aliens floated in the air, rotating slowly for all of them to see. "They don't communicate in normal phonetic patterns like you and me. Instead, they use melody, rhythm, and pitch. So don't even bother trying to start a conversation. Anything you say will sound like nails on a chalkboard to them. Most importantly, they're going to introduce each one of you to the Forest of Light—"

"Forest of Light?" Bull said with a smirk hinting at condescension. "What the hell kind of place is this? Chippyville?" he asked, referencing the popular kids' holoshow-turned-theme-park space stations.

"Doesn't sound near as scary as y'all make it out to be," Lonestar added.

"We'll see what you think when a Forinth is dangling you over the mouth of a live volcano knowing that if you scream, they'll drop you," Tag said. The marines shifted, eyeing him nervously. "Been there, done that. And it's not as fun as it sounds."

Sofia continued as they listened with now rapt attention to an overview of the Forinths' camouflage abilities and the scything, bony claws that could extend from the end of each of their tentacles. She explained their fanatical devotion to the balance of life within the underground Forest of Light and their efforts to keep the ice gods from entering their paradise-like domain.

"Ice gods, ma'am?" G asked. "Pardon me, but these things are real?"

Sofia laughed. "A little bit too real."

"We barely survived an encounter with one," Tag added.

"Did you kill it?"

Now Tag laughed. "Gods, no. We threw everything we had at the damn beast, and all we really did was piss it off."

Sofia gestured, and the viewscreen displayed a rough sketch

she had drawn of the creature. Despite her talent, Tag wasn't sure she had fully captured the horror of the menacing teeth, each large enough to grind an air car, or the dozens of beady black eyes gracing its sharp-lined face and contrasting starkly with its white fur. Tag could almost hear the creature's roar blasting his eardrums and feel the plume of hot air exploding from its mouth as it chased him.

"Looks like a snake got frisky with a spider and this was their bastard child," Lonestar said.

Gorenado's brow creased into a series of deep gorges. "Weaknesses?"

Sofia looked at the creature as it rotated on the holoscreen. "Only thing that's weak when it comes to an ice god is us."

FOUR

Tag watched Sofia brief the marines on the Forinths and Eta-Five for a while longer. Once she had finished imparting the necessary tactical knowledge of the aliens and environment they would soon encounter, the marines' questions became increasingly more esoteric.

Sofia seemed positively delighted. "Yes, the Forinths have family units. But they're not anything like you or I would ever expect."

Tag took that as his cue to check on Alpha and Coren's progress, eager to dig into the nanite lab work after he finished with them. His mind whirred through all the experiments to run: more chemical analyses, biochemical profiles, electromagnetic stimuli responses, and most importantly, theoretical simulations to see if the nanites could be deactivated without killing their Mechanic hosts. All of the computational simulations and studies that he and Alpha had performed had resulted in activating the built-in genetic modifications of the nanites that triggered organ-wide cell suicide. That meant anything they tried to do to the Drone-Mechs would result in their deaths, causing a virtual genocide without a chance of reverting the Drone-Mechs to their uninfected Mechanic selves. Not exactly the results they had hoped to achieve.

A hand grabbed his shoulder, breaking his thoughts. "Commander."

Tag spun to face Bull. "Something wrong?"

"I want a moment to speak to you." From the mess's open hatch, Tag heard Sofia answering a question about what caused the plants in the Forest of Light to glow. "Alone."

"Maybe it's best we use the officers' conference room?" Tag asked.

"Maybe," Bull said.

Tag led him up the ladders to a hatch outside Captain Weber's quarters. "Through here." They entered an anteroom with a view into an open hatch of the private quarters as well as the conference room. While the SRE had emptied the quarters of Captain Weber's possessions, the space remained uninhabited.

Bull eyed the quarters. "You haven't moved in there?"

"No, it felt a little strange to claim Captain Weber's quarters."

"But you're the captain now," Bull said, looking both nonplussed and slightly perturbed. "Why wouldn't you assume the proper quarters?'

"Is that what you wanted to talk to me about? Where I'm sleeping?" Tag asked, motioning to the conference room. It hadn't taken long for Tag to realize Bull had a thing about order and rules. Tag wondered if Bull was the kind of guy who might see the Forest of Light as just unimpressive trees and rocks instead of the exotic and colorful array of plant and animal life it really was.

"No," Bull said, following Tag to the six-person oblong table within the otherwise empty conference room. He stood beside a seat until Tag motioned for him to sit. "Of course not. If I may speak freely."

"It's a standing order to do just that," Tag said. "We're an unorthodox crew, and as such, I don't want to waste time with too many formalities."

"That's just it," Bull said, sitting straight in the conference chair. "This isn't a goddamn joyride. We're flying back into enemy territory. I'm supposed to trust a green captain with my life—and those of my men—and half your crew is alien."

"The only alien on this ship is Coren, and it's because of him you and I are both still alive. Without him, the *Montenegro* wouldn't be anything more than flotsam and frozen bodies floating in vacuum."

"His alleged actions don't make me any more confident in his allegiances," Bull said. A burning, cantankerous red crept into his cheeks, highlighting his subtle freckles. The marine seemed to sense the heat of his own anger and was silent for a moment. He began again with a calmer tone, but his eyes glowed no less fiercely. "We have no formal alliance with his species, no military relationships. All I've seen of them is an attack on the *Montenegro*, and you want me to believe he's on our side."

"Of course," Tag said. It took everything in him not to explode in frustration. He had been over this with so many people in the SRE. He knew the science; he had performed the experiments himself. Still, they seemed skeptical of the nanite explanation for the Drone-Mechs' actions. He could appreciate their skepticism, but it made the task of explaining the Drone-Mechs' enslavement over and over no less enjoyable. "Their actions were not their own."

"I know, Captain. I've heard the story. I've seen the briefings.

But Admiral Doran gave me one mission. She said I'm to support your efforts by whatever means necessary. And while I'll follow my orders, I want to be honest with you." He paused. "It's not often that I get those orders from a medical officer rather than a—"

"A real commander?" Tag finished. "Is that what you're looking for? I get your concerns, Bull. But I've served in the SRE longer than you have. I know how things work."

Bull looked ready to fight, his chest puffing up. "But frankly, you don't—"

Tag cut him off again. "I'm not a marine. Never was. But if you'll trust my judgment on the ship, I'll trust yours on the ground. I'm not the type to micromanage squad tactics and fire-fights. I'll gladly leave that to you. Admiral Doran tells me you're more than capable."

Bull's expression remained fixed somewhere between a frown and a scowl. Over the few days Tag had known him, the marine's mood seemed to run the canyon-wide gamut of pissed to slightly less pissed.

"Thank you, sir," Bull said. "That's the least I can ask for."

"Anything else?"

"No, sir."

Tag waited a beat. If this were a conversation with Coren or Sofia—even Alpha had started to pick up on social cues—then he would expect them to saunter off at this point. Bull didn't move until Tag said, "Dismissed."

Bull saluted and disappeared into the corridor. Tag massaged his temples as he listened to the man's footsteps fade. When the *Montenegro* had needed saving, he had barely pulled his ragtag team of Alpha, Sofia, and Coren together in time to stop the Drone-Mechs. It had been challenge enough to learn his crew members' strengths and overcome the personal conflicts that had cropped up throwing two humans, a half-droid sentient being, and an alien together. Now he had added another five crew members on a mission even more ambiguous than before.

It couldn't be any harder than surviving the Forinths and the ice gods, right?

———

Undulating green-and-purple plasma coursed over the bridge's view screen, and Tag wrapped his fingers tight around his armrests. He let the murmurs of the terminals on the bridge and the creaking of the bulkheads wash over him. His pulse resonated in his ears like war drums beating in preparation for battle, and he reminded himself to take deep, long breaths. Alpha buckled herself into the ops station, and Sofia slumped into the pilot's seat, rubbing her hands together in anticipation of their entry into normal space and whatever unwelcome surprises that might hold for them.

"Weapons report," he said.

"Point-defense cannons loaded and fully operational," Coren said as his fingers danced across his terminal. "Pulse cannons at one hundred percent, and Gauss cannon magazines are fully loaded and ready to go."

"Shields?"

"Also one hundred percent, Captain," Alpha said. "Repair bots are standing by."

Tag prayed they wouldn't need the repair bots, but he couldn't help thinking about the Drone-Mech fleet that had been after them during their escape from Eta-Five. Any run-in with them would undoubtedly leave the *Argo* in a state to ensure no repair bot went unemployed. The fleet they had run into last time had wasted no effort in attempting to bring the *Argo* down. It was startling the sheer power they had brought against Tag's single research vessel.

Why were the *Argo* and its mission so important to the Drone-Mechs? It was one damn ship, hardly worth any strategic or technological value to a species as advanced and powerful as the Drone-Mechs and, he guessed, whoever was controlling them. He wished the Drone-Mechs had at least shared that information with him. If they were going to try to riddle the ship with pulse rounds again, the least they could do was tell him *why*.

Tag shook himself out of his dark thoughts. "How about our power plant, Alpha?"

"Overall, our fusion reactors and power systems are reporting normal function."

"When you say 'overall' power systems are normal, does that mean there's something that isn't?"

"Yes, Captain, that is an accurate assessment. Although it is such an insignificant variation, any statistical analyses I performed on the matter seemed to indicate informing you of such an anomaly was unnecessary."

"Ignore statistical analyses," Tag said. "I want to know about any and all anomalies."

"Any and all. Are you certain?"

"I'm certain."

Sofia raised a brow. "Careful what you wish for, Skipper."

Before he could ask why, Alpha began. "In that case, I noticed a slight uptick in heads usage by the crew and biological waste recycling following the consumption of specific prepared meals, including those with high levels of curry."

Sofia stifled a laugh, and Coren rolled his single good eye.

"Also, it would seem the marines express language you have told me is outside the normal constraints. I have asked them to maintain more polite conversations, and they told me to copulate with myself. As you know, that is quite impossible."

"All right, Alpha," Tag said. "That's the kind of stuff we probably don't need to know. Let's focus on the ship. Specifically, power systems. I thought the crew on the *Montenegro* and our bots took care of everything."

"Everything is repaired in accordance with the ship's schematics, sir," Alpha said. "But there was a small power sink, almost miniscule enough to be imperceptible, within one of the *cargo* holds."

"Know why?" Tag asked.

Sofia answered instead. "This ship was almost blown to pieces. We got repairs done in days instead of months. I'm surprised there aren't worse issues. A little power sink here or there, imperfect wires, and electrical routing are kind of in our cards."

"This wouldn't be an issue with Mechanic engineering," Coren added, his thin lips curling into a contemptuous smirk.

"You're more than welcome to use that Mechanic acumen to fix what we couldn't before," Tag said.

Coren seemed to give the suggestion some thought. "Maybe I will. But I might as well wait until we're on Eta-Five. No use repairing something that's just going to get broken when we run into the Drone-Mechs."

FIVE

THE KALEIDOSCOPIC BLUR OF HYPERSPACE FIZZLED INTO fluid darkness. Metallic groans resonated through the bulkheads, and Tag's fingers curled around the edges of his armrests as the *Argo* entered normal space with a slight boom shaking through the ship. The cold threads of anxiety wove their way through his mind and nerves, an uncomfortable manifestation of his darkest expectations.

"Shields up!" Tag commanded at once, his eyes already searching for the glaring distant flash of grav impellers that might give away a Drone-Mech ship speeding toward them.

A green shimmer glowed over the main viewscreen as the shields stabilized. A low buzz filled the bridge, and Tag waited for the shriek of alarms and whir of malicious red lights that would announce the Drone-Mechs' imminent attack. His heart thrashed against his rib cage with the powerful beat of an overloading fusion reactor.

But no klaxons wailed, and no crimson lights glared. Instead, the viewscreen showed the stark silhouette of a moon before them. Behind it cascaded a field of brilliant pinpricks, each shining speck representing a distant star. The golden fire of Eta, the central star of this system, burned bright eight light-minutes from their port side. Sofia tensed at her controls, taking the *Argo* through their predetermined trajectory behind the dark side of the moon.

"Contacts?" Tag asked.

"Negative, sir," Alpha reported.

If Mechanics sweated like humans, Tag guessed he would have seen bullets coursing down Coren's forehead. Instead, the Mechanic stared intently at his terminal, his fingers hovering above their offensive and counteroffensive weapons commands, ever vigilant.

Tag punched a button on his terminal. "Bull, you all holding together down there?"

"Yes, Captain," Bull's voice crackled back from the terminal. "Armed and ready to roll."

"No contacts sighted," Tag said. In his head, he added, *yet.*

"Copy," Bull said, sounding almost disappointed.

"Don't worry. If we're not dealing with boarders, I'm sure we'll keep you busy planetside. Eta-Five isn't exactly a pleasant stroll in the woods."

"Never been in the woods," Bull said. "Wouldn't know."

The *Argo* sailed past the moon and toward the familiar icy white atmosphere of Eta-Five. Tag found the sight strangely comforting. At least they were starting their adventures in a place he somewhat knew. The shielded atmospheric anomaly would protect them from prying eyes once they reached the planet, and still, no signs of the Drone-Mechs blipped into existence by lidar or radar. He also wasn't foolish enough to accept that they were safe. Just because they hadn't detected Drone-Mechs yet didn't mean that they weren't there, lurking nearby, ready to pounce.

"Alpha, send a courier drone to the *Montenegro* with our coordinates," Tag said. "Inform them we haven't immediately encountered any hostile contacts after a successful normal space reentry. We'll be landing on Eta-Five shortly and will be out of light-beam and sensor reach soon."

"Copy, Captain," Alpha said, her metallic fingers plying her terminal. "The courier drone has been released."

Tag watched the tiny silver drone glint across their viewscreen before it accelerated into hyperspace via its miniature T-drive. It disappeared from their radar to begin its eight-day journey back to the *Montenegro* with its encrypted message.

"Bull, prepare for atmospheric entry. Make sure everyone is nice and secure in their crash couches. It's not going to be a smooth ride," Tag said over the comms.

"Understood, Captain," Bull replied.

The *Argo* plunged through the stormy clouds swirling above Eta-Five. The viewscreen fizzled and went dark while red lights washed over the deck and alarms screeched in a high-pitched clamor. Tag's terminal reported system failures all across the board, and Sofia held tight to the controls, her arms trembling as she pulled back. Metal groaned and protested in concert with the roar of the thrusters attempting to control their descent. The cacophony thundered throughout the bridge as if the ship was falling apart until the shaking suddenly settled. A dull-gray light appeared over the viewscreen once again, and all around, Tag saw the icy spires and jagged mountains of Eta-Five covered in a blanket of snow.

"We're back," Tag whispered.

"Captain?" Alpha said, her hypersensitive auditory sensors picking up his muttering.

Instead of repeating himself, Tag issued a new command. "Contact the Mechanic outpost in the Forest of Light."

Alpha worked at her terminal for a few moments before the viewscreen sparked to life with a new image. A tall Mechanic with a permanent frown sterner than Coren's appeared. Her golden eyes gazed at Tag with an air of nonchalance, as if escaping the brutal barricade of Drone-Mechs, saving the *Montenegro*, and making a risky return trip to the planet were of no particular import. The iridescent, almost cloyingly cheerful fluorescent purples, blues, pinks, and greens of the Forest of Light behind the alien contrasted sharply with the Mechanic's countenance.

"Commander Tag Brewer," the Mechanic said in a vaguely feminine monotone voice. "You have returned."

"Right you are," Tag said. "And I come bearing presents. Coren, go ahead."

Coren tapped on his terminal. "Bracken, it is good to see you again."

"Is that a goddamn smile?" Sofia asked, staring at Coren. "By the gods, the guy's actually smiling!"

Any hint of a slight upturn in his lips vanished, and Coren gave her an admonishing look.

"Good to see you as well," Bracken continued. "I wasn't sure you would return. Your odds of survival with your current company were not favorable." She glanced at Tag.

Not subtle at all, he thought.

"Favorable odds or not, we made good on our promise," Tag said. "We have enough spare parts to fix the *Stalwart*, according to Coren."

Bracken looked to Coren.

"It's true," Coren said.

"Captain, I'm beginning to sense Bracken is very skeptical of us," Alpha said with robotic innocence.

"You're catching on," Sofia said with a chuckle.

"Pardon my cynicism," Bracken said, "but I don't make judgments on a single data point. We learned to trust Sofia, but you, Commander Brewer, and the rest of your species remain unknowns."

"Maybe this is another positive data point for you," Tag said with a forced smile. As a scientist, he understood the pragmatic adherence to scientific dogma and scrutiny when it came to good data. It would take far more than returning to Eta-Five with Coren to inspire the Mechanics' faith. *Hope*fully, over the next days and weeks of work on the *Stalwart*, he could do just that.

The *Argo* leveled out over an expansive plain of snow where frozen geysers peppered the landscape, and somewhere in the distance a green flash of lightning cut through the leaden sky. He briefly wondered if the storm was rolling toward them. He had had enough of the storms and avalanches that plagued Eta-Five last time, and at least for now, in the *Argo*, they could escape an ice god attack with a bit more ease than trying to run away on an air car. But the natural planetside threats Eta-Five offered weren't the worst of his fears.

"What happened to the Drone-Mechs?" he asked.

"We shut down all our power facilities, leaving only a minimal sensor array open so as not to attract any attention from them," Bracken replied, "and the last of their planetside scouts left less than twenty-four hours after you did."

"And of course you couldn't tell when the fleet left," Tag said as more statement than question.

Bracken seemed to give an exasperated sigh, as if she were a prodigious child answering an ignorant teacher. "Of course not. The atmospheric anomaly has *always* blocked both incoming and outgoing sensor and communications attempts."

"Figured," Tag said, biting his tongue so as not to reply with the same irritated manner Mechanics seemed so apt at communicating with.

Bracken's expression remained as stonelike as ever. "And though they aren't here now, that doesn't mean they won't be soon."

"Which means you're as anxious as I am to begin repairs on the *Stalwart*," Tag said. "Can we start today?"

SIX

TAG WATCHED THE SNOW AND ICE RISE TO MEET THEM. IT came at them slowly, steadily. Not like his last time landing on this planet—if he could call it landing.

"We really have to park this far from the Forest?" Sofia asked, setting the ship down. It crunched into the snow, and its still-hot impellers melted into the white fluff.

"If those bastards show up, I'm not about to lead them straight to the Forinths or the Mechanics," Tag said. "Seems like the polite thing to do."

"And your concern is appreciated," Coren said. The engines spooled down, and the Mechanic unbelted his restraints then stood, stretching. "Besides, I could use the hike."

"I look forward to witnessing the Forest firsthand," Alpha said. "Your videos and Sofia's holofeeds have been educational, but there is much data missing from the biological forms present there."

"Everybody's a critic," Sofia said. She brushed a hand through her hair then clasped the back of her neck. "But damn, I'm really not looking forward to carrying all that space garbage to the *Stalwart* crash site."

"Nice of you to plan on carrying it," Tag said. "But I was thinking, if we aren't about to face any Drone-Mech threats, the marines might want something to do."

"Until the ice gods come," Coren said drily. Tag couldn't tell whether his remark was morbid sarcasm or certain despair. He decided to ignore the lament.

"No major life-forms detected within the immediate vicinity," Alpha added from the ops station, "which suggests the ice gods are not yet present."

"Oh, good," Coren said again with no change in his tone. "I cannot wait for our reunion."

"Think that one is still mad about you popping all its eyes?" Sofia asked, giving Coren a playful elbow to his side.

"Are ice gods known for their forgiveness?" Alpha asked, her silver head tilted. "I cannot imagine any reason they would not retain some anger for what you have done to them."

"Exactly," Tag said. He pictured the ice god's teeth bearing down on them. "So let's try not to waste too much time on the surface. Don't want the ice gods or anyone else finding us out here. Which, just to be safe, Coren, activate that camouflaging tech you made last time we were on Eta-Five. I'd prefer no one knows the *Argo* is here besides us."

"Will do," Coren said, his slender fingers tapping across his terminal.

Tag undid his restraints and led the others off the bridge. Their EVA suits rattled and rustled as they prepared themselves for the short journey ahead. This time, Tag was happy to be venturing onto the unforgiving arctic landscape with a crew behind him and a firm destination in mind. Through his wrist terminal, he hailed Bull. "Meet in the *cargo* hold for immediate departure."

"Copy," Bull replied.

Tag opened the hatch to the *cargo* bay. Unlike his last foray on the planet, there were no gaping wounds in the hull, and the ship was full of enough supplies to keep their crew traveling for decades in case they didn't reunite with the SRE in the near future. He certainly hoped it didn't come to that, but there was no way of knowing how long it would take to find the monsters responsible for the nanites and Drone-Mechs, along with completing Captain Weber's enigmatic mission, whatever that turned out to be.

Soon the clatter of footsteps announced the entrance of Bull and the rest of the marines. Ammo belts were wrapped around their power armor suits. Heavy rifles and multiple sidearms were secured over their backs and along their legs. Every usable surface contained some strategic piece of equipment to complement the marines' arsenal. Yellow lights glowed inside each of their helmets, providing a small if distorted glimpse of the humans encased by the formidable gear. If it weren't for that view of their faces, Tag would have thought they were more machine than Alpha.

"You took Sofia's warnings about the ice gods to heart, huh?" Tag remarked to Bull.

"A good marine doesn't go into any situation unprepared," Bull replied. The other four lugged even more weapons onto the air car, and Bull's eyes traced over Coren. "It might be more than ice gods we face."

Coren returned Bull's suspicious glance as he helped Sofia load a crate full of repair materials for the *Stalwart* onto the air car. Tag understood Coren's skepticism, but he also couldn't help recalling Kaufman's body and how he had failed to save her life. The *Argo's* previous marine detachment had been decimated by just a few Drone-Mechs. Even though weeks had passed, the time hadn't seemed to slow the recurring memories that would awaken at the slightest provocation. Images of the crew being annihilated under a storm of pulsefire and acrid smoke haunted Tag's waking hours. In sleep, it was even worse. Knowing Bull and the other marines were at least a little better prepared in equipment and intel provided Tag some temporary comfort.

"I trust your judgment," Tag said to the marine, hoping to win some favor.

"You should," Bull said with an edge. He marched past with a slew of mini-Gauss rifles slung over his shoulder. Tag glared at the back of the marine's head but was unable to come up with the proper response, unsure whether he needed a good dressing down or simply a stern warning. The moment passed, however, as he struggled with the right move, and he cursed inwardly, reminding himself to review the *Argo*'s digital library of military leadership books and information.

Sofia sidled up to him, seeming to read his thoughts. "Remember, we're still eggheads to them. I'm behind you one hundred percent, but you've still got to *show* them what's up."

Tag nodded. She was right, of course. Trying to study leadership as if he were memorizing biological theorems for a science lecture wouldn't be enough to earn their respect. It was like attending virtual lectures and scouring texts and expecting to improve your Turbo game without ever playing the actual sport. He needed to prove his worth to them. For better or worse, he figured he would have ample opportunity soon.

When the air car was filled with equipment and the crew found their places within it, Tag took his seat in the front. Sofia slipped into the driver's seat and turned the engines on. The car rose from the deck and hovered before the *cargo* bay door. Tag punched a command on his wrist terminal, and the whoosh of air sounded all around them as the *cargo* bay depressurized slightly. A heavy metallic groan accompanied the slow march of the opening *cargo* bay doors. Harsh wind peppered the air car with the relentless ringing of hail against alloy, but between eddies of ice and snow came beams of filtered light glowing through the windshield.

"Eta-Five, we're ready for you," Sofia said.

The low electric whine of the car's initialization motors grew into a steady roar with the activation of the thrusters, and they blasted forward from the *Argo*. It took Tag's eyes a moment to adjust as his pupils contracted, shielding themselves from the harsh light reflecting off every snowflake and icy protrusion across the landscape. Gasps sounded behind him. Lonestar whistled, her eyes glued to a porthole. Gorenado pressed a large hand to a window as he leaned toward the glass, peering through his helmet at the stark world. Even Bull seemed less a hardened warrior and more like a kid visiting a space station sweets emporium. His eyes were wide, dancing back and forth, soaking in the planet.

Tag recalled his first venture out of the *Argo* onto Eta-Five. He had been born on Earth, so he preferred the blue skies, moderate temperatures, sprawling megacities, and strips of vegetation that crawled over most of the planet he had once called home. But after a few years in space confined to metal tubes and artificial gravity, the white-washed iciness of Eta-Five was still a welcome sight to behold. Land and ground, no matter how foreign or exotic or dangerous, held a certain allure to Tag and, he supposed, the other members of his crew. True, the human soul could survive in cramped metal cans hurtling through space, but the soul *thrived* in the great wide open of wilderness and atmosphere.

They traveled over what appeared to be a frozen riverbed winding through a valley formed in the snow. Severe winds buffeted and battered them at every twist and turn, dousing them with shards of ice. Tag remembered driving alone through these conditions before, his nerves wild with fright, but now Sofia guided them almost effortlessly.

"This baby sure handles better than the *Argo*," she said offhandedly as she skirted a pillar of ice and rock. "Makes me wish I was back flying fighters again."

"According to my map," Alpha began, "it seems we are approaching the entrance to the Forest."

"Strange," Tag said. Last time he had been here, the tunnel entrance had glowed a fluorescent blue, beckoning to him like a lighthouse. This time, there was nothing but the monotonous whites and grays of the forsaken planet. "I don't see it."

"Mechanic defenses," Coren said. "Visible-light–scattering apparatus." He spoke into a terminal through his EVA suit. "Bracken, we've arrived."

In the distance, Tag saw a snowdrift shimmer slightly. Then it dissolved, almost as if it had evaporated all at once. Blue light pulsated from a cave where the snowdrift had been only moments before, and Tag knew they had found their way back to the world of the Forinths. The air car coasted through the tunnel, where the colorful lichens, mosses, and other plants lining craggy rock walls flew by them. The vegetation grew denser and shone more intensely with each meter they descended until they entered the enormous underground forest.

Tag had been in the place only weeks before, but still a warm feeling of awe flooded through him with electric vigor. So many plants and trees illuminated the space that it was easy to forget they were underground. Above them, tendrils of foliage draped from the high ceilings, casting their light down, and beside them, vast trees stretching as high as Earthside skyrisers spread their warm glow across the ground in wide swathes. Creatures with all manner of strange bodies retreated into the forest at the arrival of the car, escaping and melding into the shadows or changing the hue of their skin to emulate the intense light around them. Birds took flight, their leathery wings shimmering with hypnotically shifting pigments as they fled. The only creatures that stood in their path contrasted sharply with the lush landscape. Each wore a suit of black armor and cradled a rifle.

"How's that for a welcome home?" Sofia asked.

"My rudimentary knowledge on Mechanic body language suggests these individuals are adopting an aggressive stance," Alpha said.

Tag gulped. "That would be my assessment as well."

The clink of restraints being released sounded from the troop hold of the air car. Tag turned to see Bull staring straight through the windshield.

"These are the people we came to help?" Bull's fingers tightened around his mini-Gauss. "You'd think they'd show a little more appreciation."

Tag's stomach twisted over itself. It couldn't be possible. Could it? Had the nanites infected what might have been the last free Mechanics? If so, there would be no talking with them to put down their weapons. There was only one way to reason with Drone-Mechs. The mechanical rustle and hum of the marines' power armor suits was punctuated by the click of magazines into rifles.

Sofia looked between the Mechanics and Tag. "What now, Skipper?"

SEVEN

OREN WAS THE ONLY ONE IN THE VEHICLE WHOSE posture remained relaxed as the air car slowed in front of the other Mechanics. "If I were to guess, they are reacting this way because the nanites have their origins in human technology, and you are in fact humans."

"Three hells, but we've gone over this," Tag said. "The SRE banned weapons like that."

"A Mechanic's trust is hard to earn," Coren offered matter-of-factly. "There is little I can say to convince them otherwise."

"What do you mean? Did you not bother to tell them we aren't the enemy?"

"I sent them only the facts from our findings. But before I left with you, I did warn them to be cautious upon our return, in case we were compromised while away from Eta-Five."

"So you prepped them to think we might be the enemy? Not helpful, Coren."

Bull undid his restraints and moved toward the door. "Let me get them to put down their goddamn weapons."

"No," Tag said. "Stand down. That'll only make things worse." The Mechanics outside inched closer, their weapons trained on the air car. Tag looked at Coren. "You want to let them know we're all good here?"

Coren pressed something on his EVA suit and talked into it. Tag hated it that the alien still had a private channel to the other Mechanics he couldn't patch into. Nonetheless, he watched the Mechanics outside lower their weapons and back away.

"We're all clear," Coren said.

"Good," Tag said. "Remind me to kill you for that later, Coren, okay?"

"Do you want me to set a reminder?" Alpha asked. "Although that is a rather unorthodox thing to say to a crew member."

"Sarcasm," Tag said. "Mostly."

Alpha's silver mouth made an O shape as she nodded.

"Bull, let me and Coren out first," Tag said.

"Don't like it, Captain," Bull said, still peering out the window in the door. His hands wrapped tighter around his rifle.

"Trust me," Tag said. "I've dealt with these people before."

"Before we go out there, there are some conditions from Bracken," Coren said. "They don't want you to come out armed."

Bull scoffed. "You kidding?"

Lonestar glowered at Coren. "I didn't go through three years of training to confront the enemy with my willy hanging out."

"You don't have a willy to worry about," G said. Then, thinking, he added, "Do you?"

"First off, the Mechanics are not our enemy," Tag said. "We need them; they need us. If they wanted us dead, we'd be dust already."

"That's not the way marines do things," Bull said. "We would've cut them down before they had a chance to lay a finger on us."

"According to Captain Brewer," Coren said, "the marines on the *Argo* had no such success."

Bull's face lit up redder than any volcanic pit in the Forest, and he lunged at Coren. Tag reacted by instinct, throwing himself between the Mechanic and the marine. He braced himself for Bull to slam into him like his namesake, but the heavy impact never came. Gorenado, his huge arms wrapped around Bull's narrower chest, grunted, holding the marine back.

Sumo stepped beside them with a decidedly calm expression, as if she were impermeable to the heat of emotion. "Best to ignore the xeno. Don't want to start any more wars than we have to."

"Let me go," Bull said, his face the color of autumn leaves. When Gorenado hesitated, he said, "That's a goddamn order." Gorenado loosened his grip, and Bull stood, staring at Coren and still fuming. "That was uncalled for."

"Agreed," Tag said. His own internal wounds at the slight throbbed. "I know you're all about facts and reality, but try to have a bit of human sympathy, all right?"

Coren's face belied no emotion. "Apologies, Captain. I didn't mean it as an insult, only as an unfortunate fact."

Tag watched Bull, waiting for him to come at Coren in a flurry again, but the marine didn't take another step forward. Instead, he glared with a furious intensity that rivaled the burn of the sun Eta.

"Screw the xenos," Bull spat, full of spark and vitriol. The marines clung to their weapons even more fiercely than before. This mission was already off to a wonderful start, and they hadn't even encountered their real enemy yet.

"Sarge is right," Lonestar said. "Foolish thing to do, walk into the arms of an armed stranger with no gun of your own."

"Look, they aren't strangers. They *are* frightened for their lives, though. We're here to show them they can trust us," Tag said. A couple of weeks ago, he hardly would have believed he would be defending the Mechanics. "You're getting off and leaving your weapons behind."

"Bullshit," Bull said. "Look at those monsters out there. And what about the Forinths? You're telling me they aren't dangerous either? We should just trust them because you and Sofia are still alive?"

"That's exactly what I'm saying," Tag said. "Now drop your weapons and move out."

G looked nervously between Tag and Bull as if he wasn't sure whose orders to follow.

Tag felt like he was dangerously close to losing control of the marines. Once, there had been a time in officer training where he had felt confident in his ability to run a ship and its crew, when he had known he would one day be commanding at least a destroyer. His failure during bridge officer training had put an end to those plans—and that self-assuredness—and now he looked back at his naiveté with a hint of guilt and shame. His career in science and medicine had at least allowed him a newfound passion, and leading teams in the lab and med bay had come to him naturally, granting him some semblance of achievement. Fate and circumstance had had different plans for him, and once again, he found himself trying to force a misfit team together. This wasn't how he had pictured his career decades ago. Three hells, this wasn't how he had pictured it last week.

"Look," Tag began, trying to feign a confidence he wasn't sure he felt. Entreating Bull to his side with any pleading, calls to reason, or well-intended discussions wasn't going to work. The man saw things in black and white, and he had to give him black and white. "I'm losing my patience. I am the goddamn captain. I hold rank in this mission, and I am ordering you to leave your weapons here and follow me. You are not to provoke any conflict with either the Mechanics or the native species of this planet. Is that understood?"

G's head bobbed first, and one by one the other marines gave a "Yes, sir." Only Bull, nostrils flared and a vessel in his forehead bulging, did nothing. Tag stared the shorter man down for what seemed like minutes before the grizzled marine finally muttered a "Yes, sir."

"Good," Tag said. "Follow me."

Tag punched the release to the air car's hatch and undid his EVA helmet as the warm, humid air blasted into the vehicle. The succulent atmosphere carried with it the taste of fresh fruit, clean water, and lush vegetation. With Coren by his side, he stepped out of the car and onto the soft ground, where the creeping moss and leaves under his feet gave way to loamy earth. He strode to the tallest Mechanic of the bunch with her visor peeled back, and he recognized Bracken. Her narrow face and prominent cheekbones gave her a slightly more human look than Coren. As he approached, she slung her rifle over her back and raised a hand to signal the other Mechanics to lower their weapons.

"Hell of a way to say hello," Tag said. "I thought bringing parts to repair the *Stalwart* would be a welcome gesture. Is it not?"

Bracken's golden eyes flitted between Coren and Tag. Her lips remained straight, and she offered no sign of emotion, relief or otherwise. "It is welcome." She gestured at the marines. "Those are not."

Sofia and Alpha sauntered ahead of the marines. Alpha scanned everything around her, mesmerized like a child at a zoo. The Mechanics seemed to relax at the sight of Alpha's innocence and Sofia's familiar presence.

"They aren't here for you," Tag said, referring to the marines. "We weren't sure what kind of resistance we'd face getting here or further along in our mission."

Bracken said nothing, letting the uncomfortable silence between them stretch.

"Look," Tag said, stepping forward. Out of the corner of his eye, he saw one of the Mechanics raise his pulse rifle. "I made it off Eta-Five with more luck than skill before. I don't want to rely on chance this time."

"Your race is responsible for the nanites," Bracken said. If the words had come from a human, Tag would've expected them to be dripping with poisonous malice. Instead, they came out flat and calm. His skin prickled at the cold delivery of the accusation. As much time as he spent with them, he doubted he would ever get used to the Mechanics' demeanor. They were more emotionless than Alpha. "Pardon me for not welcoming you and your armed party with open arms. Coren's words mean little to us when, for all we know, you may have infected him with the very nanites your people created."

Tag could sense the tension between his crew and the Mechanics with an almost palpable thickness. A stab of panic pierced his gut, with a fear that this was all about to go south in a fusillade of pulsefire. He couldn't let that happen for the sake of humanity's—and the Mechanics'—future. "It's in our best interest to find out who is behind the nanites. If they are human, they're operating outside SRE law with technology more frightening than we could've ever anticipated. If they're not human, then that means they've somehow stolen tech from us. All without us knowing. Either way, it doesn't look good for us. So I'm not going to pretend we're coming to help you out of the goodness of our hearts. We share a mutual interest in stopping the Drone-masters responsible for enslaving your people."

Bracken seemed to consider his argument. Her eyes never left his, and he halfway wondered if the Mechanics had some kind of mind-reading tech she was using to scan his brain. It was probably paranoia, but then again, with everything else that had happened around him, it wouldn't be entirely surprising.

With one arm outstretched as if she was going in for a handshake, she finally stepped forward. "Take them in."

It took Tag a second to comprehend the meaning of her words. Then they fell over him like shards of icy pillars collapsing on Eta-Five's surface. The Mechanics surged forward, surrounding him, Alpha, Sofia, and the marines. Bull charged one of the Mechanics, knocking the lithe alien away with a hammering fist. Gorenado punched another in the gut, and the alien reeled over, absorbing most of the impact through its suit. The Mechanics swarmed them, unintimidated by the marines' show of force, and slapped metal bands around each of their wrists, dodging the rest of the powerful blows and furious assault with relative ease. Each time one of the bands wrapped around a marine's wrist, the marine's suit seemed to power down, standing still and straight with the marine trapped within it. The Mechanics yanked Tag's arms behind his back and secured his wrists together with a similar metal band that sent shivers through his flesh.

"What are you doing?" Tag yelled.

Bracken ignored him, signaling the Mechanics to take their prisoners deeper into the forest. Tag wrenched his head around enough to see the marines struggling in their power armor suits. Coren, too, was taken prisoner and gave Tag a sorrowful look, as if he truly felt regret for what had just transpired. The look lasted only a second before more Mechanics churned between them, and Tag lost sight of Coren.

"Bracken!" Tag yelled, a hot ball of rage growing in his stomach at Bracken and at himself for trusting her. He lashed against his restraints and struggled against his captors' grip. "I demand you tell us what's going on!"

The Mechanic looked at him with her cool eyes, conveying no sympathy or anger. She gave a slight nod to a Mechanic next to Tag, and a heavy pain shuddered through his skull. Red snowflakes danced in his blurred vision, then his world went black.

EIGHT

THE CACOPHONOUS SOUND OF SOMETHING SLAMMING against metal pierced Tag's ears. He blinked, slowly making sense of the world as the ringing continued. Each high-pitched rattle sent knives through his ears and into his brain, twisting the pain inside his skull until he felt ready to explode. At first, when his pupils focused on the silver metal above his head, he thought something was wrong with the *Argo*. The cloying scent of the Forest of Light rocked him back to his senses. He pushed himself to his feet, almost losing his balance. His hand shot out and found the smooth coolness of a metal wall, his head pounding as he gazed around him.

Sofia stood. "Skipper, you okay?"

"Alive," Tag managed.

She ran to his side and helped him as he teetered forward. His memories of everything that had just happened hit him at once, from arriving in the Forest to the bash that had sent him reeling into unconsciousness. Another wave of vertigo rolled over him, and he leaned on Sofia for support.

The marines were clustered around what looked to be a doorway to their makeshift prison cell. Bull continued drumming his fist on the wall, and Lonestar hurled epithets and curses at the clear polyglass door. Gorenado sat near the entrance, his eyes closed as if he was meditating, and G and Sumo paced around Bull. Beyond them stood Coren.

"Can you quiet down with that racket?" the Mechanic said.

Bull twisted to face him, his face no less flushed than usual. "This is your fault, xeno." He jabbed his finger into Coren's chest.

Coren made no indication he was alarmed or at all frightened by the marine's posturing. "I didn't know it would end up like this, that they wouldn't believe me when we got here. But that hardly matters." Coren indicated the polyglass door with a wave of his hand. "No matter how much you yell, they won't hear you. This is sealed with acoustic barriers. Mechanic technology."

"I don't give a flying rat's ass what you or the gods might say," Bull said, using the choice phrase so common at makeshift station bars full of gutfire and other home-brewed alcohol. "I'm not stopping until they answer my questions."

"The least you can do is be considerate of your captain," Coren said with a sigh. He gestured at Tag.

Tag curled his fingers through his hair, gripping at his scalp as if that would disperse the lingering headache pulsating through his brain.

Bull appeared no less angry, but he stopped punching the cell's wall. "Captain, I hope to the gods new and old that you've got a way out of this mess."

Tag wanted to make a smart remark. He wanted to say he had the key to this place sitting in his pocket. No big deal. Like he was supposed to have all the answers or something. But he didn't. That wasn't what he *should* say, whether or not his agonized brain was telling him Bull deserved it.

"Give me a minute," he said instead.

Bull didn't like that. And when he didn't, neither did his marines. A fire burned in Bull's eyes that spread to the others, radiating in furious glares, all except G. Tag could understand their frustration. They had endured a surprise assault on the *Montenegro*, had helped start the rebuilding process, and then were sent away on what must seem to them like a wild goose chase. Now, before they had even started any real mission, they were prisoners of the alien species they were supposed to be helping, betrayed by their captain's trust.

"Look," Tag said. "If you want out of here, hear me out. If you won't do it out of respect, I'll damn well order you to." He glanced at Bull. He hated continually pulling rank like this. It wasn't how a leader truly earned respect, but he didn't have time for relationship building: they were in prison. Mission number one was getting out. "I know I'm just a CMO turned captain and this isn't what you signed up for, but you've got to listen to me on this one."

"After all," Sofia added, "can't get much worse than being stuck in prison."

"Not helpful," Tag said.

"Fine," Bull said. "You got us in here, you get us out. This is your rodeo now."

Lonestar smiled at the comment. "If it's a rodeo, count me in."

Gorenado huffed in agreement, and G looked as eager as a puppy to please its family. Sumo leaned against a wall, her sinewy arms across her chest.

"The Mechanics are nothing if not practical and logical," Tag said.

"He's got that right," Sofia said. "They place about as much importance in pure emotion as a navigational AI system on a warship does."

"Exactly," Tag continued, "so we have to appeal to their—" He stopped then looked around the cell. A sickening feeling stormed through him, settling in his gut. "Speaking of AI, where's Alpha?"

"The xenos took her away," G said. "Said they wanted to check her out."

Alpha had started as an experiment, having once been nothing more than a dish of cells growing in a cell incubator. Tag had nurtured life and sentience out of those cells, and in the short time since her virtual birth, she had saved his life numerous times against the Drone-Mechs. All notions of formulating and executing a plan to appeal to the Mechanics suddenly seemed inadequate and far too slow.

"What are they doing to her?" he asked.

"Don't know," Sumo said. "For some reason, they didn't care to explain."

"I don't think they planned on hurting her," Coren said, as if he could read Tag's thoughts. "I think they were just curious. You know, as much as I hate to admit it, Alpha is a work of technological prowess. I'm sure they could hardly believe a human created her."

Tag wanted to take pride in that reluctant admission of Coren's, but all he could think about was the Mechanics taking Alpha apart in some kind of mechanical vivisection to study how she worked. "They can't treat her like a machine. Not now. She's fully sentient."

Pushing aside Bull, Tag started to bang on the polyglass door, their previous conversation forgotten, overwhelmed by thoughts of Alpha's torture. The tremors resonating through his bones made the headache worse, and the noise didn't help either. He ignored the hammering sensation on his brain as he watched a pair of Mechanics strolling by.

"What did you do to Alpha?" he yelled, knowing full well what Coren had said earlier. But he had to try. He couldn't just let them tear Alpha apart. Not like this. Gods, no. "Don't hurt her!"

Then, to his surprise, the door opened.

Tag's heart leapt, and he waited to be escorted out, waited for the guns to be drawn or maybe for the pulsefire to fly.

None of that happened. Instead, Bracken stood before him, alone and no longer wearing her power armor.

"I was wrong," she said simply. No apology. No explanation.

Her velvety fur waved under the caress of a soft wind curling between them. It carried the distant beat of the drum the Forinths used to keep the ice gods out of the Forest. The sound should have made Tag's head pound all the more furiously, but instead, it brought him only relief. He was out of the prison cell, facing Bracken. A strange expression traced itself across her face. Her thin lips were slightly downturned, and her golden eyes glowed a little less brightly than before.

"Wrong about what?" Tag said. He heard the footsteps of the others as they cautiously approached the exit, and he took a step out the door. His boots sank into the wet earth and foliage.

"Your people." She eyed the marines. "Or more accurately, you."

"No shit," Tag said. He took another step toward her, his fingers clenching into fists. She didn't flinch. "What did you do to Alpha?"

"She's fine," Bracken said, "and she's what saved you."

———

When Tag neared the shelter Bracken was leading him to, he saw Alpha seated inside on a table with a gaggle of Mechanics surrounding her. Several of them peered into an open panel on her chest. Tag's heart climbed into his throat, and he broke away from Bracken, his feet pounding through the vegetation. The fluorescent plants and trees blurred by until Alpha turned his way. She lifted a hand in an awkward but distinctly human "hello." Her mouth contorted into the best simulation of a smile she could muster.

"Captain!" she said. The ease in her tone slowed Tag, but his heart still raced as he approached her.

The Mechanics around her backed away upon his arrival, and Tag studied the open panels, revealing the work he had put into integrating her life-support units with the M3 droid chassis.

"What's going on?" Tag said. He heard Bracken's light footsteps as she caught up to them.

A shorter, younger-looking Mechanic stepped forward. "We were just examining the electroneural connections you created to serve as the biosynthetic conduits with her external control systems."

"Why?" Tag asked, not hiding the suspicion in his demand.

"The technical aspects of this machine are quite a bit more advanced than I suspected from a human of your rank and talent."

Tag ignored the derisive words. The insult wasn't what worried him. "You do realize she's more than a machine, right? She's sentient. You have to respect that."

The Mechanic stepped back, his brow twitching slightly as if nonplussed.

Bracken scoffed. "I fear it is much too difficult for my people, talented as they may be, to see your invention as anything but a machine. Biological components or not."

"I find satisfaction in knowing you appreciate Captain

Brewer's work," Alpha said, "but I must agree with him that I do not appreciate being referred to as a machine."

The young Mechanic backed away from Alpha, glancing among Tag, Alpha, and Bracken like a lost tourist trying to figure out which corridor of the space station to take. "I suppose I regret my choice of words. I will have to think about the ramifications of biological organisms within machines."

"Yeah, you do that," Tag said.

Alpha closed her chest panel, muffling the humming and clicking of her internal workings by her outer chassis. "I didn't mean to cause a conflict."

"Not your fault," Tag said. "But did they hurt you?"

"No, Captain. I was merely showing them how you accomplished the task of bringing me to life."

"You actually consented to that?"

"Of course," Alpha said. "But only after I convinced them you and the others weren't here to initiate any type of nanite enslavement protocols."

Tag turned to Bracken.

She regarded him for a moment before speaking. "The good thing about her being part computer is that the data don't lie."

"Although I am quite capable of lying organically," Alpha said proudly, "she is correct that my internal data storage is quite difficult to alter without leaving behind significant markers of such alteration."

"You breached her internal memory then," Tag said.

The realization of what that meant hit him with enough force to make his pounding headache worse. Not only had the Mechanics found access to everything Alpha had experienced firsthand, but they would also have had the opportunity to delve into the trove of the *Argo*'s databases. Every vid and audio feed, every bit of experimental data and security, every conversation he might have shared between crew members, for better or worse, could have been accessed through Alpha's connection with the ship's main AI and computer systems. He wanted to interrogate Bracken, to find out what else she knew about them in this breach of privacy. He felt almost naked in front of them now. No more secrets. Nothing he could hide from them.

Bracken didn't seem the least bit bothered by what they had done. "We did believe her internal memory," she repeated. Then, to quell any shadow of a doubt he might have about her indiscretion into their data-sifting, she said, "The theories you and Sofia shared certainly align with our own suspicions that your species is somehow responsible."

"But the SRE isn't?" Tag asked hopefully.

"I have not put it past your current governing body or any of your rebellious colonies," Bracken said, "but I can say with a fair amount of confidence that you and your crew are acting in our best interest and not that of the Drone-masters responsible for the enslavement of our people."

"You're damn right," Tag said. "Why not let my crew go, and then maybe we can get to work?"

"Yes," Bracken said. She gestured to the younger Mechanic, and he jogged out of the shelter toward the prison cell. "It's clear that the first order of business is getting the *Stalwart* in working order. But after that, what exactly did you have planned, Captain Brewer?

NINE

CONSTRUCTION ON THE *Stalwart* HAD BEEN UNDERWAY for a couple of weeks now with no interruption by ice gods or Drone-Mechs. The routine of managing repairs and doing research on the nanites and Drone-Mechs, while strenuous, was a welcome reprieve from being stuck on a cramped spaceship traveling the stars and constantly watching for a surprise attack. Scanning his terminal, Tag was seated at a table in the improvised home Sofia had lived in over the past five years of her residency on Eta-Five.

The open windows of Sofia's home let in the otherworldly warble of alien birds and insect-like species, and each breath Tag took was another reminder of the strange planet he was on. The thickness of the humidity and the scent of the damp soil reminded him vaguely of the wet earth and fog of the early mornings when his father used to drive him from Old Houston to the Gulf of Mexico. They would wake up before the break of dawn, take a passenger pod from their 127th-floor apartment in the midtown skyrisers, and fly down the coast until they reached the protected coastlines where water lapped the sliver of a beach. The call of gulls had rung out through the humid air, piercing the gray smog above them, and ten-year-old Tag would follow his father past the blinking holoscreens advertising VR simulations ranging from intense combat to sensual experiences, skirting their way to a fishing spot on the Preserves, the largest faux-nature franchises operating in the SRE. Supposed "fresh" air was pumped into the bubbles where they fished surrounded by holoscreens that gave them the illusion of being on a secluded dock on the bay. And though the visual and auditory effects were almost convincing, the artificial fresh air scents had never convinced Tag.

"It smells like Grandma's perfume mixed with sugar and seaweed," Tag had said.

His father had laughed, almost letting his fishing reel fall into the saltwater. "Who knows? Maybe that's what it actually smelled like before."

"Then I don't want to breathe fresh air," Tag had said.

But now, far from the overpopulated planet filled with humans and their industry and outside the ships and space stations with recycled and filtered atmosphere, he welcomed fresh air. He was even more thrilled that it smelled nothing like the "fresh air" from the Preserves.

Tag took another deep breath, and Sofia apparently noticed.

"That's what I loved about this place," she said. "After growing up on Paragonia during the terraforming efforts, stuck in the tunnels and domes all day, I couldn't imagine what it would feel like to take a clean breath of air."

Her brown eyes focused on a point only she could see as if she were caught in a trance.

Alpha looked up from a terminal she was working on.

"Captain Brewer, do you think it's possible we can install scent receptors on my chassis? I would like to experience this scent as well."

"Be careful what you wish for," Sofia said, "because you'll regret it after a freeze-dried-bean night on the *Argo*."

"Is that due to the human proclivity for gaseous discharge?"

"Farts," Tag said. "We call them farts."

Sofia burst out laughing while Alpha nodded as though she were a student being taught an important lesson. Tag couldn't help the grin cutting across his face. But when Coren showed up at the door, his short fur in disarray, the humor vanished as quickly as a Forinth changing colors.

"Is it done?" Tag asked. The dark reminder of the mission before them fell over him like an ominous shadow, eliminating the momentary reprieve any immature jokes had provided.

"The *Stalwart*'s reactors are all in working order again," Coren said. "It will fly now. If we took it to space, the *cargo* decks, half of engineering, and some of the crew quarters would be unusable."

"Understood. As much as I like Eta-Five, fourteen days here is enough. It's about time we carry on," Tag said. "Any chance we can take off early and use some of the *Argo*'s repair bots to help expedite things on route?"

"Maybe," Coren said. "But by the time we reprogrammed the bots to work on our ships and retrofitted them to accommodate the alloys of a Mechanic ship, our own bots and engineers would be finished. It's best we stay the course to ensure optimal repairs."

"Still don't trust human tech to help with the job?"

"In a manner of speaking, no," Coren said. Tag thought he detected the hint of a good-natured grin twitching at the corner of the Mechanic's thin lips. Maybe hanging around with humans was wearing off on Coren. "But I do appreciate the offer."

"Good to hear," Tag said. He stood from his seat on a tree

trunk serving as a stool. "I'm going to go check on our friends with the guns. Alpha, if you could keep searching for any way to deactivate the nanites without killing their hosts, that would be greatly appreciated."

"Happy to oblige, Captain," Alpha said, still hunched over her terminal. Tag had no idea whether it was in the realm of possibility for Alpha to find any such solution, but at least it kept her busy. She seemed to appreciate having something, anything, to keep her mind active.

"I'll be meeting with the Forinths," Sofia said. "Want to let them know we're a few days from takeoff. I'm sure they'll be relieved when all these crazy aliens are out of their hair."

"I thought Forinths didn't have hair," Alpha said.

"Human phrase," Tag replied.

Alpha mouthed an O and continued staring at her terminal.

Tag followed Sofia out of the shelter and then paused, watching her delve into the verdant Forest. Even though she wore the crisp, clean white-and-blue uniform of the SRE, she appeared at ease on Eta-Five, gingerly stepping over the knotted roots and between the vines, walking as if there were a path where there was none. Her voice warbled between the trees even as the foliage enveloped her into its colorful embrace. The singsong language of the Forinths chorused back in reply, emanating from all around like the siren call of wood nymphs beckoning a traveler into their clutches.

As Sofia diverged and Tag followed a trail the Mechanics had made, he felt the gentle tugging of the Forinth song on his mind. He couldn't fully understand their language like Sofia, and the translation tech the SRE had developed was unable to comprehend the intricacies of a language built on a complex blend of intonation, melody, rhythm, and pitch, especially when compared to the more commonly spoken languages of the universe. Still, like a moving piece of symphonic orchestration, the haunting song of the Forinths played on his emotions. He felt a strange mix of nostalgia and an almost intoxicating giddiness, like he was drunk on gutfire without the burning sensation in his stomach or the knowledge that a debilitating hangover was on the horizon.

"Captain," G said, snapping to attention.

Tag shook himself from his reverie. "At ease."

The marines were scattered about a courtyard of sorts and were trying on their power suits. Nothing looked different about the suits the marines had arrived on Eta-Five with, but Tag was all too familiar with their new features. As a halfhearted apology, Bracken had ordered a couple of Mechanic engineers to retrofit the SRE marines' suits with the same shielding system that came standard on Mechanic foot soldier power armor suits. The SRE had installed energy shields on all their spacefaring vessels in the navy, but they had as of yet been unable to miniaturize the technology. Bull had been resistant to the idea of Mechanics tampering with his power suit but had eventually acquiesced when Bracken had demonstrated the capabilities of the energy shield by having her foot soldiers fire a fusillade of pulsefire at a Mechanic power armor suit.

Bull examined the wrist controls of his upgraded suit, turning the shield on and off. "If these xenos can make this kind of tech, our scientists should be doing it, too."

He gave Tag an almost accusatory look.

"I'm all AI and bio," Tag said. "It's out of my league, but we'll send the schematics to the *Montenegro* next chance we get."

Sumo strutted back and forth in her suit as if trying it on for the first time. "I'm just happy to be one of the first members of the SRE to try these things out."

Gorenado looked like he wanted to say something, but before he could, a violent rumble shook the Forest. Birds began squawking, taking flight, and flitting between the trees, and a small herd of the buffalo-like spirit oxen with color-changing hides stampeded through the Forest, charging deeper into the vast caverns. Their long fur flashed a fierce crimson, and they bellowed a flurry of strangely high-pitched growls.

"What was that?" Bull demanded. He secured his chest plate with a snap and clipped his helmet onto his suit. The other marines assembled their armor, and the clink of magazines jamming into weapons pierced the cacophony erupting around them.

"That the ice gods?" Lonestar asked, rotating with her rifle pressed against her armored shoulder.

Tag's fingers inched toward the holstered pulse pistol at his hip. "I don't know."

"Thought you said that Forinth drum-thing keeps them out," Bull said. He stepped toward the opening to a forest trail. Lizard-like creatures scurried from the trees, hissing and spitting. They traveled on six legs, their muzzles scrunched in snarls as if they were prepared to fight. But they didn't bother with any of the marines, instead charging into the undergrowth where the spirit oxen had gone.

"What are they all running from?" G asked, uncertainty lacing his deep voice.

The caverns' trembling crescendoed until the quaking was loud enough to resonate through Tag's bones. Dirt and rock started tumbling from cracks in the high ceiling of the cave. Bioluminescent leaves and plants shook free, floating down like fluorescent confetti. The rumbling suddenly stopped.

"Bracken, Coren," Tag said through his comm line, "what's going on?"

Bracken's voice crackled. "We've got contacts. A whole—"

Before she finished, an explosion echoed from near the Forest entrance. Tag saw the resulting concussive force wash over the

Forest like a tremendous wave, and he turned to duck with the rest of the marines. But he was too slow. He was lifted from his feet and thrown backward, his teeth chattering. He pushed himself up against his swimming vision and the dull pain throbbing from deep within his torso. A creaking caught his attention, and he rolled to the side, dodging a falling tree. It crushed a Mechanic shelter, sending up a cloud of dirt. The aliens ran between their squat black buildings, gathering weapons and assembling near several of the ground vehicles they had been using since making their refuge on Eta-Five. Tag's eardrums screamed in pain, and he yelled a command at the marines to follow him back to Sofia's shelter, back to Coren and Alpha. He couldn't tell if they had heard him or not. His voice was muddled by the persistent ringing in his ears. The marines seemed to have understood his intention, and they fell into formation around him as they barreled back to Sofia's.

The ground still shook under Tag's feet, threatening to throw him off balance. Adrenaline surged through him, churning him onward, and his vision became tunneled on the path ahead as he hurdled over fallen logs and vegetation that had plummeted from the high roof of the massive cavern. Slowly his hearing returned as they approached Sofia's shelter. Alpha burst from the door, her mini-Gauss rifle at the ready. She lowered it when she saw Tag, and her tinny voice greeted him, beckoning to him, although her words sounded like a jumbled mess to him, like he was hearing her through water in a pool.

Coren was already busy inside, zipping into his EVA suit. He tossed Tag his helmet with one hand, and Tag caught it, securing it into place. As the helmet drowned out some of the external noise and the ringing in his ears died, he could finally make out the voices flying back and forth over the comm system.

"—attack!"

"Four, no five—"

"—entrance now!"

Mechanic voices. All of them.

"Bracken," Tag yelled, establishing a private channel. "What is it? What's going on?"

"The Drone-Mechs," she said, her voice uncharacteristically high. "They found us."

TEN

THE SQUEAL OF SOME POOR CREATURE WAILED AMID THE din exploding around the Forest. Tag wasn't sure if the animal had been hurt by a falling tree or caught in the crossfire somewhere. Something like remorse moved through his chest, almost painful. He couldn't help but think it was his fault the Drone-Mechs were here, destroying a sanctuary for all kinds of unique life-forms that had eked out an existence on the ethereal, beautiful, and decidedly fragile biosphere of Eta-Five.

How had the Drone-Mechs found him? How had they seen past the atmospheric shielding of Eta-Five? For the gods' sakes, how had they known he was even back in the Eta system?

Tag and his crew hadn't seen any drones, much less scout ships to let them know the Drone-Mechs were here, watching and waiting for him. He wondered if the Mechanics had somehow been complicit in helping the Drone-Mechs find them. Or maybe a stealth ship had followed them after they saved the *Montenegro*, perhaps a ship that had survived the battle and skirted all the SRE sensors. Both scenarios made him shudder uncontrollably, but nothing frightened him more than the voice screaming over his comm line.

"Skipper!" Sofia cried. "They're everywhere!"

"Sofia, where are you?" Tag asked.

"Near the volcanic field. The Forinths are freaking out."

"It seems like the Drone-Mechs used the main entrance to get down here. Is there another exit? Some way we can take to the *Argo* and the ship without having to fight through their forces?"

"Yeah," Sofia said. "There are a few tunnels that lead to the surface. They're a few kilometers from your position, though."

"Understood. We're coming to you."

Another explosion sounded from behind them, and it was rapidly followed by the scream of pulsefire scorching the air. Tag snagged one of the mini-Gauss rifles from where it was leaning against the wall. His return to Eta-Five had been brief and already overstayed. "Bull, keep the Drone-Mechs off. I'm leaving security up to you."

Unable to nod in the bulky power armor, Bull lifted his fist in acknowledgement. The other marines were too large to fit into the small shelter with their armor, so they had formed a ring around their doorway as they bristled with weapons, looking into the rest of the Forest for enemies.

"Remember, our pulse weapons are virtually useless against these guys," Tag said. "Overloading their energy shields is next to impossible with the SRE weapons we've got, so you've got to use kinetic slugs."

Tag half-expected Bull to sneer and give him a smartass remark about how he had paid attention to Sofia's briefing. To the marine's credit, all he did was raise his fist again.

"Alpha, stay down and close to me," Tag said.

"Yes, Captain." She stood, never letting her mini-Gauss down. She was as fierce as she was intelligent, but her chassis wasn't built from a battlemech.

"Don't engage if you don't have to, got it?" Tag said. "That's what we've got these guys for." He motioned to the marines then looked at Coren. "You with us or with Bracken?"

For the duration of the mission to the *Montenegro* and back, Coren had been, more or less, an official crew member of the *Argo*. Now with that mission over, the fate of Tag's engineer was up in the air.

"Right now, I'm very much physically with you," Coren said expressionlessly. "And I'll be staying with you so long as our main goal here is to evacuate my people."

"That's the damn reason we came back," Tag said, "Drone-Mechs or not, that's what we're going to do."

Coren gave an assenting nod, no relief or gratefulness painted across his face. Bull looked almost disappointed to hear the alien was still tagging along.

"Bull, we need to get to the air car, then"—he paused and tapped a command on his wrist terminal—"travel to these approximate coordinates to rendezvous with Sofia. She'll help us get the hell out of here." He switched to a private channel again. "Bracken, how are your people holding up?"

"So far, we're managing," Bracken said. "I don't think they expected to see *us* down here. The first wave of scouts was nothing more than a half-dozen soldiers in light exo-suits. But I don't think that's all they brought. They want you badly, Captain Brewer, and I wish I knew why."

Me too, Tag almost added. He refrained from saying it aloud. "Can you start to fall back? Organize an evacuation to your ship. We've got to get you all out of here."

Bracken huffed. "I am already organizing our retreat. We just need to know where we can escape to."

"Understood," Tag said. He motioned for the marines, Alpha, and Coren to follow him. They started at a jog for the air car. More mechanical groans and whines echoed through the trees, emanating from the entrance near where Bracken's resistance was stationed. "I'm sending you the coordinates of our first stop. From there, we'll navigate our escape."

"If I'm to borrow a phrase we learned from Sofia, this sounds rather half-assed."

"We don't have time to sit down and flesh out a full-assed idea, so unless you've got a better one, this is what we're doing," Tag said.

"Fine," Bracken said, sounding exasperated "Here I am, trusting a technologically and intellectually inferior race to be our salvation again. I suppose I should find some irony in that."

"Yeah, maybe you should," Tag said. "Sofia ever teach you the human phrase, 'fool me once, shame on you, fool me twice...'"

"No, we haven't had the pleasure."

"Good. But who knows, maybe you'll learn about it today."

Another fusillade of blue pulsefire ripped through the air, trailing up the wall of the cave. Tag was far enough from the blasts to avoid the shrapnel of rock spraying from the impacts, but the distance didn't assuage his fears of getting involved in a gunfight. The faster they escaped and were back on their ships flying out of here, the better. He just prayed the *Stalwart* was actually as spaceworthy as Coren had estimated, but there was no better way to find out than trial by fire.

"The air car!" Bull yelled, pointing with one massive armored fist toward the vehicle. G and Sumo sprinted ahead, drawing away from the pack to secure it. As they did, something rustled in the glowing blue and orange bushes near one of the abandoned

Mechanic shelters. Three Mechanics in sleek black armor appeared. Their suits looked untouched by wear and extended use like Bracken's Mechanic forces. They froze in apparent surprise before wheeling their rifles on G and Sumo. Tag swiveled to fire on them, joining the marines in lobbing a flurry of rounds at the enemy. Kinetic slugs ripped into their armor, and black liquid poured out.

But the Drone-Mechs still had time to fire. A wall of pulse rounds sizzled through the air, splashing against G and Sumo and sending them wheeling backward.

There was no avoiding conflict now.

ELEVEN

G AND SUMO HAD FALLEN UNDER A MESS OF DEADFALL
behind the shrub- and tree-covered berm when they had
been shot. Tag didn't have time to worry about them. Movement
between the emerald and crimson plants caught his eyes, and he
adjusted his aim. Between leaves speckled with blood, another
half-dozen Drone-Mechs cut through the foliage, stepping over
their downed compatriots. Pulsefire rang out around Tag, peppering the ground and tearing bark from the trees. He dove for the
ground, with Coren and Alpha beside him. The remaining marines circled up, kneeling behind logs and twisting around trees,
firing back at the Drone-Mechs.

"Bracken," Tag yelled over the gunfire. "I thought you said you
had them at the entrance."

"We did," Bracken said. "Or we thought we did. They tore a hole
from the entrance tunnel into the wall. They've been trickling in
around us. We're moving now, but I think they've got us surrounded."

A round skimmed above Tag's head, and the heat radiated through his EVA suit. *That was way too close*, he thought while the marines fired back into the forest. They now had the benefit of heads-up displays utilizing built-in AIs that would automatically mark their enemies. With Coren's help, all the AI systems related to the *Argo*, including these, had been fitted with Coren's anticorruption code to protect them from Drone-Mechs overriding their computer systems. Even with these safeguards, however, the density of the plants and trees prevented them from getting a clean shot on their enemy. The remaining three marines would have little chance against an enemy overwhelming them in firepower and numbers.

Tag needed to do something, anything, to get them out of this mess.

"I'm getting to the car," Tag said. "Bull, cover me."

"You got it, Captain," Bull said. He fired a burst of kinetic slugs into the brush. Leaves and twigs sprayed with the impacts. Each shredded plant glowed in changing scarlet, amber, and sapphire hues, as if expressing the pain of a slug ripping through it. Tag hated seeing this place get torn up by relentless invaders, but what else could he do short of killing them all or escaping to stop the destructive madness?

"Alpha, Coren, ready?" Tag asked.

Coren grunted a terse acknowledgment.

"Aye, Captain!" Alpha said, childishly enthusiastic.

"Go, go, go!" Tag yelled.

He dashed toward the car, winding between trees and keeping his body low. A torrent of pulsefire slammed into the trees, and he threw himself to the ground, sliding, before jumping up and sprinting again. Approaching the car, he dove into the wide trail where it was parked. Rounds careened against the side of the car and left singe marks on the scarred alloy. The smell of wet dirt and burning plants kicked up around him, making it through the air filters of his suit, as more pulsefire streamed everywhere. He reached for one of the air car's hatches, ready to tumble inside, when movement in his peripheral vision caused him to drop low. Five Drone-Mechs marched toward him, weapons hammering the earth around him, and he scuttled toward the front of the vehicle. The air seemed to morph, wavering like heat rising from asphalt on a summer day as the pulsefire grew in intensity. Pounding footsteps announced that the Drone-Mechs had split up, coming at the car from either side.

Coren, Alpha, and Tag were stuck in the middle, trapped against the air car. Tag leaned around to fire at one of the Drone-Mech groups but was quickly dissuaded by a burst of orange rounds.

"Son of a—Bull!" Tag yelled. "We're pinned down!"

"I know!" Bull shot back. "We're trying to help, but we're surrounded! Can't lift our goddamned heads without getting shot at!"

Tag felt a layer of sweat form between his palm and his gloves, his nerves twitching with anxious energy. They needed to move; they needed to be inside the damned air car. At least it would offer some protection and get them out of here, get them to Sofia and to the rest of the Mechanic forces. Another round zipped by him, slashing into a tree. Smoke wafted up from the fresh hole in the trunk, and ravenous tongues of flame leapt up the bark.

Everything was going to shit. The Forest of Light would be gone, destroyed in a few minutes. The remnants of the surviving free Mechanics would be rounded up and either slaughtered or enslaved. And Tag's crew would be massacred.

But whatever the Drone-Mechs wanted from him, he wasn't going to give it to them easily. He tightened his fingers around the mini-Gauss rifle. "Alpha, Coren, on my count, we give it our all on the right side, got it? Knock these guys out then make our way into the car."

"The odds of us succeeding against their numbers and weapons are rather low," Alpha said. "Would you like to know the numbers?"

"No," Tag said. "Here we go. Three."

Coren grimaced, his single working golden eye narrowing in determination. Tag's pulse raced in his ears as the blood rushed through his vessels, carrying with it the invigorating elixir of adrenaline.

"Two."

Alpha's servos whined. Tag could practically see the calculations running behind her beady eyes, measuring the best course of action in a battle they seemed to have already lost.

"One."

Tag led Coren and Alpha from behind the car. Time seemed to slow as bolts of pulsefire crossed his path, and his vision focused on the targets standing meters from him. His finger squeezed the trigger of the mini-Gauss, and each shudder of the rifle in his hands, each electric hum of the magnetic coils charging and releasing, traveled through his body with an energy that almost calmed him, made him ready for whatever the fates had in store now. He watched in brutal satisfaction as the slugs punched into the armor of one Drone-Mech, sending the spindly alien careening backward.

But one Drone-Mech down didn't turn the tide of the oncoming forces. Pulsefire rained down on Tag like a blizzard on Eta-Five's surface. Even he wasn't suicidal enough to continue forward, and he prepared to retreat again, to find a modicum of shelter for his last stand.

Then a smattering of hisses sounded from one of the Drone-Mechs. Black liquid dripped from freshly shorn holes in its armor.

Some of the Drone-Mechs started to turn, drawing their attention away from Tag, Coren, and Alpha. But they too were plastered by an unseen force that cut them down from the tree line. Tag took advantage of the momentary confusion and fired at the remaining Drone-Mechs bearing down on them, with Coren and Alpha joining his counterattack until the last of their enemies fell. A determined giddiness swept through him as he found himself on the winning side again.

Branches and bushes at the tree line moved, and Tag turned, facing whatever dared confront them next. Instead of Drone-Mechs, G and Sumo emerged. A shockwave of confusion muddled Tag's thoughts until Sumo explained.

"Those damn shields work great," Sumo said. "The pulsefire knocked the air out of me. Might've lost a few brain cells hitting the ground. But I'm alive!"

G swiveled around, not sharing in the same joy. Sweat beaded down his forehead, visible through his visor. "There's going to be more. Got to be more," he said, his nerves tingeing his voice with trepidation.

Those worries were answered by a pulse round flying into his chest. His fingers splayed, and he almost lost the grip on his rifle as he flew backward. But the round never pierced his armor. Instead, it fizzled in electric-green sparks on the energy shield the Mechanic engineers had installed.

Sumo hooted in excitement, aimed, and fired on G's attacker. "Bet you xeno scum didn't see that coming, did you?"

"Come on!" Tag yelled, opening the hatch to the air car. A cool wave of relief coursed through him as he boarded the vehicle with Sumo and G still alive and well. But there was no time for celebration now. "We need to get to the others!"

Alpha and Coren spilled into the front seats, with G and Sumo hopping into the back.

Bull's voice crackled over the comm line. "Captain, it's getting bad out here. I could use some support!"

"On it!" Tag replied, settling into the driver's seat. The controls hissed as they moved toward him, and he grabbed them, ready to jockey the air car again.

"Old friend, you and me have been through some rough times," he muttered as he punched the throttle and the car took off. "*Hope* you're up for more."

TWELVE

Tag leaned forward in the driver's seat. It wouldn't help him speed down the meager trail through the Forest any faster, but he couldn't help it. Luminescent plants and trees whipped by in a psychedelic fury of visual stimulation that threatened to distract him at every twisting turn. Even amid the dissonance of colors, it didn't take long to locate Bull, Gorenado, and Lonestar. The trio was caught in a raging storm of pulsefire. Blazing azure rounds pierced tree trunks, cutting through a swathe of the Forest like an overzealous logging operation.

On their approach, Tag hit a button to open the hatch on the roof so the marines could fire out of the car. Sumo and G popped out of the top, firing into the ranks of Drone-Mechs who had thought their battle against the isolated marine squad was already won. Kinetic slugs tore into their armor, and returning pulsefire raged against the air car. The vehicle was tough, but Tag was reminded of his first trip on Eta-Five when an unlucky shot had debilitated it. It could only take so much abuse before they would be stranded here, too.

With a path cleared from the marines to the air car, Bull stood. A barrage of pulsefire slammed into his position, and a few rounds caught him, knocking him over, but dissipated in his energy shields. He scrambled to his feet with Gorenado and Lonestar leading the charge. Coren threw open a side hatch, and they tumbled in, the heavy weight of their power armor shaking the vehicle. Their labored breathing sounded through the public comm channel as they settled into positions and opened portholes around the vehicle.

"Time to turn this little pony into a goddamn bronco!" Lonestar yelled. She peppered one of the Drone-Mech's positions with a burst of kinetic slugs, kicking up dirt and chunks of plants. Each hit plant flying up from the impacts rippled with color as if it were on fire.

Tag shoved the throttle forward, and the car took off, leaving a wake of leaves curling into the air. The bursts of blue pulsefire around them became more sporadic as they accelerated away from the Drone-Mech foot soldiers. With a little more distance between them and the enemy, Tag's medical officer instincts overrode his adrenaline-fueled warrior rage.

"Anyone hurt?" he asked. "We've got autoheal gel and med packs in the first aid kits."

"Think we're all good, Captain," Bull said gruffly. Then his voice dropped lower. "Hate to say it, but the xeno tech saved our asses."

The corners of Coren's lips twitched as if to suggest a slight grin. "That is certainly no surprise."

"Mechanic shielding technology is far superior to that of human energy shields," Alpha said.

"Thanks for the support," Coren said.

"I'm merely stating a fact."

Bull shook his head as if he already regretted the reluctant compliment.

Tag swerved the car hard to the left, avoiding a fallen tree he had barely noticed in the aggressive glow of the foliage. Now more than ever, he wished he had Sofia piloting them out of this mess, and that made it all the more important to get to her soon.

"Sofia," Tag said, "we're on our way."

"Hurry!" Sofia said. "Forinths are reporting Drone-Mech activity all over the Forest. They're spreading out, forming a dragnet to catch you guys and the Mechanics."

"Understood." Tag switched channels. "Bracken, we're two minutes out. Where are you?"

The screams of pulsefire a few hundred meters to his right answered before she did. A plume of fire and black smoke stretched into the air like the fist of a demon erupting from the three hells. Screeches from Mechanics and unseen animals alike rent the air.

"We're taking casualties," Bracken said. "There are too many."

Coren bowed his head at the news of his brethren's deaths. "The machine remembers, brothers and sisters."

"Copy," Tag said. He dug through his mind for something else to say, something else he could offer her. He had returned to the Mechanics promising an escape from the planet and seemed to bring with him only their massacre. If Bracken shared the same thought, she at least didn't express it.

"We will do the best we can," she said. "Whoever is responsible for doing this to our people will pay."

The venom and malice in her voice shook through the comm line. In his mind's eye, Tag saw her eyes narrow and her snake-like nostrils flare.

Ahead of him, a familiar shimmering marked an area of rising heat in an open plain. The undulating air emanated from a protrusion in the ground, one of the many budding volcano-like holes that heated the Forest of Light. Near the edge of it, Sofia was ducking into the rise of the volcano. She fired at a squad of Drone-Mechs with her pulse pistol, but the cobalt rounds flying from her pistol were hitting the Drone-Mechs impotently, shredding against their energy shields as they advanced.

"Suck on these, you zombie bastards!" Lonestar yelled.

The marines opened fire on the Drone-Mechs, catching them by surprise. Most went down in the first salvo of kinetic slugs, while others scrambled for cover. A few pulse rounds crashed over the plain near the air car, but the marines fought back the lone Drone-Mechs that had survived the initial attack. Sliding through the air near the volcano, Tag slowed long enough for Coren to whip open a hatch and grab Sofia's arm. With his help, she jumped aboard.

"Thanks," she said, almost wheezing. "Wasn't sure how much longer I'd make it there."

"Glad to have you," Tag said, "because I'm getting tired of driving."

He relinquished the driver's seat to her. She jumped into it, spitting into her palms and rubbing them together.

"Oh man, feels good to be in here instead of running my ass around out there," Sofia said.

"Before you get too comfortable," Tag said, "I need you and Alpha to plot us a way out. Bracken's on the way."

"Can do. Only problem is, I, uh, don't know the exact locations of the exit tunnels. Just a general approximation. A guess, you know?"

"A guess?" Coren asked, his voice shaking slightly. "Our only escape route is a guess?"

"I'm an extraterrestrial anthropologist, not a cartographer!" she said.

"I don't care what you are as long as you find us a way out of here!" Bull yelled.

Bracken's voice came through again. "We're almost—"

The sounds of exchanged pulsefire cut her transmission short.

"Bracken?" Tag asked, fighting the surging panic climbing up his throat. "Bracken? Are you there?"

"We—hold on!" she said.

The trees and plants on the plain's perimeter started to shift. Sofia rotated the air car around so they could get a view of the approaching Mechanics. A few burst through the woods, but they didn't wear the worn suits of Bracken's people, nor did they drive the sleek vehicles she was using to evacuate them. *Drone-Mechs,* Tag realized, his stomach dropping. Foot soldiers poured out along all the edges of the plain, cornering the air car. They started taking shots as they crossed the plain in an all-out charge. Even with the advantage of the volcanic cover and the marines firing back with a deluge of kinetic slugs, they would soon be overwhelmed.

"This is what the Forinths warned about," Sofia said ruefully. "We can't hold up any longer. We're going to have to run."

"And leave my people behind?" Coren said, anger tingeing his voice.

"We can't. We just can't abandon them," Tag said, staring out the windshield. "But what choice do we have?"

THIRTEEN

THE SOUNDS OF BATTLE ECHOED AROUND THE PLAIN, AND THE heaviness in Tag's gut thickened. "Bracken, where are you?"

"We're pinned down and cut off by the—"

Her line went silent again, and Tag turned to Coren. Where the Mechanic's face had once showed as much expression and emotion as a boulder, now something else played across his visage. Something akin to horror. Maybe the realization that the last free members of his species were dying—or already dead.

"We have to go back!" Coren yelled. He forced himself between the marines and laid down a stream of fire at the approaching Drone-Mechs. The marines joined him, but their salvos only delayed what Tag saw as inevitable.

A voice sparked over the comm line again. "Hold your fire! Hold your fire!" *Bracken.*

The marines ceased firing, but incensed, Coren still poured out his anger in a fusillade of powerful pulsefire.

"Hold your fire!" she repeated.

"Coren!" Tag yelled, urgency threading his voice. "Coren! Stop!"

The Mechanic seemed too caught up in his own fervor, and Tag had to tug on the alien's shoulders, pulling at his suit to get his attention. Snarling, Coren turned, his fingers quivering and the short fur across his face bristling.

"Don't hurt the Forinths!" Bracken said. Her voice sounded almost gleeful, a far cry from the panic that had shaken it before.

Tag was about to ask her to clarify why they would hurt the Forinths. Then he heard the reverberating humming from the tree line. Sofia perked up in her seat and leaned toward the windshield.

"They're here," she muttered. "I didn't think they would. I told them not to...but they're here."

"My biosensors are detecting new life-forms within the ranks of the Drone-Mechs," Alpha said, "but I see no new targets in the visible light spectrum."

"Just...watch," Tag said.

A few dozen Drone-Mechs continued firing on the air car. Their shots mostly hit the budding volcano Sofia had parked the vehicle behind, and dirt and mud flipped through the air. One Drone-Mech started to crest the volcano. Its armor shimmered in the heated, sulfurous air escaping the vents, and it aimed a rifle directly at the air car. Before Bull or another marine could so much as squeeze the trigger, the Drone-Mech's neck split. Dark, black fluids intermingled with blood as the Drone-Mech's body collapsed, twisting and plummeting into the volcano. The head, still in its helmet, rolled back down the incline.

"What was that?" Sumo asked.

Lonestar whistled. "Is that...is that..."

The air seemed to undulate where the Drone-Mech had been. If Tag squinted, he could make out the cephalopod-like shape of a

Forinth. It vanished again as it utilized its camouflage to disappear like a wraith, and again another Drone-Mech went down. Then another, and another. The number of Drone-Mechs diminished faster than a ship escaping into hyperspace. Bodies fell, cut apart by invisible forces leaving long gashes in flesh and power armor.

Coren slumped into his seat, watching the massacre play out. The only gunfire was that of the Drone-Mechs firing blindly at the unseen predators that were ripping them into so many ribbons of meat and armor.

"Goddamn if I ain't glad they're on our side," Lonestar said.

All the while, the haunting wail of the Forinths carried up around the forest. Tag shivered uncontrollably, and for no particular reason, he felt ready to break down in wracking sobs. The Forinths' language played on his human emotions like a pilot controls a ship. He was helpless to the chorus.

"What...what are they talking about?" Tag asked.

A wet sheen had formed over Sofia's eyes, visible beneath her visor. "They're mourning the loss of life. They're singing prayers to welcome the Drone-Mechs into their version of the heavens."

"You got to be shitting me," Gorenado said. "Those bastards are out there ripping us apart, and the Forinths think their souls are going to some kind of alien paradise?"

"That's exactly it," Sofia said. "All forms of life are sacred to them, and they see life as a precarious balance. Having to destroy so much of it at once is hurting them. They didn't want to take sides in this war, but I told them what the Drone-Mechs were."

"They are, more or less, walking corpses of my people," Coren said.

"I guess that actually convinced the Forinths to help protect us," Tag said. Then, as an afterthought, "And Bracken, too."

A stray blast of pulsefire caught one of the Forinths. The creature wailed in a tone and rhythm that hit something deep in Tag's chest, squeezing it with an almost palpable force. He watched the alien writhe. Its tentacles whipped, and its colors changed in shades more dazzling than the bioluminescent foliage around it. When it settled, its body turned a dreary gray, all color draining from it except for the crimson-and-black blood congealing on the curved blades protruding from the end of each serpentine arm.

Soon a cadre of black air cars and smaller vehicles that looked to Tag like hoverbikes spilled from a path in the Forest. A few lumbering personnel carriers trailed them. Smoke wafted from several of the vehicles, and gashes in the armor showed where they had barely survived the Drone-Mech onslaught.

"Hold your fire!" Tag said, raising his fist until the marines lowered their weapons. "It's Bracken's forces."

Tag counted the vehicles as the convoy lined up near the air car. He guessed at least a half dozen or so were missing. Already they had taken heavy casualties trying to hold the Drone-Mechs back. Somewhere in the distance, mechanical thumping echoed through the trees, while debris still sprinkled from the vast cavern's ceiling.

"Do we have everyone here now?" Tag asked over the comm line.

"We are prepared for departure," Bracken replied.

"Good," Tag said. "The plan is to leave together. There's at least one exit Sofia thinks will fit our vehicles. We'll aim for the closest one. Worse comes to worst, plan B is to go on foot." He saw Sofia shiver at the prospect of hiking all the way to the *Argo* and the *Stalwart*. "But I don't want to do that. Getting caught with our pants down in the middle of a blizzard with Drone-Mechs on all sides doesn't sound appealing."

"No, it most definitely does not," Sofia said.

"We can handle anything," Bull added. Tag nodded but still thought the man was overestimating their prowess against the

Drone-Mechs. They had survived mostly on luck, the benefits of Mechanic shielding technology, and some unexpected aid from the Forinths so far.

Tag chinned off his comm line. "Coren, you coming with me or Bracken? This might be your only chance to change ships until after our hyperspace jump."

"Captain," Coren began, "I believe you are stuck with me. No one here, besides yourself, has weapons experience on the *Argo*, and you need an engineer aboard that ship now more than ever. No one here can do what I can for the ship."

"I was hoping you'd say that," Tag said, "although I could've done without the pretension." He gave Coren a slightly playful smirk to let him know he was joking. Kind of.

Coren's skinny shoulders lifted in a slight shrug.

"Okay, Sofia, get us the hell out of here," Tag said, facing out the front of the air car once more. "To the *Argo*."

"Aye, aye, Skipper," she replied. "Your wish is my command."

"I believe that was not a wish, but a command," Alpha said. "So his command is your command. That's rather redundant."

"Semantics," Sofia muttered. "How about we worry about getting out of here before poring over my word choice?"

"Let's go!" Tag said, settling into his seat. The air car took off, and the Mechanic convoy followed, winding through the Forest. The mourning songs of the Forinths echoed all around them, accompanied by the occasional scream of a Drone-Mech going down under a flurry of scything blades. Tag imagined the invisible creatures were following them like a ghostly wake escorting them to safety. He wanted to thank them for the kindness, for their mercy, but no words would be enough for these beings.

Something else began accompanying the Forinth's calls. Tag strained to listen. There was a distinctly mechanical sound, a whining like servos and motors straining against immense forces.

"Exo-suits!" Coren jolted upright in his seat.

The first few exo-suits lumbered into a jog, narrowing the distance between themselves and the convoy. In their metallic claws, they carried huge cylindrical weapons. Tag knew what those things could do from his time aboard the Drone-Mech dreadnought, and in case he needed a reminder, the closest exo fired on the nearest personnel carrier. An intense green laser struck the side of the vehicle. Its touch melted alloy, and slag flew from where it hit as the beam cut a wide swathe through the personnel carrier, then pierced its fusion core.

A booming explosion sent pieces of the personnel carrier and the Mechanics inside scattering into the trees. Metal shards and charred remains of Mechanics showered the rest of the convoy. Forinths jumped atop the exos, scratching at the polyglass and alloy, but their blades couldn't penetrate the gargantuan defenses of the Mechs. The Mechs simply ignored them, or, when the Forinths shimmered particularly brightly and could be spotted, swatted at them like insects. Mechanics and marines fired back at the armored juggernauts. They took down one, then two, but a renewed assault on the convoy left another personnel carrier in flames that rivaled the bioluminescence of the Forest.

Tag felt his stomach drop at the sight. He didn't think it could, but it plummeted lower when a swatch of trees cracked and fell, crashing through the forest.

"No," Coren said, his voice tinged with horror. "No."

"What?" Tag asked. "What is it?"

"In your language, a Death Walker," Coren said.

A behemoth of black metal and orange polyglass galloped toward them. Its long legs stretched over the exos, making the intimidating armored suits look puny in comparison, and weapons bristled off of it everywhere. The eight-legged walking tank fired pulsefire cannons, kinetic slugs, and explosives, raining hell around the convoy. The Mechanic vehicles and Tag's air car were shielded only by the dense foliage. That soon wouldn't be a problem when the mechanical spider caught up to them.

Sofia pushed the throttle forward, carrying it to its limits while she wove dangerously between the trees. "Well, Skipper, it was nice while it lasted."

FOURTEEN

THE DEATH WALKER CLOSED IN ON THEM. TAG FELT LIKE A helpless fly caught in the web of this giant arachnid. The marines continued their assault on the exos and managed to bring down a few more, but the Walker relentlessly repelled their fire as if the rounds pinging against its armor were nothing more than pebbles slung by the Forinths.

"What do we do now?" G said, his voice shaking.

"Fire, goddammit, fire!" Bull roared.

But Tag knew it wouldn't be enough. Nothing they could throw at this contraption would be enough. At least, not until they reached the *Argo*, and the gods only knew how many Drone-Mechs would be swarming around the ship. Tag's only hope was that the camouflaging algorithm Coren had developed last time they were on Eta-Five was still working. They had enabled the antilidar and -radar tech before they left for the Forest of Light, and if all was well, maybe, just maybe, the Drone-Mechs hadn't found the *Argo*. Still, none of that would matter if the Walker got them first.

"Where's that damn exit?" Lonestar yelled as she joined the fusillade against another gaining exo.

"I'm working on it!" Sofia said. "Unless you want to pilot this tin can!"

Tag tried to ignore the anxiety-ridden banter between the crew. There had to be something they could do, something even the Forinths could do to stop the Drone-Mechs.

Then it hit him.

"Sofia, engage the external speakers on the air car," Tag said.

"Why me?" she asked. "How about someone less busy?"

"Because I need you to do this." He explained his plan to her. It wasn't much, and it relied mostly on powers outside his control. But it was all he had.

Sofia began singing through the speakers. Her voice carried loud and booming over the sounds of exos and the Walker trampling through plants and trees. The slight shimmering of the color-changing Forinths disappeared from the mechanical monsters, and Tag saw them fade into the forest as they abandoned their attack.

"Captain?" Bull asked.

"Stay the course!" Tag said. "Keep firing! I need their attention on us."

"On us?" G asked, gulping.

The ground continued to tremble as they raced toward an opening in the stone wall of the gigantic cavern where blue light filtered in. Sofia aimed straight at it. The tunnel looked as if it would easily fit the whole convoy just as Sofia had promised, but it would also be no problem for the Death Walker and its minions to follow as well. Soon the tunnel swallowed them, and they traced its rocky path while glowing, moss-covered walls sped by in a colorful blur.

"Bracken, when your last vehicle gets in the tunnel, throw everything you've got at it," Tag said. "I want it collapsed."

"That was already the plan," Bracken replied coolly.

Tag couldn't see when the last of the Mechanic convoy reached the relative safety of the tunnel, but eventually he heard them unleash a salvo of explosives and pulsefire into the stone walls. Planet-shaking rumbles chased them onward, along with the sound of rocks crashing against each other.

"It's done," Bracken said.

On and on they shot toward the surface. A faint glow caught Tag's eye from the end of the tunnel, where sheets of white blew into it. Snow and ice, a frigid welcome back to the reality of Eta-Five's surface.

"You think the Forinths did it?" Tag said to Sofia.

"I have no doubt they did," she replied.

Bull looked like he wanted in on their conversation, but there was no time for Tag to explain. An explosion erupted from behind them as if the planet itself were releasing its pent-up energy in a fiery bellow. Stone and rocks pinged against the convoy and the air car. One chunk of earth collided with a hoverbike, taking the vehicle and rider out, while smoke, fire, and debris swallowed another lagging vehicle.

Tag watched for the vehicle to escape from the cloud of black and orange. It never did. Instead, in its place marched the Death Walker, cannons firing rapidly, blasting and shredding another member of the Mechanic convoy. Coren punched the dash of the air car, cursing under his breath.

"Damn!" Bull said. "They're relentless!"

But Tag thought they might still make it. They could escape the tunnel, race across the landscape, and return to the *Argo*. Just a little farther. Soon they burst from the underground passage and sliced through the landscape, accelerating over the frigid desert of snow and ice, where a blizzard swirled in full force. Grainy white and gray flecks peppered the windshield, making it look to Tag like he was viewing the world in some antique 2-D black-and-white film.

The rest of the convoy had made it out of the tunnel with the Walker trailing them and exos teeming at its feet. Pulsefire cut through the air, melting through snow and ice, and green beams lanced around them. Another Mechanic vehicle vanished in a mist of billowing flames. Then one of the exos turned its sights on the little car leading the convoy. Tag's car. A tightening sensation gripped Tag's chest, and he braced himself for the incoming fire.

"Evasive action!" he yelled.

Sofia swerved hard to the right.

It wasn't enough. The blinding emerald beam caught the back of the air car. G disappeared in the laser, his body turned to ash before he could so much as scream. Every one of Tag's nerves lit up at the sight, his eyes going wide, his mouth opening to yell, to cry out for G as, in an instant, memories of Kaufman and the others slaughtered aboard the *Argo* overwhelmed his senses. The other, more fortunate, marines tumbled against each other, their power armor rattling, as the car flipped end over end. Tag's restraints pressed on his EVA suit, forcing him back into a reality as harsh as the nightmares haunting him, and he struggled to retain some semblance of orientation. The snow flurries and dancing ice clouds obscured which way was up until the remains of the air car finally settled, with warning lights and bleak alarms blaring, muddling the world around him.

"Critical failure," a robotic voice said. "Fusion core overload reported."

FIFTEEN

TAG UNDID HIS HARNESS, HIS HEART HAMMERING AGAINST his rib cage. "Everybody, move!"

He scrambled from his seat, ushering Coren, Sofia, and Alpha out before him and directing them toward the *Argo*'s location. Gorenado helped Lonestar out from beneath the wreckage of the air car, and Sumo climbed over a broken seat. She fired at the oncoming horde of Drone-Mech armored troops.

"G," Gorenado said glumly as he searched for a body Tag knew wasn't there. The young marine was gone, erased by that goddamned monster of a laser beam as if he had never existed.

"You got to go," Tag said. "G's gone."

"Sarge," Lonestar said, "we moving?"

But Bull stood in place, his eyes wide behind his visor.

"Bull, you good?" Gorenado said. "We got to move."

"You all go!" Tag yelled as the alarms blared from what was left of the air car. When they hesitated, he raised his voice. "Go!

That's an order!" He clambered over a piece of broken bulkhead and grabbed Bull's shoulder. "Come on, Sergeant!"

A look of abject terror was painted across Bull's face. Tag was reeling from G's sudden death, but he didn't expect the trained marine to react like this.

"Bull!" Tag shouted.

The marine looked at him as if his spirit had left and all that remained was his shell of a body. His limbs shook as Tag tried to drag Bull from the car, but the armor was too heavy, too bulky to move all by himself. Alarms continued to wail, bolstering the surging panic flooding through Tag.

"Get yourself together!" Tag yelled. "We need to move!"

Then he understood.

Bull wasn't frozen in terror from watching G die. No, not at all. He'd seen the deaths of his comrades aboard the *Montenegro* and likely plenty of other ships and space stations. But that was just it. He'd only ever been on a spaceship or station. His entire life, he had been surrounded by four solid walls, a roof, and a ceiling. Enclosed spaces. Tag had heard about it before: the fear of open spaces. Of suddenly being unprotected. The duration of Bull's time spent on Eta-Five had either been spent inside an air car going to and from the *Argo* or under the looming embrace of the cavernous ceiling of the Forest. The concept of being exposed to an open sky was foreign to people who hadn't lived or traveled to planets where the only thing preventing you from becoming one with the universe and floating away forever was a little invisible thing called gravity.

"Bull!" Tag yelled. "You need to move! If you don't, you're dead!"

He punched Bull's armor. The blow would barely be felt through the alloy, and the armor's automatic stabilizers hardly allowed the motion to move Bull. But it was enough. Bull's eyes lost their glaze, and his wide-eyed expression filled with shame before the visor went dark. No doubt Bull was hiding his embarrassment with the color-changing polyglass.

"Apologies, Captain," Bull said, taking off in a run beside Tag. "I was—"

"I get it," Tag said as they loped off after the others.

The air car exploded behind them, tossing shrapnel and forcing them to duck into the snow. A concussive force rolled over Tag and Bull. Hot, slagged metal melted into the ice and snow around them as the rest of the air car burned, tongues of plasma jutting up through the wreckage.

"Do you need a pickup?" Bracken asked.

"Yes!" Tag said, still running toward the *Argo*.

Her convoy barreled their direction with the exos and Walker not far behind. One air car veered off from the pack. Two of the exos gave chase as the Death Walker targeted the brunt of Bracken's force. Tag's lungs were on fire by the time the air car reached him. A door slid open, and three Mechanics pulled him and Bull inside. They sped away, catching up to the others, and soon all of the *Argo*'s crew was within the Mechanic air car. All except for G.

"Can't believe they got him," Sumo said. "Can't believe he's gone."

Gorenado shook his head. "Like he wasn't even here..."

The shaking ground behind them calmed as the Walker doggedly pursued the main thrust of the fleeing convoy. Tag felt certain they were actually going to make it to the *Argo*. And once they did, he was already prioritizing what they needed to do to bring all the systems, engines, and weapons online as fast as possible. If they were quick enough, they could provide air support to Bracken's crew. Luckily, whatever ships had dumped the Drone-Mech ground forces hadn't descended on them yet. They might have a few minutes' advantage to pull this all off.

"Bracken, we'll power up the *Argo* and cover you when you get to the *Stalwart*," Tag said. "Anything else we can do now?"

"Not unless you can get the Death Walker off our tail, Captain Brewer," she said in a far calmer voice than he had expected.

As if on cue, the Walker changed course. Its thumping footsteps took it away from the convoy, and it careened toward the air car.

"That was not what I had planned," Bracken said.

"Neither did I," Tag said. "They're listening in. They're tapping into our comms and just pinpointed us!"

"We had comms encrypted!" Coren said.

"Guess your tech isn't that much better than ours after all, huh?" Lonestar said.

"Now's not the time, guys." Tag turned to the Mechanic crew on the car. "Can you go any faster in this thing?"

"We are already at our limits," the Mechanic driving the vehicle said.

"Bull, can you guys throw some firepower at it?" Tag asked. "Maybe blind it or something?"

Bull seemed to sense a hidden implication of inferiority in the question, though Tag didn't intend there to be any. "Sure as shit we can."

The marines joined the Mechanic fire teams at the portholes and mounted weapons stations within the vehicle. Pulsefire and slugs flew from the vehicle at the Death Walker. The wall of rounds would be enough to take down an exo, but it hardly scratched at the Death Walker's armor.

"When you guys made these things, did you think about making something to destroy them?" Sofia asked Coren.

"The whole intent behind their design was such that they couldn't be destroyed easily," Coren said.

"Well, you all aced that one."

The air car flew over a sheet of ice, and the ground began to quake with renewed vigor. At first it seemed like the trembling earth was from the Death Walker, but Tag would never mistake the characteristic groan and buckling of the ice and ground for anything other than what it actually was. He'd had his own close encounter with the entity responsible for such tearing of the earth and resounding roars.

"What in the three hells is that?" Sumo asked.

Tag grinned back at her when he replied. "An ice god."

SIXTEEN

AN ICE GOD BURST FROM THE GROUND WITH ITS JAW SPREAD wide, revealing a mouthful of jagged fangs, each capable of crushing the meager vehicle Tag and his crew were in. Hundreds of beady black eyes traced the monster's face, and its tongue whipped, throwing spittle that froze almost immediately in Eta-Five's atmosphere. The monster dragged itself from beneath the ice and earth, carrying its serpentine body in a rushed charge on dozens of insectile legs, its tail thrashing behind it.

"It's here," Tag said.

"But the Forinth drums were supposed to keep these creatures away, were they not?" Alpha said. "I thought the radius of effect was larger than this."

"It is," Tag said.

"Which is why he asked me to tell the Forinths to stop the drums," Sofia said.

"So those ice gods are on our side?" Gorenado asked.

"Uh, no...no, they aren't," Tag said. "But as far as we can tell, they're attracted to sound and vibration. The Death Walker and those exos are a bit louder than us."

"You're just hoping that's the case then," Bull said.

"More or less," Tag said evasively. "The ice gods are about the best reinforcements we have right now."

"Or the best way to die," Lonestar said glumly.

"Focus on going forward," Tag said. "Let that thing do our dirty work."

The ice god barreled over a Mech. Tag expected a small explosion, maybe limbs and chunks of broken metal thrown into the blustering wind. Instead the exo simply disappeared, swallowed whole. The ice god didn't so much as gulp.

Other exos turned on the ice god, and their beams cut into its flesh, leaving a score of deep black singe marks. Charred skin peeled away in spots to reveal coursing red muscle where mist rose from the revealed tendons and sinew, freezing almost instantly. Even though the ice god bled like a mortal, its fury was that of a titan. It crushed another exo with all the ease of a man rubbing his boot across a cockroach.

"Did you ever realize how fortunate we are?" Coren asked Tag in an almost reverent voice.

Tag didn't have to clarify what Coren meant. When they had barely escaped with their own lives before, it was because they'd had the speed of an air car with a skeleton crew and the insight to blast out the ice god's eyes. Evidently the Drone-Mechs hadn't thought of that strategy yet and had relegated themselves to strategies of brute force.

Another salvo of desperate fire leapt from the exos and bore into the ice god. A wave of unexpected sympathy coursed through Tag for the giant creature. As he watched the Death Walker levy blast after blast of slugs and energy weapons into the monster's hide, he couldn't help but feel sorry for the creature, which had unknowingly walked into the worst day of its terrible life.

It didn't seem to want Tag's sympathy. Instead it threw its bleeding, shredded body into the legs of the Walker, and one of the Walker's legs crumpled as if it had been made of toothpicks.

"That monster makes it look easy," Sumo said. "Can we keep it?"

"If you can find a place on the *Argo* for it," Tag said. "It might be a tight squeeze, though."

"While the *Argo* may be inadequate, the *Montenegro* has capacity for such a creature," Alpha said. "But the odds that Admiral Doran would approve of bringing it are rather dismal, according to my data analysis."

"You're spot on again," Sofia said. Her hands were thrown behind her head in an almost relaxed pose. Tag absolutely hated that in the midst of such tension, dealing with a multitude of threats to their lives, she could exhibit such calm. Then again, she had somehow lived with the Forinths for five years without getting killed. Keeping calm and going with the flow must have been something she had mastered.

Right now, Tag found it difficult to even fake nonchalance as he watched the ice god coil around the Walker. The monster threw its fangs into the limping Walker's metallic skin. It let out a frustrated bellow that shook the air car's cabin, and Tag thought he could see Coren and the other Mechanics' fur stand on end through their glowing orange visors. Tag imagined it was wondering why it couldn't tear into the Walker's silver flesh or spill the thing's blood. The Walker's weapons tore into the ice god, unable to miss at such short range, and the monster started to lose its grip. Many of its legs were broken and twisted, and the gashes in its side bled with flash-frozen blood. The Walker began picking up speed again despite the weight of the dying ice god pulling it down.

"Something we can do, Captain?" Lonestar asked, her trigger finger tapping on her rifle.

"Pray, if you believe in it," Tag said. They were only a klick or so away from the *Argo*. Even with the Walker gaining, they might still make it to the ship in time to activate the point defense cannons. The depleted-uranium rounds should have no problem punching a hole or two in the Walker.

At least, that was what Tag hoped.

Snow, ice, and rock spewed in geysers around them as the Walker took potshots, but the Mechanic driver deftly avoided the incoming fire. Sofia had finally lost her cool demeanor. Her hands clenched and unclenched as if she wanted to be driving the car. She probably felt as helpless as Tag being a passenger and nothing more in this hell ride.

Another chain of pulsefire ripped into the snow and ice. The air car almost slid sideways from the concussion of the impact, but the pilot somehow maintained control.

"That was too damn close," Bull said. "Next time you drag me onto a planet like this, I'm bringing high-explosive rounds. Something better to blast those xeno assholes into the atmosphere."

But it looked as if explosives wouldn't be necessary. Another ice god exploded from beneath the planet's surface in a shower of debris and barreled into the Death Walker. Its body curled around two of the legs, crunching them together, tripping the weaponized behemoth. The Walker could no longer struggle on against the combined efforts of the two ice gods, and the beasts dragged it to the ground. It hit with a sickening thud of metal screeching against rock. A huge puff of frost billowed into the air, and the ice gods writhed, attacking the Walker relentlessly. Stray pulse rounds still burned through the blizzard, and several low blasts sounded as Tag and company raced away from the violent scene.

"We would have appreciated it if you had sent one of those creatures our way," Bracken said over the comm line.

"I don't control 'em. I just call 'em," Tag said. "You still got a tail?"

"Exos, mostly. A few squads of foot soldiers. No Walkers. It would appear they really wanted you."

"Strange thing, that," Tag said. "Not sure why I'm of any value to them."

"Then again, maybe you aren't that important," Bracken said. "Maybe it's not you but rather your ship."

It sounded like one of those honest Mechanic statements that were delivered as a half insult. But Tag couldn't deny that she might be onto something. "I suppose so. They tried to annihilate the *Argo* before, so I wouldn't expect them to treat it any differently now."

"They better not destroy it before you give us some support," Bracken said, her voice rising in sudden alarm. "Because from what's showing up on our scanners now, we're going to need it."

SEVENTEEN

A KNOT TWISTED IN TAG'S STOMACH. HE WAS ALMOST AFRAID to ask Bracken what she saw out there, but ignoring the threat wouldn't make it disappear.

"What do you see?" he asked.

"Looks like several dropships are circling Eta-Five within the troposphere," said Bracken. "They're flying low—presumably to avoid the atmospheric anomaly so they can still communicate with their ground forces. The signals I'm picking up also show they dropped troops all over the planet. I'm guessing they dumped Drone-Mechs everywhere they saw a heat signature since they couldn't find your ship."

"Damn," Tag said. "So they've got more Death Walkers and Mechs descending on us."

"That certainly is part of it," Bracken said, "and I wouldn't be surprised if they've already sent a courier drone up the gravity well back to whatever fleet they came from. Who knows what in the machine's name is waiting for us above those clouds."

"I suppose we'll find out soon enough," Tag said as they drew near the *Argo*'s location.

"Captain Brewer, you're positive it's here?" one of the Mechanic crew asked.

"Yep," Tag said. "Just buried under some snow." He was proud to see the sensor-camouflaging strategy not only fooled the Drone-Mech sensor arrays, but it was just as good against their Mechanic friends. It made sense of course, given they were operating the same technologies, and he refrained from gloating in the power of their new tech. It was Coren after all who had masterminded it, and Tag would be damned if he made the alien's head any bigger than it already was.

"Stop here, and let us out," Tag said. "You're welcome to join us aboard the *Argo* if you don't think you can make it back to your own crew in time."

The Mechanics seemed to take that as a challenge. Tag should have known.

"Our abilities and vehicle are more than adequate to return us to the *Stalwart* before it launches," the driver said.

"Suit yourself," Sofia said, opening one of the side doors. A harsh blast of air cut through the cabin, and Tag was immediately thankful for the self-heating EVA suit he wore. Wind, snow, and ice beat at Coren, Alpha, Sofia, and the marines as Tag led them from the car. He noticed Bull's eyes never left the ground. Likely the marine didn't want to remind himself he was at the mercy of uncontrollable gravity and a magnetosphere to protect him against the vacuum and radiation of open space.

"Captain, pardon me, but where is the goddamn ship?" Lonestar asked.

"Coren, do the honors," Tag said.

Coren activated his wrist-mounted weapons, and a blue flame licked out of its barrels. It cut into the ice and snow like a plasma cutter through alloy, and he tunneled down into the depths of the icy buildup until he hit the glimmering silver surface of the *Argo*.

"All clear," Coren said in a monotonous voice.

Tag ushered the crew down into the fresh void. He scanned the horizon for any glints of metal, any signs at all that the Drone-Mechs were approaching. But he saw nothing. At least, not yet. Scrambling down after Sumo and Gorenado, Tag entered the *cargo* bay. Bull seemed to have recovered from his planetary phobia and had initiated the *cargo* bay closing and repressurization procedures.

"Alpha, Sofia, Coren, to the bridge," Tag said. "Initiate ops, weapons, and get those engines running hot. I want to map a hyperspace jump as soon as we get off this planet. We'll need to share it with Bracken, too."

"Yes, Captain," Alpha said, jogging ahead of the crew up the ladders and down the corridor. She was the youngest member of the crew, yet she had proved herself more than capable of the tasks Tag had handed her. For a moment, he realized how insane it was that he was trusting the lives of his crew and the *Stalwart* with trajectories and flight plans drawn up by a synth-bio AI he had created only weeks ago. Three hells, if he thought too much about that, he would probably scare himself as shitless as Bull had been seeing a real sky for the first time.

Once the crew reached the bridge, they settled into their respective positions. Tag reveled in the growl of the engines and the thrusters as they warmed up.

"How are weapons looking?" Tag asked. "And more importantly, countermeasures?"

"We're at one hundred percent," Coren said.

"Ops?"

"Shields are at one hundred percent strength. I have charted a course off the planet—now passed along to Sofia. The computers are waiting for us to leave the planet before they'll be able to calculate an accurate hyperspace course."

"Excellent," Tag said. "How does it feel to finally be taking a fully intact ship into battle?" He almost couldn't help the boyish excitement tingeing his voice. Every other time they had encountered the Drone-Mechs to this point, something had been wrong with the *Argo*.

"Still feels like we are operating a woefully downgraded vessel," Coren said. "Mechanic tech—"

"Yeah, yeah, we got it, Coren," Sofia cut in. "But how about we focus on kicking some Drone-Mech ass?"

"I propose we do indeed, as you say, kick some Drone-Mech ass," Alpha said. She paused. "Captain, incoming transmission from Bracken."

"Put her through."

Bracken's face lit up on the viewscreen. Behind her were the dull-red glow of battle lights and a dozen Mechanic forces, bouncing around inside the belly of one of their vehicles. "Brewer, we could really use your assistance. A little human firepower, no matter how unreliable, could go a long way toward covering us as we get the *Stalwart* spacebound."

"On it," Tag said. "Coren, take down the camo. Divert that energy to your active countermeasures. I have no doubt we're going to be taking some fire."

"Understood," Coren said. His thin fingers worked across the holoscreens faster than Tag could follow. The screens might have been made for a human, but Coren probably navigated them more quickly than any human weapons officer in the SRE.

"Bull, you guys strapped in back there?" Tag asked over the comms.

"Yes, Captain."

"Sofia, take us up."

"Roger, Skipper," she said.

The ship shook, healthy vibrations resonating through its bulkhead. Tag's crash couch trembled slightly on its gimbals as he watched the viewscreens and holoscreens around him. Snow and ice melted off the ship or else slid off in huge white sheets. Soon the gray skies, cut by vivid arcs of webbing green lightning, showed everywhere around them. Mountains and pillars of ice and rock like enormous stalagmites speared up from the landscape.

"Captain, we've got contacts zeroing in on our position," Alpha reported.

Sure enough, several red dots on Tag's holomap were rushing to the green dot representing the *Argo*. A flood of smaller red dots broke off from the pack, accelerating toward them.

"Torpedoes incoming," Alpha said.

"Goddamn if this isn't familiar," Sofia said.

"You guys know the drill." Tag braced himself as Coren launched point defense cannons and antilidar and -radar chatter to drive off the incoming ordnance. Sofia twisted the ship as if it were a fighter, and the *Argo* groaned under the duress. "Let's go save ourselves some Mechanics."

It didn't take long for the *Argo* to catch up to the Mechanic convoy. In between shooting torpedoes down, Coren raked the surviving exos and foot soldiers rushing the *Stalwart*. The *Argo* circled above the vessel as the *Stalwart* swallowed the black personnel carriers, cars, and hoverbikes. After a few minutes of the *Argo* providing a barrage of high-powered energy rounds and kinetic slugs to ward off any approaching troops, the *Stalwart* lit up on Tag's holomap. Its power plants had gone online, and the thrusters were warming up.

"*Stalwart, Argo*," Tag said. "What's your time to takeoff?"

"Three minutes and counting," Bracken said. "Countermeasures aren't yet fully operational. We're having intermittent energy shield shortages."

"But you can fly?"

"We can fly."

More red dots flashed across the holomap, and Tag had to remind himself to breathe as the Drone-Mech dropships glared over the holoscreen, converging on them. Through the viewscreen, he could actually see them in the distance along with the pinpricks of light indicating incoming fire. *Dropships.* The ships weren't meant for space-to-space or air-to-air battle. From everything he knew about them, they were better equipped to support ground forces. That didn't stop them from being dangerous.

"Good," Tag finally said to Bracken. "Because we should start moving real soon."

EIGHTEEN

THE FIRST ROUNDS OF BLUE PULSEFIRE HIT THE *ARGO*'S
shields. Energy dissipated in a splash of colors, vaguely re-
sembling the celebratory World Unification holiday fireworks Tag
had once watched with his parents in Old Houston. The emotions
flooding him now were a far cry from the awe and jubilation he
had felt then. Emerald fissures formed over the energy shields,
appearing with each absorbed blast, and his crash couch quaked
while crimson letters glowed on the holoscreen, reporting incoming fire.

Damn smart computer you are, Tag thought.

In his head, he inventoried the missiles and torpedoes they
had at their disposal. They could no doubt knock the dropships
down with a sustained volley of warheads. But the *Argo* was a research vessel. Its capacity for storing ordnance couldn't match that
of a destroyer, and expending their stores now would mean less
for later, rendering them at a much greater disadvantage against

whatever Drone-Mech fleet awaited them off planet. He preferred to act on the conservative side should they run into some real trouble beyond Eta-Five.

"Coren, return fire with Gauss cannons," Tag said. "Prioritize dropship weapon systems."

"Copy," Coren said before initiating a barrage of slugs. They cut through the sky at hypersonic speeds, leaving contrails of vapor where the heat of the slugs slicing through air turned ice and snow into mist.

Through his holoscreen, Tag zoomed in on the nearest dropship, revealing gas venting from one of its cannon batteries where the slugs had penetrated. Another dropship started to tilt sideways, smoke wafting from a huge hole in its side as gravity tugged at it, beckoning it toward the land of ice gods.

"See ya, suckers," Sofia said. She kept the *Argo* rapidly maneuvering to thwart the incoming fire, but her efforts couldn't contend with the sheer quantity of rounds. The shields lit up as they absorbed the rounds.

"Eighty percent of full," Alpha said. Another blast of pulsefire rocked the *Argo*. "Now sixty-eight."

"Bracken, what's going on down there?" Tag asked.

"Impellers are online, but we're facing another energy shield drop," she replied. "If we rise into oncoming fire like that, we'll be torn apart."

"You need help?" Tag asked.

Bracken actually let out a laugh. "No, not from your crew. My engineers are on it. We just need time."

Coren shared a knowing look with Tag. "I trained the engineering crew. Of course they don't need our help. They're one of the best technical teams in the Mechanic navy."

"No surprise there," Tag said. Another salvo hit the *Argo*. "Now why don't you focus on our crew? Start with keeping us alive."

The dropships began flying lower, and in their wake, snow and ice plumed up in huge waves, kicked up as they accelerated toward the *Stalwart*. There was something strange about the dramatic decrease in altitude that bothered Tag. The move didn't give the ships a better vantage point for their cannon batteries; instead, it seemed to have worsened their shooting position.

"Coren," Tag said, "what are they doing?"

"It's a fast-drop maneuver for deployment."

"They're unloading more ground forces?" Tag asked.

"Death Walkers don't do much good when they're on a ship, do they?" Sofia asked, leaning into the controls.

As the dropships regained altitude, they left behind a storm of black dots. Tag magnified his view, centering on one of those figures to see exactly what their enemies had deposited: more Death Walkers and exos, as Sofia had predicted. These appeared better equipped for battle against airborne forces as lasers and missiles flew from the ground troops, rocking against the *Argo*'s shields. The PDCs were having trouble keeping up with all the incoming ordnance, and warheads were exploding closer to the *Argo* than Tag would have liked. Beams tore into the energy shields, draining them as they fought to absorb the intense loads.

"Twenty-two percent," Alpha said.

Tag clenched his jaw hard enough for his teeth to hurt. "Sofia, I need you to avoid more of the incoming fire."

"Getting difficult, Skipper," she said, her voice terse and strained. "Not sure it's possible."

"Make it possible," Tag said. "We don't have any other choice unless we want to abandon Bracken out here."

"I do not think she would be amenable to such a plan," Alpha added.

"No," Coren said. "Most definitely not."

Tag's mind drifted toward the lives of the Mechanics, the

Forinths, and G. *We've already left too many behind*, he thought but didn't say.

Bracken's voice cut over the comms. "Captain Brewer, what are you doing? The ground down here is—"

An ice god thrust itself from the bowels of Eta-Five and rammed its head into the *Stalwart*.

"I suppose they weren't our friends after all," Sofia said, not taking her eyes off the viewscreen showing the flash of pulsefire and kinetic rounds streaking toward them.

"Nope, we're not catching a goddamn break," Tag said. "Should be used to it by now." He chinned his comms. "Bracken, is that going to hamper your shields?"

"As long as it doesn't get into the ship, we should live. Might put a dent in the outer hull, but the *Stalwart*'s armor is better than that of the Death Walkers."

"Speaking of which…" Tag focused on the onslaught of ground troops moving their direction under the cover of the dropships. Ice gods began to sprout around the concentrated forces, but the Drone-Mech reinforcements proved too much for the monsters. Most of the huge beasts would grapple with a Walker or two and then be put down by a flurry of fire from their compatriots.

"I'd offer to shake that one off for you," Tag said, "but I don't want to riddle your ship with any accidental friendly fire."

"We would appreciate that," Bracken said, "given that your targeting systems are likely not as accurate as ours."

"Really, you don't let up," Tag said. "I mean, we are trying to save your asses."

Bracken didn't seem to know how to take it and was silent for a moment. "It appears you can be relieved of 'saving our asses' duty, Captain. Our energy shields are fully functional."

"Great," Tag said. "Then let's get off this planet and make a jump."

The *Stalwart* rose from the snow like a waking giant. Tag had never seen the whole ship except in holos. All the work they had performed on it had always been done when the ship was half buried. It dwarfed the *Argo*, and the ice god's insectile legs scratched against the moving ship, struggling for purchase. The huge beast fell away, crashing to the ground, and the *Stalwart* lashed out at the dropships and torpedoes flying toward it and the *Argo*. Its cannons thumped the air with blasts of pulsefire and a spray of flak to detonate the incoming warheads, illuminating the sky in violent flashes and resounding explosions that boomed even in the *Argo*'s bridge.

"You said this was a research vessel, didn't you?" Tag asked Coren.

"It is."

"Hell of a science ship," he muttered. "Bracken, Sofia, let's get spaceside."

Together the ships wound through the air and burst into the grim clouds encasing the planet. Jagged sparks of electricity broke against their energy shields in a display of blinding energy. All the instruments and viewscreens went dark intermittently as alarms shrieked. The shaking bulkheads whined, the sound hammering against Tag's eardrums.

But this wasn't Tag's first rodeo, as Lonestar would say. None of it worried him too much. Rather, he was more eager to discover what was waiting for them on the other side. Soon the viewscreens stabilized, and the alarms quieted. A bejeweled darkness stretched before them, greeting their entry into space. One pinprick of light burned brighter than the rest. *Eta.* Then several more pinpricks lit up around it. More and more appeared. Red dots spread over their holomap.

"Captain, we have thirty-four contacts incoming," Alpha reported.

"T-drive status?"

"Spooled. Ready for a jump. Computers are finishing calculations," Alpha said. Her metallic fingers tapped across her terminal. "And they are finished. Sharing the trajectories with the *Stalwart* now."

Coren looked at Tag expectantly. "We've got incoming fire. Swarms of fighters are assembling outside one of the Drone-Mech ships. Orders?"

"Stand down. No need to waste anything," Tag said, feeling confident in their odds for once. They wouldn't stand a chance against the horde of Drone-Mechs floating around the Eta system. But that didn't matter. "We're about to get the hell out of here anyway."

"Yes, Captain," Coren replied.

"Bracken, ready to do this?" Tag asked.

"Unfortunately, Captain Brewer, we have a slight problem."

Suddenly Tag no longer felt so confident.

NINETEEN

TELL ME IT ISN'T YOUR CORONAL ENGINES," TAG SAID, referencing the Mechanic version of a T-drive.

"It is precisely that," Bracken said. "They are unable to charge. We will not be able to make a jump."

"Gods be damned." Tag pounded his terminal. "Can they be fixed?"

"It would take us a day to diagnose the problem and, presumably, fix it. Proceed without us."

Tag admired the absolute adherence to pragmatism in the Mechanic's mindset, but it clashed with the more human notion to protect and defend even against the most perilous of odds. "Not going to happen. We'll stay and fight if we have to. We came to Eta-Five to get you people off that planet, and that's just what we'll do."

"You have fulfilled that part of your promise," Bracken said. "We are off the planet."

Coren's face was wrought with determination. He was as ready for a fight as Tag. "Captain, countermeasures online. Weapons at the ready."

"It's suicidal to stay here," Bracken said. "Even with our aid, you will not survive the onslaught."

"Then we'll die trying," Tag said.

Both ships were still moving away from Eta-Five. They were headed in the same direction they would have traveled had they been able to make the jump. Tag watched as the red dots on their holomap grew closer to the *Argo* and the *Stalwart*, his fingers trembling. Sweat stung his eyes, and he had to force himself to keep his breathing slow and steady.

"Coren, fire countermeasures at will," Tag said. He knew it was probably futile. Maybe even foolish. But what could he do? Abandon the Mechanics? Until he came up with a better plan, he resolved to stand beside them. There had to be a way out of this. There had to be. Maybe they would get lucky and outrun the Drone-Mechs. Stranger things had happened.

"We have fifty-four incoming torpedoes," Alpha reported. Several seconds later and a slew of countermeasures fired by Coren, she amended that to forty-five.

The first torpedoes slid past their chaff screen. At least they had their energy shields. Maybe they could survive for a while. Then what? Help from the *Montenegro*, if he sent a courier drone now, would take days or weeks to arrive if it could come at all.

No, help wasn't coming. They were most definitely alone.

Tag knew their next steps to prolong their survival: fire back at whatever the Drone-Mechs shot at them, prioritize any on-the-fly repairs with the bots waiting for his signal, and coordinate defensive and counterattack efforts with Bracken. It was all by-the-book strategies that he had learned in his ill-fated days in officer-of-the-bridge training before he had been passed over and sent to a new program.

But nothing had quite prepared him for what to do when he was in a team of two science vessels against thirty-four well-armed hostiles. Was there even a page in their training manuals or a program in their sim software that dealt with odds like this? Or did it just say "tuck yourself into a ball and kiss your ass good-bye"?

Tag felt an almost silly, impractical urge to ask his father what he should do. It was what he had always done before the SRE navy took him away from Sol System Prime, and he found himself missing his father now, wishing he could say another good-bye and tell him how he had saved Tag's career. Given him a new purpose in life by advising Tag to pick himself up and find a different trajectory in the navy. The one that had led him to the seat he sat in now.

His father couldn't save him now if he were here.

As Tag watched the Drone-Mech fleet approach, his heart sank. They had come so close to saving the Mechanics, so close to saving all that remained of their species. And even if they jumped without Bracken, Coren might suddenly become the sole free being of his race in existence. The desperation coursing through Tag's mind was only a fraction of the worry he saw in Coren's frantic motions. Tag needed a solution. They needed some way to fight back, to change the paradigm.

"Remember how I said it was damn near impossible to dodge all that incoming fire on Eta-Five?" Sofia asked. "Well, what's more impossible than impossible? Because that's how hard it's going to be for me to avoid everything coming at us now."

"The T-drive is still spooled and ready to go," Alpha said. Even she sounded nervous, urgent.

Bracken had given them explicit permission to leave her. Tag could still make their sacrifices worth something. Maybe find out who was responsible for the mind-altering nanites and put a stop to it. Figure out who had been behind the Drone-Mech assault on the *Montenegro* and why. He would do it all in honor of Bracken and her crew. Alarms continued to remind him of the incoming onslaught, and it was in that moment he knew he couldn't sacrifice the *Argo* in some noble but ultimately foolish pursuit of honor and fraternity.

This decision would haunt him for the rest of his life. He would be responsible for singlehandedly giving the Mechanics hope and then letting that hope be dashed like icicles against the *Argo*'s hull.

"Trajectory to hyperspace still clear?" Tag asked solemnly.

"Awaiting your command," Alpha responded.

Coren gave Tag only a brief look over his shoulder before turning back to his weapons terminal. There was that Mechanic pragmatism again. Coren might already be mourning the loss of the crew he would be abandoning to die in a storm of streaming plasma and uncontrollable explosions, but he still had a job to do, and he would be damned if he didn't do it well.

And likewise, Tag had a job to do. He was captain of the *Argo* now, and he had to protect the ship and its crew. Finish their mission. A painful stab of regret tore through his gut as his finger hovered above the holoscreen to execute the hyperspace jump Alpha had prepared.

Then he took his finger away. "No, no, we can't leave them here."

"But Skipper, there's no way we can win this battle," Sofia said.

"I know," Tag said. He started scanning through the available commands on the terminal. His father had once told him he was a highwayman, always had an alternate exit, another choice. And by the gods, he had been so damn focused on fighting or fleeing without the *Stalwart*, he had forgotten the other alternatives. "Dad, I'm going to do things right now," he said under his breath. Then, louder, "Alpha, recalculate the hyperspace jump using our T-drive. Instead of using only our ship's mass, incorporate the *Stalwart*'s."

"Captain?" Alpha said. The rest of the crew, even Coren, shared her nonplussed expression.

"Can our T-drive handle it or not?" Tag asked, his voice rising.

Alpha's fingers whirled through the holoscreen. "Yes, it can accommodate a load that large, but I don't understand how that helps." She paused, and her faux eyes seemed to widen. Comprehension shone through her droid features.

"You see where I'm going with this?" Tag asked.

Alpha nodded, working vehemently at her terminal again. "It's a risky maneuver. According to the SRE fleet history guides, it has been attempted only once, and it failed then."

"Let's prove history wrong."

TWENTY

Alpha, engage the grav tether," Tag said. "Bracken, we're going to make a modified docking attempt with the *Stalwart*."

Bracken's face appeared on his holoscreen. Apparently using voice communications wasn't good enough. She wanted to see him to ensure he was actually serious about this. "Do you really believe you can drag us through hyperspace?"

"I don't know, but I'm willing to try."

"Your T-drive is inferior to our coronal engines," Bracken said, as if that alone explained her reluctance.

"Did you run the tests, or are you just assuming?" Tag was a bit tired of the Mechanic's superiority complex. "Because the way I see it, you stay here and get slaughtered like hopeless martyrs, or you try this jump with us. Worst-case scenario either way is we lose your ship. Best case, we *all* make the jump."

Bracken's golden eyes narrowed. "We'll clear our energy

shields enough for you to secure the tether. I must advise you to take the jump slower than normal. I'm not sure the tether will hold during such abrupt acceleration."

"I've got the best mind on our ship working on that challenge," Tag said. "Won't be a problem. Right, Alpha?"

"Technically I am relying on the *Argo*'s AI systems to incorporate these extra variables, so it is less my mind and more the ship's," she replied.

"That makes me feel infinitely better," Bracken said with a touch of sarcasm.

Tag thought he heard a snigger from Coren as the Mechanic sent a fresh wave of chaff into the oncoming torpedoes. The explosions looked brighter, closer in their viewscreen. Pulsefire pounded the energy shields, increasing now that Sofia had taken the ship in closer and slower to the *Stalwart*. A loud clunk reverberated through the bulkheads, and a voice chirped over Tag's terminal, "Tether connection engaged."

The energy shields shimmered as a fresh round of pulsefire crashed against them.

"Are we secure enough for a jump?" Tag asked.

Alpha gestured over a holoscreen, and a three-dimensional holo of the *Argo* and the *Stalwart* appeared. Between them was a beam of light representing the grav tether. Alpha expanded the holo to examine the connection between the two vessels. "Computers are reporting a ninety-five percent attachment efficiency."

"Is that going to be enough?" Tag asked.

"Better be enough!" Coren yelled. "Because I don't think that I can hold this up for much longer."

"Second that," Sofia said. "I'm as cornered as a mouse in a station apartment with a broom in my face."

"Alpha?" Tag asked. "Got a prediction for me?"

"I'm sorry, sir, but we don't have any computational models for this. The AI needs some kind of data to run off of."

"Then I suppose it's time we give it some," Tag said. "Bracken, we're about to initiate the jump. Are you ready?"

"I am not sure how to prepare for anything of the sort," Bracken said. "Let's get it over with."

"That's the spirit," Tag said. "Alpha, initiate!"

The *Argo* jolted forward, and Tag was forced into his crash couch. Rapid acceleration pulled at his flesh and organs, making everything seem as if it were pressing against his spine. The inertial dampeners caught up before nausea got the better of him and he passed out. His stomach found its rightful place in his gut again as the purple and green waves of plasma began coursing over the ship in a hypnotic dance.

"Jump completion is at forty percent captain," Alpha said, "but the tether is—it's gone!"

The *Stalwart* disappeared from Tag's viewscreen, and his hand sprang out at the Abort Jump command. This time his body was thrown forward against the couch's restraints, and he heard groans from all over the bridge. He watched Coren's hands fly out, but at least this time the Mechanic finally had a couch that fit him properly from their time on the *Montenegro*. In an abort maneuver like that without the couch, the Mechanic would have been dead, no matter how well the inertial dampeners tried to compensate for the sudden change in acceleration.

"What in the three hells are you all doing up there?" Bull asked over the comms. "We're being tossed around like shots of gutfire down here."

"Flying is tricky," Sofia offered. "Why don't you guys just sit back and enjoy the ride?"

Tag ignored the crew's banter. "Bracken, do you read? *Stalwart*, anyone there?"

The attempted jump had propelled the *Argo* hundreds of thousands of klicks away from the Drone-Mech fleet. Still, they weren't out of danger. It wouldn't take long for the ships to identify and track them down now that they were in normal space again.

"*Argo*, we read," Bracken responded. "It appears your ninety-five percent tether attachment efficiency was inadequate."

"I would support that assertion," Alpha said in her most helpful voice.

"Then let's make it one hundred and try again," Tag said. His fingers tapped along the armrests. He was unable to keep them from remaining still with the electricity and adrenaline coursing through him.

"Captain, I just got a lock on their position," Alpha said. "They're about a hundred thousand klicks behind us. It appears the Drone-Mech fleet is also moving in their direction."

"Then let's get there first," Tag said. He wasn't sure whether the Drone-Mechs were actually interested in the *Stalwart* or the *Argo* instead. The *Stalwart* simply was between the fleet and him. Either way, he didn't think they would go any easier on the *Stalwart*.

"Can do, will do," Sofia said.

The impellers roared, and the resulting vibrations resonated through the crash couch and into Tag's bones as they rocketed toward the *Stalwart*.

"We have a problem," Bracken said.

Each time Tag heard those words, they sounded like nails scratching across an alloy bulkhead. "Don't tell me an ice god is hitching a ride or something."

"That would be preposterous," Bracken said, evidently missing the joke. Maybe she thought humans were so dull that he was serious. "But the force of the grav tether ripping from our portside damaged our attitude control thrusters. We're rolling and have difficulties course correcting."

"Mechanic technology, eh?" Sofia said.

Coren sighed. "That doesn't get old for you all, does it?"

"Nope," Tag said. "Sofia, that means you've got to match their motion. And Alpha, we're relying on you to make a proper connection."

"I'll do my best," she replied. If droids could sweat and they weren't wearing EVA suits, Tag imagined there would be beads streaming all across her forehead.

"As long as your best means we've got a one hundred-per-cent-efficient grav tether, that's good enough for me."

The blip representing the *Stalwart* grew closer on Tag's viewscreen. So did the entire Drone-Mech fleet. Once again a hail of smaller red dots separated from the main fleet, signifying a deluge of fighters and warheads, all of it headed their direction.

My gods, Tag thought, *they really, really want to see the* Argo *dead.*

When the *Argo* reached the *Stalwart*, the first salvo of Drone-Mech rounds was closing the distance.

"Countermeasures," Tag said with no further explanation.

Coren activated the PDCs, and the cannons fired a rapid barrage of depleted-uranium rounds. Distant explosions of rounds striking warheads bloomed in the holoscreen.

"Matching thrust with the *Stalwart*," Sofia said. Instead of holding a straight trajectory in parallel with the *Stalwart*, she was forced to simultaneously match its speed and direction with its axial rotation.

"Alpha, let's do this again," Tag said.

"Aye, Captain."

The grav tether extended from the *Argo*. Several energy rounds shook against the shields, and the tether missed.

"Sorry!" Sofia said. "Nothing I could do about that. Not while trying to trace their movement."

More fire hit them, and the thought cropped up in Tag's mind that they might be forced to leave the *Stalwart* behind after all.

"Can you make this happen with the distractions?" Tag asked Alpha.

"We will see, Captain."

Her beady eyes focused intently on the holoscreen before her. For a moment, he marveled at the strange neural interfaces and interactions blossoming in her synth-bio mind. The intensity of her concentration radiated off her like UV rays from Sol: invisible but powerful nonetheless. On the holoscreen sim, the tether showed a successful link between the spiraling ships.

"One hundred percent efficiency!" Alpha said.

"Then spool up the T-drive," Tag said. "Let's get out of here!"

As the T-drive began its ascending growl, Coren glanced back at Tag. "What's that human expression? Third time is a charm?"

"Oh, three hells, no, Coren," Tag said. Rounds sprayed against the shields. Only a few hundred thousand klicks stood between the Drone-Mechs and the *Argo*. They were well within range of almost all their cannons now. Space lit up with projectiles and glowing pulse rounds careening toward them. "Two times has to be it for us. It has to be."

And with that, acceleration pressed Tag into his crash couch.

TWENTY-ONE

THE *ARGO* BUCKED AND GROANED UNDER THE IMMENSE gravitational distortions guiding its passage into hyperspace with the *Stalwart*. Tag's fingers tightened around the ends of his armrests, and he had to remind himself to keep breathing. The sounds of the *Argo* struggling to make the hyperspace jump were good signs. It meant that the *Stalwart* was still tethered, still being pulled along in their feverish escape from the Drone-Mechs. Under the ebbing and flowing glow through the viewscreens, all of the ragtag crew members sat at their terminals in focused silence. Alpha was the only one moving, rapidly scanning the status on the tether, the *Argo*'s T-drive, and their precious *cargo*.

Everything started to settle once they had completed the jump and reached traveling velocity within hyperspace. The waves of plasma now coursed more like the sea lapping gently on a soft, white sand beach. The *Argo* itself seemed to quiet, and Tag breathed normally, letting the adrenaline fade from his blood.

The tether was still attached and reporting one hundred percent efficiency.

The *Stalwart* had made it.

"Captain, we may need to alert the SRE," Alpha said, breaking the silence.

Tag's pulse resumed its accelerated pace. "What? What's wrong?"

"The hyperspace astronav guidelines are," Alpha said. "We just proved that a ship can indeed tow a considerable *cargo* without both vessels imploding."

"Oh, right, that little thing," Sofia said with a laugh.

"I wouldn't rewrite the books yet," Coren said, rising from his couch. "After all, we were lugging a Mechanic vessel. I'm sure its design and fortitude helped the effort somewhat. Dragging a human ship into hyperspace would, as the books suggest, almost assuredly end in tragedy."

"We can always count on you for lightening the mood." Tag unlatched his own restraints and strode toward the Mechanic, then placed one hand on the alien's shoulder. "But seriously, thanks for coming with us. You were right down there. We needed our engineer and most definitely our weapons ops officer."

"Of course I was right." Coren undid his helmet, revealing a slight smile. "What do you need from your talented and intelligent engineer now?"

Tag refrained from rolling his eyes. "Well, I think we're in a pretty good spot. Seems like the *Stalwart* will need a bit more work than us. Everyone, go take a break. You deserve it, and then, in one hour, I want to meet in the conference room."

———

Coren, Alpha, Sofia, and Bull were seated with Tag in the conference room near the captain's quarters. A sixth person sat at the table with them, albeit through holopresence.

"The *Stalwart* is stable, despite the repairs that must be made," Bracken said. "I thank you all for your efforts. We could not have escaped without your crew's actions, Captain Brewer."

"Please, really, Tag is fine," Tag said. "And we're happy to prove ourselves useful. We've got some time before our scheduled normal space drop to get things in working order. How does two weeks sound to you?"

"That should be adequate," Bracken said.

"Good," Tag said. "Because I've been thinking about the next order of business."

"You've had time to do that?" Sofia asked with a dubious grin. "Because I barely had time to shower and grab a coffee."

The idea of a coffee practically made Tag salivate. For the first time since embarking on their escape, he realized just how heavy his eyelids felt. The strain and lingering burn in his muscles begged him for a break. Now wasn't the time. "It's clear we're not going to put up much resistance against the Drone-Mechs as is."

He waited a beat for some smartass remark from one of the crew, but they stared back with somber expressions. Even Bull looked crestfallen, his eyes no longer full of the vigor and anger they usually possessed. The hardened warrior had seen enough and lost enough already to know that what they were facing was no idle threat. Bracken, her gaze only slightly downturned, appeared just as depressed at the prospects of roaming the galaxy in flight from the Drone-Mechs. She had been far less fortunate than Tag, losing damn near half the surviving Mechanics in their crew.

"What do you propose?" Bracken asked.

"You all escaped becoming Drone-Mechs because your last

scientific mission was on Eta-Five. None of your crew was infected with the nanites, correct?"

"That's right," Coren said. "We knew nothing about the infections until we arrived at Meck'ara."

"My suggestion would be to rally any free Mechanics on far-reaching expeditions or colonies. I'm guessing the nanite infections were spread similar to a planetborne pandemic. Maybe, if we're lucky, there are some colonies or ships of yours that might have survived, avoiding infection like you did."

"You might be onto something," Coren said. "We have active expeditions and budding colonies all over that could have survived. If your hypothesis is correct, if Meck'ara was the epicenter of the nanite pandemic, then it may be worthwhile."

"If we do find free Mechanics," Bracken began, "what do you suggest then?"

"I'm approaching this like any good epidemiologist would," Tag said. "I mean, my training is in AI and synthetic biology, but the most basic principles of tracking a pandemic would suggest following the disease—or in this case nanites—back to its roots, back to patient zero. Back to where it all began."

"You're proposing we infiltrate the Mechanic home world?" Bull said, his brow furrowing into a gorge of wrinkles. "If that's the case, I'm in. Those goddamn Drone-Mechs deserve everything they have coming."

"That is an enormous risk," Coren said. "We have no idea what we'll be facing or how many Drone-Mechs might still be there."

"Right," Tag said. "That's what makes recruiting as many Mechanics as possible so crucial. On top of that, we'll have time to do more research on disabling the nanites. We've got the power of our science team and yours put together for this mission."

Alpha piped in. "Captain, if I may."

"Please."

"I do remember another fact from going through the data Coren provided. The nanites did not infect all free Mechanics. My databanks are showing a reported approximate two-thirds infection rate."

"That's true," Coren said. "There were many of the Mechanics who remained free aboard space stations and ships. From the messages we intercepted, they were simply slaughtered by the Drone-Mechs."

"It's my hope that all the free Mechanics weren't killed," Tag said. "Maybe your planet is overrun by the Drone-Mechs, but you're an intelligent people. I would be surprised if there aren't resistance groups around your planet, all around this sector, for that matter, that would rally to our cause. Do you think any free Mechanics would back down from a call to retake their planet?"

"No," Bracken said. "They would not. They would realize it is imperative to our survival that we overcome the Drone-Mech menace and stop whoever is behind it. It's only logical."

"Then rally your troops," Tag said, "because we're going to take the fight straight to the Drone-Mechs."

TWENTY-TWO

Do we need to prioritize any work on the *Argo*?" Tag asked his crew.

Bracken had already signed out of the conference. From the repairs on Eta-Five that had been cut short to the damage they had sustained during the escape, the Mechanics had enough to keep them occupied in their flight to the first Mechanic outpost. Not only that, but the casualties they had taken exacerbated their problems as the Mechanics struggled to fill jobs left vacant by the dead. They desperately needed the aid he hoped they might find in the far reaches of Mechanic space if they were going to mount any kind of resistance against the Drone-Mechs.

"All systems are reporting near one hundred percent efficiency," Alpha said. "The hull breaches we experienced are minor. Internal hulls withstood enemy fire thanks to our shields."

"And, I'd like to suggest, my piloting," Sofia said.

"And Sofia's piloting," Alpha added. "I apologize for neglecting to recognize your contribution."

Bull sat in cold silence, his lips straight and his arms across his chest. Tag could practically see the storm of emotions raging behind the man's eyes. Bull had lost someone whose life he had been responsible for. Tag knew what that felt like. He remembered watching his crewmates being slaughtered by the Drone-Mechs. He remembered Kaufman, the last person alive on the ship besides him, dying in his arms while he tried fruitlessly to save her. G hadn't just been Bull's responsibility; Tag's new role on the *Argo* meant everyone who stepped aboard this ship was entrusting their life to his leadership, to his mission.

"As long as the repair bots are taking care of everything and nothing else is critical," Tag said, "we can't forget G. Or, for that matter, all of the Forinths and Mechanics who sacrificed their lives in our escape. I know we don't have a body, but I want to give G a proper burial in space." The scarlet in Bull's face began to fade. The thought of paying their respects to G seemed enough to allay some of his grief and anger. "Sofia, Bull, I want you to prep for the ceremonies. Coren, let them know if there's anything we can do to respect the Mechanic traditions."

"You got it, Skipper," Sofia said.

"Thank you, Captain," Bull said.

"Unless you two have anything else for me, you can get started right now."

"Will do, Captain," Bull said. He snapped up from his seat, and Sofia followed him into the passageway.

Coren leaned forward, placing his furry black elbows on the table. "I take it that means you do have something else for Alpha and me."

"I do. Once you two finish queuing repairs for the bots and weapons maintenance, I'm going to need your help in the med bay.

I want to get a head start on our research to disarm the nanites. I'm afraid Bracken has her hands full bringing the coronal engines online, along with getting their ship in shape for any other fun the Drone-Mechs might have in store for us."

"I'm on it," Coren said. "Shouldn't take long to reload all PDC and Gauss cannon magazines. Is that all?"

Tag nodded, and Coren left. Alpha didn't seem ready to get up yet.

"Something else you got for me?" Tag asked.

"Yes, Captain." Alpha said. "I'm still seeing some strange but minor fluctuations in power. Specifically, there was the power leak in the *cargo* hold."

"Yeah, you mentioned that before. Is it anything significant?"

"No, nothing significant."

"Good," Tag said. "Then let's keep an eye on it. Sounds like it's just one of the light banks going bad."

"That would be consistent with the readings," Alpha said. Still she sat like a statue in her seat. It was unlike her. Most of the time Tag asked her to do something, she was quick to carry through with his commands.

"What's bothering you?"

"Disarming the nanites," Alpha said. "From our analyses, tampering with the nanites would lead to the death of all the Drone-Mechs."

"That's true." Acknowledging the simple fact felt like a Forinth running its claw-tipped tentacles through his gut. The massacre that would result from disarming the nanites would be enormous, but there was little else they could do to stop the Drone-Mechs.

"We know that the Drone-Mechs are simply Mechanics whose neurological systems have been overridden."

"Also true."

Alpha hesitated a beat. "I don't like the idea of creating

something that attacks the nanites. It's like developing a weapon of mass destruction. A weapon that would almost assuredly enact a genocide. It's one thing when they are threatening our lives, but if they aren't attacking us, it is difficult for me to justify their complete annihilation—based on the human legal, philosophical, and moral precedents I've studied."

"That's understandable," Tag said.

"I know I've done it before." Her robotic voice actually dropped, sounding remorseful. "I know it may be logical, but I am finding it challenging to understand the strange feelings associated with the act of killing. It is almost like a weight is pulling down my chassis and my limbs are filling with lead when I think about it."

"I know that feeling," Tag said. "That's your human side. It's what drives us. It's what makes us think about what's really right or wrong."

"I am well aware, Captain," Alpha said. Her silver mouth tightened. "And I know that killing in general is wrong. Everything I told you is true." Even for a droid, she looked pained. "But even so, in the middle of battle, when your life or Coren's or Sofia's is at risk and I kill a Drone-Mech, I don't feel those things."

"What do you mean?"

"I feel glad, Captain. I feel powerful. Knowing I can end their life and they can no longer end mine." Alpha actually shuddered. "I like that feeling. And I don't want to like it."

———

Tag thirsted now more than ever for a long swig of gutfire. His conversation with Alpha still swirled among his thoughts. He had no idea how to comfort her or to dispel her concerns. He tried reaching into his own mind to pull apart how he felt when he pulled the trigger and watched a Drone-Mech explode in a mist of black and red. It never had felt *good* ending a life, and he wasn't sure he liked the power of it like Alpha had described. Staying alive and defending himself and his crew felt good or at least right.

But the act of killing itself?

Even in those moments when he had ended the lives of the Drone-Mech squad that had pirated the *Argo*, his victory had felt good, but not killing them.

Right?

He shook his head as he entered the mess hall. Gods, yes, he could really use a splash of gutfire.

"Captain," a voice called, breaking his reverie.

Tag looked up to see Lonestar. A blond curtain of hair hung over her face, and the steam from a mug wafted up from her cup.

"Mind if I join you?" Tag asked. She shook her head, and Tag grabbed a cup for himself from the autoserv bay then sat across from her. "You wouldn't happen to have something stronger to add to the coffee, would you?"

"Sure wish I did," she said. "The taste is bad enough. Miss the blends my pops used to trade on the ranch. Damn good stuff. Three hells, I miss the *Montenegro*'s. Not nearly as burned. Don't know how you drink so much of this."

Tag took a sip and waited for the hot liquid to wash away some of the heaviness in his eyes. "I wasn't exactly thinking about the taste." He drank a gulp again. "I'm sorry about G."

"Me, too," she said. "Kid was young. Shouldn't have been him. Not that I wanted anyone else to die, but gods be damned."

"No one deserves to go like that," Tag said. He curled his fingers around the mug. The warmth crept into his hand. "Can I ask you a question?"

"Shoot."

"Besides learning the basics, I was never trained to be a soldier like you. Never taught how to survive in shipboard combat or in a ground skirmish."

Lonestar looked up from her mug with a skeptical expression.

"But—gods I hope I'm not offending you—you aren't trained to like killing, are you?"

"No, can't say that we are. And, I mean, it's part of our job and all, but I don't like it. I really don't think you're supposed to like it. You'll run into a gunny every once in a while who loves his job. Who likes the violence a bit too much, but *damn*. Even killing xenos doesn't always feel good, you know?'

Tag nodded.

"Something on your mind, Captain?"

"No, just asking," Tag asked. He could see she didn't believe him, so he finished off his coffee. "Again, sorry about G. I'd sit longer, but I've got some work in the med bay."

TWENTY-THREE

THE EFFECTS OF THE COFFEE BURNED THROUGH SOME OF THE fog hovering over Tag's mind. He still felt a sticky oiliness covering his body left over from the sweat of their escape. As much as he longed for a shower and a change of clothes, he couldn't take a break while his crew worked overtime. Besides, even if they had not been around, the call of the laboratory was too great. It was where he felt at home, where he felt most confident, and when he had an experiment to run or research to perform, the med bay's lab beckoned like a seductive siren calling to him.

"Captain," Coren said when Tag entered the bay. The Mechanic was hunched over one of the terminals. "Alpha seemed like she had a handle on everything at the bridge. Acted like something was on her mind, though. She wasn't much for conversation, so I started on the nanite disarmament strategies."

"Appreciate it," Tag said. "I still can't figure out how to reverse the genetic changes the nanites cause. I'd need some kind of enzyme to knock out the hundreds of bits of genetic code integrated into the Drone-Mech's genome. Then we'd have to use an insanely powerful bioweapon to infect every Drone-Mech with DNA vectors, and that's just the beginning. I mean, I know you're not a medical scientist, but I'm sure even you can appreciate the impossible hurdles we're facing to make that happen."

"Thank you for your confidence in my ability to understand your rudimentary scientific knowledge," Coren said. Tag thought he could see a slight smirk in the Mechanic's expression, but he wasn't sure. Coren gestured to a holo displaying the brain structure of a Mechanic along with the antenna embedded within it formed by the self-assembling nanites. "After reviewing everything, I think that solving this problem from a biological or biochemical approach is the wrong way to do it. You're right. Trying to reverse the genetic changes is an impossible task, even by Mechanic standards. Species-wide DNA vector delivery is, I regret to say, beyond our most advanced capabilities."

"Damn," Tag said. "I was actually hoping you wouldn't say that. Retaking Meck'ara—" He stopped. Something inside the back of his skull itched. It was an almost tangible feeling, as if there was a bug scratching at his conscience. And then, his mind reverting back to chief medical officer mode, he realized what it was. "We always took extreme caution when handling the nanites. You never got infected by them. I'm not sure whether that's because you're immune or because we were careful or another something else entirely."

He felt something tighten in his throat, and he had to gulp before continuing. "But I'm not sure what will happen when we bring a ship full of free Mechanics to a planet full of nanite-infested Drone-Mechs. Whatever infected the Mechanics there in the first place might still be active."

"You think we may as well be committing suicide by heading straight back to Meck'ara."

"Exactly," Tag said. "We need a way to vaccinate you all. Something to prevent the nanites from entering the nervous system—or at least from allowing the genetic changes to take root. Something to ensure when we bring the fight to the Drone-Mechs, all the free Mechanics don't turn sides on us."

"That is an idea worth pursuing I had not yet fully considered." Coren's eyes traced over the chemical formulas of the nanite constituents displayed on the side of the holo. "It appears we have our hands full. Do you have any idea how we might expedite the search for a vaccine?"

"There is something that would accelerate our progress," Tag said. He recalled when he had first met Coren and Sofia in the Forest of Light and their attempt to fill him in on all that had transpired regarding the Drone-Mech pandemic. "The reports you and Sofia showed me indicated almost a third of Mechanics weren't affected by the nanite outbreak. We need to find one of them to figure out why they might be immune."

"Of course." Coren paused as if in thought. Then his healthy eye lit in a radiant golden glow. "Even if we do find a vaccine, that doesn't solve the problem of the vast number of Drone-Mechs we'll face."

"I take it you have another idea to deal with them."

"The nanites respond to grav waves. And yes, I understand grav-wave communications are only a theoretical subject in human technology. Mechanic science has advanced further than your current grav-wave tech."

"Where are you going with this?"

Coren let out what seemed like an exasperated sigh as he motioned to the holo of the Mechanic brain and nanites. "Someone's controlling the Drone-Mechs. That means, theoretically, we could, too."

Grav waves—and physics in general—were beyond Tag's realm of expertise.

"As far as I know, the SRE can detect grav waves from natural phenomena," Tag said, "but I don't think we can manipulate them coherently enough for any real mode of communication. Why not just create some kind of shielding effect to block the signal? Surely that's easier."

"Are you thinking of something like an EMP blast that disables electronics?" Coren asked.

"Maybe."

"Grav waves are capable of penetrating matter, and electromagnetic radiation wouldn't interfere with their signal. So unless you humans have something we don't, I'm not sure of any reasonable way to stop the signal."

Tag sat on a stool in front of the Mechanic brain holo. He rotated the image, studying the spiral pattern of the self-assembled nanites. "So the best you think we can do is send a different signal to the Drone-Mechs."

"Exactly," Coren said. "And since the *Stalwart* avoided the Drone-Mechs altogether until Eta-Five, we have no samples or models to base our research on. Can I send them the holos and data you have on the autopsied Drone-Mechs?"

"Yes, of course."

Coren nodded and initiated the data transmission at his terminal.

Collaborating freely with the Mechanics could be their saving grace. After all, that was the way the scientific community had prospered for centuries. The sharing of research papers and data packages provided a constant stream of new knowledge for anyone to tap into. Now that scientific tradition was spreading to another technically adept species. The mere thought that this single act could connect SRE science with Mechanic technology practically made Tag salivate. All the new advancements they could make…installing the personal energy shields in the marines' armor was just the first step in what Tag hoped would be a fruitful relationship.

"You said Mechanic grav-wave technology is beyond SRE tech," Tag asked. "How far along is it?"

"There's a research institution near our capital city called the Lacklon Institute for Physical Sciences. One of the premier research groups within the organization developed a grav-wave generator." Coren gestured over the holoscreen, and an oval-shaped facility glowed between them. It appeared almost as large as the *Montenegro*, dotted with rows of windows and all kinds of satellite dishes and antennae. "Most of the research performed there has been studying natural phenomena, and to my knowledge, only a few experiments have considered grav waves as a focused communication medium.

"But the *Stalwart* has some of the best scientists, physicists, and engineers in the Mechanic navy." Coren paused then added more dourly, "At least, it did before the Drone-Mechs. My hope is that my people can reverse engineer the nanite antenna technology. If they are successful, we could determine how best to deliver a signal to the Drone-Mechs. We might not be able to bring the Drone-Mechs back to full consciousness as free Mechanics, but we can at least disrupt their programming and interfere with the signals driving them to kill."

"That would be perfect," Tag said. "But that poses some challenges. We've got to develop the technology, hope that the Lacklon Institute still exists, and make it to the facility."

"Which makes reaching out to any free Mechanics all the more important," Coren said. "But I'm also worried that their help may not be enough."

A heavy silence weighed between them for several long

moments. Tag understood the implication without Coren saying another word.

"I'll certainly contact the SRE, but you saw what disarray they were in after the attack on the *Montenegro*," Tag said.

"That's all we can ask."

The holo of the Mechanic's brain captivated Tag. He thought of the Drone-Mech bodies they had once had aboard the *Argo*. Coren and Tag had relinquished the corpses to the *Montenegro* for the SRE to analyze, but not before Tag had completed a full autopsy, run a biochemical profile, and secured a few samples of the neural tissue infested with nanites. "If we need to, we can always use the samples we have to run some of the grav-wave tests. But that still doesn't give us a lot of dead Drone-Mech specimens to work with."

"I'm sure as we make our way back to Meck'ara," Coren said, his twelve fingers knitting together, "we'll have the opportunity to retrieve more samples."

TWENTY-FOUR

THE CEREMONY FOR G WAS BRIEF BUT HEARTFELT, WITH the marines telling stories of the young soldier, from his first taste of gutfire to the time he twisted an ankle trying to prove he could jump as high as any Turbo player. Without a body, they had been forced to load one of G's old uniforms into the torpedo bay and launch it into space. Tag watched as the marines consoled each other. Bull never wavered, though Tag swore he could see a slightly wet sheen over the man's eyes. Gorenado, Sumo, and Lonestar didn't quite hold back like Bull did, and Tag felt like a stranger presiding over a ceremony for a man he had only known for a matter of days while these four might as well have spent a lifetime with him.

After G's symbolic funeral, Coren said there was little they needed to do to pay their respects to his Mechanic brothers and sisters other than continue the fight and free Meck'ara from the grasp of the Drone-Mechs. *Easy enough*, Tag thought ruefully.

He had felt like he was cheating those who had sacrificed themselves by not doing something at that moment to honor them, but Sofia had insisted this was Mechanic tradition, and there would undoubtedly be a proper remembrance ceremony once the battle against the Drone-Mechs ended and the Drone-masters were defeated. Tag said a short prayer for them anyway.

The days following G's burial in space bled into each other as Tag almost lost himself in the pattern of laboratory work. The med bay had been his home long before his abrupt promotion to command of the *Argo*, and it was too easy to forget his responsibilities to the rest of the crew. He had run dozens of simulations with the help of the ship's AI to test various biomolecule and nanoparticle compounds to see if any would inhibit the self-assembly of the nanites or their effects in the Drone-Mechs. Nothing he had tried produced any desirable results, and from his communications with Bracken, the science team on the *Stalwart* hadn't made any breakthroughs either.

Alpha worked at a nearby terminal. They had shared conversations on science and the status of the *Argo* but little else over the past several days in hyperspace. He waited for her to bring up her concerns over the psychological effects of combat from before, but she never did, and he didn't press her. They mostly continued their efforts in silence.

"Captain," she said, breaking the quiet. "We're thirty minutes from transition."

Tag closed the holoscreen he was using, letting the blue-and-green light fizzle away. "Alert the crew."

"Yes, Captain," Alpha said. She sent a message over her terminal, and a voice sounded over the shipwide comms, calling all crew members to their stations.

Tag jogged to the bridge and settled into his crash couch. Sofia and Coren were already secured, and Alpha found her spot. The holomap displayed in the center of the bridge showed a rotating image of Nycho Station, their first destination in Mechanic space. The station had been used as a resupply and research station for expeditions within the Fidelity sector.

"What do you think, Skipper?" Sofia said. "Going to run into hostiles or friendlies?"

"Either way, they'll no doubt be surprised to see us," Tag said. He pressed the comms for the *Stalwart*. "Bracken, are you all ready for normal space transition?"

"We are," she replied. "And we look forward to no longer being towed behind the *Argo*."

"I take it your coronal engines are fully repaired and ready to go," Tag said.

"We do not make the same mistake twice."

"Good," Tag said. "Because we better prepare for a fast exit if things go south."

"At the first sign of Drone-Mech conflict, we'll be prepared to embark on Trajectory Beta to our next destination."

"It's a shame we couldn't contact Nycho Station ahead of time somehow."

"That would've been most unwise," Bracken said. "The likelihood of Drone-Mechs intercepting any messages outweighs the benefits of risking message transmission."

Tag agreed. He still didn't like it. His stomach flipped as he considered exactly what they were getting themselves into. There was no telling whether they would be welcomed with open arms by a fleet of free Mechanics waiting to enact vengeance on the Drone-Mechs or if a horde of Drone-Mechs had taken up residence at Nycho to ensure the death of any humans or free Mechanics who passed by.

The plasma coursing over the ship gave way, and Tag gulped as the *Argo* began its descent into normal space. His body sank into the crash couch, and the inertial dampeners fought against the rapid deceleration. White flecks of light peppered black space on the viewscreens.

"Alpha, hostiles?" Tag asked.

"Negative, sir," Alpha said.

The crew seemed to breathe a collective sigh of relief. The only other ship that cropped up on the holomap was the *Stalwart*.

"Untether the *Stalwart*," Tag said.

"Yes, Captain," Alpha replied. The *Stalwart* started to put distance between itself and the *Argo*.

"Feels good to have some breathing room again," Sofia said, taking over the controls. "It's a hell of a lot easier flying this thing when it isn't towing a million tons of spaceship and Mechanic ego."

A single huff escaped Coren. A laugh, maybe.

"I'm glad we don't see any Drone-Mechs, but where is Nycho?" Tag asked.

"We should be able to see it," Coren said. "It orbits Lanon-Four." He pointed a skinny finger at the planet on the map. "Lanon itself is uninhabitable. We never bothered terraforming it because it was simply easier to mine the nearby asteroids and put together Nycho. But..." He cocked his head as he studied the ghostly sphere of Lanon-Four on the map. "Nycho was built to be transportable. Kind of a slow-moving spaceship in case we decided to relocate where our research vessels in the area resupplied."

"You think they moved then? Maybe to escape?" Sofia asked as they approached Lanon-Four.

Tag felt a mixture of hope and frustration. On one hand, maybe that meant the free Mechanics had survived and were out there somewhere. On the other hand, if they were, then he had no idea where to begin looking for them.

"Captain!" Alpha said. "I'm picking up a signal! An

unidentified vessel, approximately the size of Nycho Station, is four hundred fifty-six thousand three hundred and four klicks from our location. There are no signs of grav impellers engaged, and electromagnetic radiation signals emanating from the ship are minimal."

"Precise as always," Tag said. "Bracken, did you get a read on the ship ghosting out there?"

"Yes," Bracken replied. "That seems to match Nycho's profile. We would like to make the approach."

"I'm sensing some hesitancy. You see something we don't?"

"It's strange that we aren't getting so much as an encrypted SOS from the station. If they were fleeing an enemy, we would expect them to have done exactly that."

"Maybe they're not trying to attract much attention," Tag said.

"Maybe," Bracken said. Tag could tell she was skeptical of his suggestion. He wasn't sure he believed it himself.

They drifted toward the vessel. Coren was bristling at the weapons station. All countermeasures were hot, ready to be engaged at any sign of a single energy round glimmering from space. Slowly they approached Nycho, and Tag recognized its halo-like shape from the images Coren had showed them. Based on those pictures, Tag had expected to see thousands of portholes glowing with light as the station spun around its central pylon.

Nycho was completely dark, and as it rotated in their viewscreen, Sofia gasped. An entire chunk had been torn from the ring. Flotsam floated around the broken segment like the detritus of a beast attacked by an ice god and left to die.

"No," Coren said. "I truly hoped…I can't believe it."

Alpha magnified the image on the viewscreen to get a closer look at the debris littering the vacuum around the station. Uncoiled snakes of wire and chunks of bulkhead glided by. Tag forced himself to watch as the bodies of spaced Mechanics lazily drifted in the spinning station's wake. Singe marks and gaping holes across the station revealed the story of a battle that had taken place here. All the docking stations lay empty except for three. Those three tunnels were connected like umbilical cords to Mechanic science vessels similar to the *Stalwart*. But each appeared broken in pieces, barely hanging on.

"The Drone-Mechs were here," Tag said. "Good gods, no doubt about it."

Coren's fingers twitched. Tag imagined him filled with rage at seeing more of his people massacred and their bodies ignobly left to float on through space for an eternity. There was nothing here for them after all. Tag was ready to initiate the next jump.

"Captain!" Alpha said. "I'm getting a signal! Someone... someone on there is alive!"

TWENTY-FIVE

BRACKEN, ARE YOU GETTING THIS, TOO?" TAG ASKED. He watched the *Stalwart* lurk around the opposite side of Nycho.

"We are," Bracken said. "It's coming from a prox comm device."

Tag looked to Coren for a translation.

"It's for short-range communications. Kind of like a two-way radio or your intersuit comm lines."

"Got it," Tag said. Then to Bracken, "The AI translation here is telling us it's a Mechanic asking for help."

"That is correct," Bracken said. "We think there is a not-in-significant possibility that this is a trap. All the same, we hope to proceed. Drone-Mechs or not, we want to know what happened on Nycho."

"Count us in," Bull said over the private link to Tag. "We're itching to get the hell off this ship."

Tag weighed the prospects of finding free Mechanics here, dead or alive. Although it seemed morbid, even dead Mechanics could be useful. If this was indeed a site of the nanite outbreak, then any free Mechanics who had perished in the resulting battle would be worth examining. Samples from their tissues could prove instrumental in figuring out how their bodies resisted the nanites, which might give their vaccine production research a leg up.

"We're going to proceed as well," he said. "Alpha, see if you can get us docked."

"Will do, Captain," Alpha said.

They floated toward Nycho. Ahead of them, streams of vented gas created white crystalline swathes from the docks where the *Stalwart* was making a connection with the station. Alpha used her hand to trace a circle around another empty docking bay on the station. It was situated next to one of the decrepit science vessels still bleeding frozen bodies and debris into space.

"We can fit in here, although the seal won't be airtight," Alpha said. "You will need to wear your EVA suits."

"Planning to anyway," Tag said. "It'll keep out any potential nanites." He sucked in a deep breath. This was it. "Sofia, handle maneuvers. Let's get in there."

A metallic groan reverberated through the *Argo*'s bulkhead as the ship slid into place. Then a clang sounded.

"We're docked," Alpha said.

"Bull," Tag said, "have your marines ready in five and meet me at the docking port."

"Already there, Captain," he replied. "Locked and loaded and ready to go."

Clicks echoed through the bridge as Tag undid his harness and stepped from his crash couch. "Alpha, Sofia, you stay here. Keep the ship hot. I want energy shields ready to go, the T-drive spooled, and impellers ready to blast us out of here. First sign of Drone-Mechs, you let me know."

"You got it, Skipper," Sofia said.

"Understood, Captain," Alpha said. Her robotic voice sounded particularly monotonous as she settled back at the ops station. She certainly seemed disappointed, but Tag refused to dwell on what that meant.

"Coren, you're with me," he said.

Together they jogged from the bridge and stopped by the armory to pick up their weapons. They joined Bull, Sumo, Lonestar, and Gorenado at the docking port. Coming in just under two meters in height, Tag had towered over most of his former crewmates. But next to the marines in their power armor, he felt grossly undersized. Their bulky armor made their already-muscular bodies appear like weapons in and of themselves. For a moment, he compared the research-oriented EVA suit he wore, which was intended more for exploration than it was combat, against the heavily armored marine suits. The stark contrast between his protection and that of the marines didn't help the unsettling thoughts drifting through his mind about what they might face aboard Nycho and how he would hold up against whoever—or whatever—else might be on the station besides any free Mechanics.

But he refused to let those emotions show.

"Ready?" he asked.

Bull jammed a magazine into his mini-Gauss rifle. "Gods be damned, you bet we are."

"Bull, I'm leaving combat operations up to you. First priority is locating the source of the distress signal. Second is obtaining a sample of a free Mechanic."

"Dead or alive, sir?" Bull clarified.

"I'd prefer if we found living free Mechanics. Then a voluntary blood sample would suffice. Failing that, a deceased Mechanic should work. We just need to somehow make sure it was actually a free Mechanic and not a Drone-Mech."

"Understood. Lonestar, take point," Bull commanded. "Gorenado, you're on rearguard. Captain, Coren, you two stay between me and Sumo. Lonestar, go!"

"For G," Lonestar said, striding forward. She slammed her fist on the docking port release terminal, and the hatch dilated. Air from the pressurized docking chamber rushed out, rippling past Tag's suit. Lonestar led into the station with her rifle. A bright light from her helmet shone into the cylindrical corridor, casting long, ghoulish shadows from the scaffolding and debris covering the passageway. The docking tube was Spartan, with little more than a few metal benches and lockers coated in the sleek black paint the Mechanics seemed to favor. It was utilitarian to a fault.

Boot steps echoed down the passage behind them. Tag almost jumped as Gorenado's beam swung around to coat the incoming party in a brilliant blast of light.

"Put that damn light down," a Mechanic said. Like every other Mechanic in his squad, he wore black power armor that looked right at home in Nycho Station. The only difference between his uniform and his squadmates' was a slight purple band on his left upper arm that glowed when the light hit it. "I'm Sharick, leading the rescue operations on the *Stalwart*'s behalf." Sharick pushed his squad of six past Lonestar. "We triangulated the distress signal to a location within the station's library. Follow us."

Bull shot Tag a distrustful look. Evidently the marine didn't like taking orders from a Mechanic.

Tag chinned over to a private channel with the sergeant. "These guys know their station better than us. They have the lead."

"It's not that," Bull said. "I just want to have a fair chance at bringing down any Drone-Mechs we run into. Can't let them have all the fun."

"I'd be careful what you wish for."

They continued in silence, following the Mechanics through the passages. Sharick led them on as if he'd once lived here. Probably had, for all Tag knew. And he was damn thankful the Mechanic knew the tortuous route to the library. The station couldn't have been abandoned for much more than seven or eight months according to the information they had on the nanite outbreak, but the place looked like it was a relic of a civilization past. It was battered and broken, with wires hanging loose from the ceiling, panels torn from bulkheads, and all manner of refuse scattered across the decks.

They gingerly stepped over the remains of Mechanics whose bodies had been shredded and singed by pulsefire. There was no telling which side these Mechanics had fought for. Frosty icicles hung off their open, glassy eyes and from their slack jaws. Tag shivered. It wasn't from the cold; his EVA suit protected him against that. But it didn't protect him from imagining the ghosts of the dead wandering the station, looking for a way off, looking for the bridge to whatever heavens came next. Then he remembered the predominant Mechanic cults and religions didn't include any-thing so optimistic as an afterlife. They had nowhere to go. All these souls were stuck here in this wasteland adrift in the void.

Onward they went, passing a bank of terminals with broken holoscreens. A couple still buzzed on with emergency battery power somehow still leaking to them. One flickered on and off in an ephemeral image of a Mechanic ship departing, then docking at Nycho, over and over. Soon they entered a larger room full of tables in what looked to be a mess hall of sorts. Bodies were strewn against the walls near an exit hatch as if they had been slaughtered while attempting an ill-fated escape. Stains around their frozen corpses somehow made the floor appear darker.

Sharick wove between the dead and opened the hatch they

had been concentrated around. It made Tag's skin crawl to see that door so easily opened when so many around it had died evidently trying to escape through it. He imagined the Mechanics here reaching out for the hatch as pulsefire tore into their flesh. The panicked screams. The shriek of gunfire. The spilling blood. Tag shuddered. One by one, the Mechanics and humans made their way out of the mess and into another large chamber. This one had several sitting areas and massive windows that revealed the space outside the station.

Tag supposed the windows had once looked out over Lanon-Four, where it would have been easy to catch glimpses of the dead planet and the stars beyond it. Now a cloud of flotsam and the occasional body drifted by, providing a macabre tableau that made him recoil from the polyglass. They snuck through the atrium, Tag trying to avoid looking out the windows, until Lonestar suddenly stopped.

"Good gods," she said.

Tag followed her line of sight until he saw what she was staring at.

Nausea gripped him like a vise tightening on his stomach.

"Oh," he offered lamely.

Coren glanced at what had captivated them then quickly turned away, staring straight ahead again. Somehow the Mechanics didn't seem nearly as concerned as the humans, and Tag couldn't help but find it strange, despite all he knew about the way Mechanics viewed life and death. His eyes lingered on the scene. It was something he had never seen, something he realized was foolish not to have considered before, especially in a self-contained city like Nycho Station. The dead free Mechanics scattered about the room were no more than half the size of Coren, some much less. It physically pained Tag to see them caught up in this strange war, victim to an enemy neither they nor their parents knew. The terror they must have felt. The horror of what they had witnessed before their young lives were cut short.

A new fire burned in Tag's gut, and he turned forward, following Sharick once more into another room. Now more than ever, he knew the Drone-Mechs had to be stopped, and unless the gods intervened, he was going to damn well do his best to find a way to make that happen.

TWENTY-SIX

"THROUGH HERE," SHARICK BOOMED THROUGH THE COMMS.

The Mechanics flitted through the hatch like shadows through darkness. If Tag didn't pay attention, their black armor made it seem almost as if they were part of the station come to life, giving them the illusion of disappearing when they stood still, the alloy and polyglass surging like a fluid melding in and out of the bulkhead when they moved.

With their fingers hovering next to their trigger guards, Gorenado and Bull constantly swept the floor and bulkheads behind them. It was as if they expected something to come careening from the branching passages or jumping from the overhead airshafts at any moment. Tag didn't blame them. Walking through the widening chambers and corridors leading to the library made the hair on the back of his neck stand on end. He felt like he had when he had first set foot in the Forest of Lights, back when the Forinths had had their eyes on him, stalking him as they skirted through the foliage with camouflage that made them almost completely invisible. The thought of them and what the Forest must look like now sent a pang of regret and sorrow through him. He didn't let the thought burn on for long. As much as he wished for their safety and future well-being, his own safety and well-being might be at risk here. It wouldn't do him any good to let the morose thoughts distract him from the nightmarish reality he found himself in now.

They crept down another passage with a series of rooms on either side. Most of the hatches were stuck open, revealing berths and shelves with few belongings, fitting with the typical décor of the Mechanics. They passed through the quarters, ignoring most of the rooms. Then a glimmer of blue light caught Tag's eyes. Sharick continued past it, and for a second, Tag considered doing the same.

But his curiosity got the better of him. "Sharick!"

The Mechanic paused. Several in his squad turned, their rifles raised. Lonestar and Gorenado aimed their weapons in concert.

"Just wanted to investigate something," Tag said. He pushed the hatch open wider and stepped into the room. Bull followed, watching over Tag's shoulder. He sensed the marine's unease at separating from the pack. "There."

Tag pointed to a blinking light from a terminal. It was still on. Next to it was another dead Mechanic. Its arms were folded across its chest as if to protect itself. But its feeble attempts to defend itself had failed. A gaping void cut through its chest, and Tag tried to keep his gaze from lingering on the fatal wound, instead focusing on the terminal. He pressed a small button on it, and a holo glowed in the center of the room. Sharick stepped in beside Bull. The azure glow of the holo reflected on Sharick's orange visor as a recording began playing.

On the holo, the dead Mechanic appeared alive, huddled in these very quarters. The retort of pulsefire pinging and scorching around the station played in the background. Intermittent, distant screams burst through the audio as the Mechanic's eyes darted between the hatch and the terminal.

"I'm recording this in hopes that someone will find it useful. Something has happened to the crew. Some kind of mutiny." The Mechanic spoke in hushed, trenchant words. "I don't know what's going on. Instead of demands, they've been killing those of us who aren't like them. Those of us who resist. It doesn't make any logical sense."

The Mechanic sighed. "Without warning, people turned on each other. The massacre I saw was unlike anything I would've expected from our people. The mutineers took our armory then raided the life support systems and engineering. Once they started absconding with all the docked ships, I thought it would be over." Her eyes locked with the camera, making it appear that she was looking straight at Tag. "But that wasn't the end. If you're listening to this, there's got to be a reason for this disaster. Maybe it's scientific. A disease or something." She catalogued the various experiments and research projects underway at the station, wondering aloud if one of these projects had led to this mutiny. Nothing sounded remotely similar or related to the nanites from Tag's point of view. "Please, you must—"

Then the Mechanic's hatch blew open in the holo. Tag had to keep himself from jumping.

"No, stop!" the Mechanic shrieked. Tag's pulse raced as he watched her get cut down by gunfire from what must have been Drone-Mechs. The Drone-Mechs left, and the holo continued recording empty air. The sounds of faraway battles went on until Sharick turned the holo off.

"I want a copy of that holo," Sharick said. A Mechanic stepped past them and waved his wrist over the terminal to transfer the data onto his onboard computers.

"Us, too," Tag said. "And there's something else I need." He moved closer to the Mechanic's body. Her eyes were still frozen open in fear. The moment the Drone-Mechs had entered her chamber would be memorialized for an eternity in her thousand-yard stare.

Coren understood what Tag wanted and knelt near him. "She was a free Mechanic. Even through all of this, she didn't succumb to the nanites."

"We have to get a sample," Tag said. "Sharick, Bull, can you post guard?"

The two exited the quarters, giving orders to their charges. Tag took a specimen collection kit from a shoulder-mounted pack. With the use of a miniature plasma drill and a few slices with a laserblade, he collected blood and neural tissues within a few tiny vials. He made short work of the procedures. It was less gruesome and messy than he had anticipated since her blood was frozen solid.

"Do you think this will be good enough?" Coren asked.

"It's a start," Tag said. "Thanks to her recording, at least we can be fairly certain she wasn't a Drone-Mech."

"I would guess most of the bodies we've seen today weren't Drone-Mechs," Coren said. "But at least for her, we have proof she wasn't. Will you need more samples?"

"It wouldn't hurt," Tag said. He thought he heard the faint scurry of something above them. Like mice going through vents. Only he knew no mice—at least no earthborn mice—could survive here.

"Is something wrong?" Coren asked.

"You didn't hear that?"

Coren gave him a blank look.

"Never mind."

They rejoined the others waiting outside, and Tag couldn't help the creeping sensation tickling along his spine that they were being followed. Maybe it was the creepiness of the place. He wasn't superstitious, but he couldn't help imagining this place was still haunted by more than just the memories of those who had died here. The group traversed another series of chambers and passages until they arrived at a large hatch. The doors here continued to half dilate then close a few centimeters, causing a continuous clicking. It appeared they were stuck half open.

"The library is through there," Sharick said.

"Alpha, Sofia, any contacts?" Tag asked over the comms.

"Negative, Captain," Alpha replied.

"Good. Let's check this place out."

"Gorenado, Sumo, stand watch out here," Bull said. "Captain, stick close to me."

Seeing Bull leave a pair of marines on watch, Sharick followed suit with his Mechanics. The rest went through the half-working hatch one by one. Tag jumped through as quickly as possible, finding it difficult to avoid thinking of the hatch closing around his middle and slicing him into two bleeding chunks.

"This is the library?" Tag asked, gazing around the new chamber.

"Affirmative," Sharick said.

Maybe it was an antiquated notion from watching too many old holofilms, but Tag had been envisioning shelves of digital texts or datacubes—something more in line with the human definition of a library. Instead, the Mechanic library was a mazelike room full of pods. Each pod appeared as if it could fit a single person on an uncomfortable-looking flat cylinder Tag assumed was a seat. In front of each seat was a single holoscreen and terminal. The pods were stacked atop each other, accessible by ladders.

The library wasn't free from the horrors that had played out in the rest of the station. Several of the pods held the bodies of Mechanics who had apparently sought refuge here.

Sharick started to lead the group between the pods and under the ladders. Tag forced himself to ignore the grisly images they passed, focusing instead on the hope that maybe there was actually someone alive here. Someone who had survived the massacre.

"Fat chance we're going to find the person who recorded the distress call," Lonestar said, as if reading his mind and ready to squash the remnants of his fading optimism.

They followed the winding paths into another half circle of pods. The squad bristled, their rifles pointed in every direction. Sharick walked toward a ladder and began climbing it.

"This should be…it. There's no one here. Just an abandoned wrist terminal." Sharick paused at the third pod from the ground then turned and looked around at the others. "Does anyone see any bodies?"

The words sent a chill through Tag, and he spun on his heels, looking for who could have left the terminal behind. But there were no Mechanics, dead or alive, anywhere in this section of the pods.

"Gods be damned," Tag said. His ears perked, waiting for the hiss of Drone-Mech troopers descending on them in power armor, the blare of pulsefire screaming past them, and the clatter of boots from all around. "We got what we came for. Let's get back to the ships."

"Sumo, Gorenado, how's it look out there?" Bull asked.

"Clear as the sky on a sunny day," Sumo replied. "Not so much as a peep out here."

Tag's nerves started to fire, his vision growing narrow as they returned to the library's exit. Something wasn't right. He strained to hear footsteps or heavy breathing or something to let him know they were being watched, that the Drone-Mechs were here. The hatch appeared before them, still trying to close on itself and meeting with the same failure, over and over. Sumo, Gorenado, and one of the Mechanics waved at them from the other side, signaling that all was clear.

One of the Mechanics reached the door first and started to slide through. The door's clicking stopped. It slammed shut with a resonating thud and cleaved the Mechanic at his torso before he could so much as yelp. Lonestar bounded forward with another Mechanic at her side. The Mechanic tried activating the door terminal. When that failed, together they pried at the door using a discarded piece of singed bulkhead.

"Can't get it!" Lonestar said.

"Can we override it?" Tag asked.

The Mechanic at the hatch shook his head. "I already tried, but I'm completely locked out of the terminal."

"Son of a bitch!" Bull boomed. "Sharick, there's got to be another way out."

"Yes," Sharick said. "But it's that direction."

Tag followed Sharick's pointing finger. Something was floating in the air, bathed in the shadows. It let out a shriek then flew straight at them like a wraith come to collect its debt.

TWENTY-SEVEN

SHARICK'S RIFLE BARKED BEFORE HE SAID ANOTHER WORD. Blue pulsefire coursed through the library from the other Mechanics, joined swiftly by the kinetic slugs exploding from the marines' rifles. Tag barely had time to shoulder his own weapon. The flying thing tried to dodge the fusillade, but it didn't stand a chance against the pure quantity of rounds pouring in its direction. Energy rounds burned against its flesh, but to Tag's surprise, they didn't pierce it. The rounds must have done something to it, though, because the thing crashed into the ground, bounced, and rolled toward Tag's feet.

"What is that thing?" Tag asked. "Is this from one of the research projects?"

"No," Sharick said. He and the other Mechanics were still tense, their rifles searching the shadows and space around the pods. "We call them Dreg."

"Dreg?" Tag kicked the body of the alien. The Dreg was no

larger than a human head. Its slimy skin glistened under the light from Tag's helmet. The alien's body appeared somewhat like a slug except it had six thin arms protruding from under its mouth. A long tongue lolled out of the creature's mouth between rows of serrated white plates that approximated teeth. From the back of its fat neck sprouted a pair of fibrous, translucent wings, somewhere between those of a housefly and a bat.

"Ugliest goddamn butterfly I ever saw," Lonestar said. She raised her boot above it, ready to stomp it, then stopped. "These things poisonous or anything? Like if we get splashed with that green stuff oozing out of its wounds, is that bad?"

"In the wise words of Lieutenant Sofia Vasquez, it would smell like shit," Coren said, "but no, the Dreg aren't poisonous. They're a menace but not poisonous."

The sounds of buzzing wings echoed throughout the library, but still they couldn't see another Dreg. Instead of venturing into the unknown and risking an ambush, Sharick ordered two of the Mechanics to burn a hole through the hatch with their wrist-mounted plasma torches. Sparks bounced off the alloy as they cut through it, and the light wavered off the torches, casting flickering shadows all around the pods. It made trying to track down any Dreg even more challenging.

"This isn't your first time running into them?" Tag asked.

"Not at all," Coren said.

"What in the hell are they?" Bull asked. "Damn things seem impenetrable to pulsefire. Almost as good as our energy shields."

"Don't be fooled," Coren said. "The skin does burn, but most importantly, the heat is transferred and cooks their insides. They die easy enough."

"Then why do we need to be scared of 'em?" Lonestar asked. "They look like bugs to me."

"Underestimating your enemy can be deadly," Coren said.

"They're a sentient race. Parasitic, as if that's a surprise. Their ships look and work worse than a human's. What they lack in sophistication they make up for in sheer numbers. Where there's one, there's a hundred."

"Shit," Bull said. "So they're like bedbugs."

Lonestar visibly shivered. "Remember when we were headed to the *Montenegro* on the *Condor*? Whole ship got infested with bedbugs, and it took months to zap every last one from between the walls and air vents and…gods, it was terrible."

"That sounds about like a Dreg infestation," Coren said. He never took his eyes off his rifle's sights.

"You think they set this trap? Not the Drone-Mechs?" Tag asked. The Dreg were disgusting, and he would take Coren's advice by not discounting their danger, but he was glad they weren't Drone-Mechs.

"I told you they were decently intelligent," Coren said. "Maybe not individually, but they possess a swarm intelligence."

"Smart or not, they're still disgusting," Lonestar said, "and by the gods, I grew up on a goddamn ranch."

"Don't make me tell you how they breed," Coren said.

The buzzing of the Dreg intensified, and Tag thought he saw movement in the shadows. Every time he swept his light to disperse the darkness, he found nothing.

"What's the progress on the hatch?" Sharick asked.

"Almost there," a Mechanic said over the din of the unseen buzzing wings and the growl of the plasma torches.

"What are these goddamn things waiting for?" Bull asked. "Come on, you ugly pieces of shit, you want something, you come and get it!"

The buzzing became a boiling roar, and a cloud of Dreg rose above the pods. It was impossible to pick a single alien out of the amassing horde, so Tag squeezed his trigger over and over, shooting into the storm of winged abominations. Pulsefire screamed all around him, drowning out the plasma torches, and Dreg bodies flopped against the deck with sickening thuds.

But like a descending tornado, the flying creatures swirled toward Tag and the others. Adrenaline pumped through Tag faster than he could shoot as the aliens blurred together. He braced for the impact of the creatures as they slammed through the barrage of gunfire. Soon enough, the creatures would cover them in a flood of grimy bodies, and Tag feared their battle would be short lived. Maybe it would have been easier to face Drone-Mechs after all.

"Captain!" Sofia's voice cried out in alarm over the comms. "We've got incoming contacts. Dozens of air car–sized ships just started pouring from the wreckage of Nycho."

A two-armed assault. The Dreg were smart indeed. Divide and conquer while the ships were docked and the forces spread thin.

"We're through!" a Mechanic voice yelled over the unholy chorus of rushing, shrieking Dreg.

Bull and Sharick covered the others as they hurtled through the freshly shorn hole in the hatch. Once everyone else had cleared the hatch, Bull came through first, and the Dreg overwhelmed Sharick, covering his suit.

"Go!" Sharick boomed over the comms. His limbs were coated in Dreg as they sank their teeth into his armor. The scrape of their teeth-like protrusions against the alloy was jarring enough. Adding that to their wailing war cries, Tag was forced to reduce the volume on his environmental audio sensors. The Mechanics had already started off in a jog, following Sharick's order with no hesitation.

But Bull didn't follow their lead, and Tag couldn't fathom leaving Sharick behind either. Somewhere in the mass of squirming brown bodies, Sharick was being smothered. Bull reached an arm into them, grabbed Sharick, and yanked against the force of their beating wings as they pulled Sharick back through the hatch toward the rest of the swarm. Bull's boots slid on the deck, and if he didn't let go, it appeared he too would be tugged into the library with the Dreg. Tag ran to the hole in the hatch and forced a hand through the Dreg to get a handhold on Sharick. Several started to gnaw on his suit, and others who hadn't landed on Sharick flew toward Tag and Bull.

Tag's muscles burned with an agonizing fire as he struggled against the creatures. The vessels in his neck bulged with the effort, and his mind was screaming to let go, that he was putting his life in too much danger and Sharick was already gone. Tag and Bull continued fighting against the Dreg, but their combined strength was quickly being overcome. They would have to give in, have to follow Sharick's last command after all.

Someone grabbed Tag from behind.

"You're not going anywhere, Captain," Gorenado said.

Sumo, Lonestar, and Coren soon joined them, with the Mechanics finally relenting to go against their leader's orders and assist in a death-defying match of tug-of-war. Their belabored breathing and curses ringing over Tag's comm, the combined Mechanic and human forces prevailed over the Dreg. Sharick popped through the hole in the hatch. Dreg still covered his suit, their teeth grinding and squealing against the alloy. The Mechanics and marines made short work of the grotesque slug-like beings, peeling the aliens off and firing at them point-blank or smashing them between their boots and the deck. Still the rest of the horde funneled through the hole in the hatch like so many angry hornets.

"Fire!" Bull roared. The marines levied salvo after salvo into the Dreg. The Mechanics defaulted to taking combat orders from

Bull and joined the marines' efforts. Most of the disgusting creatures perished under the fire, impaled by slugs and pulsefire ripping through their ranks. By the power of sheer mass and quantity, they continued surging forward and pushed past the bottleneck.

"We need to move!" Tag yelled over the heat of the battle. He started dragging Sharick away from the maelstrom of Dreg and gunfire. "Come on, Sharick, we got to get you out of here."

Gas vented from holes in the Mechanic's armor. It froze almost as soon as it hit the air and fell over Sharick like a miniature snowfall. As Tag lugged Sharick away and the others provided cover fire, the holes slowly stopped geysering atmosphere as the self-regulating redundancies built into the suit clotted the compromised sections of the armor. With the holes closed off, Sharick used a hand to push himself to his feet. Tag could hear him gasping through the comms, trying to catch his breath after having lost so much breathable air. When he put weight on his right foot, he tumbled until Tag caught him. Black liquid had frozen along a laceration in the armor that stretched from the Mechanic's knee to his ankle. The gap appeared much too large for the self-healing components of the suit to fix on their own. It seemed the blood and coagulating oil had clogged the hole by freezing, and the sheer amount of blood loss made Tag recoil, wondering how Sharick could even be alive.

"Leg's hurt," Sharick said with a wheeze. "Think I'm still bleeding."

Bull paused from shooting and held out an open palm to Sharick. Sharick grasped at his hand feebly, and Bull helped the Mechanic stand.

"Thank you," Sharick said.

"No problem, brother," Bull said. "We've got a thing in the SRE. Never leave a man behind."

Tag marveled at Bull's sudden compassion for the Mechanics.

He didn't have long to dwell on whether this was a permanent alteration in Bull's attitude toward the aliens or just a temporary way of the marine showing his moral warrior superiority over the Mechanics.

"You and you!" Tag yelled, pointing at two of the Mechanics. "Help Sharick. He's injured. Get him back to your ship. We'll cover!"

The Mechanics slipped their arms around Sharick and helped him limp forward, back down the passages and past the bodies they had passed on the way here. As the Dreg wound out of the library in a tendril formation, their shrieks and droning wings roaring louder, Tag hoped he and his crew wouldn't soon join the eternal slumbers of the Mechanics around them. Like a sledge-hammer, the swarm of Dreg fell on them.

TWENTY-EIGHT

AG AND THE MARINES SCRAMBLED AWAY FROM THE swarming Dreg. The little flying aliens hit the deck where Tag had been moments ago, thudding and slapping against it in a cacophony that sounded like a fisherman unloading a catch large enough to keep him set for life. A few of the Dreg struggled to fly again, scrambling over each other and making sickening slurping noises. In a wave of muddy brown, they roiled toward Tag. His boot landed on one of the creatures, and he slipped, falling backward. His shoulder and hip slammed against the deck with a boom that echoed in his suit. Pain rocked through him as Coren stepped to his side.

A few of the grotesque monsters latched onto Coren's suit, but he paid them no heed as he aimed his wrist-mounted weapons at the swirling masses still flooding from the hatch. Blue-and-orange tongues of fire licked from Coren's wrists and swallowed a swathe of Dreg. The monsters shrieked in high-pitched wails that felt like someone was hammering a nail into Tag's eardrums. Their bodies shriveled and crisped, but still they pushed against the flames.

"Little shits are tough as nails," Sumo roared, firing into the slowed-down masses.

"How do you think they survive in this atmosphere?" Coren asked, the glow of the flames flickering over the front of his suit.

They retreated into a narrow tunnel, forcing the Dreg into another funnel. The fire allayed the assault somewhat, but it hadn't turned the tide of their numbers.

"They're suicidal!" Sumo said. She jammed a fresh magazine into her rifle.

"Their individual lives are nothing compared to the life of their colony," Coren said matter-of-factly, as if he weren't roasting a swarm of ugly flying slugs.

A Dreg, still on fire, crawled forward using its insectile legs. Its wings burned, making it look like some kind of rejected demon banished from the three hells. Tag put four rounds into the Dreg, and it wheezed like a balloon deflating. Thick black-and-brown fluid oozed from its slack mouth. Tag kicked its leaking body back into the horde, and the little beasts flew out of its way, still churning into the wall of fire.

"Alpha, Sofia, how are we holding up?" Tag asked.

"I can't do a damn thing until we're no longer docked," Sofia said. "Alpha and I are filling the air around us with PDC fire and chaff. But these ships are so damn small it's hard, even up close, to get these assholes. Like trying to shoot a fly with a pulse rifle."

"What about the energy shields?"

"We cannot engage the energy shields at full strength since we are docked," Alpha said.

"Right, right," Tag said. "Dammit. We're about halfway back to the ships. Hold them off as best you can."

"We will attempt to do our best, Captain," Alpha replied.

The flames spurting from Coren's wrists started to sputter. "I'm almost out!"

Another Mechanic took his place, and fire jutted from his wrists. Tag was relieved to have something to stymy the Dreg assault, but the barrier of fire wouldn't protect them much longer. They appeared to be losing narrow passages to escape through and were approaching a much wider chamber. This chamber was filled with benches and had a river cutting through the middle. It was frozen solid, and all around protruded the husks of what once looked to be plant life. A park. The Mechanics actually had a park aboard the station. For some reason, even in the literal heat of battle, the notion that Mechanics would expend the resources to preserve a park in their station was strange to Tag.

"When we hit the open field," Bull said, "I don't want any of us wasting our time trying to pick these things off. It's too open to establish any worthwhile resistance. Charge straight for the opposite side. We need to make it to that passage. Mechanics, we'll give you a head start. Marines, I want you on me. We're going to hold them in the tunnel as long as we can. Set up a line of fire on the park's perimeter."

But like all good plans, Bull's didn't stand up to reality.

The buzzing of the Dreg echoed from all around, as if they had somehow passed the barricade of fire the Mechanics were laying down. Tag searched the bulkhead and the quarters they passed with open hatches. But he couldn't see them.

"Shit!" Tag yelled. "Check the ducts!"

One of the Mechanics raised his wrist at a vent. Flame started to roll from his wrist-mounted barrels. The puff of fire did nothing to stop the pillar of Dreg bursting from the vent and slamming into the Mechanic's body. Tag fired into several of the Dreg then used his rifle to bat them away and smash them against the bulkhead. The Mechanic was being buried under the aliens. Flames spurted intermittently from his flailing limbs, but he was quickly losing his battle.

"Oh no," Gorenado said. He started charging, building up momentum, and threw himself into the pile of Dreg. He burst from the other side, clutching the Mechanic by one arm.

"Keep going!" Tag yelled. "Run!"

Bull bounded ahead and barreled into the oncoming Dreg. He shoved through their bodies like a man fighting a gale. A Mechanic next to him matched his stride and used his flame-thrower like a shield, breaking the ranks of Dreg before them. The group ran across the park, firing periodically in wild volleys as Dreg swirled down from the ceilings and descended on the squad like ravenous locusts. Carried by inertia and unbridled ferocity, the Dreg flung themselves at the group, and the impacts of their bodies smashed against Tag's armor, over and over. Through his suit, the grinding of their saw-blade–like teeth resonated in his ears. Their weight dragged on him as they plopped onto his suit and stuck to him like leeches. Lactic acid built up in his muscles as he pushed himself across the dead lawn. He willed himself to fight past the pain creeping into his legs, and even with fresh oxygen pumping into his suit and adrenaline flowing through his blood, his lungs burned. A coppery taste filled his mouth.

"We're almost there!" he yelled, his throat raw and scratchy. He said it as much to his crew as to himself. *Get to the next corridor, slow the flow of the Dreg, lose a few of the bastards clinging to my suit. Just put that on repeat for a little longer.*

The grinding and gnawing sounded louder until he heard a pop. Air rushed from a hole in his left leg, and coldness snuck in to replace it. The sounds of gunfire and the yells of the crew were muffled by the din of the Dreg attack. One of the aliens slapped onto his visor, and he reached up with a Dreg-covered arm to rip it off. A hatch appeared before him, just ten meters away. There it was, their escape, their temporary refuge. Two forms sprinted ahead, each covered in squirming Dreg. It was impossible to tell if they were Mechanic or marine. More shapes rushed past him, and flames hissed through the blizzard of Dreg behind him, providing an ephemeral barrier against the rest of the swarm. The Mechanics and marines beside him flung Dreg off each other, throwing themselves against the bulkhead to smash them and stomping those that came loose. Tag gasped as he struggled against the aliens. Each breath seemed weaker than the last. He was losing too much air too fast.

A sharp agony tore into him, and lightning zigzagged up his nerves. He let out a tormented yell. His vision churned in pulsating shades of red, and he reached down to grab the culprit. One of the Dreg had punctured the leg of his suit and was boring into his flesh. Tag peeled the creature off, and blood drizzled from its circular jaws, forming crimson icicles. The cold worked itself into Tag's torn skin, and dizziness muddled his senses, the whole station fading and tilting around him. He fell against a bulkhead, fighting the blackness threatening to overtake his consciousness.

They were almost there. Almost back to the ships and almost off this hellhole. They had to make it. Had to.

And if they did, then finally they'd be—

"Captain!" Alpha's voice pierced the rampant confusion flooding his mind. "We have incoming contacts. More hostiles!"

"Dreg?" Tag managed. The word felt clumsy on his tongue as he staggered forward.

"No, not Dreg. Drone-Mech!"

TWENTY-NINE

Drone-Mech?" Tag repeated. He must have heard her wrong. The agony, the lack of oxygen. It was all adding to the confusion drowning his brain. There was no way the Drone-Mechs had randomly followed them here. No way.

"Yes, Captain," Alpha said. "The Drone-Mechs. They...they found us."

"How did they find us?"

"I have no idea. They transitioned into normal space without warning, and they're headed straight for us. Approximately twenty minutes out."

Something spiked through Tag's body. A final wave of energy. Desperation, maybe. Alpha and Sofia were stuck in the ships, completely immobile, without so much as the full protection of the energy fields. Not to mention Bracken's ship was in an equally vulnerable position.

"We've got to move faster!" Tag said. He dashed ahead of

the group. Every loping step he took sent shuddering waves of agony coursing through his calf. He began to hyperventilate, his mind reeling from the lack of oxygen. Dark stabs of pain pierced his brain, an increasingly violent reminder that he needed to do something about his suit, something about the loss of atmosphere.

But the buzzing behind him, the Dreg still clinging to him, and the Mechanics and the marines around him kept him going. There was no stopping now. They would be devoured. It was either do or die.

His sight seemed to fade in and out, and he blinked, trying to settle his double vision. The corridor to the docking ports finally appeared before them, but the proximity to his refuge didn't quell the burgeoning pain. Tag's limbs started going numb, turning colder and clumsier. Vaguely he felt an arm slide under his shoulder.

Coren.

Together they limped into the *Argo*'s docking port and through the hatch. Tag watched, relieved when Bull, Sumo, Lonestar, and Gorenado came in after him. The hatch shut, and the sounds of the Dreg throwing themselves at the door echoed throughout like a shower of miniature asteroids pinging against the alloy. As the docking bay repressurized, Tag gasped for air. Warm atmosphere filled in around him, and he welcomed its comforting embrace. It didn't allay the pain from the Dreg wounds, but it helped against his frozen flesh.

A few Dreg still gnawed at the marines' armor, and the group finished them off with satisfying stomps. Sumo fell to her knees, chest heaving. A large gash on her upper right arm glistened with red. Gorenado wiped the sweat off his forehead with the back of his hand. Lonestar started to stand next to him, then her eyes rolled up into her head. Tag dove forward and caught her before her head slammed against the deck. Something wet, sticky, and warm dripped over his fingers. *Blood.*

"She's hurt!" Sumo said.

"Bull, Gorenado, grab a hoverstretcher," Tag said in as calm a voice as he could. The blood seeped between his fingers and puddled at his feet, giving off a ferrous odor. It was a wonder she had even made it to the ship alive. When the marines returned with the stretcher, Tag gently laid Lonestar on it.

Something slammed against the *Argo*'s hull, and the reverberations echoed in the *cargo* bay. Tag braced himself as something else hit. A series of six or seven growling bangs sounded from around the ship.

"Alpha, Sofia, we're all aboard," Tag said. "Take us away from this damned station, and tell me what is going on."

"We've got Dreg ships attaching to our hull," Sofia said. "They aren't even bothering to aim for hatches. I don't know what they're doing."

"I don't think they need hatches to get into the ship," Tag said. The pain in his leg lit up as he started ushering the stretcher with Lonestar to the passageway. "Bull, you know how to operate a regen chamber?"

"No, Captain."

Tag wanted desperately to be at the bridge. The threat of the two-pronged attack of Dreg and Drone-Mech caused a rash of anxiety. His heart raced fast enough to propel the *Argo* into hyperspace. He couldn't just let Lonestar die, either.

"Alpha, engage energy shields. Shoot off as many Dreg as you can. Coren's coming to take over weapons shortly."

The Mechanic nodded and dashed off.

"Captain," Alpha said as Tag rushed Lonestar to the med bay. "Some of the Dreg ships have attached themselves in blind spots or areas we cannot risk firing at."

"Son of a..." Tag burst through the hatch into the med bay. He ran to a regen chamber and slammed a fist on its terminal to initiate the system. Constant whining like drills through metal reverberated throughout the ship. If the Dreg ships were anything like the Dreg themselves, they would be forcing themselves into the ship, and there was no telling how many of the little bastards would come pouring in to wreak havoc. "Bull, you hear that? I need you guys to suit up. Mag boots and rocket launchers if you have them, too. We want these bastards off our ship before we go hyper."

"Understood," Bull replied. "Suiting up now."

The regen chamber hummed. Its internal lights glowed blue, and Tag opened the cylindrical chamber's door and then gently pressed Lonestar inside. He waited for the door to seal shut and the diagnosis and healing regimen to begin before taking off toward the bridge. The regen chamber's AI would have to finish the job.

"We're outside," Bull said. "Headed to the first Dreg vessel."

"Good. Stay sharp out there," Tag said.

He hated sending them out there while the Drone-Mechs were bearing down on them. It was goddamned dangerous. Near suicidal. As soon as the Drone-Mechs started firing, they would be as defenseless and vulnerable out there as a courier drone against a Mechanic dreadnought. He couldn't wait until they went into hyperspace. Once there, if they so much as tried to leave the ship, they stood a damn good chance of being destroyed by the gravity distortions, coursing plasma, or simply losing their footing and being lost somewhere in the black eternity of space.

On the bridge, Coren was already firing at the Dreg he could safely shoot with the PDCs. Alpha was spooling up the T-drive and entering a trajectory for their escape to the next Mechanic station. A holoscreen map showed in red the locations of the smaller Dreg ships leeching onto the *Argo*.

"Sofia, take us around the other side of the station," Tag said. "Put it between us and the Drone-Mechs."

"You got it," Sofia said. On the holomap, the *Argo* was swinging around the huge U-shape of Nycho Station's remains.

"Bracken," Tag said, "we're not ready to jump. Got to take care of the Dreg first, then we're going hyper. If you need to jump before us, we'll meet you on the other side."

"Copy," Bracken called back. "We are currently engaged with the Dreg as well. So far they haven't penetrated the hull, but it has been challenging trying to shake them."

A jarring clang exploded against the hull, and the bridge quaked slightly.

"What was that?" Tag asked. The Drone-Mechs were still out of pulsefire range, and their holomap hadn't detected any incoming rounds or warheads.

"Took care of one of the Dreg ships," Bull said. "Bastards don't seem to much like rockets."

"Good," Tag said, willing his heart to settle. "Keep it up."

"We have five more to go," Alpha said.

"Get me a live feed."

Alpha entered a few commands on her terminal, and the holoscreen around Tag split up into live video feeds. He saw the beetle-like shapes of the Dreg ships. Scaled plating covered their exteriors, giving them a distinctly organic, almost animalistic hide. He shuddered, wondering what the interior of those ships looked like, imagining a slimy, claustrophobic anthill look to them.

An alarm screamed from one of the screens, and a warning flashed in red. "Exterior hull breach near port quarters detected."

"Did you get that?" Tag asked Bull over the comms.

"Just popped up on the HUD. We'll make that asshole our next target."

A few minutes later, he saw three humanoid shapes saunter around the portside hull toward one of the Dreg ships on the cam feed. They hid behind an outcropping of alloy, and a marine lifted a tube-shaped weapon on their shoulder. Before the marine could fire, a volley of spikes shot out of the tube-like vents on the Dreg ship. Tag flinched. He didn't dare tear his eyes away from the cam feed, as if doing so would ensure the enemy hit their target. All the shots seemed to have gone wide or else burst against the outcropping the marines had sheltered behind.

"Everybody okay?" Tag asked.

"So far," Bull said. "Didn't know if these assholes would fight back."

"Now that they are," Sumo said as if she was gritting her teeth, "this is going to be a bit more *fun!*"

She added special emphasis to the last word as a rocket accelerated from the tube and smashed against the Dreg hull. The ship cracked open like an egg, and black-and-brown slime oozed out, freezing in space in long, whiplike tendrils. Dreg spilled out with the slime, their gossamer wings flapping wildly until they slowed and froze. Grotesque bodies drifted away from the site of the blast. The Dreg ship didn't detach, but from the sounds of it, it seemed the drilling had at least stopped.

"Four more ships, marines," Tag said. "Alpha, how close are the Drone-Mechs?"

"They're—Captain, they just fired their first round of torpedoes. Estimated time of impact in five minutes."

"Countermeasures ready. Chaff going out," Coren said.

"Very good. Bull, I have faith in Coren, but by the gods, let's finish the cleanup out there and be back in the ship before then, got it?"

"We'll do our best," Bull said, "but trying to use these mag boots to stay attached to the ship means we're clumsily and slowly making our rounds. Not exactly a fast process."

"Understand," Tag said. "All the same, let's try not to get nuked by the Drone-Mechs today."

Three more Dreg ships exploded in clouds of floating slime and slug bodies. The remaining shells of the ships stuck to the *Argo* like the carapaces of cicadas that had molted and long since flown away. One ship was left, and the marines crested the hull toward it. Several of the Drone-Mech warheads shooting toward them had already been knocked out by PDC fire, and Coren was bent forward, leaning into his terminal, trying to engage the rest.

"Three minutes until first impact," Alpha said.

Tag stared at the stream of projectiles glaring across the holo-map. A bead of sweat dripped down his forehead. He desperately wanted to flick it away, but he had already locked his helmet into place again. Another part of the holoscreen brightened as a rocket trailed from one of the marines' launchers and shot toward the final Dreg.

Then Tag saw something that made it feel like someone had thrown a rock at his stomach. A spike flew out of one of the Dreg's protrusions. Even as the rest of the ship went up in a plume of debris and freezing slime, the spike flew straight at the marine that had launched the rocket. Tag wanted to do something, anything, but he didn't have time to cry out a warning. The spike impaled the marine, cutting into the right side of their chest, and the body was flung off the ship, carried by the impact.

Tag watched the holoscreen reporting the marines' blinking vital signs. There was a sudden arrhythmia and drop in blood pressure in Gorenado's reports—he had been the one that had been shot. Tag expected the EKG spikes to flatline as Gorenado cartwheeled into space. They never did.

He was still alive.

And with Bull and Sumo desperately reaching for Gorenado, their fingers outstretched, unable to grab the man as momentum carried him away, the Drone-Mechs closed in. They had already lost G, and now this. Tag gulped, finding it difficult to swallow. He could leave Gorenado behind. The marine would probably die anyway. He could order Sumo and Bull inside. Jump to hyperspace. Avoid the Drone-Mechs and carry on with the mission.

He knew that was what he should do. What Admiral Doran would want him to do.

But he also knew he couldn't do it.

THIRTY

"BRACKEN," TAG SAID. "WE HAVE A MAN ADRIFT. HIT BY the Dreg. We're going in for a recovery maneuver."

"By the time you reach him," she replied, "the first salvo of the Drone-Mech weapons will be hitting."

"I know," Tag said, checking over the holoscreen to see the energy shields still at one hundred percent. "We're going to survive it."

"At least we're going to damn well try," Sofia helpfully clarified.

"Bracken, get to the next objective," Tag said. "We'll meet you there."

There was a pregnant pause before Bracken spoke again. "Normally I would find that course of action prudent. In fact, I agree that is what I should do now. But I will not. I believe it was one of your marines who Sharick owes his life to. And to paraphrase him, we will not leave a human—or a human ship—behind."

The *Stalwart* maneuvered in front of the *Argo* like a whale putting itself between a harpoon and a hapless fish. Energy rounds coursed through the void, glowing across the darkened Nycho Station. They connected with the distant warheads, and space seemed to be filled with brilliant dying stars.

"Focus your efforts on your crew instead of countermeasures," Bracken said. "We can handle them for now."

"Mech tech is better than human tech anyway," Sofia said in a mocking tone.

"Let's hope," Tag said. "Alpha, calculate Gorenado's trajectory. Sofia, take us in gently. Bull, I want you guys to be ready to catch him."

"Yes, sir," Bull said.

"We're on it, Cap," Sumo said. "Let's do this!"

Blazing light continued to glare as Bracken's crew provided temporary cover from the Drone-Mechs. Tag's fingers tensed around his armrest. The *Stalwart* might be able to hold off the first wave of the incoming volley for a few minutes, but they couldn't withstand much more. The closer the Drone-Mechs pressed, the harder it was to fend them off. The *Argo* and the *Stalwart* had barely had time to lick their wounds from their last encounter with the mind-jacked aliens.

"Coming in a little fast," Bull said, his usually stern voice wavering.

"Don't you worry your little bum," Sofia said.

Tag stared at the cam feed. Air recyclers buzzed overhead, and the thump of cannon fire and chaff launching beat like a pulse through the ship. He had to remind himself to breathe as he watched Gorenado's limp form slowly grow larger in the feed. Sumo and Bull's arms stretched for Gorenado. The ship slowed, a metallic groan reverberating through the hull.

"We got him!" Bull roared. Even in happiness he sounded angry.

"Perfect," Sofia said. She let out a long sigh and shook her hands. "Got to remind myself not to hold the controls so tight. Fingers go numb."

Bull and Sumo began loping toward the hatch.

"Bracken, we've got our man. As soon as my crew is situated, we'll be ready to jump."

"That is excellent to hear," Bracken said. "We are prepared to jump at your signal."

Tag undid his restraints. "Sofia, you've got the bridge. I need to get Gorenado into a regen chamber."

"Aye, Skipper," Sofia said.

Tag ran to the hatch where the marines had exited. Through the polyglass, he watched them close the hatch to space behind them. Hissing air poured into the chamber in white clouds until the room had repressurized and the interior hatch opened. Bull and Sumo didn't bother taking their power suits off.

"Bring him with me!" Tag commanded.

Their heavy footsteps crashed behind him as they rushed to the med bay. Tag initiated a second regen chamber beside Lonestar's as the marines unsuited Gorenado as best they could. When the regen chamber was open and ready for Gorenado, Tag turned back to them.

"We can't get the armor off without removing the spike," Bull said. Besides the incident on Eta-Five's surface, Tag had never seen Bull look so frightened. "What do we do?"

"Will he bleed out?" Sumo asked.

All the severed arteries and veins the spike currently blocked would spill blood across the med bay's deck when it was removed. Death was certainly a highly probable risk.

Bracken's voice broke over the comms. "Captain Brewer, we're requesting an update on jump status. More Drone-Mechs have arrived. We cannot withstand their fire much longer.

Nycho is falling apart, and soon we won't have a station to hide behind."

That made Tag's decision for him. "Tear the spike out."

Sumo gave him a worried look.

"Tear it out!"

She and Bull loomed over Gorenado and used the augmented strength of their suits to squeeze the spike. They groaned and strained until the spike came out with a wet plop. Crimson liquid immediately began to pool around Gorenado. Tag knelt and peeled off the rest of the man's armor.

"Help me out with him," Tag said. The marines grabbed Gorenado under his shoulders and deposited him in the regen chamber. They started to head toward the exit hatch, back to their personal quarters for their crash couches. "We don't have time. Grab one here!"

Tag secured himself into one of the patient crash couches. The other two marines settled in near him.

"Bracken, Alpha," Tag said. "Initiate coordinated jump. Now!"

———

After the *Argo* completed its hyperspace transition, Tag unlatched his restraints. The pain in his leg was persistent but manageable. He applied autoheal gels and bandages to his leg and Sumo's arms then went to check on his new patients, whose injuries were significantly worse. The marines followed him like shadows, peering into the regen chambers where Gorenado and Lonestar were kept in stasis.

"Will they be okay?" Sumo asked. She played with the end of her long ponytail. "These things pretty much always work, right?"

Bull grunted. Maybe in agreement. Tag wasn't sure.

"Most of the time, yeah," Tag said. "I would be surprised if

Lonestar isn't out of there by our next stop. Might not be ready for another mission, but she'll be healing well, I'm sure."

"And Gorenado?" Sumo asked.

Tag checked the readouts from the regen chamber's terminal. "He's in critical condition. The AI isn't giving me an estimate yet." That wasn't a good sign. No estimate usually meant the AI wasn't even sure if the regen chamber would be sufficient to heal the patient's trauma. He left that part out. "Don't worry. I'll keep you both updated."

Sumo left, seemingly satisfied, but Bull lingered near the hatch. Tag retrieved a tissue sample of the free Mechanic they had encountered on Nycho from cryostorage.

"Something up, Sergeant?" Tag asked. He took the plastic container and deposited it in the biochemical analysis port. A few buttons glowed on a terminal, and he programmed the machine to run chemical and genetic profiles on the tissues, comparing these samples with that of the Drone-Mech samples he'd analyzed before his return to the *Montenegro*.

"Yeah, Captain," Bull said, sauntering toward Tag. He spoke in a rolling growl that set Tag on edge. "There is something on my mind. I lost one marine already. Might be losing another one."

"They're both—"

Bull cut him off. "I know what it means when the regen chamber doesn't give an estimate. As Lonestar would say, this ain't my first rodeo."

"You've made that clear," Tag said. "But don't lose hope. If the regen chamber can't do it alone, Gorenado's got me and Alpha. Sometimes a human touch can do more than a computer." He realized the irony of the statement as soon as he said it. But he didn't care. "I promise you, I'm not giving up on him."

A vessel in Bull's temple still throbbed.

Tag initiated the protocols on the terminal, and the

biochemical analysis machine began humming. "Something else?"

Bull exhaled, running a thick hand through the red stubble on his head. "You're a smart guy, Captain. I think you know what else I'm worried about."

The analysis machine chirped as it dissected the sample to determine its molecular constituents. Encountering the Dreg had been bad enough, but even worse had been the Drone-Mech ambush. They had expected a trap by the Drone-Mechs, but they had been nowhere on the station itself. Instead, they had popped out of hyperspace without warning right on their position. The *Argo* hadn't detected any outgoing signals or courier drones from the station to send an alarm, so there was no obvious explanation for how the Drone-Mechs knew the *Argo* and *Stalwart* had been there.

"I think I do," Tag said. "During our conference with Bracken, we'll discuss how the Drone-Mechs found us at Nycho."

"Damn right," Bull said. "Fishy thing, too, when the only ones who knew where we were going were Bracken's crew."

Bull's suspicion of the Mechanics was back. So much for his calling Sharick a "brother" in the heat of battle. All the same, maybe Bull's skepticism wasn't so misplaced. What if a Drone-Mech had somehow infiltrated the *Stalwart*? Tag shuddered. How were they supposed to mount any kind of formidable resistance when their forces might already be compromised?

THIRTY-ONE

SUGGESTING ONE OF MY CREW MEMBERS IS INFECTED is preposterous," Bracken said. Her holo shimmered as if radiating the anger from her actual body.

Around the conference table sat the usual crew: Coren, Sofia, Alpha, Bull, and Tag.

"I realize it's highly unlikely," Tag began, "but there must be some explanation for the Drone-Mechs finding us so easily."

"I am slightly offended that you would doubt me," Bracken said. "Especially after we risked our ship to protect yours."

"I understand," Tag said, trying not to raise his voice. Bracken's golden eyes appeared wide, her pupils dilated like a feline focused on prey. "But we've got to take all precautions."

"How do you know one of your people isn't the culprit?" Bracken asked.

Coren held up his hands defensively. "I've been tested."

"I wasn't talking about you," Bracken said, "rather the more technologically inept around there."

Gods be damned. Bracken really didn't like Tag expressing any suspicions regarding her or her crew. He needed to defuse the bomb he'd just set off. "I'm sorry, Bracken. Really, I am. I'm just trying to cover all our bases here, any possible leak. I'm more than happy to entertain your theories. But we've found no evidence that the nanites are capable of integrating into human hosts."

Bracken glared at Tag for a moment. With a huff, she admitted, "That's true. Our researchers report much the same results. That's not to say there aren't other methods of manipulating the human mind."

"I'll give you that," Tag said, "and we'll be on the lookout among the crew. Right now, I don't even have a whole lot of suspects outside my officers. We've got two incapacitated marines, and we've only got one other to spare."

"Being an officer and being a traitor are not mutually exclusive," Bracken shot back.

"I know, I know," Tag said. "We'll do our due diligence here. All I ask is that you run the assays Coren sent you to detect nanites. Trust me, I'll be as happy as you are to see that no one is infected."

"Fine," Bracken said. "But we will not forget that you subjected us to this."

"And neither will we," Bull said under his breath, "when we find the traitor on your ship."

Tag shot him a look he hoped conveyed his disapproval. Luckily, it didn't seem the audio receptors had picked up the whispered comment, or else Bracken had ignored the insubordinate suggestion. Either way, Tag needed to quickly change their focus.

"Any chance this is all a terrible coincidence?" Tag suggested. He doubted it, but he wanted to spur some new discussion away from pointing fingers at each other. "Maybe they were returning to Nycho for something."

"Probability analysis would likely yield an exceedingly low chance that the Drone-Mechs sent a strike group of ships by happenstance to our location," Alpha said.

"She's right," Coren said. "There are too many other Mechanic space stations out there, too many colonies and planets for them to just randomly show up precisely when we're around."

"What about those little Dreg assholes?" Sofia said.

"Dreg are not typically known for forming alliances with other species," Bracken said. "I find it doubtful they'd be working willingly with the Drone-Mechs."

"Keyword is 'willingly,'" Bull said.

"That's right," Bracken said. "It's possible they have been hijacked much like the Drone-Mechs."

Coren's fingers tapped on the table in a steady staccato. "Certainly. But I have my doubts about that. One thing about Drone-Mech behavior: they act differently than free Mechanics. They're more robotic and admittedly stupider. Their tactics aren't as good, and the only reason we've really lost ground to them is sheer numbers."

"This is true," Bracken said. "There is no other way we would be able to withstand their forces if it weren't."

"So I take it the Dreg were acting like their normal parasitic selves?" Tag asked.

"Exactly," Coren said. "Their behavior was no more indicative of being possessed by nanites than yours."

"I suppose that's reassuring," Tag said.

"If I were to hazard a guess, I'd say they were feeding off the Drone-Mech scraps left behind," Bracken said. "Their entire species has a habit of salvaging and pirating, and they've been a constant plague on our exploratory and research teams."

"Hence the well-armed research vessels, right?" Sofia clarified.

"That is correct," Coren said.

"Maybe the Dreg are allies with whoever controls the Drone-Mechs," Tag said. "I think we can't write off the possibility. But I can understand your arguments." He pictured the husks of Dreg ships clinging to the *Argo* like barnacles. "At our next stop, maybe we can spend some time on a spacewalk retrieving some samples. Test them for nanites or something."

"That would be helpful to rule out possibilities," Bracken said. "We will do likewise."

For a moment, Tag's crew and Bracken looked around the table. All seemed preoccupied in their thoughts, stretching for alternative possibilities.

"How likely is it that they're simply following our drive signatures through space?" Tag asked.

"Extremely likely in normal space within certain proximities," Coren said, "but Mechanic technology in hyperspace, much like your tech, isn't capable of those extremes. There was no one here when we arrived at Nycho. I suppose maybe someone or something was set up on the station to act as an alarm of sorts."

"What about the Drone-masters?" Bull said, his voice gruff. His red eyebrows scrunched together like angry, fiery caterpillars. "Couldn't they have technology like that if they developed the nanites?"

"Maybe," Bracken said.

"Is there anything we can do if that's the case?" Sofia asked. "I like fast flying, but it'd be nice not to get shot at every once in a while."

"Without knowing how they're doing it," Coren said, "I have no idea if there is any possibility of avoiding them."

"I suppose we'll see if they really are following us," Tag said. "Next stop is Herandion Station. We've got four days to prepare for another encounter. Maybe we'll get lucky and we'll find some free Mechanics."

"Maybe," Bracken said. "In the meantime, my researchers are formulating models for gravimetric control of the Drone-Mech nanites. They have made some progress in the theory. Much of it builds on the machinery and technology at the Lacklon Institute on Meck'ara."

"Good to hear," Tag said. "Alpha and I will be working on the biological components. I started analyses on our free Mechanic samples earlier today."

When Bracken's holo fizzled out from the meeting, Tag dismissed his crew back to their stations. Alpha followed him in silence to the med bay. His muscles still hurt, sore from overexertion on Nycho, and a headache began pulsing behind his eyes. Maybe it was from exhaustion or the long-term effects of exposure to the cold, loss of blood, and who knew what the hell he might have picked up from the Dreg attack.

"Captain?" Alpha asked. Tag looked at her, and she pointed to his leg. He hadn't done anything other than apply some autoheal and coag gel since they'd made the jump, and spears of distant pain still stabbed up through his nerves as his suit-provided painkillers wore off. "You're bleeding. Do you require medical assistance?"

"Looks that way," he said. Alpha's acknowledgement of his injuries seemed to accelerate the waning of his meds, and he stood, his muscles quivering under his weight.

While Alpha helped him amble to the med bay, he was still unable to separate Alpha's current concern for his well-being from the conversation he'd had days ago with her. He wished he had created her in a time of peace during the mission the *Argo* was supposed to be on. Shaping her conscience while on a search for new knowledge across the galaxy would have been far more favorable than throwing her into a war. She'd had a violent birth and a short, tumultuous life so far. As they wandered into the med bay and she began sifting through supplies, he took comfort in knowing that at least she still had the capacity to heal others.

And, hopefully, herself.

THIRTY-TWO

Alpha walked toward the regen chambers. Each chirped and hummed as if conversing in a language only it knew. She checked the status on Lonestar and Gorenado even though Tag hadn't asked her to. He watched her beady eyes scan the terminals next to them, surveying vital signs and machine reports on their injuries.

"Gorenado may not survive," she said. Tag wanted to believe she said it with sorrow or concern. But wanting to believe it didn't make it so.

"What do you think about that?" Tag asked. He might have been a doctor, but he was no psychologist. Even so, he couldn't help probing into Alpha's psyche. It must have been the scientific part of him, the side that was ever curious, ever wondering. He got off the patient crash couch where he had been sitting while Alpha had applied the autoheal gel and bandages to his legs and the frostbitten portions of his skin. When he reached her, she turned to him.

"I am concerned," she started, "that the regen chamber will not be sufficient. I'm concerned you and I will need to perform our own interventional surgery on him to expedite tissue closure and restore blood flow to his heart."

"And what about Gorenado's life?" Tag asked. "Does it bother you that he might die?"

"It will bother me if we fail to save his life."

It wasn't quite the answer Tag had hoped to hear. But it was a start. He wanted to delve deeper with Alpha, to help her realize again what it was like to feel a wide range of emotions rather than just the extremes she had displayed so far. He had to remind himself it was a temporary distraction. An entire race might be depending on their progress in the lab.

"Shall we?" Tag motioned to the lab equipment and terminals on the other side of the bay.

"I look forward to the challenge."

"If we can't disable the nanites," Tag said, "then hopefully we can at least prevent free Mechanics from succumbing to them."

"Yes, hopefully," Alpha said. She bent over the terminal to retrieve the results of Tag's earlier analysis. A bevy of chemical formulas and molecular structures floated in the air between them. Alpha gestured through the holoscreen until she came upon the neural tissue samples. "This is promising."

"Yes." Tag peered closer at the chemical components. "No match for nanites anywhere within the Mechanic's brain. At least we know she's a free Mechanic. That might just mean she never came into contact with them, so I don't know how useful she'll be. We need to know if she was actually exposed to them."

"True." Alpha selected the results of the blood sample next. "And it looks like a trace amount of nanites were in fact found in her blood."

"Really? Well, that's certainly interesting. She was infected, but she wasn't affected."

"It would seem that way. Reports show a rather high concentration of nanites within her tissues, too, consistent with levels of nanites in our Drone-Mech samples."

For comparison's sake, Tag scrolled through the data on the Drone-Mechs and selected a scan of the Drone-Mech's blood. "Computer, tag the nanites in this sample."

The view magnified past the collapsed discoid shapes Tag approximated to be red blood cells and the occasional spherical cells that composed the Mechanic's immune system. Protein structures and other small, granular components loomed into existence until the magnification had reached the level of displaying nanites. Silver lines appeared around the edges of the nanites as the computer highlighted them, giving them a metallic gleam on the holoscreen.

"Fascinating," Tag said. "Look at how the nanites are already assembling in the Drone-Mech's blood."

Alpha nodded as she studied the images. The nanites seemed to be coalescing into spiracle structures, looking like tiny starfish swimming through the bloodstream.

"These must serve as the seed for the self-assembly process," Alpha said. "And once they reach the neural tissue, they link together into the rest of the antenna."

"That's my guess," Tag said. "Computer, show us nanites in the free Mechanic's blood."

Tag expected to see a similar image on the holoscreen as the Drone-Mech's as the display's magnification zoomed past the blood cells and into the realm of the nanoscopic. But there they were greeted with a very different sight.

"Didn't you say there was a comparable concentration of nanites in the free Mechanic's blood as the Drone-Mech's?" Tag asked Alpha. "There are none of those coalescing seeds."

"That's correct." Alpha leaned toward the image as if it would suddenly become clearer to her.

"Then where are the nanites? Computer, identify nanites."

The computer highlighted the location of the nanites. Unlike the Drone-Mech's, there weren't any in starfish-like formations. Instead, the silver nanites appeared to be individually trapped. Cubic molecular protein-based structures surrounded each.

"Those structures," Alpha said, "appear to be subcellular in nature."

"I think you're right," Tag said. "Maybe they're like human platelets. Something to do with the Mechanic immune system. I'm going to send this data to Bracken and see if she can have some medical professional there confirm our findings."

"And then if we are on the right track," Alpha said, "we can use what we learn about the Mechanic immune system to develop a vaccine."

"Right. There must be something different about this Mechanic's acquired immune system—or maybe their DNA—that we can track down into the immune system." Tag sighed. "But whatever it is, I've spent my life studying humans. I'm not sure how much of my knowledge or experience is really going to translate here. *Hope*fully the Mechanics have an answer for this one."

———

Even after a couple days into hyperspace travel, Lonestar and Gorenado were still in the regen chambers. Tag was studying their status, switching the cartridges that fed the regen chambers' nutrients and engineered stem cells, when the hatch to the bay opened behind him, and before he even looked, he recognized Bull's heavy footsteps and self-assured gait rattling toward him.

"Sergeant," Tag said in a perfunctory greeting as he perused the regen chambers. Gorenado's terminal still reported that there was no estimate for when he would be healed enough to leave the chamber. Lonestar's indicated her body was fully stabilized, with complete replacement of lacerated tissues. She would need a modicum of physical rehabilitation to get the new tissue feeling less like rubber and more like living flesh, but she would be fine.

"How long do we give Gorenado?" Bull asked.

Tag let out a long breath as he snapped a cartridge into place on Gorenado's chamber. "We don't have much time until we reach the next station. I'd rather focus on the mission at hand than add another complicated variable right before we enter normal space."

"Your complicated variable happens to be my man."

"Trust me, Sergeant, I understand. Remember my training is all about saving lives. Taking your man out too early could put Alpha and me in a situation where we have to choose between giving him the proper treatment or being at the bridge if the Drone-Mechs—or for that matter something else like the Dreg—shows up. Not a choice I want to make."

Bull inhaled with what sounded like a slight snarl, and he placed a hand on the regen chamber holding Gorenado. "Don't let him die."

The marine didn't give Tag time to respond and turned to leave. The hatch opened again as Alpha entered with an air of nonchalance. Bull shouldered past her, and she watched him, a glimmer of surprise in her black eyes.

"Captain, he appears to be distressed," Alpha said. "Does he need medical attention?"

"He might need attention of some sort," Tag said, replacing the second cartridge on Gorenado's chamber. "But I don't think there's anything you or I can do to make him less distressed right now."

"That is curious."

With the threat of running into more Drone-Mechs or Dreg and the challenge of finding a vaccine for the Mechanics hanging over him, Tag wasn't ready to spend several hours explaining human psychology to Alpha. Thankfully, she dropped the subject and turned her attention to one of the lab's terminals.

"We received a report from Bracken's medical team," Alpha said. "Would you like me to go over it?"

"Please." Tag undid the almost-empty cartridge of engineered cells from Lonestar's chamber. "You know, this used to be your job. Back before you had a brain."

"Should I do that instead of go over the report?"

"No, a little mindless physical labor is good every once in a while."

"I am not sure I follow your logic."

"It's not always about logic." Tag pursed his lips as he tried to pull out the nutrient cartridge. It seemed to be stuck. A slight buildup of salts and grimy liquid sealed the cartridge to its port.

"I will log this conversation for analysis later. I sense that I should prioritize our discussion regarding Bracken's report."

"Your senses aren't leading you wrong."

"I am pleased to know I am more capable of picking up on the subtleties of human communication."

"Great." Tag clenched his jaw as he peeled the cartridge back. It finally came off with a plastic pop. He wasn't sure he was being too subtle, but he wasn't about to distract Alpha anymore by telling her that. "Now how about that report?"

"Ah, yes, Captain." Alpha's fingers tapped against the terminal, ringing out with a metallic clicking. "It reports that our initial suspicions were correct. The cubic structures we witnessed surrounding the nanites are indeed part of the Mechanic acquired immune system."

"Very interesting." Tag faced Alpha, holding the fresh nutrient cartridge in his hand. "That's an extremely important distinction. If it's part of the acquired immune system, then it means the

Mechanics somehow developed resistance to the nanites. There might not be any innate or genetic difference that gave these Mechanics their ability to stall the nanites."

"From Bracken's team's description of the cubic molecular structures and my *acquired* knowledge—do you see what I did there, Captain? That's humor." She allowed herself a forced and rather uncanny smile.

"Yeah, sure. Funny. Go on." This was a different Alpha than the one who had talked with him about the power of killing your enemy.

"From my knowledge of the human immune system and this new report, I believe the cubic molecules to be akin to a human's antibodies. They are attracted to specific antigens, sequester those antigens, and signal the Mechanic body to rid itself of the offending antigen. In this case, the antigen would be the nanites."

"Good deductions," Tag said. "But there's one thing we've got to consider. Antibodies are around in a person's body because a person has already had to overcome a particular disease. So, for instance, I had chicken pox when I was a kid. I've now got the antibody for chicken pox."

"I think I see where you are going with this."

Tag plugged the fresh cartridge into Lonestar's chamber. "Do you?"

"Yes, the presence of this Mechanic's cubic antibodies would indicate that those Mechanics with the ability to resist the nanites would have at some point encountered the nanites before."

"And that begins to pose a problem," Tag said as he leaned against Lonestar's chamber. "How did these Mechanics come across these nanites before? And who introduced them?"

Alpha's black eyes seemed to be staring at a point Tag couldn't see. He waited for her to come up with an answer to his questions. From the way she seemed to be frozen in thought, he worried he might have somehow short-circuited her neural-computer interfaces.

But then a smile cracked across her face. "Those are trick questions, aren't they, Captain?"

Tag grinned. "And why do you say that?"

"You mentioned to me once before your greatest weakness is your tunnel vision," she said, parroting the words his dad had once told him. "You sometimes forget all the available paths and avenues you have to approach a problem." A cold spring seemed to well up in Tag as he recalled his father's advice to take a step back from problems and think outside the options he had limited himself to. It sounded strange coming from her. "And I think you told me that so I wouldn't be limited by shortsightedness."

"Where are you going with all this?"

"Edward Jenner."

"What about him?" Tag asked.

"He was a scientist and physician—not too unlike yourself—in the eighteenth and nineteenth centuries. And he discovered the first vaccine for smallpox."

"Nice history lesson. You've paid attention to some of the encyclopedias on store here." Tag checked Lonestar's terminal to ensure the new cartridges were working before he joined Alpha at the laboratory terminal.

She continued. "He discovered that people who experienced cowpox, even though it is a different disease, became immune to smallpox. Exposure to cowpox enabled the creation of antibodies that actively responded to smallpox. Because of this, cowpox could be used as a vaccine."

"You got it." Tag started walking toward the hatch and nodded for Alpha to follow him. "My hope is that we can find out what gave those Mechanics their acquired immunity to nanites in the first place. It's very likely that it isn't, in fact, the same nanites that control them. And if we can identify this analogue, we don't have to invent a vaccine."

"Because it already exists," Alpha said.

"Exactly. We just have to find it."

THIRTY-THREE

TAG AND ALPHA BRIEFED THE OTHER MEMBERS OF THE CREW on their findings. After sending a report to Bracken, they made final preparations for entering normal space, and Bracken provided them a holo of their next target, Herandion Station. This one had a similar halo-like structure reminiscent of Nycho, though it was almost half the size. It had served as a trading port with other species in the far reaches of Mechanic space. Tag wondered if its differing role had mattered at all to the Drone-Mechs or those that had controlled them. He somehow doubted it.

If the Drone-Mechs had been to the station, it was probably a wreck like Nycho. But Bracken had been the most curious about Herandion because of its relationship with other races. She promised the Mechanics had connections with sentient, spacefaring races that were more amenable to trade and communication than the Dreg. And maybe, if they were lucky, they would come across some of them. There stood a small chance, however miniscule, that a species looking to establish economic ties to the Mechanics and unaware of their current nanite blight might be heading into the area to do business at the station. Or maybe if the Drone-Mechs had already been through and left the place vacant, one of those species had set up shop to replace the gap in the current interstellar economy.

Tag reminded himself not to be nearly so optimistic. Jumping from station to station seemed like a good way to depress their moods further. If they knew the locations of the stations, surely the Drone-Mechs did too. He wished there was some way they could better contact research and military vessels that had escaped like the *Stalwart* had. Sofia suggested sending out several courier drones in varying trajectories, but trying to send out courier drones randomly throughout space was like throwing a message in a bottle into one of Earth's oceans and hoping it somehow made it to Luna.

The med bay hatch hissed open, and Tag entered with Alpha close behind.

He strode to Lonestar's regen chamber and exhaled slowly. "Time to wake her up. You ready?"

"I have emergency sedation supplies prepared in case she has a negative reaction."

"Here we go."

Tag tapped on the terminal, each press of the touchscreen sounding a light blip. A single command blatted across the screen, asking him to engage the awakening process. He confirmed his choice, and the blue fluid in the regen chamber drained. The chamber's door glided open, and Lonestar's body started to slump forward. Tag undid the clasps holding her in and gently lowered her onto a nearby patient crash couch.

Her eyelids flickered, bulging with the movement behind them as if she was still asleep and caught in some nightmare. The muscles in her arms tensed and relaxed in unpredictable spasms, her fingers clenching tightly, digging into her palms.

"Is this normal?" Alpha asked, leaning over Lonestar.

"Everyone's reawakening is different, but it's normally not this intense."

Tag drew a blanket over Lonestar. Her thrashing threatened to fling it off. For a heartbeat, he wondered if whatever violent dream she was in would end. Another heartbeat passed, and her body went still. Sweat beaded down her forehead, and a tear budded from the corner of one eye. Pallor sucked the vibrancy from her expression, and her eyes pinched hard together, causing wrinkles to spring from the corners of her closed lids. She still seemed to be in pain, though to Tag it looked more emotional than physical now.

"Lonestar?" he tried, softly. "You're all right. You just came out of regen. Can you understand me?"

Her eyes shot open, and she clutched the sheet to her chest, squeezing herself against the slightly inclined crash couch. For a woman built with genetic enhancements and a disciplined weightlifting regimen, she looked strangely tiny and afraid.

"What…how did you…" Her breathing settled, but she didn't let go of the sheet. "You aren't…you aren't…"

Tag had never had a patient stuck in such a confused state for so long. Then again, with the *Argo*'s initially peaceful mission up until he became captain, patients needing a regen chamber were pretty damn limited.

"I'm not what?" Tag raised an eyebrow. "Lonestar, do you know where you are?"

"The *Argo.*"

"And do you know who I am?"

Her nostrils flared almost imperceptibly, but Tag noticed it. He'd been looking for any symptoms of something wrong with her and continued to study her every movement. "Tag Brewer. Commander Tag Brewer, former chief medical officer, and now… now captain of the *Argo*."

"That's right," Tag said. "We're in hyperspace. We just had an encounter—"

"With the Dreg." Lonestar relaxed her hold on the sheet, letting it drape lightly over her body again. The light-brown hue returned to her face once more, washing away the ghostly pale. "I was attacked. I remember making it back here, but then it all went black."

"Your memory recall is accurate," Alpha chimed in cheerfully.

"Are we returning to normal space soon?" She swung a leg over the side of the crash couch as if she was ready to get suited up.

"We will be," Tag said, "but you're not up for it yet."

"The three hells I'm not!" Lonestar said. "Get knocked off the horse, you get back on."

Tag placed his hand on her shoulder, trying to gently coax her back down. She shoved him off, let the sheet fall, and stood. When she straightened, her face screwed up into an agonized wince, and she flopped back into the bed.

"Good gods," she said, arching her back. "My spine."

"Yeah," Tag said. "Alpha, let's get some pain meds for her." He tried to put on his best bedside manner but found forcing a calm expression slightly awkward. Even though it hadn't been much longer than a couple months since he'd had a patient, so much had happened between then and now that it might as well have been a decade. "Lonestar, I know you hate to hear it, but the nerves and muscles under that fresh skin are going to need some work. You aren't going to be one hundred percent immediately. Your new cells and tissues need a few days out of the chamber before you can hit the weights again."

Alpha placed a patch on Lonestar's arm and then pressed it

to ensure the insertion of the hundreds of microneedles within the patch would inject her with pain relievers. All the tightness in Lonestar's expression faded.

"How long's that going to take?" Lonestar asked. "I don't want to sit this stuff out."

"If you do what I prescribe, you'll miss one station mission, maybe two, tops."

"If everything heals the way it's supposed to."

"If everything heals the way it's supposed to," Tag confirmed. He selected an exercise regimen for her on his wrist terminal then flicked his finger to transfer it to hers. "Take this to the fitness facilities when you feel up to it. No earlier than two days from now, got it?"

She nodded.

"I'm serious."

"All right, all right." She held up her hands in a placating gesture.

"The AI in the fitness facility comps will keep an eye on you. Listen to it. That's a damn order."

"Captain, we have our final briefing with Bracken in fifteen minutes," Alpha said.

Tag faced Lonestar again. "Take it easy. Let Alpha or me know if you need something. You're going to feel good enough to stand up before the end of the day, but don't. Give yourself a little more time. Trust me."

Lonestar gave him a skeptical furrow. "I'll try."

"Good," Tag said. He started to follow Alpha out the hatch. As he exited into the corridor, Lonestar called after him.

"Doc…er, Captain?"

Tag turned. "Yes?"

Lonestar was staring at Gorenado's chamber as if she had finally noticed it. "What about him?"

Tag let a breath go before speaking again. "It's a bit unclear, but we're doing what we can."

Alpha's footsteps clanged out behind him as she followed him up the ladders to the captain's conference room. He steeled himself mentally for his talk with Bracken. Once again, they planned to drop into normal space with uncertain prospects for finding free Mechanics. And once again, Tag wondered if they would find the Drone-Mechs there first—or if the hijacked Mechanics would come to ambush them as they had at Nycho. If they did, Tag wondered if he would even get a chance to save Gorenado.

Or the rest of the crew, for that matter.

Tag took his seat next to Sofia and Coren. Bracken's holo fizzled into existence next to Alpha, and Bull seemed to be glaring at the ghost of someone or something that hadn't yet appeared in the room.

"So," Bracken began, "are we prepared for our next outing?"

Tag tried to swallow, but his throat was dry, scratchy. They had barely squeaked out of the last mess. With two marines out for the next mission and the Mechanics similarly disadvantaged, he wondered if there was any way he could realistically and unreservedly answer Bracken in the affirmative.

But now wasn't the time for doubt or nihilistic thoughts. Not with so much at stake.

Tag clenched his jaw. "Absolutely."

THIRTY-FOUR

ERANDION STATION FLOATED BEFORE THEM LIKE A mechanical jellyfish, the lines of hull plates and debris spreading from the central ring like tentacles. The station rotated on its central axis with a wounded tilt, but lights still shone and glimmered sporadically from portholes across the massive piece of engineering. Several Mechanic ships drifted nearby, detectable by the *Argo*'s lidar and radar. Magnified images revealed that each seemed to have been gutted like an animal after a successful hunt. The scene was eerily similar to Nycho.

"No sign of those slug assholes ready to jump my ship, are there?" Sofia asked. "I'm not interested in gunking up the exterior any more than it already is."

"I've recalibrated our sensors to assess the presence of Dreg ships," Alpha said. "There are none I can detect in the vicinity."

"But that still won't account for the ones that hide their ships in the husk of the station or other ships," Coren added. His fingers hovered over the weapons terminals.

"Keep the T-drive spooled, and keep us a safe distance from the station," Tag said. "Any other signals, distress or otherwise?"

"Nothing, Captain," Alpha said.

Tag initiated a connection to the *Stalwart*. Bracken's face appeared on his holoscreen. "We're reporting no activity on Herandion. Doesn't look much different than Nycho."

"Attempts to hail the station or any vessels nearby have gone unanswered," Bracken said. "All Mechanic frequencies have been met with the same result."

Tag sighed. He hadn't really expected to find any free Mechanics, but disappointment still filled him as if to dismantle the only shreds of optimism he had left. "You know the station better than me. Should we proceed with our intelligence-gathering objective?"

"It would be prudent," Bracken said. "Even if there are no living free Mechanics aboard, I would like to tap into the computer system. Most systems appear to be shut off, but we might be able to pull data from them if we can gain physical access."

"What's the game plan? Go to the administration center and see what we can grab?"

"Yes, that would be the so-called game plan, though calling it a game trivializes the matter."

"Sorry," Tag said, waving a hand defensively. "Just an expression."

Bracken's face remained impassive. "We'll prioritize our data, scouring for any intel on other species' ships that may have passed through the sector recently on trade or other endeavors. Resuming contact with them may prove worthwhile. Maybe they will have information on the Drone-masters or at least what happened here."

"It might also give us a sense of how the nanites are spreading," Tag said. He hated to admit it as he did. "Or if other species are being similarly affected."

"Yes," Bracken said. "I also want to know if they've encountered any free Mechanics."

"That, too." Tag studied the holoscreen image of Herandion. "Seems like the docking ports are mostly shot to hell."

"Maybe it's best we board via spacewalk anyway," Bracken said.

Tag nodded, understanding the implication. Docking their ships had left them defenseless against the Dreg before. They wouldn't make that mistake again, especially when a station with more holes and craters bored into it than Luna made this place a perfect hiding spot for a score of small Dreg ships, regardless of what their sensors said.

A quick tap on the terminal, and Tag called up a line to the armory, where Bull and Sumo were waiting. Tag imagined himself down there with Coren. The boarding party had already been cut in half since Eta-Five. A heavy weight crept into the back of his throat. It took him a moment to comprehend the strange sensation before he decided it was something akin to dread. "Bull, prepare for a spacewalk. We're not risking docking. Going to go EVA all the way."

"You got it, Captain," Bull said. He turned from the terminal connection before it even ended, already donning the components of his power armor.

Tag undid his restraints as Herandion loomed larger in the viewscreen. He stood at the hatch to the bridge, taking in the devastated structure, wondering how many tens of thousands of Mechanics had once called it home. How many had passed through here. How many other species Tag could only vaguely imagine docked at those ports, walked through those corridors, and went on their way, charting the unknown.

And now how many of them were dead—or puppets of the nanites?

Those thoughts weighed on his mind as he made for the hatch. "Coren, let's do this. Sofia, you've got the bridge."

"Aye, Skipper," Sofia replied.

Coren strode toward Tag in that characteristic fluid gait Mechanics had with their hyperflexible limbs. As they exited together, Alpha abruptly stood from her station.

"Captain," she said, "if I may make a suggestion, I believe that your current boarding team's chance of surviving an assault like last time are drastically reduced given your smaller number. May I suit up to join the incursion?"

For a second, Tag wondered if her concern was truly genuine or if she simply longed to hold a rifle in her own hands against an enemy. He forced aside the image of her grinning manically as she peppered slugs into the Dreg or a Drone-Mech. *She's always been about protecting you*, Tag reminded himself. He imagined her again, this time when she had thrown herself in harm's way, grappling with an exo when they were defending the *Montenegro*. Back when she had saved Tag at the last moment aboard the Drone-Mech's dreadnought.

"Sorry, Alpha," Tag said. "Our probability of survival is even lower if we don't have you and Sofia here to take care of the ship. Besides, Bracken's promised to double the number of Mechanics for this one."

Alpha stared at him expectantly, as if she wasn't satisfied. He nodded a good-bye before leaving. As he did, he felt the burn of her eyes on the back of his neck. He hoped she was wrong. That they wouldn't run into any surprises here. That their probability of survival wasn't diminished.

But hope had led him astray far too many times. When he reached the armory and squeezed into his EVA suit, beside his normal armament of a Gauss rifle and a pulse pistol, he secured a rocket launcher to his back. If hope didn't pan out, he had seen what the rocket launchers could do.

Bull raised a single eyebrow in a look of skepticism. "Captain?"

"I'd advise that all of you grab one, too."

Tag led Coren, Sumo, and Bull to the docking port. They waited outside the first airlock as the *Argo* slipped near the Herandion's docking port. Metallic groans and pops sounded over the deck as the altitude impellers activated, slowing the ship. The images on the docking port's viewscreen displayed the ruined airlocks that ships had once attached to. One particularly cavernous hole stood out. It appeared large enough to fit a Dreg ship or two, and he shuddered. The rocket launcher jostled on his back, gently reminding him that at least they were better prepared this time. But it wasn't just the Dreg that worried him. This might be another Drone-Mech trap. Or there might be some other gods-forsaken species lurking about this corpse of a Mechanic space station.

"We're as close as I'm going to get," Sofia said.

"Good," Tag said. He hit the airlock, and the first hatch opened, letting the group in. "Sofia, when we're in hyperspace again, remind me that I want a full briefing on every known species the Mechanics have data on. Everything you learned about from your time on Eta-Five with the Mechanics."

"Am I not a good enough source?" Coren said, hidden behind his orange visor as the hatch closed. The hiss and huff of air sounded as the airlock was depressurized.

"I just want, you know, a human perspective on what Sofia's learned," Tag said. "Thought it might be helpful, but, yeah, you'd be a great source, too."

"What he's saying is you Mechanics think you're so damn superior to everyone else that you might fail to mention just how dangerous these other aliens are to humans," Sofia said over the comms.

Coren let out a curt laugh. "Oh, I'm well aware of human weaknesses, both technological and otherwise."

Bull stared him down. "You want to back that up in the gym?"

"I wouldn't," Tag said to him, the memories of his own sparring match with Coren still fresh enough to cause the bruises and welts to sting. "Best to save your energy for whatever's waiting for us on that station."

Tag felt the ship lose hold on him as the gravity generators ceased their function within the airlock. He used handholds to pull himself toward a terminal near the exterior hatch. With a few taps, he lined up an aiming reticule with Herandion's docking bay then fired a tether into it. He saw the anchor point clunk into the station, kicking up a cloud of debris. But under vacuum, he only imagined a sound as it dug into the metal and refuse.

"Follow the line down," Tag said. "Try not to use your thrusters. I want to save all our juice just in case."

"Just in case we run into some slimy bastard down there and need to shoot back up here?" Sumo asked.

"More or less."

The exterior hatch to the docking bay inched open. Bull took the lead and clipped himself to the tether first. He pushed off from the edge of the docking port and began drifting toward the station, the tether guiding him. With one hand, he corrected his path using the tether, and with his other, he held his rifle, never letting it stray from the blackness of Herandion. Coren went next, followed by Tag. Sumo took the rear.

"Still no signs of life?" Tag asked. From his periphery, he could see the *Stalwart* in parallel with the *Argo*. Mechanics exited the ship and drifted toward the nearest docking bay. Their black armor gleamed crimson under the malicious red glow of the *Stalwart*'s battle lights. They looked like demonic apparitions descending on unwary prey, and Tag felt a glimmer of appreciation knowing they were on his side.

"Nothing, Captain," Alpha said.

"Not on the station or anywhere nearby," Sofia clarified.

"Good," Tag said. The first few Mechanics made it into the station and disappeared in the shadows. "Sharick, you got eyes in there?"

The Mechanic boarding party leader called back. "So far, everything's quiet."

Tag slid into the station, unclipped himself, and crouched beside Bull, almost wishing it weren't so quiet and dark. If they had an enemy lying in wait, unseen, and ready to rip out their throats, it would be a hell of a lot nicer to see their face and kill it without all the suspense.

Sharick's group of Mechanics joined up with Tag's forces. The Mechanics had doubled their boarding party this time, and Sharick paused when they stood next to Tag's group. The *Argo*'s measly four-member squad seemed even more anemic when Tag saw the two dozen Mechanics flowing through the corridor.

"Straight to the administration core," Sharick said. It sounded halfway between a question and a statement.

"Straight to the administration core," Tag agreed.

He let his squad be enveloped by the Mechanics as they pulled themselves through the station at zero-g. At least at Nycho, the grav generators and centripetal force had been enough to make their jobs slightly easier. Herandion was holding nothing back in creating obstacle after obstacle for them. The passages were no different. A hatch lay closed, immobile by force or electric means. One of the Mechanics activated his wrist-mounted weapons, and a plasma cutter glared in the dark passage like a miniature sun. It tore into the alloy hatch with the ease of a pulse round burning through flesh. Mechanics and marines bristled with weapons as they waited for him to clear the route for them. Tag could practically taste the tension in the air, dripping with a mixture of anxiety and excitement, fingers hovering near trigger guards, eyes glued on what lay ahead.

But as they worked to clear their passage, the enemy didn't come from ahead after all.

THIRTY-FIVE

Sofia and Bracken's voices filled the comms at once in a garbled rush of words. The only thing Tag could plainly hear through the mess was the panic evident in even Bracken's voice. He had to chin down the volume on the open channel.

"Say again, Sofia," Tag said.

"Drone-Mechs just jumped in," she said. "We've got four contacts. Not as many as before, but they're definitely Drone-Mechs."

"You're sure they're not free Mechanics?" Tag asked.

"Bracken's sure, and I'm going to take her word on this one."

Tag switched to Bracken's channel. She was already giving orders to her troops to return to the ship. "Bracken, what happened?"

"The usual Drone-Mech inquiry into where our loyalties lie, Brewer," she replied. "They just opened fire. Fourteen minutes until the first salvo hits."

"Only four ships, though," Tag said, reaching for a loose air duct. He used it to propel himself back down the corridor to-ward the docking bay. The Mechanics and his crew were shooting up around him like fish swimming for their spawning pools. He thought to use his thrusters, but if everyone tried to do that in these confined spaces, it might turn their escape into one deadly game of pachinko. "At Nycho, there were at least three times that many."

"Yes," Bracken said. "And from our impeller drive analysis, these ships are different from the others."

Tag curled his arm in to avoid a Mechanic shooting for a nearby tangle of wires. He bit back the knot of worry threatening to close his throat. They still had more than ten minutes. This would be no problem to escape. The exit appeared at the end of the passage with the threadlike tether silhouetted against the be-jeweled void of space, slightly illuminated by the battle lights from the *Argo*. Sumo led the group to the ship, following the tether up first. Tag ushered Coren up second. Then he clipped himself to the tether and pushed off from the station. The rocket launcher slapped against his back as he crossed the abyss.

Eight minutes to go. A stream of brilliant blue fire traced from the *Stalwart*, followed by a salvo of small rockets. They disap-peared into the black, targeting the warheads. He squinted, trying to make out which of the pinpricks of lights was the incoming ordnance. Then he felt something loom over him like the shadow of a giant blotting out the sun. There were no shockwaves in space, no sounds traveling through the vacuum. But all the same, some-thing tingled at the back of his neck. He twisted back toward the space station, still floating toward the *Argo*. Bull must have gotten a similar feeling, because he faced the same direction Tag did.

Something shot up from one of the holes in the station. It was a spaceship. No doubt about that. But its shape was that of a swan—an oversized swan a quarter of the size of the *Argo*. Some kind of sapphire-colored alloy made up its hull, and the entire thing seemed fluidlike. Two tubular protrusions aimed at Tag, then Bull, before finally focusing on Coren.

"Oh shit!" Tag said. "Sofia, Bracken, what is that thing?"

Coren appeared frozen as the tubes glowed brighter, bathing him in orange light. "I don't know…but I can't…I can't move!"

"I'm trying to hail it!" Sofia said. "Something's wrong with our computers. We've got interference."

"I am unable to establish a connection," Bracken said. "The vessel is of unknown origin. It matches nothing in our databases…and it's doing something to our computers, too."

Dread filled Tag like a fast-acting poison. He had nightmares of when the Drone-Mechs had implanted a virus within the *Argo*'s comp systems. The virus had disabled all the ship's AI systems and had stranded him on Eta-Five. With the Drone-Mechs bearing down on them now, they couldn't afford the loss of their AI systems.

"Help," Coren managed. "I feel like…I'm…I'm boiling from the inside."

The ship started to float closer to Coren. The sapphire alloy swirled like a whirlpool, and a hole opened in the side of it. Coren's body began drifting toward the open maw of the vessel. His clip pulled on the tether between the *Argo* and Herandion, and the tether went taut. Sumo had already made it up to the hatch, and she reached desperately for the line as if she could fight against the sapphire ship's pull. Then the line snapped. Tag and Bull spilled into space, tumbling end over end. Tag tried to straighten himself out, operating the thrusters on his suit. He managed to stabilize himself enough to see Coren shaking as if every muscle in his body was fighting the pull of the sapphire ship. The Mechanic's thrusters streaked on, plumes trailing behind them uselessly. They did nothing to interrupt the invisible grip the ship had on him.

"No!" Tag yelled. The ship was too close to the *Argo*, hidden under its belly in a blind spot, and the *Stalwart* was still loading Mechanics as the seconds ticked down until Drone-Mech contact. He couldn't let Coren get swallowed up by that ship. They'd already lost G. Gorenado's life might be forfeit. No way was he losing another crew member.

"Captain!" Bull shouted over the comms. His thrusters glowed behind him as he steadied himself and caught up to Tag. His gloved fingers grasped Tag's shoulder. "We've got to get back to the ship."

"Not without Coren!" Tag pushed Bull's hand away.

He started to accelerate toward Coren but then abruptly stopped. There would be no way to physically yank Coren away from whatever traction was sucking him into that ship. He had to try something else. The rocket launcher unclipped from his back with ease, and he shouldered the weapon, held in place by intermittent bursts from his thrusters. Firing a gun with any amount of kick would send him careening backward, and using a weapon in zero-g went against all his instincts. But the rocket launcher used self-propelled rounds suitable for this environment. All that was left was to lock onto his target. A targeting reticule popped up on his heads-up display, and he aimed at the open mouth of the sapphire ship.

Then he pressed the firing mechanism.

A self-propelled rocket exploded from the launcher, making a straight line for the azure ship. The vessel didn't even seem to notice as the rocket slipped into the opening. A moment later, Coren stopped then shot backward from the ship, his thrusters firing and pushing him away. The hatch swirled shut like waves crashing together, and the sapphire hull of the spacecraft appeared smooth and fluid once more.

Bull and Tag spiraled toward the *Argo*, joining Coren. As Tag reached to grab a handhold on the airlock, he waited for the sapphire ship to explode into a spreading cloud of jutting plasma and melted alloy.

But it never did. Instead, the brilliant blue alloy shifted to orange, as if a fire was spreading just under the surface from where the rocket had hit. The orange shifted into a dazzling sunset of colors until the entire ship went black. Abruptly, the vessel turned and raced into space, speeding away from the *Argo*, the *Stalwart*, and the oncoming Drone-Mechs in a vivid blur more striking than a lightning bolt. Tag shook himself from his shock and hoisted himself into the airlock. Bull stood next to him, holding Coren in place. The Mechanic's limbs still trembled as Tag hit the terminal command to shut the airlock. A slight quaking resonated through the airlock's bulkhead as the hatch shut. Air rushed in around them, and the grav generators reactivated within the space, tugging them all back to the deck.

Coren still seemed shell-shocked as they each rushed from the docking port, back toward their stations aboard the *Argo*. When Tag secured himself into his crash couch on the bridge, Alpha reported two minutes until contact with the Drone-Mechs. A thousand questions flew through Tag's mind in a typhoon of uncertainty, curiosity, and frustration.

"Alpha, initiate jump," Tag said. "Now!"

One burned brightest in his mind as waves of plasma broke across the ship.

What in the three hells just happened?

THIRTY-SIX

Different Drone-Mechs. Different xenos. No Dreg." Bull summed up their failed outing to Herandion rather curtly. The muscles in his jaw worked as he stared around the conference table. "Don't tell me this is just a coincidence."

"I certainly would not offer such an assessment," Alpha said.

Sofia brushed a sweat-matted strand of hair from her face and then let out a sigh. "I checked all our files and all the data the Mechanics have. That Sapphire ship is unlike anything we've ever seen. Not even a close match to another species."

"The theory still stands that the Drone-Mechs or the Drone-masters are cultivating a coalition of nanite-infected species," Tag said.

"Or, for that matter," Sofia said, "maybe the so-called Sapphires and the Dreg are simply accomplices. Maybe the Sapphire ship is from the Drone-masters."

Tag shuddered to think they had come so close to what might

be the Drone-masters. But he had his doubts. Had the Sapphire ship been in league with the Drone-masters, he couldn't imagine they would have been allowed to escape like that. "Whatever the case, we can't rule out those possibilities based on what we've seen."

"And we're still left with a couple of unresolved theories as to how the Drone-Mechs are tracking us," Bracken said. "One is that the Dreg and these Sapphires are complicit somehow. Perhaps they are serving as sentries or lookouts of sorts."

"Viable answer," Coren said.

"On the other hand," Bracken said, "there is a very real possibility that someone aboard our ships is compromised."

"Thing is," Sofia said, "Alpha and I have been looking for outgoing signals. I haven't spotted a damn thing." She looked at Bracken's holo expectantly.

Bracken's serious expression never wavered, but Tag could hear the defeat in her voice. "We also have not detected any signal."

"And again," Tag said, "with a crew my size, I've pretty much got my eye on them at all times. You're looking at all of 'em in here save for three marines who have risked their life time and time again for us. I can assure you it's not us."

"Don't you dare insinuate it's one of my people," Bull said, practically snarling at Bracken before she could get a word in. "Admiral Doran and I hand-selected them."

"I hate to reiterate a known fact," Alpha said, "but the nanites do not affect human biological systems. In fact, I have run simulations that demonstrate the nanites possess no self-assembly ability within a normal human physiologic environment. They are merely expelled."

"All the same," Bracken said, "we've run the assays and tests you sent us. We haven't identified any traitors in our midst."

"Then this should be a good thing, right?" Sofia said. She

adopted an almost dreamy expression, which Tag found strange on its own. "Imagine the hundreds of species we don't even know exist." Ah, there it was: the ET anthropologist side of her kicking in. The scientific wonder of the unknown. Her thirst to learn about new species, study their cultures. Didn't fit into a war room briefing like this, but then again, as Tag looked around, who did? "The Drone-masters have technology none of us could have fathomed. It stands to reason that they're flying around out there in places we don't even know yet meeting peoples we couldn't even think up in our wildest dreams."

"Or nightmares," Bull added.

Sofia shrugged. "Or nightmares. And they're forging alliances and enslaving people left and right. Maybe they have an established network, and we're just the little flies that keep bumping into their spider web."

"It is not an illogical point," Alpha said.

"No, no, it's not," Tag said. "And I think it's worth testing."

"How do you propose that?" Bracken said.

"Our next stop is Chronamede," Tag said, gesturing to a holo of the planet rotating in the middle of the table. The planet had been under investigation as a candidate for terraforming when the nanite outbreak hit. There were supposed to be only two ships—one military, one research—stationed at the planet to commence the operations. "I propose we skip past it."

"Do you mean we won't return to investigate it?" Bracken asked.

"No, not at all. I think it's a worthwhile candidate. But I don't want to transition into normal space anywhere near there. Let's recalculate a route that takes us an extra five days in hyperspace past Chronamede."

"That will take us well beyond sensor range," Alpha said, "and there is absolutely nothing out there within a day of hyperspace travel."

"That's my point," Tag said. "We transition there. Where everything is wide open to us. No space stations. No planets. Not even a damn asteroid. We won't be crossing any known trade routes or science expedition trajectories. Just us and the emptiness."

"Ah," Bracken said. "Very well. The chance of any alien species, Drone-Mech or otherwise, randomly existing in such a spot would be virtually zero."

"Right," Tag said. "So if we transition there and wait it out a day or two, we shouldn't see a damn Drone-Mech jump anywhere near us."

"Assuming another species is responsible for signaling them," Sofia said.

Tag nodded. "Which is what we think is most likely. I know it prolongs our mission of scouring space for free Mechanics by a few days, but I think it would be worthwhile to test this."

"Ever the scientist, Captain Brewer," Bracken said. Her thin fingers clasped together. "Very well. Let us examine this hypothesis. I hope we can lay to rest any doubt that one of our crew members is causing the signal."

"Well, that's not exactly true, is it?" Bull said forcefully. "If it's one of us in this room, they know what we're doing…then this whole plan is already fucked." His eyes danced between Bracken and Coren.

"Once again, I don't appreciate the wild accusations," Bracken replied, her tone colder than the vacuum of space. "But at least we'll have narrowed down our pool of suspects." Her eyes met Bull's. Even through the holo, the distrust radiating between them stung Tag as if it were a leak from the fusion reactors powering the *Argo*.

"Good," Tag said. "Then it's decided. In the meantime, how is the development on the grav wave program?"

"Theoretical models have been implemented," Bracken said.

"We have several physicists investigating the matter, and they believe it's possible to disrupt the signal without killing any Mechanics infected with the nanites. But we're still weeks from a practical solution to using the Lacklon Institute to disable the Drone-Mechs."

"But that means you think there is a solution?" Tag asked.

"I do," Bracken said. "Preliminary simulations…" She let her words trail off and inhaled as if preparing to subject herself to some kind of pain. "Preliminary simulations, thanks to the data your team has provided, suggest an overlap between the Institute's technology and that of the Drone-masters' nanites."

Tag couldn't help the smile spreading across his face. "I'm happy to hear we could do something helpful."

Bracken's slightly defeated expression turned ever so slightly sour. "How about the vaccine?"

A knot formed in Tag's gut. "Good news and bad news. We've confirmed that the free Mechanic we found had an acquired immune reaction to the nanites. She was infected, but her body more or less fought them off."

"Bad news?"

"We have no idea how she acquired this immune reaction," Tag said.

"No idea *yet*," Alpha added a bit too cheerfully, emphasizing the "yet."

Even though Bracken's expression had hardly changed, Tag had found he had gotten better at reading Mechanics' expressions. There was clear disappointment etched in her slightly downturned lips and flat-pressed fur.

"We need a vaccine," Bracken said. "If we figure out how this mess of Drone-Mechs is following us and manage to find any remaining free members of my species, the last thing I want to do is drag them all to Meck'ara and make it that much easier for the Drone-masters to finish their work of eradicating my brothers and sisters."

A weight heavier than the *Argo* settled over Tag. "Trust me, I understand." A brief thought flitted through his mind regarding the state of the *Montenegro* and what his own species was up to. He had sent the SRE constant updates via drone courier. But between their sporadic mission schedule and the fact that they never sent their next destinations via courier for fear of interception by the Drone-Mechs, they had been unable to receive any messages back. For all he knew, the entire human race had already been destroyed or enslaved by the Drone-masters. He had no doubt the Drone-masters were attempting to spread through the universe like some kind of galactic disease, and all they had was a single sample from a free Mechanic to develop a vaccine against them.

Then it hit him. They had far more data than he'd ever realized. His sudden epiphany must have made its way into his expression judging by the shrewd look Bracken was giving him.

"You look like you just solved the issue of developing a vaccine," she said.

"As a matter of fact," Tag said, "I might have."

THIRTY-SEVEN

Sofia, Coren, and Alpha were gathered in the med bay with Tag. Lonestar looked at them with passive interest as she performed a couple of light exercises Tag had given her.

"I am thrilled to finally be included in the club," Sofia said, "but I'm not big on needles."

"No needles," Tag said.

"And you're not strapping me with some kind of droid work—no offense, Alpha."

"Why would I take offense?" Alpha asked. "I'm not a droid."

"No," Tag said, looking between Coren and Sofia. This was going to be a long shot, but it might actually work. He recalled his epidemiology courses and seminars once more. He wasn't looking for a patient zero this time. Rather, he wanted to know more about the people who hadn't been affected. "On Eta-Five, you two played a whole bunch of recordings and holos. Every one of them featured a Mechanic or a group of them who were under attack or trying to escape from Drone-Mechs."

"Ah." Sofia was already calling up the data on her wrist terminal. "I get it. You think at least most of them are probably free Mechanics, right?"

"That's my hope," Tag said. "I want to dig up as much data on them as possible. Maybe there's something they share in common. If there are any patterns in their medical histories or something, we might identify what it was that gave them immunity to the nanites."

"Tracking down all this data will not be easy," Coren said. "Especially given that our connection to Mechanic databases outside what we have on the *Stalwart* is tenuous at best."

"I know. We're not exactly in a great spot, but at least we have something to go off of."

"And I suppose combing through these databases will be my responsibility?" Coren asked.

"Sofia's, too, and Alpha's when she's not helping me with our patients," Tag said. "If I've got free time, I'll be right there with you."

"Data mining and data entry duty?" Sofia asked with a mock expression of disgust. "This is definitely not why I studied ET anthropology."

"We can drop you off with the Dreg instead," Tag said. "I'm sure a five-year immersive xenopological study on those guys would be a blast."

"The only part of that plan that would be a blast is when I shoot every goddamn one of those little assholes that try to drill into our ship again," Sofia said.

"Harsh."

"Hey, they left their grimy little prints and broken ships all over the *Argo* for me to clean up."

"I thought the repair bots were responsible for extraship maintenance and repairs after the Dreg assault," Alpha said.

"Don't get smart with me," Sofia replied. Alpha's face remained immobile as if she was trying to figure out exactly what Sofia meant. "Humor, again. Anyway, point taken. Happy to help with the free Mechanic study."

"Good," Tag said. "I'm sure you'll find the work vastly rewarding."

He left Coren and Sofia to begin scouring through the data they had compiled from the initial nanite outbreak. With a gesture, he had Alpha follow him to Gorenado's regen chamber. The terminal still glared with a bleak "N/A" next to the estimated time of healing. Normally by now, tendrils of red blood vessels and ligaments would be crisscrossing the void, serving as a scaffold for the other tissues and replacement organs to regenerate. But the hole was still a hole. Tag could peek straight through the polyglass and see the back of the regen chamber through Gorenado's injury. Something was stopping the regen chamber's AI from filling in the devastating wound on the marine's chest.

"Should I prepare the surgical suite?" Alpha asked as if she could read Tag's mind. For all he knew, maybe that wasn't so far-fetched with her built-in biosensor arrays. He wished he had some way of knowing what *she* was thinking.

"Yes," Tag said. His heart started to climb into his throat as he imagined the surgery ahead. An image of his deceased med bay assistant, Curtis Morgan, scraping at the med bay hatch during the initial Drone-Mech attack on the *Argo* floated through his mind. Some extra medical experience around here would have been nice. If the AI couldn't figure this one out, he wondered what the odds of him and a weeks-young synth-bio life-form helping Gorenado were.

As it was, the only thing keeping Gorenado alive in any

semblance of the word was the mechanical blood-pumping and breathing control offered by the regen chamber. Alpha returned to Tag's side with a hovergurney attached to a mobile life-support system. Seeing the life-support system reminded Tag of his failed attempt to save Staff Sergeant Kaufman.

I won't let you down, Tag said as he disengaged the regen chamber. This time, the marine in his charge would live. He promised himself they would save Gorenado. He couldn't imagine the outcome any other way. Whatever it took, Gorenado would open his eyes again and walk through these passages with the rest of the crew.

The regen chamber hissed open, and Tag lowered Gorenado's body onto the hovergurney. The biomonitors attached to Gorenado blatted with high-pitched alarms reporting systemic organ failure. Tag ignored the reptilian part of his brain screaming in fear in response to the alarms and let his medical training prevail. Deliberately and carefully, he secured the life support system around Gorenado's chest. Electric signals passed through Gorenado's skin from the system, telling his cardiac muscles what to do. A tube down his trachea ensured proper oxygen flow, and rivulets of blood seeped from parts of the wound that had opened again from moving his body.

Tag led the hovergurney into the surgical suite after undergoing a sterilization spray. He could feel the eyes of the others glancing in at him from their work. Lonestar pressed her palm against the polyglass. The unnatural red glisten of Gorenado's wound stared back up at Tag. The procedure ahead would require every ounce of focus he could muster, and the last thing he needed was the distraction of all the emotions radiating at him from onlookers.

With a gesture over a terminal, the clear polyglass turned solid white. Lonestar might be put off by the sudden opacity, but

Tag didn't care. The *Argo* was safely in hyperspace, and his crew was embroiled in the most pressing tasks to ensure the success of their mission. The only things that mattered to him now were in the surgical suite.

He took a deep breath. Alpha stood stock still, almost as if she had reverted to the droid she had once been, and gazed at him expectantly. "Let's begin."

THIRTY-EIGHT

Tag began the procedure using a plasma blade to cut away some of the excess tissue that had grown over Gorenado's wound. He looked at Alpha as he did, half-expecting her to cringe like a first-year medical student at the smell of burning flesh. But without activated scent detectors, she simply stared at the procedure with curious interest.

"We'll get a better sense of what we're dealing with by cleaning the wound up a bit," Tag said.

"I see," Alpha replied.

Tag gestured over the nearby surgical terminal. A holo shone a green latticework of translucent vessels, muscles, tendons, bones, nerves, and organ structures over the hole in Gorenado's chest, showing what his natural physiology should look like.

"Problem is," Tag said, "usually the AI system gives me some clue. Some reason it can't complete the regen process without human intervention. Right now, we've got nothing." Tag handed her the plasma blade and vacuum tube. "Can you do a bit more of the edgework?"

Alpha paused a second. "My training algorithms suggest that I can."

"You certainly could when you were just an M3 droid. If you have to, you can load up an old sequence from before I implanted the synth-bio brain."

"Yes." Alpha nodded, leaning over Gorenado. "I've got it."

She began working at the tangles of vessels and nerves, the torn muscles and fractured bone. Tag studied the wound. Half of this work should have been done already. Had the AI systems in the regen chamber not worked for some reason? Maybe the regen chamber was suffering some lingering effects of the virus the Drone-Mechs had infected the *Argo*'s comp systems with. That might explain its poor functioning.

"Something wrong, Captain?" Alpha asked.

"Just trying to reason things out here," he said.

Alpha turned back to her work, and Tag's mind raced. All the tiny bone fragments from Gorenado's busted ribs should have already been washed clean. The regen chamber shouldn't have had a problem cauterizing the blood vessels either. Yet each torn vessel stared at him like a snake with its mouth open. Stranger than that, they weren't bleeding. He probed the wound with a wormlike holocam. It projected a magnified image of Gorenado's shredded anatomy onto a holoscreen, and Tag studied the bizarre attributes of the completely unhealed mess.

"Captain," Alpha said, "I'm having trouble cleaning the debris from Gorenado's wounds."

The plasma blade couldn't dislodge the bone fragments. Instead, the blue energy on the blade simply fizzled and popped when it touched the fragments.

"Let me see that," Tag said. He wanted to believe Alpha's

procedure wasn't working simply because she hadn't recalled it properly. His own efforts were met with the same failed results, and he highly doubted he had suddenly forgotten how to clean wounds. Frustration cut through Tag like a scythe through grain. "What is going on?"

Something in Gorenado's body was resisting the plasma blade. It made no sense. Plasma should slice through even the toughest of human tissues like a battlecruiser sliding through space. But for whatever reason, Gorenado's tissues seemed to have become impervious to the standard-issue surgical equipment.

"It's almost as if he is made of some kind of alloy," Alpha said. "Like he has his own innate energy shield. Nothing in my databases or brain is coming up with a solution for this type of physiological phenomenon."

Tag worked feverishly at various spots within the wound. But nothing he did with the blade made a difference. The plasma kept sparking out, as if the blade were losing power. Or—

His mind raced now, a sudden realization crashing over him like an avalanche. "What did you say again?"

"Nothing in my databases—"

"No, before that."

"I remarked that Gorenado seemed as if he was made of some kind of alloy. Maybe had his own energy shield. But it was merely a metaphor. Nothing literal, Captain."

"Oh, you might actually be more right than you realized," Tag said. He dropped the plasma blade into a pan and picked up a more antiquated metal surgical blade. Twisting his wrist, he rotated the stainless-steel blade before him. It caught and reflected the light of the surgical lamps. Willing his hands to remain sure and still, he cut gently into the coagulated blood around one of the tiny bone chips.

Alpha made a soft tutting sound—maybe a droid's version of

a gasp. But he didn't share in her surprise and instead continued cleaning the wound. As he did, blood finally flowed back into the opening as if a glacier had just melted and rivers were released down the mountain.

"Suction and coagulation, now," Tag said.

Though Alpha still appeared shocked by the apparent magic of using the stainless-steel blade, she complied. With Gorenado's wound suddenly unhindered by whatever had clotted it before, his vitals went wild. Alarms bleated periodically as Tag and Alpha worked frantically to fight each fire as it cropped up. Torn artery here. Retracted muscle there. All they had to do was stabilize Gorenado enough that they could load him back into the regen chamber.

And if Tag's hypothesis was correct, the regen chamber would take it from there. There wouldn't be a blank time-esti-mate-to-healing window. Instead, he felt damn certain the AI would quickly diagnose and fix the issue now. With Alpha's help, he placed coagulating microparticles around the wound, and when he judged the bleeding at a minimum, he guided the hov-ergurney back to the regen chambers. Alpha assisted in removing the life support system, and they hoisted Gorenado into the regen chamber.

Once the chamber's door locked shut with a mechanical whir and click, Tag initiated the regen process on the terminal. Blue light and liquid filled the chamber once more, covering Gorenado and soaking his injury. The holoscreen blinked. A progress bar showed in the air between Tag and Alpha. It filled and restarted over and over, with words like Diagnosis and Treatment Regimen floating above it.

Then it disappeared, and a timestamp appeared. Tag's eyes went wide, and his chest felt lighter, almost as if it were filling with helium. Alpha clenched her silver fingers in a gesture of victory.

Approximately two weeks, the machine reported, until Gorenado would be whole enough to leave the chamber.

Lonestar limped to their side, drawn by the apparent victory. "He's going to make it?"

"He is," Tag said with pride.

"Gods be damned, you did it. You saved his life." She took a step back, growing quiet and contemplative. Far different from the reaction Tag had expected.

"You look like you don't believe me."

"No, it's not that," she said with her slight drawl. "It's just… Thanks, Doc. Whatever you did, thank you." She limped away, stretching her back and testing her own healing tissues. Tag was slightly confused by the interaction, but Alpha tugged at his sleeve and prevented him from lingering on the issue too long.

"Captain," Alpha said, "I'm still at a loss for what happened. Why did the stainless-steel blade work? After all, with the blade, the process was extraordinarily simple."

Tag wiped the perspiration from his forehead with the back of his hand, finally able to take a breath without Gorenado's life hanging in his hands. "You said it yourself. His wounds were like an energy shield. And you also said we didn't have anything like that in our medical databases. Nothing us humans have ever encountered before."

"Just like the Dreg," Alpha said in sudden comprehension, her metallic head bobbing. "That is where you drew your hypothesis from."

"Right," Tag said. "That Dreg spike that impaled Gorenado must've coated whatever it touched with some kind of polymer that's inert to intense energy sources."

"Which makes sense," Alpha said. "It had a distinctly biological look to it, but it somehow was being fired off in space through what appeared to be a rather powerful cannon. Judging by its use as an interspace weapon, I would guess it is capable of piercing energy shields as well."

"That would be my guess," Tag said. "So when we pressed a plasma blade—which isn't that much different from a pulse round—to the microscopic coating that was stuck around Gorenado's wound, it simply absorbed that energy like an energy shield would."

Alpha indicated the regen chamber. "The regen chamber didn't recognize the coating because the SRE had never encountered the Dreg. It simply couldn't detect it. Have we disposed of the spike that we removed from Gorenado after Nycho?"

"No, we still have it. Mind performing a little chromatography on it? I'd like a full spectral analysis run up so we can load the data to our med bay AI."

"Consider it done, Captain." Before she traipsed away, she locked eyes with Tag. "That was truly thrilling."

"Sorry?"

"Solving a problem like that to save a life. To save Gorenado's life," Alpha said. "I can see why you trained to become a medical scientist and physician. Having the power to save a life is a far better, a far more difficult skill to master than taking one. I will relish this victory of ours."

"Good," Tag said, welcoming her enthusiasm for the medical profession. Her mind was young and malleable. He reminded himself to reward this behavior of hers, to offer her more opportunities to save lives rather than take them, to show her the great responsibility that came with the ability to do just that. There was still hope for Gorenado—and there was still hope for Alpha.

Staring through the polyglass at Gorenado, Tag took a moment to revel in what they had accomplished. It was a reminder of how things had changed out here. How pushing the frontier of human knowledge and space and teetering on the precipice of war with unknown species provided unknowable challenges. His dad would probably smile at seeing this win, this shining shred of competence overcome an otherwise dark and grim situation. He could almost hear the words in his head: "Tag, you're a highwayman. Got all the opportunities ahead of you, all the possibilities you could ever dream of. You've just got to keep looking side to side instead of just straight ahead. Keep those eyes open. Keep that brain working."

Coren and Sofia were still poring over the data on the free Mechanics. He strode toward them, ready to move on to the next challenge.

"Captain, I'm going to request that you at least take a short break," Coren said, not bothering to look up from his terminal. "I cannot imagine what you just did was easy."

"No, I promised I'd help," Tag said. "I'm going to help."

Sofia paused. "What he's trying to say is that you look like shit, could probably use a coffee, and then a second to chill your brain before you bumble through all this data with us."

"I liked the way he said it better," Tag said.

A shit-eating grin crossed Sofia's face. "Is it better with a smile?"

THIRTY-NINE

IN THE MESS HALL, TAG TOOK A SIP OF COFFEE AS HE LET HIS mind wander. Darkness surrounded him except for the massive viewscreen showing an outboard view of the ship, brightened by the coursing plasma of hyperspace. A dull glow washed over the bulkhead, tables, and seats, almost as if it were a reflection off oceanic waves. But instead of having a blue tinge, it glowed purple and green.

Tag wondered what staring at the screen with a belly full of gutfire would be like. Drunkenness and a dazzling light show would probably keep him entertained for a solid hour or two. But he was long past shirking responsibility and reality by allowing himself such a debaucherous pleasure. A metallic clink caught his attention, and a triangle of yellow light spilled in from the corridor, silhouetting a tall, muscular figure. His eyes took a second to adjust until he recognized Lonestar limping toward him.

"Kind of creepy that you're just sitting here in the dark," she said. She walked with an awkward gait to the coffee maker and poured herself a cup. With steam rising from the cup, she slumped into the seat across from Tag. Her face twisted in a slight grimace. "This whole healing business is a bit more painful than I thought it'd be."

"You were wounded pretty badly. Busted vertebrae, shredded muscle."

Lonestar held up a hand. "Damn, I've seen some shit, but I don't like imagining that on myself, you know?"

Tag laughed. "I sometimes forget. That kind of stuff becomes pretty casual by the time you're done with medical training. Three hells, when we had anatomy labs and cut up old cadavers for surgical practice, the professor would walk between our tables with a sandwich in hand, taking bites and critiquing our sutures while spitting crumbs at us. I swear he did it just to annoy us."

"Can't you just use VR for practice? Or for that matter, use some kind of synthetic bodies?"

"It's not the same. Might sound a bit morbid, but when you're around people enough, you can tell what's a person and what's not. It takes a combination of senses when you're performing a surgical procedure. It's not just the sight, but also the feel, and, I hate to say it, even the smells that clue you in to working with the human body."

Lonestar pushed her coffee cup away from her. "I grew up on a ranch. Animals can be gross, but Captain, that really takes the cake."

"Again, sorry." Tag sipped his coffee. He felt the tightened grasp of tension leave his muscles as the warm beverage slipped down his throat. Coren and Sofia had been right; he had needed the short break. After draining the last few drops, he started to stand. "I really need to get back to Sofia and Coren."

"Before you do, can I ask you about something?"

"Okay." Tag sat back down. "Shoot."

"Before Nycho, you asked me if I ever liked killing."

Tag let the silence carry between them, waiting with a tickling sense of apprehension lurking at the back of his throat.

"Why did you ask me that?" she said.

"I'm sorry," Tag said. His face felt hot, and he regretted drawing her into his moral dilemma with Alpha. "It was just something I heard from someone else. I wanted to know, I guess, if it was normal."

"Right, because you weren't a trained foot soldier. A trained killer." Her tone sounded almost accusatory.

"I'm not."

"But you have killed now. You've fought the Drone-Mechs. The Dreg. And gods know what or who else you might have to deal with."

Again Tag let her words fall on him like little hammers pounding his psyche. Everything sounded rushed and angry. Like she had been letting that brief conversation simmer in her mind until it boiled over, exploding like a failing fusion reactor. He hadn't expected such an intense reaction.

Lonestar's chest heaved as if she had just finished a marathon—or, taking into account her genetic enhancements, three of them. She began again in a softer voice. "Now that you have killed. Now that you have acted like a soldier, do you..." Her eyes met his. A relentless stare. Unbreakable. Fierce. "Do you like taking lives?"

The inflammatory question burned in his conscience. He wanted to scream that of course he didn't. He had devoted his life to saving others, to preserving life. He thought of Alpha. For that matter, he had *created* life. That was his gods-ordained mission in life. That was why he had become a scientist. Why he had joined a research team. Why he had found satisfaction and a new purpose when his prospects of being trained as a bridge officer had broken like shards of ice against alloy.

All those thoughts hurtled through his mind faster than the *Argo* through hyperspace. But all he said was, "No. Never."

"Not once?" she asked, a brow raised. She didn't take her eyes off him. Didn't blink.

"Not once," he repeated, as calmly as possible.

Her gaze fell to the table, tracing over her hands draped around the cup. "Okay." He couldn't tell whether she believed him or not, but interrogating her now to determine what this was all about would likely be a fruitless endeavor. Better to bring it up with Bull later.

Lonestar emptied her coffee cup and then chucked it into the trash receptacle. "Thanks again for saving Gorenado." She got up and left Tag with no further explanation. Without looking him in the eye again. The hatch to the corridor clicked shut behind her.

A lot of strange things had happened since the *Argo* had first circled Eta-Five and they had run into the Drone-Mechs. But this conversation—or whatever it was—with Lonestar had to be one of the strangest.

FORTY

THE *ARGO* WAS ONLY A DAY FROM ENTERING NORMAL SPACE.
The crew hadn't spoken much about what they would find
when they got there, but Tag could sense their apprehension.
It was apparent in the rushed way they focused themselves on
other work. Coren and Sofia delved into the mystery of the free
Mechanics. Alpha helped them when she wasn't performing experiments on the Dreg data. Lonestar relentlessly pursued physical therapy—and when her body was worn out, she ran simulated
missions in VR. Sumo and Bull constantly trained in the gym and
joined Lonestar in the VR missions.

Sleep seemed to be something to which every one of them
had grown a stranger. Tag had experienced the restless sleep shifts
in his bunk like everyone else, trying to find sleep, trying to succumb to the exhaustion seeping through him, bone deep. But
whenever his eyes started to close, flashes of the *Argo* exploding
under a fusillade of Drone-Mech fire sparked beneath his eyelids.

The last free Mechanics turning on him, rabid with nanites. The *Montenegro* falling apart in a cloud of alloy and spikes of released plasma. His crew, slaughtered by Dreg or Drone-Mechs or that strange sapphire ship. Each relative night on the ship brought some new horror forth from his imagination.

Coffee. Burned, watered-down coffee was all that kept his body going.

Slightly invigorated by a fresh round of caffeine, Tag joined Coren, Sofia, and Alpha in the med bay. They were still sifting through mountains of data. A multitude of patterns had been spotted from the demographics and histories of the presumed free Mechanics they had identified, but sorting through the false positives and the strange coincidences required a human (or Mechanic) touch.

"They all share similar medical histories," Coren explained, "but so does just about every Mechanic. Ninety-six percent of them were on the correct vaccine trajectory."

"Could one of the vaccines you take prevent nanites?" Sofia asked.

"I doubt it," Coren replied. "To my knowledge, Tuffet's syndrome, limb paralysis shock virus, and the mutagenic organo vector are caused by pathogens that are nothing like the nanites."

"Maybe there are other diseases with pathogens that are similar to the nanites," Sofia said.

Alpha gestured to a holodisplay. "I have performed the simulations according to the data Coren and Bracken have shared with me. There are no known disease-causing agents that share a biochemical or structural similarity to the nanites."

"Damn," Sofia said. "So what did these people come down with that created nanite antibodies like this?"

Tag moved past them and used his hand to scroll through the data on the holoscreen. "Maybe we're headed in the wrong direction." He thought of Gorenado again. How the effect of the alien technology on his wound had stumped traditional AI medical approaches. How it had taken thinking outside the human medical paradigm to develop a solution. "Maybe there's something we're missing."

"Uh, Skipper, I thought antibodies and the immune system are supposed to react to pathogens. So what are we missing?" Sofia asked.

"Evolutionarily speaking, yes. Our acquired immune systems are geared to fighting whatever our environment throws at us that might harm us," Tag said. He racked his brain to remember his seminars on the pre-interstellar history of medicine. "But sometimes that causes problems."

"Such as allergies. Unnecessarily violent reactions to an innocuous contaminant or material," Alpha said.

"Exactly. Healthcare workers, back in the days before spray-on sterilization wraps, used to wear gloves made of latex. Sometimes they would wear the gloves so much they developed a latex allergy."

"Even though latex isn't harmful to human biology," Coren said. "Interesting. This isn't generally a widespread problem in our species."

Sofia lowered her wrist terminal. "Oh, so the Mechanic immune system is superior now, too?"

Coren gave her a noncommittal shrug.

"Anyway," Tag said, "I'm guessing there's something in the environment. Something these people were exposed to that led to their acquired immunity toward nanites." He held up his hand and raised a finger with each suggestion. "Look at their jobs, where they grew up, where they traveled, what their parents did, what foods they ate. That's where I think we'll find an answer."

The group turned back to the terminals, working in strained

silence. Tag started searching through their occupations and positions within the Mechanic navy. He found engineers and educators and scientists and marines and exo-suit operators and pilots. No clear patterns emerged. Their ranks and time spent in the navy, too, proved to be a dead end.

"Any luck?" Tag asked the others.

"Unfortunately not," Alpha said. "Family history and age are proving to be nonfactors."

"It's extraordinarily difficult to find any type of patterns within extracurricular activities," Coren said.

Sofia pointed to a map of the Mechanic home world with cities across the globe highlighted. "And place of birth and where they lived isn't really helpful."

"Damn," Tag said. "What else can we look at?"

Coren's golden eye glowed as if he was struggling to retain something within his head. "I think...I think there is a pattern." His fingers danced over the cities on the globe, and he rotated it, scanning each city. "These cities highlighted in orange signify their places of birth, right?"

"Right," Sofia said. "All over the damn world."

"Yes, true," Coren said. "But these cities are all similar."

"Their populations are different, and their geolocations aren't nearly close together. What's the similarity?"

Coren waved his hand over the map. "Almost all of these cities are bubble communities."

"Bubble communities?" Sofia asked. "I don't remember you telling me about these before."

Another wave of Coren's six-fingered hand, and the holoscreen provided a magnified view of a bubble community. The entire city was a latticework of tunnels and tall buildings, not consequentially different from a modern human city. It was considerably greener than Tag had expected. Plants seemed to cover every available space with gardens and parks on top of buildings, on balconies and outcroppings, and even in dedicated suspended platforms between buildings. But the most startling aspect of the city was the enormous bubble that covered the entire community.

Tag pointed to the bubble. "What is that for?"

Coren zoomed out of the city slightly. Now Tag could plainly see the city was situated at the bottom of an ocean floor. "That seems like a rather difficult place to build a city."

"Hell of an engineering feat," Sophia added. Then quickly, "But don't let it get to your head."

The holoscreen's view expanded again to display the globe.

Coren was already copying the names of each bubble community to a new document. "These communities were built to separate us from the environment as an early experiment in our colonization efforts. It protected us from the outside elements, which was crucial on planets we had not yet terraformed. Pursuing these technologies had an unintended consequence at home." He finished transcribing the names and transmitted the document back to Bracken. "Most importantly, we realized the communities did something else important. They limited our impact on the environment. On an overpopulated planet, we could use our bubble communities to build civilizations deep underwater, past where most other native species could even survive. We could better filter the air, control what waste and refuse was recycled and that which we emitted into the environment. It saved our planet and, as a result, saved our species."

"Interesting," Tag said. He recalled the urban sprawl of Earth. People everywhere. How some parks, once protected by their individual nation-states, had been deforested to provide more living spaces. The gray skies. The occasional smog, despite the SRE's best efforts to control the changing environment. He imagined what it would be like if humans had started colonizing the ocean floor like the Mechanics rather than devouring all the land available to them. But as much as Tag wanted to mull those thoughts over, none of them affected his current dilemma. "So what do these bubble communities have to do with nanites?"

FORTY-ONE

Tag sat in the captain's station at the bridge. Soon they would be transitioning into normal space. His fingers curled and uncurled around the armrests. He clenched his jaw hard enough that the first tendrils of a headache were wrapping around his brain, but he couldn't help it. The tension building inside him was like an energy round charging in a cannon with nowhere to go.

"Incoming message from Bracken!" Alpha practically shouted.

Adrenaline jolted through Tag. Not an emergency. Not now. They were minutes from transitioning, and the T-drive was already spooling down.

"What is it?" he asked.

"She says they identified the compound they believe may be the center to our nanite immunity mystery." Then Alpha turned back to her screen.

"Well?"

"That's it."

"Three hells," Tag said. "Do Mechanics enjoy teasing like this?"

"Only if it proves we are indeed better than you," Coren said.

Tag sent a connection request to Bracken, and her image showed up on his holoscreen.

"Captain," she said as if he had interrupted something.

"What's the deal with the nanites?" Tag asked.

"We had a bet on the bridge you humans couldn't handle suspense," Bracken said. "I'm proud to say I won." There was a sense of victory in her tone, though her outward expression remained as void of emotion as a black hole. "We found a similar particle—at least in size—that shares some of the trace elements found in the nanites."

"And what's the particle do?"

"Always the curious human."

"I'm a medical scientist. Curiosity is what I do."

"The particle is from our air recycling units. I'll share more if we have a chance in normal space or else at the next debriefing."

"Looking forward to it," Tag said as he ended the communication.

"Transitioning...now," Alpha said.

Sofia tensed at her controls, and Coren hovered above the weapons commands. Tag felt the tug of momentum pulling him forward as the inertial dampeners fought to keep him restrained. The bridge rattled, and the waves of plasma on the viewscreen dissipated.

They floated in a vast expanse where distant constellations sparkled in the viewscreen. Their lidar and radar detected nothing except for the *Stalwart* beside them, floating in their periphery. The sight of the emptiness before them stretching into an expanse of stars inspired a reverence in Tag he wasn't prepared for. It was a reminder of just how alone they really were in this mission, both literally and figuratively. A reminder of just how little their tiny spaceships were, like dust motes blown in the wind, when compared to the unimaginable numbers of other life-forms carrying on somewhere around those random stars peppering the deep void.

And he wondered just how long they would be alone.

"No signs of Drone-Mechs?" Tag asked.

"Nothing yet, Captain," Alpha said.

Bracken appeared on the holoscreen. "We have not detected any other ships within our vicinity."

"Let's set the timer for five days and see what happens, shall we?" Tag asked.

"We shall."

For some reason, Tag felt his nerves flickering with more anxious energy out here than he did when they were investigating a space station or traveling to Eta-Five. There was something unnerving about not knowing whether a ship would transition into normal space near them. There was no space station or planet to orient themselves against, nothing to hide behind in case they found themselves mired in an unexpected battle.

He tried to reason that the nearest Drone-Mechs were probably situated somewhere around Chronamede, which was five days' hyperspace travel away. Nothing should, he hoped, surprise them until somewhere near the two-day mark. The likelihood of the Drone-Mechs arriving sooner, already being positioned nearby, was infinitesimally small.

Then again, stranger things had happened.

"Want to talk about those recycler particles?" Tag asked over the comms to Bracken. He never took his eyes off the holomap. No matter how he tried to distract himself, it would be impossible to quell his worry.

"Certainly," Bracken said. He could almost see a glimmer in her golden eyes. She must be studying the holos back on her bridge, watching, waiting. Just like him. "There really isn't much to them. The particles help to sequester pollutants."

"Simple enough. And I take it they are harmless to Mechanics?" His eyes gazed at the viewscreen, then the map. Still no contacts.

"The particles are indeed designed to be inert within healthy Mechanical bodies. However, my medical staff did note that there are documented cases of air recycling particle allergies."

"Which makes sense. Given we now believe those particles might elicit an acquired immune response." Tag's fingers drummed over his armrest. "So we've got some time to test this theory."

"Between sitting here, waiting for the Drone-Mechs, and the rest of our hyperspace travels to gather free Mechanics, I would say 'we've got some time' is a vast underestimation. But I would expect nothing less from a human." On the holoscreen, Tag thought he could see Bracken's lips twitch slightly.

"Was that humor? Is Bracken really making a joke?" Tag asked with a grin.

"Don't test the limits of my well-rounded humor."

"Wouldn't dare," Tag said. "I can set up some experiments to test if we can use these particles to inoculate you all. Do you happen to have any of these particles on hand?"

Bracken lowered her eyes, appearing decidedly rueful again. "Unfortunately, those that we did have on hand were used in our facilities on the Forest of Light. We of course had hoped not to pollute their ecosystem. With the Drone-Mech attack, we didn't have the time to salvage any of our homesteading or community-building technologies."

"Understood." The defeat echoed through Tag like a desperate yell ringing through his skull. "So without these particles, we're more or less back to where we started."

"Ah, human, don't look so disappointed," Bracken said. "We don't need the particles."

Tag's confusion must have been clear through the holo.

"We can make more. We've got the materials, the recyclers, and the fabricators to produce as many of those things as we want." She paused, staring at Tag through the holo. Her thin lips were pursed tight as if she was refraining from saying something.

Tag sighed. "Go on, say it. Mechanic technology is superior, yadda yadda."

"Thank you, Captain Brewer. You said it for me." She turned away from the holo and barked orders to someone else unseen on the bridge. "We'll begin production immediately. I can also send you the fabricator program for the recycler particles, although it will not be compatible with your own machinery."

"Coren, can you handle translating it into something we can use here?"

Coren's good eye twitched like he was raising his brow, his black fur rustling, and he chuffed.

"I'll take that as a yes."

Time passed tediously as the crew took shifts on the bridge. Coren updated the 3-D fabricator in engineering between shifts at his weapons terminal. He and Alpha took turns writing a script to translate the Mechanic code into a workable program for the *Argo's* fabricator. After performing some spacewalks to clean off the remnants of Dreg ships and recover samples of a few dead, frozen Dreg still secured in those ships, the marines joined them on the bridge occasionally. Lonestar's gait had grown steadier and healthier. Bull hardly spoke a word, and Sumo hung somewhere in the balance between acting like Bull and trying to maintain more amiable relationships with the rest of the crew. Sofia often sat with her legs dangling over the side of her crash couch while she used her wrist terminal to write up her observations on the Dreg, Mechanics, and the gods only knew what else. Tag had hoped analyzing the samples of the Dreg would occupy more time, but all the scans he and Alpha had performed yielded no sign of nanites anywhere within the ugly aliens. Once they had finished, there was little else to do but wait.

What had started as an exercise testing Tag's apprehension and dread had turned into one of tedium. Staring at the same blank holomap, the same star-studded viewscreen had quickly lost its luster.

That was, until several new shapes exploded into view.

FORTY-TWO

"Gods be damned!" Tag yelled, his fist slamming on the terminal. He called up the alarm, and red lights danced across the bridge. The rest of the ship would be alight in similar frenzied crimson flashes as a computerized voice alerted, "All hands to battle stations."

The red dots on the holomap began closing in on them. Alpha looked at Tag, waiting for the signal to jump to hyperspace. But while the unidentified ships grew closer on the holomap, no smaller dots zoomed toward them signifying incoming fire.

"Anything, Bracken?" Tag asked.

"No, no comms yet. We're hailing them. Maybe…" She let the rest of her sentence trail off.

Tag could sense the longing in her tone, the hope that maybe this time, for some insane reason, these were free Mechanics and not the Drone-Mechs. But then Bracken looped them into her incoming transmission.

"Where does your loyalty lie?" the droll Drone-Mech voice asked.

"Son of a Dreg!" Sofia yelled, slapping the controls. "Damn it, damn it, damn it."

A sick realization poured over Tag. He gave Alpha a perfunctory nod to initiate the coordinated hyperspace jump. The *Argo* quaked, and the bulkhead hummed in shifting harmonics as waves of plasma started lapping over the viewscreen. The crew remained still and silent even as the ship settled into a stabilized transit through hyperspace in parallel with the *Stalwart*.

But though they had escaped the Drone-Mechs again, Tag couldn't escape the dread that came with it. They had never seen another alien, another Mechanic, or anything, for that matter, in the emptiness they had sat in for five days. No signal that anyone else had identified them. No random drones happening by. No scout ships.

Just a contingent of Drone-Mechs dropping in on them. And sure enough, they had come at around the five-day mark as predicted. They must have been stationed near Chronamede, but there was no way they had simply spotted the *Argo* or the *Stalwart* from there.

Tag shook his head as the others studied their stations. Their current theory that there were allies of the Drone-Mechs stationed around waiting to signal the Drone-Mechs didn't explain what had just happened. It looked more likely than ever that someone, somehow, was aboard either the *Argo* or the *Stalwart*, signaling the Drone-Mechs. And all the paranoia Tag had once felt when he had first met the Mechanics came flooding back.

But as he looked around the bridge, he couldn't imagine Sofia, Alpha, or Coren doing something like this. And by the gods, he had seen the dedication of the marines. G had already paid the ultimate price, and that hadn't stopped the others from devoting themselves to their missions on Nycho or Herandion.

"Bracken," Tag said in a low voice. "Do you have an alternate hypothesis?"

Bracken's face appeared stern on the holoscreen. There was no humor to be seen in it now. "Someone has crossed us. Aboard your ship or mine. There is another way we can determine whose ship—"

The hatch to the bridge slammed open. Bull charged in wearing his power armor. His visor was peeled back to reveal his face, red with anger, and his words spit from his mouth like venom.

"You!" he boomed, a finger outstretched toward Coren. "It's you! Isn't it? You're the only one who could do this on the ship. The only one that knows how!"

Tag undid his restraints and rushed down from the captain's terminal. "Bull! You can't just throw around accusations like that."

"No," Bull said, "you're right. I can't. Not without evidence."

He chucked something at Tag, and Tag held his hands out instinctively, catching it. He opened his fingers. In his palm rested a disc-shaped device with several long wires flopping from it as if the thing were a dead, mechanical spider.

"What is this?"

"It's not human," Bull said. "I'll tell you that much. Never seen human tech made from black alloy like that. But I do know where I've seen it. Found it in the *cargo* bay. I remembered that power leak Alpha mentioned before, so I did a bit of investigating. Figured if the repair bots hadn't fixed it, maybe something funny was going on. And sure enough, it was."

Tag rotated the disc-shaped device in his hand. It hardly reflected the light, appearing more shadow than metal. Bull was right. It looked like it belonged on a Mechanic's armor. "What is this?"

Coren still held his hands up in a defensive gesture. His eyes traced from Bull to the object Tag held between his fingers. "It looks like a transponder."

"I told you," Bull roared. "I told you it's Mechanic tech!"

Tag wanted Coren to deny it, to say it was all a misunderstanding.

"He's not wrong," Coren said. "It's no wonder we never saw its encrypted transmissions. We use these types of devices on our stealth ships." He paused, looking introspective for a moment. "Somehow the camouflaging algorithm I wrote must've interfered with its signal. That's the only explanation for why the Drone-Mechs didn't find the *Argo*'s exact location on Eta-Five. Still, I have no idea where it could have come from."

Bull seemed only to hear the first statement. He rushed at Coren and threw his body into the Mechanic. Coren went down with a thud and tried to counter Bull's attack. But Bull wrapped Coren's arms behind his back in a way that would have shattered a human's joints in a flurry of limbs and grunts.

"Goddamned xeno!" Bull said. "Admit what you've done! Admit it!"

"I have nothing to hide from you," Coren said.

Tag ran at Bull and Coren, but Bull dragged Coren into the corridor and through a maintenance hatch. He threw Coren into an airlock as Tag caught up with them. The footsteps of the other sounded behind them.

"Don't!" Tag yelled.

Bull's hand hovered above the command to open the airlock to space. Chest heaving, Coren stood in the middle of the airlock. His eyes never strayed from Bull's.

"I did not set that transponder." Coren stomped toward the polyglass hatch between Bull and him.

Tag's heart beat faster, and he took a step toward Bull. "Take your hand away from the terminal. That's an order."

Bull never took his eyes off Coren. "I can't do that, Captain. My orders were to protect this ship. That's what I'm doing now."

Tag took another tentative step. Alpha and Sofia rustled behind him.

"Bull ..." Sumo said, joining the commotion with Lonestar at her side.

"Not now," Bull said. He faced Coren. "Tell them. This was Mechanic technology. You put it there."

"I'm not a Drone-Mech," Coren said. His nostrils flared as he glared through the polyglass. His voice came out slightly tinny through the internal airlock speakers, but there was no mistaking the menace in it. "You can space me if you want, but that will not solve your problem."

"It'll solve your problem just fine!" Bull said.

"Stop it!" Tag yelled. He lunged for Bull and grabbed the man's arm. Bull's muscles tensed as Tag tried to drag him back from the airlock. Alpha threw herself at Bull, aiming for his feet. He crashed forward, but as he fell, his free hand hit the terminal, initiating the depressurization process. Even through the polyglass, Tag could hear the rush of air escaping the chamber before the exterior hatch would release.

Pain coursed through the back of his head as he struggled with Bull. Alpha secured his legs, but it didn't stop the marine from flailing as the counter continued to tick down until the exterior hatch would be released.

A shape flew by the tangled mess of Bull, Alpha, and Coren, lunging over them and slamming a fist on the terminal. The countdown stopped, and the crew member hit another command that repressurized the chamber and opened the inner hatch. At first Tag thought it was Sofia. As Bull realized his gambit was over and ceased struggling against Tag and Alpha, Tag saw Lonestar wincing in pain over her temporary overexertion. One hand was bracing her back, the other keeping her upright by holding onto a stanchion.

The hatch soon opened, and Coren spilled inside, coughing and gasping for air. He was doubled over, still glaring at Bull.

"I didn't do it," he managed.

Bull grunted under Alpha and Tag's grip. His face burned a brilliant shade of scarlet. "You can fool them, xeno. But you can't fool me."

"He's not lying," Lonestar said.

Bull looked at her. An expression of betrayal seared through his fury. "How do you know that?"

"Because I did it. I placed the transponder."

FORTY-THREE

Tag brushed himself off as he stood, signaling for Alpha to keep Bull secured. "What did you say?"

"I did it," Lonestar said. "If you're going to space someone, space me." She gestured toward Coren. "This has nothing to do with him."

"Why? Why would you do that?" Tag couldn't decide whether to be more angry or confused. His emotions clashed in his head like two stars pulling each other into their gravity wells. He fingered his holstered sidearm instinctively as he wondered what other treacherous surprises she held in store for him.

"Because of him," Lonestar said, indicating Coren, "and you."

Bull had ceased resisting Alpha. The vessel in his forehead still throbbed, but his face appeared drained of its normal red hue. "To think that I personally recommended you to Admiral Doran."

"I know," Lonestar said. She slumped against the bulkhead. A wet sheen formed over her eyes, and her voice wavered. "I thought

I was doing the right thing. I was told…I was told that Captain Brewer and Coren had been compromised. That there might be others compromised by them. And after seeing evidence of the Drone-Mechs, after seeing what happened to the Mechanics, it was too easy to believe."

"Who told you this?" Tag asked.

"An SRE intelligence official. Gave me his credentials, but of course they were time sensitive," she said. "Gods, I'm stupid. I thought I was helping. Thought I was doing the right thing." Her fists balled up, shaking, and her fingers turned white. "It was a guy named Ken Morris. Told me that this would allow the SRE to track the *Argo* to make sure bad shit wasn't happening. To make sure everyone here was actually loyal."

"He was a human?" Bull asked.

"Yes, of course he was a human," Lonestar said. "He even told me not to trust *you*. Not to believe you. That every goddamn person aboard this ship might be infected with those nanites." She placed a hand on her chest. "And I knew, I knew it might be true because, three hells, I knew I wasn't infected. I was the sane one. The one in control. I knew I wanted to save the SRE. To save these Mechanic people if I could."

She collapsed to the deck, drawing herself against the bulkhead and putting her head on her knees. "Space me, if you have to. Space me if that's what it takes." Between the strands of her matted hair, she caught Tag's eyes. "After our talks, after the way you acted around the Mechanics, around us. Saving Gorenado. I could tell you weren't compromised. You wanted the same thing I did. To find out what is going on and to protect the SRE at all costs."

"You're damn right that's what he wanted," Sofia said. "What all of us wanted. For gods' sake, how could you believe a random spook?"

"He had evidence. Documents. Looking back, I should've

realized they were forgeries. There was even a fake holo of Captain Brewer's brain that made it look like he had been infected with nanites."

"We have to send a courier drone and alert the SRE," Bull said. "We have to tell Admiral Doran."

Tag was furious at Lonestar. Furious at being betrayed. But he was even more furious at whoever had convinced Lonestar of his fake insurrection against the SRE and furious at how far that could have spread. He wanted to tell Admiral Doran everything Lonestar had told them. He wanted answers. He wanted the *Montenegro* to know a traitor was in their midst.

But now with someone on his own ship unknowingly betraying him, who could he trust on another distant ship filled with thousands of potential suspects?

"We can't send a courier drone," Tag said. "We can't let them know what we found yet. We don't know who we can trust there, and we have no way of ensuring Admiral Doran gets the message without someone intercepting it."

"Then what do we do?" Bull asked. "Turn around and give up?"

Tag signaled for Alpha to release the marine. Bull didn't say thank you or apologize to Coren, but he stood still. Tag could tell the man wasn't going in for another attack. His confidence had been ripped out from under him.

"We won't give up," Tag said. "We continue as normal. Coren, can you deactivate the transponder?"

"Certainly," Coren said. "And if he wants to watch"—he gestured toward Bull—"he is more than welcome to ensure I'm not simply reprogramming it."

"Why not destroy it altogether?" Sumo asked.

"I want Coren and Alpha to dissect it," Tag said. "To see, first off, how it works, and, second, if they can use any intel we grab on it to figure out who might've been responsible for it. Why, for example, Mechanic technology fell into human hands when the SRE officially has no record of even knowing Mechanics existed until Sofia and I encountered them."

"What should we do in the meantime, Captain?" Alpha asked.

"Carry on as usual. We'll debrief and apprise Bracken of the developments. Then continue on our mission to our next stop. Probably need to skip Chronamede, but we'll discuss that later."

"And me?" Lonestar said. She stepped in front of the airlock hatch as if she was about to space herself.

Tag considered her question. Their strange interactions now made sense. Looking back, he saw her caution around him, her skepticism. He didn't doubt that she had acted in what she thought was the SRE's best interests. The layers of the nanite mystery were so thick he wasn't sure yet what he could do with her.

"I don't really have any other choice but to send you to the brig," Tag said. "Sofia, Sumo, can you take her?"

The duo nodded, and Lonestar went with them. She put up no resistance, made no expression of disagreement.

Bull waited for his sentencing in silence. For the first time, he looked strangely at ease. As if whatever came next he would accept. It was just part of life. No longer a battle for him. The man had all but declared a temporary mutiny, resisting Tag's orders. It would be a clear case if Tag had been a traditional captain, brought up on rank-and-file organization and discipline as a bridge officer. But Tag wasn't a traditional bridge officer, nor was this a traditional mission.

Bull expected stern punishment; he expected to be reprimanded or demoted or worse.

Tag wouldn't give him the satisfaction. "Next time you have a theory like that, you come to me first. I'm not putting you in the brig. Damn shame, but I need your help for our next transition.

There can be no more misunderstandings of how this is going to work. Got it, Sergeant?"

"Understood, Captain." Bull's jaw clenched, and he was silent for a beat. "I apologize for my actions."

"It's not me who you were about to space, Sergeant."

Bull turned to Coren. "Coren, I was an asshole. It's probably no consolation, but I feel pretty goddamned stupid. I do—" He swallowed hard, his face flaring crimson. "I do apologize."

To Tag's surprise, Coren held out his hand. Bull met it in a firm handshake. "Apology accepted."

Bull left Coren and Alpha in the maintenance corridor. The man walked with a sullen gait, his head lowered and his shoulders drawn forward.

"You really just forgive him like that?" Tag asked Coren when they were alone.

"To borrow a human phrase, three hells no. I can never forgive his actions or his ignorance. He's a stubborn, narrow-sighted man, as good a warrior as he might be. Trying to kill me when the problem was with one of his own people? That is something a Mechanic cannot forget." Coren's expression softened a moment, his fur wrinkling. "But I don't care at all for that man's life and how my forgiveness affects him. What I care about is our mission and crew. Resentment and constant fighting between myself and Bull will not save the *Argo*. It will not save the *Stalwart*, and it will not save the free Mechanics. As much as I dislike that man, we must get along if we stand any chance of accomplishing what we set out to do in the first place."

With all the chaos erupting around him, Tag had never been happier to have the Mechanic by his side. For all the times Tag or someone in his crew had doubted Coren's intentions, the alien had continuously proven his pragmatism and devotion to the *Argo* and their directives.

Tag placed a hand on Coren's shoulder. "I can't tell you enough how much I appreciate that kind of support, because the gods only know we're going to need it through everything coming ahead."

FORTY-FOUR

Running the experiments to demonstrate that the air recycler particles triggered Mechanic immunity to the nanites was easy. Turning those particles into a vaccine and distributing it to the Mechanics hadn't been difficult either. Carrying on with the typical ship maintenance and briefings with Bracken was no harder. But traveling between stations and colonies where the Drone-Mechs had left little but flotsam and corpses proved immensely draining. Tag could see the depression and hopelessness mounting in his crew with every routine mission. Sofia's humor had lost its spark. Alpha seemed more robotic than ever, hardly venturing into emotional exchanges or conversations beyond rote duties. Bull trained in solitude with Sumo. Tag checked on Lonestar every once in a while in the brig, but there seemed to be no change in her mood. She appeared to have accepted her position there, understanding what she had done and why she couldn't yet be trusted.

They continued to encounter pockets of the Dreg salvaging defunct stations and ships, but there were no signs of the sapphire ship or any free Mechanics. Even reminding the crew that at least the Drone-Mechs were apparently no longer following did little to boost morale. Not being chased by their enemy did nothing to stop the images of bodies floating in space or decaying in colonies. Homes and stations turned to rubble. Other spaceships drifting into the void trailing a wake of debris. Each macabre tableau of a ravaged alien civilization burgeoned the prevailing gloom leaching into everyone aboard the *Argo*. It became easier and easier to believe that all that remained of the Mechanic species now lived on the *Stalwart* and the *Argo*.

Tag had wondered if the Mechanics, with their more logical and emotionless nature, were more inured to the sights they encountered with each normal-space transition. When he had asked Bracken, she had assured him that they weren't, that seeing the utter annihilation of the space network they had once held as a cornerstone to the success of their species was undoing her crew's morale. In a private conference, she even admitted to wondering whether continuing this mission would be wise. If maybe returning to the protection of the *Montenegro* would prove more beneficial to the survival of her species.

From the captain's station, Tag once again signaled to Alpha to make a transition into normal space. His restraints dug into his shoulders, and he felt the familiar embrace of the inertial dampeners kick in. The impellers lit up with a throaty hum as Sofia took the controls, and a flash of light washed over the viewscreen as the *Stalwart* came into normal space beside them.

A huge planet, Garndon-Three, loomed before them. Swirls of white clouds draped over brown-and-green landscapes that were cut through with veins of blue water. Although it was mostly landmass, the planet evoked a nostalgia for Earth within Tag. An unexpected yearning for his home world filled him. It had been so long since he had touched ground there, so long since he had seen his family. Breathed the air he had grown up in. And in distant space, his sense of discovery and adventure had endured blow after blow from seeing the destruction of the Mechanics' attempts to make new homes for themselves. He had started to wonder if there really was anything out here for him or if returning to Earth would be the wiser choice in his career.

Dwarfed by Garndon-Three, a lone space station orbited into view. Tag's heart began beating faster as he magnified the image of the station on his holoscreen. It appeared mostly intact. But as the station circled closer, that hopeful curiosity soon morphed into the all-too-familiar melancholy pervading their mission. A trail of wreckage drifted from a massive gouge in one section of the station.

"Captain," Alpha chirped, "we have contacts!"

A dozen red dots lit up on the holomap. All were positioned on the other side of Garndon-Three.

"It's not the Dreg again, is it?" Tag asked. "I'm getting sick of those little assholes popping out from the ashes of all these stations."

"No," Coren said, "their gravitational signals seem to be much larger than the Dreg craft. They are more likely to be of Mechanic origin."

"Drone-Mech?" Tag asked.

Bracken patched into their communications. "I'm assuming you are seeing what we are."

"Contacts opposite us. Mechanic signatures."

"Correct," Bracken said. "I'll attempt contact now."

She patched her communications in to the *Argo*.

"Unidentified Mechanic vessels, this is Commander Bracken of the MES *Stalwart*. Do you read?"

The first of the ships lifted beyond the shelter of Garndon-Three. It cut through space like a shark. *A battlecruiser.*

"This is new," Sofia said. "Usually the bastards fire by now."

"Captain, we have a weapons lock," Alpha reported.

"Hmm, spoke too soon," Sofia muttered.

"Ready the shields," Tag said. "Prep PDCs and chaff. Sofia, keep impellers hot. If we need to, we're diving into the shelter of the planet."

Tag magnified the battlecruiser's image on his holoscreen. It bristled with energy cannons, and several gaping torpedo bays revealed the warheads within. All around it, smaller fighters zipped in defensive formations.

"Got a lock on them?" Tag asked.

"Affirmative," Coren said. "PDCs ready to go as soon as one of those fighters peels away."

"Good," Tag said. Electricity coursed under his skin. His heart began its ascent into his throat, and he tried to swallow hard, unable to quell the rising sensation of anticipation driving him now.

Again, Bracken attempted to hail them, but there was no response.

The rest of the Mechanic fleet slowly drifted from beyond the planet. More battlecruisers, corvettes, and even other craft that looked more suited for trade than war. Then another type of ship appeared: a dreadnought. The enormous ship drifted at the center of the fleet. The monstrosity of a ship dwarfed even the largest battlecruiser, and Tag remembered how easily a ship like that had turned most of the *Montenegro*'s fleet to shredded alloy, shattered ceramic, and escaping plasma.

"Holy shit," Sofia said. "I'm just going to throw this out there, but I really don't want to try boarding one of those again. Especially when it's just us and the *Stalwart* against that goddamn fleet."

Bracken's voice chimed in over the comms once more. This time it was a private communication. "I'm somewhat optimistic that they haven't given us the 'where does your loyalty lie' line, and they haven't launched anything at us."

"It is strange," Tag said. "I want to be hopeful, too. But why haven't they responded?"

Then it struck him. This was the first time they had seen a human ship. Outside of Coren and Bracken's crew, no Mechanics knew about the existence of humans. And with their civilization destroyed, these people were right to be skeptical of encountering new races.

"Captain," Alpha said. "I'm getting some incoming attempts to access our computer systems."

"Is it similar to the Drone-Mech AI and comp system overrides?"

"No," Alpha said. "It's simply a data request. They're trying to syphon off our databases."

Tag would do the same thing if he could. When he couldn't trust another being, what better way to find out if they were friend or foe than read their minds?

"Let them," Tag said.

"Captain?"

"Let them read all the data they want. Whatever they need to prove we're not Drone-masters or some species in league with the Drone-Mechs. If they try to do anything else, shut them out immediately."

"Understood, Captain."

Tag switched the comms back to Bracken. "I think they want to know who *we* are."

"They haven't yet responded over comms, but they are also trying to access our data logs," Bracken said. "We're allowing them read-only access and monitoring their activities."

They waited for several minutes in silence. The occasional creaks of shifting and expanding deck plates accompanied the thrum of the impellers and the electric buzz of the energy-shield generators. Each crew member remained fixed at their station, hovering above their terminals, ready to react at the slightest provocation. Tag's breaths were shallow and infrequent. All his senses were tuned into the holomap before him, waiting for the first sign of a warhead leaving one of the Mechanic's torpedo bays. He almost jumped from his seat when Alpha spoke.

"Captain, their data read stopped," she said.

"They've ceased their data syphon on us, too," Bracken said over the comms.

A single ship broke from the swarming fleet and shot across the void toward them.

"They've relinquished their weapons lock," Alpha said.

"Weapons, stand down." Tag tapped his fingers on the crash couch's armrest as the holoscreen focused on the incoming ship. It was a small vessel, no more than a short-range shuttle. The holoscreen flickered, and a flat-faced Mechanic appeared.

"Commander Bracken, Commander Brewer. I would like to request a meeting."

FORTY-FIVE

Forty-five minutes later, Tag found himself aboard the *Stalwart* for the first time. The *Stalwart*'s conference room consisted of furnishings as black as the space around them. To Tag's surprise, several lush green plants bloomed from planters built into the ship's bulkhead. At first Tag had assumed they were merely for decoration. While they had waited for the Mechanic representative from the dreadnought fleet to arrive, he had decided there must be some functional purpose as well. A careful sniff of the air revealed a sweet fragrance in the local atmosphere—not too cloying but not subtle. Bracken had been happy to explain that the plants assisted with the air recycling and freshening efforts of the normal life support systems within the *Stalwart*.

Their amicable conversation ceased when a new Mechanic arrived. He came without an escort, but that didn't stop Bull and Sumo from staring him down suspiciously as Bracken and Tag greeted the alien.

"Welcome to the *Stalwart*," Bracken said. She held her hands out at hip height, opening her palms to the ceiling. The other Mechanic placed his palms in hers to complete the formal Mechanic greeting.

"It is a pleasure to work with you," the other Mechanic said as if delivering a line from a script. "Let us strive to build our future together."

According to Sofia's brief explanations of Mechanic customs before Tag left the *Argo*, this was the proper way to respond to any formal welcome. It was all about work, function, and cohesiveness with the Mechanics. Tag opened his hands to offer his own version of the Mechanic greeting. His arms didn't bend in quite the same way, and he couldn't curl his fingers as far back as Bracken had.

The Mechanic held out a single hand. "Is it not human custom to greet another with a handshake? Did our data leech from your ship lead us wrong?"

"No, you got it." Tag gripped the Mechanic's hand, more at ease delivering a handshake than the uncomfortable bending maneuver made necessary to complete the Mechanic greeting. The alien squeezed hard until Tag feared he risked fracturing a bone. "That's…that's good. Pleasure to meet a Mechanic that isn't trying to shoot us out of space."

"We share this same pleasure," he responded.

They sat around the table. Bull and Sumo settled against a bulkhead, still cradling their weapons. Sharick and another Mechanic soldier stood next to them, equally tense.

"I am Commander Forcant," the Mechanic began, placing his hand over his chest. The black fur covering his skin seemed to twinkle with a gray-blue twinge, and patches of fur appeared less dense across his skinny arms. Tag wondered if this was what an older Mechanic looked like. "I'm here on behalf of Admiral Martix."

"He sent you as a sacrificial offering in case we were Drone-Mechs?" Bracken asked.

The blue-gray fur atop Forcant's brow wrinkled.

"Apologies," Bracken said. "I've been spending too much time talking to humans, and their phraseology is rather infectious. Admiral Martix wasn't certain of our allegiance, so he sent you, is that right?"

"Based off our data analysis, we felt confident you are not, as you call them, Drone-Mechs, and that the humans, much to our surprise, are actually helpful to our mission."

"It wouldn't be the first time we surprised a Mechanic," Tag said. "And what exactly is your mission?"

"The same as yours, apparently," Forcant said. "We seek to limit, if not eliminate entirely, the effects of the nanites and identify the Drone-masters."

"And take back Meck'ara?" Bracken asked.

"Of course. From there, we hope to rebuild our forces and mount a counterattack on these Drone-masters."

"Then include the *Stalwart* in your plans," Bracken said. "We are happy to be of assistance."

Forcant looked to Tag. "I thank you for reuniting the *Stalwart* with the rest of the free Mechanic navy, and I understand if you would like to return to your own people now."

"Not going to happen," Tag said. "We didn't come all this way to shuttle the *Stalwart* here. We're in this fight until the end. I need to know who in the three hells these Drone-masters are and why they perverted human technology to enslave your people."

"Humans are remarkably stubborn," Bracken said. "They cling to us like the Dreg."

"Very well," Forcant said. "I suppose it won't hurt to have another ship in the free Mechanic fleet. Even if it is vastly inferior."

Tag laughed. "You came from that dreadnought, right?"

"I did."

"Our inferior ship and crew destroyed one of them."

"I read the data feeds," Forcant said. "I would be impressed, but it was run by a crew of Drone-Mechs."

"Tough crowd," Tag said.

The trio continued the meeting for another two hours. Forcant explained how Admiral Martix had managed to retake the dreadnought from Drone-Mech forces. Over the past few months, he had scraped together a fleet through a combination of finding other free Mechanics and guerilla-style boarding assaults on Drone-Mech strike groups. Something slowly filled Tag as they discussed the free Mechanic navy's expansion and their efforts to retake what had been stolen from them by the nanites. The tightness in his shoulders and gut finally started to leave. Dread that they would never find another free Mechanic, that their entire mission would be scrapped, was now slowly being replaced with a new hope, a hope that began to fan the dying embers of what had been left into flames. *Hope* that said this might all be possible. They might actually stand a chance.

After all, they had a dreadnought on their side now.

When Forcant finished his stories, Bracken went on to explain their own journey, along with their encounters with the Dreg and the sapphire ship. Tag hoped to hear an explanation for the unexpected encounter with the ship. They had never seen another, and the mystery of their origin had nagged at him ever since.

"Sapphires?" Forcant asked. "We have not encountered this species before. We'll document the encounter and see if anything comes up from our intelligence agencies."

Tag summarized their findings on the air recycling particles, and Bracken described their plan to use the Lacklon Institute to transmit a grav-wave signal that would interfere with the Drone-Mech's programming.

"We were also pleasantly surprised to see your scientific efforts," Forcant said.

"Half my crew are scientists or engineers," Tag said. "It's what we do."

Bracken gave a slightly human shrug. "What the human said is true. Likewise, we may not be a military ship, but we are glad to assist in eliminating the Drone-Mech menace."

"All of this will drastically improve our current battle plan to retake Meck'ara," Forcant said.

"Good," Tag said. "I look forward to doing our part to retake it."

"I'm pleased to hear you say that," Forcant said.

"How soon do you anticipate engaging with the Drone-Mechs on Meck'ara?" Bracken asked.

The corners of Forcant's mouth twitched. Tag had come to recognize the almost nonexistent expression as a Mechanic smile. "Admiral Martix has made it clear that with your help, we may be able to launch an assault to drastically shift the tide of this war." Forcant's twelve fingers steepled together. "And given that surprise and your scientific developments may be our only options, he has indicated that we should commence our hyperspace jump to Meck'ara immediately."

FORTY-SIX

ONCE AGAIN THE *ARGO* ENTERED HYPERSPACE, BUT THIS time they were surrounded by dozens of ships. It gave Tag comfort to finally have more than just the *Stalwart* as an ally. And for the last time until they hit normal space around Meck'ara, his crew was gathered in the conference room, awaiting a final briefing from him.

There was just one person he hadn't yet invited.

"Captain Brewer," Lonestar said, standing from the crash couch within the brig.

Tag pressed a command on the nearby terminal, and the polyglass door slid open. He sauntered in and sat opposite Lonestar on the sole chair within her chamber.

"We're entering Meck'ara space soon. Admiral Martix wants us to retake the Institute with Bracken's crew. They'll be providing orbital support, but I imagine anything they can provide us is going to be pretty limited." He searched his mind again, wondering if this was the right move. If this was all a mistake. If his instincts were right. Had he really considered what he was about to do? "As it stands, we won't have much in the way of ground forces. And the truth of the matter is I need every rifle I can get when we get to the Institute."

"You want me on this mission?"

"Want" wasn't the word Tag would have used. He had felt certain her intentions were truly in the best interest of the SRE. If he was being honest with himself, he wasn't completely sure that there wasn't still some lingering doubt in Lonestar's mind about Tag and Coren's involvement with the Drone-Mechs.

"I need you out there," Tag said, evading her question. "I need another marine. Gorenado won't be in any shape to leave the regen chamber, much less leave the ship. And Alpha and Coren will both need to keep their focus on implementing the grav-wave algorithms with Bracken's team once we break into the Institute."

"That doesn't leave a whole lot of people to watch your backs."

"It doesn't," Tag said. "So you can appreciate my dilemma." Tag let her shift uncomfortably on the crash couch. The eagerness in her eyes was evident. She appeared almost like a dog looking to its master for approval. He hated it. "I don't want you to come. Your stunt almost got us killed. Almost got the *Stalwart* killed. There's no coming back from that. I still think that you thought you were doing the right thing. What you did was immensely stupid, and I don't know that I'll be able to forgive you for it. I *want* to, but I don't know if I can."

"You don't let a wild mongrel mess with your sheep more than once," Lonestar said. "I understand, Captain."

He jabbed a finger toward her. "If I let you out of here, if I bring you on the mission, I pray to the gods you don't prove me wrong."

"I won't," Lonestar said. "I won't. I know my word might not be much good to you, but I promise I'll do everything I can to protect you and the Mechanics."

"I hope so," Tag said, standing. He punched a button on his wrist terminal, and the polyglass door slid open again. As he moved to the exit with Lonestar, she paused.

"Captain?" she asked.

"Yes?"

"There's still something I don't get about you. All that grim talk over coffee," she began, "what was that really about?"

Tag rubbed the back of his neck. "It was a discussion I was having with Alpha." He didn't want to delve too deep into the most disturbing of Alpha's comments. It wouldn't be helpful to compromise her trust in him or to reveal the moral challenges Alpha's relatively young mind was grappling with. "She was trying to understand what it was like to be a soldier. What it meant to hold someone's life in your hands. And, I suppose, how that makes us human."

"Yeah. That'd be a tough thing to explain." She paused. "You know, I remember the first time my dad had me help him slaughter a cow on the ranch. I didn't like it. I still don't. Don't think he likes it either. When people eat meat, it's something that has to be done. And that's kind of how I think of all of this. All this fighting, this war stuff. I like saving people. I like knowing I'm protecting other humans, colonies. Other sentient species.

"But the killing isn't something I like. It's just something we have to do. And I don't ever want to mix those feelings up. I like the saving and defending part, but I don't like the killing. You can tell Alpha that."

"I'm sure you'll have a chance to talk to her yourself," Tag said.

"Thing is," Lonestar went on as if Tag hadn't said anything, "some people can't separate those feelings. Some people like the killing. And they scare me. I was glad to find out you weren't like that. It was the tipping point in realizing what I'd done. Because people who do like the killing, who do like the fighting, I sometimes think they're broken. That they can't be fixed."

Tag couldn't help the slight shudder, hoping Alpha wasn't broken. That her revelation after helping Gorenado had been enough to guide her moral trajectory as her synth-bio brain continued to develop.

"You don't think people can change?" Tag asked. "You don't believe in redemption?"

"I'm not sure," Lonestar said, "but right now, I'm hoping to change that."

————

Tag stood at the front of the conference room next to a holo of Meck'ara with Coren, Alpha, Sofia, and the marines watching him. He found it hard to believe this was his entire crew. That this was all the SRE could spare to help the free Mechanics. Of course, he could send a courier drone to alert the SRE, but judging by their luck so far, he expected it would be intercepted.

That wasn't all. His stomach twisted. There was a darker thought buried in his subconscious. A suspicion that maybe, maybe someone in league with the Drone-masters at the SRE would get the message and do whatever they could to ensure Tag's mission failed.

But here they were, discussing how they were going to infiltrate a battle-ravaged world and change the direction of an enigmatic war. And only three of them were actually trained for direct combat. Of course, they had Bracken's forces to complement them, but a few dozen Mechanic warriors escorting a group of scientists and engineers to implement a risky, game-changing experiment in the middle of an active battlefield didn't even sound like a great idea on paper, much less in reality.

Still, it was the best plan they had. Forcant and Admiral Martix had accumulated at least some data on the Drone-Mech blockade around Meck'ara. The information was dated, but if the Drone-Mechs had only half the fleet Martix believed they might, winning in space was going to be difficult enough. Tag hated thinking about what it would be like if the Drone-Mechs had gathered even more warships since Admiral Martix had last intercepted one of the enemy courier drones. He understood now why the free Mechanic navy didn't want to wait any longer than they had to.

"Tomorrow, we'll be in Meck'ara space." Tag tapped on his wrist terminal, and a blizzard of red dots appeared around the holo of Meck'ara. "This is what the last known fleet around Meck'ara looked like."

"Holy shit," Sofia said. "And I suppose you just want me to fly through that like it's no big deal, huh?"

"For a pilot like you," Tag said, "it'll be a piece of cake."

"You've got more confidence than I do."

"Get us to the ground alive, and try to keep the ship together. I'll buy you a drink afterward."

"It better be a drink big enough for an ice god," Sofia said.

"The good news is that we don't need to engage with these Drone-Mechs. Our objective is purely to get to the Institute. Bracken and Sharick will storm the gates with us. Since the Institute was more focused on academic research, there was never a formidable security force around it. *Hope*fully, with the Drone-Mechs in charge, that won't have changed. There may not be anyone there for all we know."

"Fat chance with our luck," Bull said. "Given everything we've seen, if the Drone-Mechs aren't marching around there, I'd expect that to be a goddamn breeding ground for the Dreg."

"Or an ice god," Sofia said.

"I'm beginning to think you might actually like the ice gods," Coren said.

"They're kind of cute."

"Ice gods or not," Tag said, "we've got to implement the grav-wave software Bracken's group is bringing." The nervous humor shared between the crew members dissipated. "The Mechanics are relying on us. I don't think it's hyperbole to say that if we don't succeed, Admiral Martix isn't going to stand a chance of overcoming the Drone-Mech navy. You all saw what happened to the *Montenegro*'s fleet from a single dreadnought and its strike group. We're going up against a force ten times that in strength.

"This is the Mechanics' last stand," he continued. "This is our last stand. Stopping them may be the only way to ensure they don't mount another attack on the *Montenegro* or, gods be damned, the rest of the SRE. Earth."

He let the words hang in the air for several long beats.

"I'm asking you all to give your damnedest out there. We don't know exactly what we're going to face. We don't know what it's going to be like on the planet's surface. And we don't know how long Martix and his fleet can keep the Drone-Mechs off our back. What I do know is that I've got the strangest team ever assembled to carry out a mission we never would've imagined a few months ago. And goddammit, we're also the best team to do it."

"If I may, Captain," Alpha said, raising a tentative silver hand. "I believe it would be appropriate for me to add something to a briefing like this."

"And what would that be?"

"Let's kick some ass."

FORTY-SEVEN

PLASMA DISSIPATED ACROSS THE VIEWSCREEN, AND inertial dampeners tugged at Tag's insides, the mix of anxiety and rapid changes in acceleration churning in his gut. His jaw set to the point that a tension headache was burgeoning behind his eyeballs, and he had to force himself to take deep breaths of recycled air within his EVA suit as his crash couch restraints tightened around his body. Something felt out of place in his trachea, and he coughed. A physical manifestation, maybe, of the worry knotting itself in his brain.

All around him, Martix's fleet transitioned into existence, rocking into normal space with flashes of light more violent than a thousand lightning strikes. For a moment, as the battlecruisers floated next to the *Argo*, and as the dreadnought lurked behind them like a foreboding behemoth, Tag felt almost powerful. This was the feeling he had once chased as a young ensign in training. The moment of glory entering a skirmish alongside a navy bristling with advanced technology and a singular monumental battle ahead of them. The adrenaline rush was exhilarating, invigorating. And Tag feared he could find himself becoming addicted to it.

But reality proved to be a formidable antidote.

Klaxon alarms blared across the bridge, and a storm of red dots flashed all over the holomap. The Drone-Mech numbers were so dense that they threatened to blot out the mass of Meck'ara beyond them. Tag's fingers curled around the edge of his armrests. If it weren't for his gloves, he knew he would be looking down at his white knuckles right now. At least, thanks to the EVA suits, his crew couldn't see how frightened he was. They had brought one dreadnought to this battle. And by Tag's cursory count on the holomap and Alpha's continuously updated data analysis on the enemy numbers, Tag saw at least a dozen dreadnoughts spread among the Drone-Mech fleet.

"Hostile contacts," Alpha said.

"No shit," Sofia said dryly.

Alpha appeared confused for only a second before she continued. "Incoming ordnance. Torpedoes detected."

"Coren," Tag said, mustering all the certainty he could in his voice. "You know what to do."

For the first part of their dive toward the planet, Martix's fleet would escort them. Their goal was to get within the atmosphere above the Institute at whatever the cost. Martix would break off only when they were certain Tag and Bracken had gotten their forces landside. As Tag's vision narrowed on the viewscreen, hundreds of glinting Drone-Mech warships speckling the distant view, he prayed for Martix's sake that it wouldn't take them long to infiltrate the Institute. He had no illusions that the free Mechanics in space would come out of this unscathed. They would undoubtedly take considerable losses. They were knowingly making an enormous sacrifice, all in faith that Tag and Bracken could disrupt the nanites and effectively turn the Drone-Mechs off.

If that didn't work, they would make a mad retreat to Garndon-Three. Of course, that was contingent on there being anyone left to retreat.

Sofia guided the *Argo* in a more or less straight path at the Drone-Mech blockade. They were still out of effective distance of Gauss cannons, energy weapons, and PDCs. That didn't stop a wall of torpedoes from glittering across the holomap toward them. In answer, outgoing torpedoes flew in volleys from Martix's fleet. The warheads and ordnance raced past the *Argo* in waves, rushing to meet the incoming fusillade like two ancient armies charging each other for a ferocious clash of blades against shields. The first few warheads met each other with violent energy. Chains of explosions glared, rippling in the viewscreen, and the number of detected ordnances on Tag's holoscreen constantly shifted as the two fleets fired wave after wave.

"We are approaching effective targeting range for kinetic slugs," Alpha reported.

"Coren, tear a hole through these bastards," Tag said.

Coren's fingers skipped across his terminal. The reverberations of the thumping Gauss cannons shook through the bulkhead, and slugs flew in straight lines at the enemy forces.

"Approaching PDC and energy weapons range," Alpha said.

"Shields up," Tag said. *Now things are going to get interesting.*

The green glare of the energy shields powering up around the ship shone for a few moments before settling into invisibility. Sofia seemed to lean forward against her restraints, and Tag imagined the sweat coursing down her forehead, through her hair. The clamminess in her palms. More than anyone in that moment, this mission would come down to her. Pearly ropes of incoming PDC fire erupted from several of the Drone-Mech ships, illuminated on the viewscreen. Sofia maneuvered around them as flashes of azure light and beams lanced from the Drone-Mech fleet. The Mechanics returned fire with equal ferocity, and orange streaks tore from the *Argo*'s energy cannon at the enemies.

All around, the dark abyss was illuminated with the almost constant explosion of warheads and the flash of energy rounds being absorbed by shields. Coren whooped when a kinetic slug punctured one of the Drone-Mech cutters he had been targeting. Plumes of blue plasma vented from the wounded ship, and it started to list as the gravity well of Meck'ara pulled it in. The venting plasma and failing impellers propelled the ship into a Drone-Mech battlecruiser, and the two ships ripped apart in a series of explosions that coursed through their hulls. Debris peppered the Drone-Mech ranks.

"Two for the price of one," Sofia shouted. "Keep at that shit, Coren!"

The *Argo* flipped and barrel rolled through intersecting lines of PDC fire, bulkheads and decks groaning in agonized protest as Sofia treated it like a bloated fighter. Blue beams speared through the space around them. Several caught the ship, and the energy shields hummed and flashed green as they dissipated the overwhelming incoming energy. Every near miss and absorbed round set Tag on edge, set his heart racing, his nerves twitching.

"Shields at seventy-five percent," Alpha said before another wave of energy rounds rocked the *Argo*. "Now at fifty-nine percent!"

Tag wondered how long they would have lasted had Martix's fleet not been helping to absorb the insane storm of incoming fire pounding around them. The thought passed through his mind right as a nearby free Mechanic cutter took a volley of energy rounds within a period of only a few seconds. Their shields shone bright green and appeared almost like fractured glass as they took the pounding. PDC fire and outgoing rounds from the cutter fired frantically, and Tag watched in horror as a single torpedo slipped through the ropes of defensive fire and past the failed energy shields. The torpedo disappeared, piercing the cutter, and gored the bowels of the ship. A second later, fire and plasma blew out of the shredded hull, and the ship turned to slag, its crew incinerated in one violent moment.

Coren continued firing at the incoming warheads while occasionally returning the favor. Between volleys, he stole a glance at the fractured remains of the downed free Mechanic ship and said, "The machine remembers, brothers and sisters."

Fighters from the Drone-Mech fleet flew in rolling clouds to meet the fighters that were now streaming from the free Mechanics' dreadnought. Tag tried to monitor the action unfolding over his holoscreen, but the chaotic dance of fighters separating and re-forming like ravenous flocks of birds was too much to follow. Another billow of blue plasma caught his eye, and he watched as a second free Mechanic ship was cleaved into three separate pieces by the resulting blasts. All around in Martix's fleet, ships were stalling, impellers destroyed, energy shields failing, or fusion cores jettisoned to prevent catastrophic failure.

The *Argo* and *Stalwart*'s escorts were fighting valiantly, but Tag feared it wouldn't be enough. When another free Mechanic ship was eviscerated, Tag *knew* it wouldn't be enough. Punching a hole through the Drone-Mech blockade by sheer force of firepower seemed horribly quixotic now. The crew appeared to feel the same despair Tag did, and he caught Coren watching him, waiting for the command to reverse and attempt a jump into hyperspace. All the sacrifices of the Mechanics, all their best efforts, everything they had fought for had led to this abysmal failure.

FORTY-EIGHT

Forcant, still serving as Admiral Martix's comms organizer, appeared on Tag's holoscreen. Tag waited for the order to come through. The order that would send them all running back into hyperspace, running away from any chance of victory over the Drone-Mechs.

But Forcant surprised him. "Admiral Martix requests the *Argo* and the *Stalwart* adjust trajectories. Follow the *Fury*, *Constitution*, and *Berserker*."

"Understood," Tag said.

Sofia confirmed she'd heard the order by giving him a brief thumbs up, and she decelerated slightly to let the battlecruisers charge in front of them. Each battlecruiser flew frighteningly close to the next. One wrong move by their pilots, and Tag envisioned a firestorm of exploding reactors and geysers of plasma erupting from their collisions.

"That's a damn crazy maneuver even for a fighter," Sofia said.

"Stay as close to their impeller trail as possible," Forcant continued. "We're using them like battering rams. No matter what, we're getting you onto that planet. There will be no retreat, no failure today."

A tightness gripped Tag's chest. He wasn't sure if it was the immense weight of the situation or the delay in the inertial dampeners trying to keep up with Sofia's flying. The *Stalwart* appeared nearby, uncomfortably close for Tag's liking. But he trusted Sofia to handle the *Argo* even as the proximity alarms wailed all around the bridge.

He watched as green blips on the holomap disappeared. Something seemed disrespectful about a few vanishing dots signifying the deaths of thousands. Each time another disappeared, he felt a knife slip further into his stomach, twisting and cutting at the tenuous bit of hope left that any of them would survive this desperate mission.

But if his crew had noticed his despair, they made no sign to acknowledge it. Martix's efforts to shift the battle in a new direction had reinvigorated them, and each was focused on their station, losing themselves in the tasks at hand.

"Shields at fifty-three percent," Alpha chimed as another energy blast rocked the *Argo*.

Bracken guided the chains of glaring PDC fire into a few incoming warheads. Despite the proximity to the *Stalwart*, Sofia continuously made small adjustments to the *Argo*'s trajectory to avoid incoming energy rounds and returning PDC fire. The energy shields of the *Fury*, *Constitution*, and *Berserker* flickered as they absorbed the brunt of the Drone-Mech fire. A spatter of blue PDC fire from a Drone-Mech ship peppered the portside hull of the *Fury*. Tag's heart beat faster than the energy rounds bursting from their cannons. For a moment, nothing happened. Then a sudden cobalt eruption sent the *Fury* listing to port, and it was pushed off its path, creating a void between the *Constitution* and *Berserker*.

Renewed incoming fire rained hell on the *Stalwart* and the *Argo*. The energy shields buzzed, and the bridge shook. Round after round exploded against the ship, and an alarm barked a new warning across Tag's holoscreen: *Hull breach, forward quarters*. Panic filtered through him as the internal redundancies sent hatches locking closed and repair bots flooding to the scene of the breach.

"Bull, you all okay down there?" Tag asked over the comms.

"Never better, Captain," Bull said, although he was speaking through gritted teeth.

Fighters swarmed at the trio of free Mechanic ships leading the charge. Dozens burst into shards of alloy, but even though more and more fell to the onslaught of the free Mechanics, the fighters continued to course between them, eating away at the shields and taking strafing runs at the *Argo*. As the *Fury* continued to veer off course, escape pods plumed from all sides of the vessel, and it crashed into the first line of Drone-Mech ships, erupting into a swirl of jagged fragments like so many metallic chunks of hail. The *Berserker* and the *Constitution* tore into the Drone-Mech ships after it, barreling into fighters, cutters, and battlecruisers alike. The impacts of the free Mechanic ships against the Drone-Mechs' was so violent Tag could practically feel the shuddering decks and distant explosions himself. More escape pods fired off from the ships before they broke apart in tongues of jutting plasma.

"Gods be damned," Sofia said. "They're throwing themselves at the Drone-Mechs like bricks through a window."

"Make it count," Tag said. "Take us through that broken window."

"Aye, Skipper."

The *Argo* blasted forward, skimming huge shards of broken hull and snakes of wires and pipes. Pieces of the free Mechanic and Drone-Mechanic ships floated among a sea of corpses. The *Stalwart* wasn't far behind them, and the broken ships protected them from some of the scattered energy rounds, warheads, and PDC fire coming at them. Most of the escape pods from the *Fury* careened back to the free Mechanic fleet, but an aftward cam view showed many of them being picked off by fighters and overwhelming pulsefire.

Coren went wild at the weapons station, lashing out left and right at fighters who dared venture into the debris field, stepping into his overzealous arms.

"Your sacrifice will not be in vain!" he bellowed.

Another blast of rolling plasma and breaking alloy caught Tag's eye. At first, he feared it was the *Stalwart* coming undone by the enemy assault. But the *Stalwart*'s signal still glared brightly across the holomap. Instead, more Drone-Mech ships flickered out. The free Mechanics were using the confusion of the sacrificial ships to regain a foothold in the relentless battle and keep the Drone-Mechs off the *Argo* and the *Stalwart*. As far as the Drone-Mechs knew, the *Argo* and the *Stalwart* were simply falling down the gravity well toward Meck'ara with the rest of the ruins of battle.

Bracken's voice came over the comms. "There are no contacts spotted at the Institute. Let's make this fast."

In his head, Tag heard the words she didn't say. *Let's make this fast so no more Mechanics have to die.*

Every second the battle raged on in space meant another free Mechanic lost. Another death closer to the extinction of Bracken and Coren's species. They leveled out their flight path as they rushed through the Meck'ara sky, immense heat from atmospheric friction making their hulls red.

Snow-peaked mountains rose above valleys and hills covered in verdant vegetation. It was almost impossible to see the Mechanic cities integrated into the rolling panorama of unbridled nature. Tag was only able to locate the cities and towns dispersed between the forests and plains and rivers because their positions were marked on his holomap. He felt both awe and surprise at the way the Mechanics had carefully laid out their civilization so as not to interfere with the planet. Based on everything he knew about them, he had expected the planet to be as bleak as their ships, mined and ravaged for every spare resource and decorated with brutalist architecture. He didn't expect the picturesque landscape he saw now, and the beauty of the planet made it even clearer why the free Mechanics wanted to take this place back. For a moment, Tag wondered if this was what Earth had once looked like. He could imagine humans fighting as fiercely, sacrificing themselves, to protect their home world just as the Mechanics had done.

"We are approaching the Institute!" Alpha said. "Still no contacts."

Sofia banked the *Argo* over the sprawling facility, and they started their descent. Tag looked up through the viewscreen, gazing at the glow and spark of distant volleys being traded between the Drone-Mechs and the free Mechanics. If they could just hold out a little longer, this would soon be over. They were so close. So close to ending this madness.

Sofia began lowering the *Argo*, and the *Stalwart* descended beside them. Then red dots suddenly glared across the holomap. Tag's heart threw itself against his rib cage, and he gazed frantically at the viewscreen.

"What in the three hells?" he yelled. "I thought you said no contacts."

"That is correct, Captain," Alpha said. "I do not understand—"

"Stealth ships!" Coren yelled.

The air crackled around them, distorted slightly by the mostly hidden silhouettes of the Drone-Mech stealth ships. Without a free Mechanic fleet to protect them, the ships unleashed a furious barrage of rounds into the *Argo* and the *Stalwart*. There was little they could do to protect themselves, although Sofia and Coren toiled relentlessly at their stations. The energy shields flickered, absorbing round after round. Then they disappeared.

"Shields down, Captain!" Alpha yelled.

Something slammed into the ship. The bridge quaked, and alarms shrieked, stabbing Tag's eardrums. His restraints dug into his suit, biting into his shoulders, and his head shook inside his helmet. Red began to creep into his vision, along with a throbbing pain.

"Main impellers down!" Alpha said. "Fusion reactors are going into overload."

If they kept flying, the *Argo* would soon meet the same plasma-filled fate as the *Fury*, *Berserker*, and *Constitution*.

"Shut the impellers and reactors down," Tag commanded. "Sofia, take us down for a hard landing."

There was no time for replies. The ground rushed up to meet them, tree branches and vines waving lazily in the wind as if they were unaware of the fiery scene about to unfold. No matter how the battle in space turned out, the *Argo* wasn't going to be getting off this planet anytime soon, and he wasn't looking forward to navigating the Drone-Mech–filled lands on foot if they failed now. His jaw clenched as they broke past the first layer of the forest canopy.

"Brace for impact!" Tag yelled.

His world turned into a hell of spraying mud and dirt, bursting trees, and fingers of hungry fire. Screeching alarms couldn't drown out the screams of a crew member, someone, yelling through the comms. Momentum carried the ship as the vessel plowed through the ground, leaving a violent gouge on the planet's surface. Finally the *Argo* came to rest, and for a moment, Tag thought that was it. They had survived, and now they would carry on.

Then the ship shuddered with the beat of incoming rounds. The stealth ships hadn't let them go.

FORTY-NINE

T AG UNDID HIS RESTRAINTS, RUSHING TO ALPHA, WHO WAS nearest him.

"Alpha! Alpha!"

She held the sides of her head with her fingers, metal scraping against metal. "My head. I feel so disoriented."

"Hold yourself together. We've got to get off the ship."

Coren and Sofia were already undoing their restraints and stumbling out of their crash couches. The ring of pulsefire pounding against the hull resonated through the bridge in an unending cacophony.

"Bull," Tag said. "Do you copy?"

"I hear you, Captain."

"Gather up all the guns you can," he said. The marines were closer to the armory, and Tag wasn't sure he had time to make a run to pick up weapons. Then a dark realization dripped over him. "And grab Gorenado."

"He's still in one of those med bay crash couches!" Sumo replied back over the comms.

"And he'll never leave it alive if we don't get him out of there now!" Tag said. "He'll be good enough to walk. It'll hurt like hell, but we can't leave him behind."

"Copy," Bull said.

"Everyone, on me!" Tag said. The bridge crew fell in line as more energy rounds raked the *Argo*. Klaxons still wailed, and a storm of warnings declaring various hull breaches flashed on the holoscreen at Tag's station. He ignored the discord and plunged down the corridor toward the *cargo* bay with his crew in tow. The bay hatch opened before them, leading them to another scene of disarray. A fire burned in one corner, the repair bots now shrapnel from a stray pulse round fired by one of the stealth ships. Sunlight filtered in through holes across the bay, and black singe marks marred the bulkheads. The air car was crushed under a section of alloy hull that was bent inward.

"Looks like we're walking," Sofia said.

The screech of grinding and shearing metal echoed through the *cargo* bay, and blue pulsefire ripped into the stacked remains of their *cargo*. The crew ducked, as if that would save them from a stray fusillade of fire. Another hatch opened to the bay. Bull and the marines came in, bristling with weapons. He tossed a mini-Gauss rifle, and Tag caught it. The others took the weapons the marines offered them. Gorenado had an arm around Lonestar. His bulk made even her muscular form appear like that of a child, but she made no outward sign of being distressed by his weight.

"Captain," she said in greeting.

"Gorenado, we're going to need to make a run for it. Can you handle that?" Tag asked.

"Do I got a choice?"

"Not really."

"Then sure, I can handle it."

Tag led the group to one of the exterior bay hatches, and he punched the terminal. The doors hissed open, letting in a flood of sunlight tinged green by the leaf canopy.

"Bracken, we're headed your direction. You got working vehicles?" Tag asked over the comms.

"We do," Bracken said. "Although the *Stalwart* will not be flying anywhere anytime soon."

"The *Argo's* no better."

Tag wound through the woods, leaping over fallen trees and flitting between the foliage. Maybe it was the threat of certain death, or maybe Bull had gotten over his agoraphobia, but Tag noticed the sergeant had no issues charging along with the rest of the group. They ducked under huge leaves and skirted past enormous insects clambering up trees. Tag eyed them as they went.

"They aren't dangerous," Coren said, allaying his fears. "The only things to watch out for are those ships."

The intermittent whine and roar of the stealth ships rushing overhead, desperately searching for survivors, plagued them as they made their way toward the *Stalwart*. Tag didn't have to look at his wrist terminal to navigate. A trail of thick black smoke drifted into the sky from the *Stalwart's* crash site.

Suddenly the snap of breaking tree branches and crunching leaves caused him to twist. With his rifle shouldered, he aimed at an approaching phalanx of vehicles.

"It's us, Captain Brewer," Bracken's voice rang over the comms.

Tag lowered his weapon. A Mechanic waved an arm toward a large opening hatch in the transport's side and beckoned them in. The group fell in, all too glad to be in the protection of the armored personnel carrier. Lonestar helped Gorenado onto one of the empty seats. He grimaced as he sat, holding the healed-over spot that had once been a hole through his chest.

Bracken turned to Tag from one of the front seats. "I am happy to see you all made it without any casualties." Her gaze lingered accusingly on Lonestar for a moment before it flickered back to Tag.

"How did you fare?" Tag asked.

"We lost one," she replied, "but we are fortunate that is all. Her death will not prevent us from succeeding at the Institute."

The transport wove between the massive tree trunks and over the rolling earth. They stuck to the cover of the forest, and Bracken's forces spread out as they made their way to the Institute. Every time one of the stealth ships blew past overhead, Tag felt his stomach twist, his fingers tightening around his rifle, and he peered out the windows nervously, waiting for pulsefire to rain through the leaves.

Bracken opened a comm line with Forcant, patching Tag in as well. "Admiral Martix, we are approaching the Institute. Once we're there, we'll need about ten minutes to complete the algorithm integration with the grav-wave generator."

"Ten minutes may not be soon enough," Forcant said, his voice wavering in trepidation. "We are taking heavy losses. We've managed to subdue only one of their dreadnoughts, and the shields on most of our remaining ships are approaching single-digit power readings."

"By the machines," Bracken said, "hold out a little longer, and I swear to you we will succeed."

"Even if we cannot," Forcant said, "you still have a chance to succeed. Do not squander it. Captain Bracken, Captain Brewer, the future of our people resides with you now."

Pressure built in Tag with the intense ferocity of a meteor burning into the atmosphere. The stealth ships continued to screech overhead, firing randomly down into the forest, razing all the foliage that covered Bracken's forces. Apprehension tightened his muscles and wrapped its paralyzing grip around his chest. An open plain separated them from the Institute. No more hiding from the Drone-Mechs. Nothing to shield them from their superior firepower. Just a bit of luck, hope, and speed.

Tag feared that wouldn't be enough. The first free Mechanic vehicle burst from the tree cover, charging straight for the Institute. The hovering stealth ships unleashed a barrage of azure rounds that lanced into the earth, kicking up grass and tearing into the air car. The vehicle burst into a ball of fire, and Mechanics ran from the debilitated vehicle. More fire from the stealth ships cut into their fleeing ranks.

"Gods be damned!" Bull yelled. He shouldered a rocket launcher, and Lonestar followed his lead, a glimmer of wild anger sparking in her eyes. "Let me at those assholes!"

"No," Tag said. "You're going to get slaughtered."

"What?" Bracken yelled. "The best thing we can do is make this fast."

Before Tag could reply, several more ships burst through the atmosphere and accelerated toward the Institute. Tag's stomach dropped. Each looked like the swanlike sapphire ship they had seen at Herandion. He recalled the way the ship seemed to have swallowed a rocket that should have torn it apart. Six of those ships now tore across the plain. Any semblance of a plan to get to the Institute now seemed worthless. Getting past the stealth ships was one thing, but these strange ships were another matter entirely.

They were done for.

FIFTY

CAPTAIN BREWER," A VOICE SPOKE THROUGH HIS WRIST terminal. It sounded as though whoever was calling him was speaking through water. A face appeared on his terminal as well. It looked gelatinous. Translucent. Tag felt a pang of repulsion staring at the strange creature with its entire anatomy visible behind its misshapen, clear outer layer. Things that looked like blood vessels and nerve clusters were bunched around what might have been three eyes and an opening that Tag assumed was a mouth.

"What…what do you want?" Tag asked apprehensively.

"We want you to succeed," the voice responded. "I am Jaroon Ka' Shorloff of the Melarrey people. Our first encounter was at Herandion. There's not much time to explain, but we need your grav-wave-generator plan to work."

"You're going to help us?" Tag asked. He hardly trusted these jellyfish-like aliens and their enigmatic, transmuting ships.

"We are," Jaroon replied. One of the Melarrey ships morphed

slightly so two ports showed in its side. A jet of strange-looking bubbles exploded from the opening. The bubbles encompassed one of the Drone-Mech stealth ships, slowly conglomerating until the entire ship was covered. It looked like a child's plaything until the bubbles expanded, crushing the ship between them. Plasma and shrapnel burst throughout the sky as the other Melarrey ships fired and spewed more of the spherical ordnance. The strange bubble weaponry would be almost comical if it weren't so deadly.

Stealth ships and Melarrey vessels clashed with volatile fury. Explosive shockwaves from both sides shook the ground, serving only to remind Tag how weak the armored personnel carrier was. Even with the Melarreys' surprise and still-uncertain assistance, Tag could see the battle hadn't completely turned in their favor. They only had a moment to take advantage of the confusion.

"Move! Now!" Tag said.

Bracken didn't bother responding and instead commanded all her vehicles across the plain at once. Air cars bobbed over low hills, and APCs tore over the open landscape, leaving a tide of crushed grass in their wake. One stealth ship turned its attention to the free Mechanics and lobbed explosive and pulse rounds into the Mechanics' ranks. Another air car fell apart in a furious conflagration that enveloped the dry grass of the plain. The wildfire licked into the air, churning up plumes of black smoke, as another air car passed and was cut to pieces by Drone-Mech weapons.

As they advanced on the Institute, trying to escape the maelstrom, a multitude of questions rattled in Tag's mind. He wanted to know why the Melarrey were here. How they had gotten here. Why they had approached them at Herandion. But no question was more important right now than whether they would succeed.

Bracken seemed to be similarly conflicted, and she activated their comm line to Forcant. "The previously unidentified Sapphires are aiding our assault on the Institute. They claim to be the Melarrey, but we are still uncertain that their intentions are purely benevolent. Please remain cautious regardless of our success down here."

"Copy," Forcant said. Over the holoscreen, red lights flashed over the gray-tinged fur on his face. He appeared shaken and disheveled. "The Melarrey have lent their assistance to us up here, as well. Their efforts may be just as suicidal as ours. The Drone-Mechs still outnumber us ten to one."

The number was almost staggering, and it weighed heavily on Tag's mind as they bounced across the plain. Any distraction now would only exacerbate the casualties out there if they didn't succeed at the Institute. He tried to push those thoughts from his head, but he couldn't ignore the overhead explosions burning brightly like fireworks in space, reminding him of the destruction just beyond the planet's atmosphere.

Soil, grass, and trees geysered around them, bringing Tag's focus back to the ground. Drone-Mech fire blasted from all sides, with the occasional return volley from the Melarrey swooshing overhead in wide arcs. Another Mechanic air car was leveled in a blast of azure pulsefire. Tag couldn't even see where the rounds had come from. Smoke hung like acrid fog from the fire scorching through the landscape.

Bull had one hand wrapped around a bar to steady himself and the other holding onto his rifle. He gaped, transfixed, through the windshield of the APC. The vehicle accelerated over the cratered terrain as the Institute loomed before them. Another round ricocheted over the APC, almost knocking it off its path. A singed hole formed in the roof, and still Bull stared straight ahead, the target ever in his focus.

As if he could feel Tag staring at him, he said, "We're going to pummel some xeno ass, Captain." Then he cast a sideways glance at Coren. "The bad kind of xeno, that is."

The APC hit a rut formed by one of the Drone-Mech barrages. It launched several meters into the air before coming back down, with a jarring scrape tearing at the undercarriage.

"Yeehaw!" Lonestar said.

"We're fifty meters to the target!" the Mechanic driver yelled.

Sharick turned to his soldiers. "Prepare for—"

An intense, fiery light cut into Tag's retinas before his EVA suit's automatically adjusting visor could compensate. He felt himself flung forward, and he landed against something soft. His eardrums rang with a fierce howl, and he grasped at the sides of his helmet, desperate to throw his hands over his ears. His tailbone throbbed, and a stabbing pain burst through his left elbow. Blinking to clear the blinding white in his vision, he struggled against the dizziness that made him want to give up, to succumb to gravity and let the planet swallow him. Rallying, he pushed himself up, and a glint of metal caught his eyes. He crawled toward it.

A rifle. He picked the weapon up and scanned his surroundings, desperate to see through his disorientation. Smoke wafted up in gray columns all around him as if he were in the midst of some ephemeral, hellish temple. Fragments of the APC lay in melted chunks. Between the lumps of alloy jutting from the ground like the teeth of a giant ice god, Tag spotted the bodies of the Mechanic crew. His heart beat in rhythm with the pounding of gunfire still battering the surviving vehicles.

"Captain!" A voice cut through his confusion, piercing his still-pained eardrums. "Your vital signs…they faded for a moment. I thought we had lost you."

Alpha. She knelt next to Tag, scanning the horizon with her rifle. She fired at something, though Tag couldn't tell what it was.

"Marines!" Bull yelled. Black burn marks marred his armor, but he stood on a metal plate from the APC's wreckage. Coils of dark smoke twirled around him as he reached out to Lonestar. With his help, she hoisted herself from under a carapace-like shell of APC armor. Together, they pushed another sheet of alloy off of Sumo and Gorenado.

"Sofia! Coren!" Tag said, hobbling forward with one arm draped over Alpha's shoulder. He found Coren hunched over the body of another Mechanic.

Coren turned at Tag's approach. "Sharick's gone."

"He was a damn good soldier," Bull said. "Didn't deserve this."

Tag wanted to say a prayer for the brave Mechanic, but there were too many others to mourn and not a second to waste. An incoming barrage of pulsefire lit up the ground near them, and they threw themselves behind the wreckage. Tag army-crawled forward, dragging himself past a piece of the bench from the APC's troop hold. Beneath it he saw Sofia. The others were moving around him, ducking and weaving behind what shelter they could find, rousing the other surviving Mechanics.

He grabbed her shoulder. "Sofia!"

Through her visor, he saw her eyelids tremor before opening.

"Something going on, Captain?" she asked, her voice groggy.

"We've got to move."

She reached out a hand, and he took it.

Before he started to drag her out and exacerbate any injuries, he asked, "Can you feel your limbs? Anything hurt?"

"Does it matter?" she shot back.

"Fair enough. Ready?"

Pulse rounds pinged against chunks of slagged APC.

"Ready or not," she said, "get me the hell out of here."

Tag yanked on her arms, and her nose scrunched up, her mouth opening as if she was ready to scream. But just as quickly, she clenched her lips closed. Once she was free of the bench, Tag could see one of her ankles was twisted beyond the normal limits of human anatomy.

"Your earlier question?" she said, her voice almost a whimper and sounding agonized. "About feeling my limbs? I can feel them."

"Alpha!" Tag said. He was already monitoring the auto-pain-killer routines on Sofia's suit through his wrist terminal and upped her conservative dose slightly. "Help her out."

"Yes, Captain!" Alpha scooped an arm under Sofia's shoulder.

Without Alpha's help, Tag limped forward on his own. The pain was slowly dissipating from his own injuries, whether it was the painkillers kicking in or the adrenaline fueling him to focus on the task at hand. Several Mechanic air cars slid to a stop in front of the Institute, and Mechanics stormed out, firing a fusillade into the main door until it caved inward. The first Mechanic soldiers plunged into the darkness of the science building. This was it. They were in. Dozens of Mechanics rushed through the entrance, relaying updates over the public comms.

"No contacts."

"Clear!"

But Tag gulped. With the explosions glaring brightly enough above the atmosphere to be seen on the planet's surface and the stealth ships and Melarrey still engaged in a vicious battle overhead, Tag knew it wouldn't be this easy. Couldn't be. Tag led his own diminutive forces up the stairs into the building, his boots clattering against the polished stone, when a resounding chorus of gun blasts barked from the depths of the building. Mechanic screams and yells echoed through the corridors and over the comms.

No, this wasn't going to be easy at all.

FIFTY-ONE

TAG PRESSED HIMSELF FLAT AGAINST THE INSTITUTE'S WALL, his eyes adjusting to the darkened corridors. Obsidian walls and floor surrounded them, making the place look similar to the Mechanic ships, only instead of the tight hallways Tag was used to navigating, rounded walkways snaked under high ceilings and between ornate sculptures of molecular models and other abstract shapes. Between the artwork installations and multiple doorways, Tag saw Mechanic and Drone-Mech bodies alike. Terminals had been ripped from the walls, lying on the floor with their wires trailing behind them as if they were eyeballs torn from the sockets of a metallic being. The Drone-Mechs didn't seem to have underestimated the importance of this place as Tag and Bracken had hoped. Instead, the Drone-Mechs appeared to be in the middle of scavenging all the research and supplies within the facility.

"Looks like we didn't come a moment too soon," Coren said. "Let's hope they haven't torn up the grav-wave generator yet."

"Can you put it back together if they have?" Tag asked as they jogged rank and file down the corridor.

"Sure," Coren said.

"Good."

"I wasn't finished."

Tag glanced at Coren.

"It would take the better part of a year to reconstruct and recalibrate it if they have altered it at all."

"Then we better hurry!" Lonestar said, bounding forward.

The distant report of Drone-Mechs and Mechanics battling in the corridors guided them as they followed the maps projected by their wrist terminals. Tag's heart leapt each time he heard another rumbling explosion, and he prayed it wasn't the generator going up in flames. As they rounded another bend, huge banks of white lights swung above them. A flash of cobalt hit one of the obsidian walls, sending down a shower of dust and debris. He pressed his rifle against his shoulder and sighted up the Drone-Mech that had fired on them. A barricade at the end of the corridor blocked what was, according to his map, the grav-wave generator. Drone-Mechs were bunkered behind various shining pieces of laboratory equipment and huge chunks of stone that looked vaguely like lab benches to Tag. A couple of entrenched free Mechanics were firing at the barricade.

"We're taking heavy fire," Forcant's voice boomed over the comms. "Half of our fleet is out of commission. Our dreadnought only has one functioning fusion reactor. The other cores have been dumped. We're running at fifteen percent efficiency."

Tag spotted Bracken behind one of the pillars. Her power armor appeared as sleek as every other Mechanic's except for the scarlet stripes accentuating her joints and signifying her rank. Tag had only ever seen her at the conference table, never suited up for battle. She towered over the other Mechanics, cutting an impressive and formidable silhouette as she fired a blast of pulse rounds into one of the Drone-Mechs.

"We're almost into the generator," she said. "We've got forces defending the facility."

"Pardon our intrusion," Jaroon said, patching into their comm lines, "but we spotted additional forces following you into the facility."

"Great," Sumo said. "In front of us, behind us."

"More for me to kill," Bull growled. "Lonestar, take that column. Sumo, Gorenado, cover us."

Bull and Lonestar darted to new positions, flanking one group of Drone-Mechs and pinning them between the two marines. Inch by inch, the Mechanics and Tag's crew pushed toward the massive door at the passage's end, leveling Drone-Mechs with gunfire as they popped out from behind stanchions and doorways. A half dozen Mechanics perished in the fight to move forward, but they didn't let a single loss slow them.

Soon enough they were at the door, and Bracken dispatched five of them to force their way through the bulky door with their plasma cutters. Boot steps from the Drone-Mechs approaching behind them clacked down the corridors, echoing loudly, and Bracken sent a squad of Mechanics to intercept the new attackers.

"It's suicide," Sofia said as she watched the six soldiers sprint back along the route they had come, leaping over corpses of free Mechanics and Drone-Mechs alike.

"They know it," Bull said. "But they won't let it stop them. Never knew xenos to be worth a damn like your people, Coren."

Coren grunted a response, his fingers nervously tapping on his rifle. A quarter-meter-thick plate of door fell away with a heavy clang, and Bracken ushered in the first few Mechanics. Bull charged in next with Lonestar and Sumo flitting in behind him. Tag followed with Coren, and Alpha helped Sofia in next. Several Drone-Mechs posted around the inner facility fell under a wave of quick gunfire, and Tag felt victory close at their fingertips. They might actually have a chance. They might actually do this. He lunged toward the center of the room, expecting to see a massive machine or *something* towering above them. Instead he saw a deep well a few meters in diameter. Within the well floated the glowing purple cylinder he had seen in the schematics provided by Bracken, seemingly unprotected other than by a crackling green energy shield that sparked around it.

All around the room were a host of terminals, each buzzing and blinking in indecipherable script. Tag used his wrist terminal to turn on the Mechanic-language translation software given to him by Bracken's team. The language around him shifted into Sol Standard, but it was no more decipherable. Instead of unrecognizable characters in an alien language, the translations were just as meaningless; all he saw were words and numbers in Sol Standard far beyond his level of scientific expertise.

"Thank the gods Bracken's got the real scientists," Sofia said as she gazed around the massive chamber.

"You and Captain Brewer are real scientists, are you not?" Alpha asked.

"We are, but not this kind," Tag said, waving to the equations and information on the holodisplays across the room. He wondered if even the best-trained SRE physicists could unravel the information seeping from these terminals.

Bracken sent her soldiers to secure various doorways in the room. Her engineers settled into terminals, already installing their software that would override the Drone-Mechs' signals. Coren and Alpha, too, found stations to assist.

"Bull," Tag said, "I want you all on that door at all times. Don't let a single Drone-Mech in."

"Aye, Captain," Bull said then turned to Sumo, Lonestar, and the still-limping Gorenado. He gave directions over their private channel, and the trio set up a defensive barrier of overturned lab tables near the main door.

Sofia stood next to Tag as they watched the Mechanics bend over terminals, furiously inputting commands or settling into defensive positions. "Glad my xeno-anthropology background is coming in useful now."

"Maybe you can write a book about the Drone-Mechs' culture," Tag said, glancing nervously between the various doors leading into the chamber. Muffled gunfire and rattling explosions shook through them.

"Already wrote it," Sofia said. "Shoot. Kill. Destroy."

"That's the title?"

"No, that's the whole book."

Tag heard the telltale screech of distant pulsefire and aimed his mini-Gauss at one of the trembling doors. "Let's try not to be a chapter in that one, okay?"

"Whatever you say, Skipper."

Coren leaned back from his terminal. "Bracken, it appears the systems aren't quite what we predicted."

Bracken hurried to his side. "How so?"

Another Mechanic engineer spoke up. "They were modifying the generator to extend its range, presumably to improve their control over the Drone-Mechs."

"Will that be a problem for you?" Bracken asked.

"No," Coren said. By the way he said it, Tag could practically see his smirk behind the orange visor. "It should make our program more effective."

"Only there is a downside," the other Mechanic engineer said. "We will have to rewrite certain software components."

"How long will that take?" Bracken asked.

"No more than an extra fifteen minutes," Coren said. "The changes should be relatively simple."

Tag hated that Coren had said "should be." Uncertainties and probabilities weren't helpful right now.

Bracken seemed to share a similar sentiment. "Our fleet is dying up there, and even those damn strange Melarrey are having a difficult time keeping the Drone-Mechs off of us. We'll be lucky if we have five extra minutes."

Coren nodded but offered nothing other than to keep working.

For several long moments the clatter of typing Mechanics filled the air. The sounds of the gun battles outside had grown quiet. Bracken attempted to hail the detachment she had sent to stave off the Drone-Mech counterattack, but no one responded to her inquiries. She paced near Coren and the other engineers. Tag stood vigil near her, vowing never to leave Coren or Alpha's side. He willed his breathing to slow, willed his mind to remain sharp, to focus on where the enemy might dare breach the grav-wave generator's chamber. Tension rose between the Mechanics, humans, and Alpha as thick as the humid air in Tag's hometown of Old Houston.

A rumbling began shaking the walls, and Bracken's soldiers bristled with their weapons. Bull stared pointedly at the main door, where the quaking seemed to be concentrated. Metallic groaning echoed all around them, amplified by the chamber's acoustics, and Tag felt his pulse increasing with every tremor.

"How long do we have until the code is implemented?" Bracken shouted over the din.

Coren replied. "We're almost—"

The rumbling erupted into sounds of tearing, shrieking alloy. One of the overhead air vents burst outward, sending fragments of slagged metal splashing in red-hot drops across the room.

Shrapnel caught one of the Mechanic engineers and tore him from his terminal.

And then they came in.

Not from the doors but from above, rappelling from the holes torn into the ceiling, firing as they went, aiming haphazardly at Mechanic and terminal alike. Tag saw one of the Drone-Mechs lining up a shot at the delicate grav-wave generator hovering in its well. Time almost stood still as he tried to sight up the Drone-Mech, tried to get the drop on the enemy before the alien ended all their efforts. Everything they had worked for. All the sacrifices, human and Mechanic alike. All of it threatened to be worthless, subverted by a single rogue, hijacked alien swinging from the goddamned ceiling.

Tag squeezed the trigger. Even as he did, the Drone-Mech fired first. His shot careened straight at the generator. Straight at their only salvation.

FIFTY-TWO

THE SINGLE PULSE ROUND BURNED THROUGH THE AIR, PAST the tumbling shards of metal and plumes of dust falling on Tag and Bracken's crew. Tag cut the Drone-Mech apart in a fusillade of kinetic slugs. But it was too late.

A blast of violent green shook through the room when the round hit the generator. Tag winced, readying himself for the resulting explosion. As the light settled, no ball of fire tore from the well and enveloped the room. Instead, the generator pulsed green for a few moments before settling again.

Of course, Tag thought. The damned energy shields had saved it. But like the personal energy shields on the Mechanics' and now the marines' armor, and like those of the ships, the shield wouldn't last forever.

More pulsefire streaked from the Drone-Mechs, hammering the generator's shields. The Drone-Mechs and whoever their masters were no longer seemed so interested in protecting and upgrading the generator. Instead, they had quickly realized the immense, immediate threat it now was to the control of the Drone-Mech forces. Streaks of blue hammered the terminals near Tag, and the Drone-Mechs fired a barrage into the generator.

"Protect it!" Bracken yelled over the comms. Her engineers continued at their stations, ignoring the chaos around them, working at their code until the end.

"Bull, on me!" Tag commanded. The marines rushed from their now useless defensive barricade to join Tag and Sofia. The crew returned fire on the Drone-Mechs streaming into the generator room, picking them off with kinetic slugs that punched through their alien bodies and right into the room's walls. For every Drone-Mech they took out, another black cord fell from the ceiling, and a new squad of Drone-Mechs slid in. Bracken issued new orders to her soldiers, reorganizing them as the Drone-Mechs descended. No matter how they changed their tactics or where they focused their firepower, nothing seemed to thwart the Drone-Mechs' relentless efforts to destroy the generator.

The shields continued to shimmer and flash with each incoming round. Arcs of plasma-like lightning jolted out from the generator. Tag recognized the signs of imminent shield failure.

When that shield went down, a stray, grazing pulse round could debilitate the whole generator. The efforts of the engineers still glued to their stations, some enduring pulsefire, some already lying at their terminals dead, would be worth nothing. The generator would never shut the Drone-Mechs down. Tag and his crew would die here beside Bracken and hers. The free Mechanics would fall from the sky, their fleet destroyed, any hope of stopping the Drone-masters lost with it. The SRE, even if they did resume the *Argo*'s failed mission, might never find the Drone-masters, might never discover how human technology had been perverted into the nanite weapons of mass enslavement. Between Lonestar's deception and the initial attack on the *Argo* that had gotten him into this mess, there was no doubt in Tag's mind someone in the SRE knew exactly who and what the Drone-masters were. That alone sent a dark terror through Tag. Those people—those traitors—had an immense, secret power: the ability to disrupt civilization and peace precariously situated within the SRE. The days of prosperity, of human expansion into the far reaches of the galaxy, of peaceful coexistence with most alien species were being threatened.

No, Tag realized, *they were already gone.* They had already passed the brink of war, the edge of interstellar conflict, and were now plummeting straight toward galactic-scale annihilation.

Drone-Mechs continued pouring into the facility, and the marines and Mechanics struggled to maintain their tenuous hold on the room. There was no way they could let this room fall. No way they could let this generator fail.

Tag swiveled, firing at a Drone-Mech as its feet hit the floor. Another three charged him, firing all the while, and Lonestar barreled at the aliens.

"Captain, look out!" Lonestar fired her rifle, plugging rounds into their bodies, but one still carried forward. Black fluid leaked from the holes in the Drone-Mech's armor as Lonestar threw herself at it before it could reach Tag, and the duo collided with a sickening crack of alloy against alloy.

Bull and Sumo fired wildly at other Drone-Mechs that had made it to the floor. Several of the Mechanic engineers were cut down in hand-to-hand combat; others didn't even have a chance to turn from their terminals. Tag looked to Bracken to see how she was organizing her last-minute resistance. She too was grappling with a Drone-Mech, tumbling in a sea of bodies and twitching limbs.

Coren and Alpha were still at their stations, working fervently, as Sofia leveled a blast that knocked a nearby Drone-Mech off its feet. Tag ran to them, signaling for the marines to follow, knowing that the duo might be their last chance at survival. Another Mechanic engineer went down in a torrent of gunfire, and Tag watched a Mechanic soldier fall to four Drone-Mechs. Bracken was pushing off the body of the Drone-Mech she had finally prevailed against when another two jumped atop her.

Tag fired at the Drone-Mechs still descending from the ceiling, but he realized he was no longer aiming at single targets. Now he was simply firing into a mob of armored soldiers. Rounds pinged near him, scorching past his suit continuously, and he ducked lower, crouching near Coren's terminal.

"How much longer?" Tag yelled above the din.

"We are almost finished," Coren said. "Just need thirty seconds to execute."

Something bubbled in Tag. Something like hope. *Just have to survive for thirty more seconds,* he thought.

A new sound pierced the unholy chorus of gunfire and agonized yells, and Tag twisted to see the main doors fall under the all-too-familiar glow of intense green lasers. Drone-Mechs in exo-suits cut through the melting alloy, and their weapons wrought new havoc on the hapless free Mechanics. Bull dropped his rifle, and Sumo, Lonestar, and Gorenado followed suit, arming their rocket launchers instead. They fired a salvo at the exo-suit soldiers, rockets leaving a wake of gray smoke until they collided with the mechanized soldiers in a brash display of deafening fireworks. The first line fell quickly but was replaced by more of the looming giant armored suits, and the Drone-Mechs continued their drive forward.

"Coren, how are we?" Tag asked.

Coren leaned away from his terminal. "We're there. We're ready!"

His finger plunged toward the command to initiate the generator, but before he pressed it, a salvo of blue pulse rounds lanced into him. His built-in energy shield wavered and crackled then disappeared entirely. Energy rounds ate into his shoulder and arm, knocking him away from the terminal, and he tumbled backward onto the floor. Alpha began lunging toward his terminal but had to dodge as an exo-suit's green laser caught the ground at her feet and swung upward, slicing through her terminal.

Without thinking, Tag ran at Coren's terminal. He ignored everything around him, and his vision tunneled as he leapt over Drone-Mech corpses. His eyes focused only on the terminal's screen, on the command that would end this all, that would deactivate the Drone-Mechs' nanites and shut them down. Stop this massacre.

"Tag!" Someone cried from behind him. *Sofia.*

She glanced at him, then back at one of the exos, firing crazily as she did. The exo brought its laser to bear on the terminal Tag was heading for.

"No!" Tag yelled. His lungs burned and his muscles strained as he raced to the terminal, using every last energy reserve in his body. He lunged, his hand outstretched, desperate to end all of this. To stop it with that single command. Activate the generator. Save his crew. Save the Mechanics.

His fingers came down hard on the terminal as the screech of the laser exploded in his ear drums. He looked down to see the laser sheering through his chest, tearing through his armor, his bones, his flesh.

There was no time to feel pain.

Only darkness.

FIFTY-THREE

A HOLLOW, PERSISTENT BEAT.
  Thump-thump.

Then the whoosh of air. Like recyclers or filters working to keep a ship alive in the cold, unforgiving vastness of outer space.

Thump-thump.

There was a dull ache. A memory unable to be placed, tickling at the edge of the mind but refusing to reveal itself, coy and tantalizing.

Thump-thump.

Flashes of light exploded in a symphonic burst of colors. First red and black then giving way to softer, calmer blues and greens. Then silver, like fluid metal flowing all around.

Thump-thump.

Tag took his first unaided breath, his consciousness flooding into him, bouncing beneath his skull, and he gasped, his hands jolting to his chest. He felt fluid draining from all sides, puddling at his feet, then being siphoned off. He was stuck inside something. Imprisoned. His breathing grew more rapid, accelerating in concert with his pulse. He pressed a palm on the polyglass, yearning to be free, to be outside this chamber. Whatever it was.

Something looked back at him. Huge brown eyes, soft and warm, shone from a face chiseled and scarred by war, dark skin traced by light lines telling tales of glancing pulsefire and piercing shrapnel.

"He's waking up!" the person boomed.

Then it all rushed back to Tag. He was in a regen chamber, and outside was Gorenado. Last time he had seen the man, the marine had still been recovering from his own debilitating injuries, limping around the battlefield on Meck'ara. As the chamber door hissed open and the man cradled Tag in his arms, Tag realized Gorenado had had plenty of time to recover, which begged the question.

"How long...how long..." Tag struggled to get the words from his lips. His mouth felt sticky, and he could taste the stench of the worst morning breath he had ever had lingering on his tongue.

"Been a few weeks, Captain," Gorenado said, gingerly laying Tag on one of the med bay patient crash couches. He turned to someone Tag couldn't yet see. "If you can handle him, I'll go let the others know. Want to tell them in person." Gorenado's heavy footsteps faded into the corridor.

A silver face loomed over him. "All biometric activity reports normal healing processes, Captain, in line with computational projections."

Tag tried to take a relieved, deep breath, but he felt a sharp sting in his chest as if an exo-suit were wrapping its metal claws around him and squeezing. He winced.

"That will cause some pain for a while," Alpha said. "It's advisable to take shallower breaths."

"No…kidding," Tag managed. The events that had landed him here started to materialize. The grav-wave generator. The Drone-Mechs. The exo-suits, and the laser that had torn into him. Judging by his mere existence, he guessed they had somehow won, but he was almost afraid to ask the question, fearing he had only survived by a miracle.

However, Alpha didn't leave him in suspense. "You managed to initiate the implementation, Captain. The Drone-Mechs were shut down. Unfortunately, that meant that some of them perished as the genetic alterations made by the nanites initiated cellular suicide. But a surprisingly sizable portion did survive and are being treated to help recover full neurological functioning. It's unclear if that will be possible. Many of the Drone-Mechs are simply husks of beings, functioning as though they do not have a brain at all. Most of the Drone-Mech ships were reinstated into the free Mechanic navy, and the Melarrey have established a working relationship with the Mechanics as they rebuild Meck'ara. Bracken survived, as did—"

"Coren?" Tag asked, his voice coming out raspy.

"Yes," Alpha said. "He suffered several pulse rounds, but nothing near as traumatic as the laser you took. The injury was rather gruesome." She repositioned a holoscreen and clicked a command on the terminal. Tag cringed at the image of his charred torso. It appeared even worse than Gorenado's wounds, and Tag was surprised he had survived at all. "You were lucky that Lonestar dragged your body away from the exo-suits' laser before it could do much more damage, or you would have surely died. She took quite a bit of pulsefire but came out of the battle looking much better than you."

Alpha's delivery left much to be desired in the way of bedside manner, but Tag appreciated the content of the message. He also made a mental note to thank Lonestar when he saw her. A twinge of relief passed through him in knowing his decision to let her in on this last mission had been a good one. She truly was a dedicated marine who had been wrapped up in a conspiracy beyond her control. Her fidelity to the mission and the SRE had been proven by her valor.

"Lonestar isn't back in the brig…is she?" Tag asked.

"No," Alpha said. "In your place, Sofia assumed command and said you would probably wish her to have open range over the *Argo*." As if she was uncertain whether Sofia had made the right choice, she added, "My objections were noted based on SRE law in such circumstances, but Sofia insisted your views on the matter would be different."

"Good," Tag said. He stretched his fingers and toes and felt a warmth in his muscles. Normally a stint in the regen chamber would necessitate a stay in bed for complete recovery, but he felt like he could get up and walk out of here. "So…Lonestar saved me from the laser, but she certainly doesn't know medical science. I'm presuming you took the lead there?"

Alpha nodded. "I did, Captain. I altered the regen chamber's healing algorithms as well, making adjustments to some of the preprogrammed simulacrum stem cells. I hope that you find the changes satisfactory, as I believe they are an improvement over the normal healing paradigm."

"I can tell," Tag said. He forced himself up straighter in the crash couch. His bones creaked, and he still had to refrain from taking too deep a breath, but he managed to swing a leg over the side with surprising ease. "How's it feel?"

"Pardon me?" Alpha said.

"To make an improvement like that. To be able to do something that helps others live."

"It currently resides as the most favorable feeling in my life, though my life is rather short compared to yours," Alpha said.

Tag smiled at that, brushing his hand through his still-wet hair. "Good. And throughout my somewhat longer life, it's still remained the best feeling I've had. Helping others even when the odds seem long and lost. Doesn't get better than seeing someone you saved recover from the brink of death."

"Yes," Alpha said, her eyes tracing the deck. "It is a much greater feeling than causing destruction. I am almost ashamed of what I told you before. What I said when I didn't realize the fragility of life." Her beady eyes narrowed. "But after seeing what the Mechanics have gone through firsthand, I can say that saving life will always be preferable to me over taking it."

"As it should be," Tag said. "Thanks to your efforts and the rest of the crew, we just saved more lives than we can count."

"Actually, I think I can offer a prediction with an exceedingly low margin of error on the exact count of the lives we saved."

"Just a saying, Alpha," Tag said as she looked at him with a robotic but certainly bemused expression. "Can I go for a stroll?"

"You must take things slowly, but I believe with my aid, you can."

"Then let's do that," Tag said. "I want to see the crew."

"They are assembled on the bridge, taking a brief break from their efforts to rebuild the Institute. Bracken believes we can use the Institute as a center of defense against the grav signals from the Drone-masters in case there are still surviving Drone-Mechs elsewhere. In addition, they've begun full-scale production of the nanite vaccine we discovered."

"Excellent," Tag said. "And besides taking care of me, what have you been up to?"

"Between coordinating the onboard repair bots, I've been scouring the records and analyzing everything on the shipboard computers to analyze any code or encrypted messages Captain Weber may have left." She let out a mechanical sigh. "I still have no leads on where Captain Weber intended to take the *Argo*, nor what he intended to do with the ordnance the Drone-Mechs stole in their initial attack on the ship."

"Damn," Tag said. "What about the Melarrey? What's their game?"

"They, too, are after the Drone-masters. The Drone-Mechs destroyed most of their home world, and the ones we've met are some of the last members of their species. They had been scouring the wreckage of the Mechanics' civilization for clues as to what the Drone-masters were after when we encountered one of their scouting ships. Jaroon was on that ship. He apologized for frightening us but said they refused to answer any incoming hails for fear their computer systems would be hijacked by the Drone-Mechs."

"Makes sense," Tag said, recalling the Drone-Mech computer takeover of the *Argo*. "But why did he decide to help us?"

"Jaroon scanned our computers, which is what caused those strange disturbances, to determine whether we were friend or foe, since they'd never encountered a human."

"And what about trying to suck Coren up?"

"That was an attempt to assess whether Coren was a Drone-Mech or not. They planned to perform a scan not unlike the one you developed to detect nanites."

"Got it," Tag said.

Words still felt clumsy on his tongue, but talking was getting more comfortable as he walked down the ship's corridors, even though he was leaning heavily on Alpha. Still, the mere fact he was walking after the injuries he had sustained gave him hope. He should have been dead. And if he could recover thanks to a little ingenuity and perseverance from his crew members, he had confidence that both the Mechanics and the Melarrey could, too. It would be difficult, perilous work, but there was a chance to succeed. And no matter how slim it was, he and his crew would work to make it happen. Because when the day came—and he knew it would—that the SRE needed help, he had faith these races wouldn't soon forget the *Argo* or its help and that they would be glad to return the favor.

Maybe it was optimistic. Maybe it was the painkillers or his stay in the regen chamber messing with his mind. At least for today, he wouldn't let anything but optimism dominate his thoughts.

With Alpha leading him, they began the climb to the bridge. He tried to come up with what he would say to his crew, how he would inspire them on the next leg of their journey—wherever it would take them—but he realized he was lacking direction. Lacking something to say that would give them a concrete next step, a concrete objective. They could certainly devote their time to rebuilding the Mechanic society and learning what they could from the Melarreys' efforts, but that wouldn't necessarily put them any closer to finding the Drone-masters.

"Damn the gods." He stopped in the middle of the ladder, perching on a step. He had been blind again, looking for answers in the exact places there would be no answers. It seemed so obvious now, so clear that it *had* to be true.

"Captain?" Alpha asked.

"Take me to the captain's quarters," Tag said.

Alpha gave him a curious glance but relented, changing direction as she helped him hobble toward the captain's quarters. He entered past the conference room and into the chamber he hadn't yet moved into. The place still felt haunted by Captain Weber's spirit, and by all accounts, it might be. He searched the room, looking for something, anything. A clue that they had missed before. He tapped in a command on a nearby terminal and opened a holoscreen view of the captain's quarters according to architectural schematics.

"Overlay," Tag commanded the computer. The holoscreen projected the images of the captain's quarters all over the physical quarters themselves. Bulkheads, shelves, secured lockers, the bunk. All were illuminated in the glow of the projection.

"What are you doing, Captain?" Alpha said, still standing in the doorway to the chamber.

"Remember how the computer reported the slight power discrepancy in the *cargo* bay?"

"Right," Alpha said. "Lonestar's transponder was leeching from our shipboard systems."

"All the computers knew was that there was a power leak. They knew nothing about what was causing it."

"I understand that, Captain, but I do not understand what you are doing now."

"Sometimes the computer doesn't know everything," Tag said, already stepping gingerly around the room and searching the holographic overlay. "Sometimes we don't put things on the computer because they might be discovered, like a secret transponder. Or they might be stolen by our enemies, right?"

Alpha's beady eyes seemed to expand as if she understood immediately. "And surely if Captain Weber's commands were as secretive as we suspect, searching in the computer will yield very few results to guide us."

"Exactly," Tag said. "There's no way he was just shooting into space without a solid plan, and even the best memory enhancements can't give you perfect recollection of everything you'd need to travel through hyperspace toward whatever it was Weber was after."

"At least that is what you are presuming."

"That is what I'm hoping for, yes," Tag said, "because that would mean…"

He let the words trail off when he spotted a panel on the

bulkhead that appeared slightly different than the holo-over-lay suggested. There was an extra indent for a rivet that hadn't been part of the ship's original schematics. It appeared innocu-ous, subtle. And that was exactly what he had been looking for. He punched it with his finger, and the panel opened, revealing a chamber within it. His fingers shook as he reached inside and felt the cover of a physical book. An actual, physical book. He withdrew it, trailing his fingers over the leather cover and smell-ing the scent of the paper. It reminded him somehow of home, of comfort, though he swore he had never known the scent of a physical paper book before.

Carefully, he opened the cover, not knowing how gently he had to treat it to prevent the thing from tearing. And there, on the first page, was handwriting that he presumed was Captain Weber's. He scanned through the lines of text detailing coordi-nates and locations to unleash certain ordnance. As he read on, his stomach sank. The optimism brooding in him earlier was re-placed with a frightening chill that started first in his gut then spread through his limbs and came to rest in his mind. The book didn't explain much.

But it was enough for Tag to know the mission Weber had been on was one of dire importance. One that might mean the survival of the human race. Surely the SRE had sent other ships, designated other missions to ensure their success. To provide some kind of fail-safe redundancies.

But how many of them had failed, betrayed by treasonous moles within the SRE? How many had perished like the *Argo* almost had?

Whatever the real story was behind this notebook, Tag knew every day he had spent recovering in a regen chamber had been a day wasted, and he couldn't delay any longer. He rushed to the bridge, Alpha barely able to slow him with pleas that he would worsen his injuries. The pain of his deep breathing and the throbbing in his barely healed ribs didn't stop him from scaling the ladder or bursting onto the bridge. There, Sofia was at the pilot's station, and Coren was busy reading something on his terminal. The marines, clustered around another station, were mired in a boisterous conversation. All went momentarily silent when they heard Tag's approaching footsteps, and as soon as they glanced his way, the crew broke into applause, cheering his arrival.

But the joy didn't last long. They undoubtedly saw the look in his face, the desperation in his eyes, and the absoluteness of all that he had felt after reading Captain Weber's notebook. He held the book in the air.

"The *Argo*'s mission was never one of science and research," Tag began, with no time for pleasantries or easing into the subject. He tapped the cover of the book. "It was one of war. Of destruction. Captain Weber had a target and a *cargo* of torpedoes and warheads more advanced than anything I knew existed in the SRE's forces.

"His mission was to launch all these weapons at a set of coordinates he described here. Even he didn't know exactly what the purpose was or what he was aiming for. But he knew it was important. That much was clear in his urgent attitude toward the *Argo*'s final destination." Tag paused. "It seems we were supposed to raze an entire planet."

Tag took a deep, painful breath. "And before we could do it, someone found out. Someone must've told the Drone-masters, and they sent the Drone-Mechs after us." He found himself gasping for breath now. So many revelations in such a short time, and his body was still weak and recovering. Every intake of air hurt, but he didn't care. "We don't have the weapons, and we don't know who the enemy is, but we must find out. This may be the closest anyone from the SRE has gotten to the Drone-masters, and I'm determined that we'll be the crew to find them. Are you with me?"

The bridge was silent for a moment. But only the briefest of moments.

"Three hells, yes, Skipper!" Sofia said.

"You have my service," Coren said.

"I am with you, Captain," Alpha said.

The marines pumped their fists, giving a unified cheer. Bull's voice growled above the rest. "Let's kick some xeno ass!"

Tag reveled in their enthusiasm as he strode toward the captain's station. It had been left empty and ready for him, and he slid into the crash couch, calling up the comm systems. He recorded an urgent message for Jaroon, Bracken, and Forcant, calling them for a conference, and he watched his crew rush between their stations, readying the ship for flight once again.

He had started this mission alone and was now surrounded not just by a crew who had succeeded against formidable odds, but also by other fleets, other races who shared a common goal in defeating an unknowable but ruthless enemy. And together, he knew, they had no choice but to succeed. There was no alternative. No other way out of the war that had already started, unbeknownst to him, the Mechanics, or the Melarrey.

But together, they would finish it.

THE END OF BOOK 2

Dear Reader,

Thank you for reading the *Edge of War*. Would you like to know when the next book in The Eternal Frontier series comes out? Sign up here: http://bit.ly/ajmlist

I love to hear from my readers. If you want to get in touch, there are a number of ways to reach me.

Facebook: www.facebook.com/anthonyjmelchiorri
Email: ajm@anthonyjmelchiorri.com
Website: http://www.anthonyjmelchiorri.com

Sincerely,
Anthony J Melchiorri

ALSO BY ANTHONY MELCHIORRI

The Tide Series

The Tide (Book 1)
Breakwater (Book 2)
Salvage (Book 3)
Deadrise (Book 4)
Iron Wind (Book 5)

The Eternal Frontier

Eternal Frontier (Book 1)
Edge of War (Book 2)
Shattered Dawn (Coming 2017)

Black Market DNA

Enhancement (Book 1)
Malignant (Book 2)
Variant (Book 3)
Fatal Injection

Other Books

The God Organ
The Human Forged
Darkness Evolved

ABOUT THE AUTHOR

Anthony J Melchiorri is a scientist with a PhD in bioengineering. Originally from the Midwest, he now lives in Texas. By day, he develops cellular therapies and 3D-printable artificial organs. By night, he writes apocalyptic, medical, and science-fiction thrillers that blend real-world research with other-worldly possibility. When he isn't in the lab or at the keyboard, he spends his time running, reading, hiking, and traveling in search of new story ideas.

Read more at http://anthonyjmelchiorri.com and sign up for his mailing list at http://bit.ly/ajmlist to hear about his latest releases and news.

Made in the USA
Lexington, KY
30 June 2017